Falling Hard

By

Lori Laine

ISBN: 978-1-911761-41-9

Table of Contents

Chapter 1:
Daisy Donaldson is not charming

Walking out of her god-awful job might just turn out to be a blessing in disguise. Lance had left that very same company a week before she quit, jumping ship to a social media firm where he was now working in marketing—and, according to him, it was the best job ever.

He was convinced Daisy should follow his lead. "I'll get you in," he'd promised, brimming with confidence. Experience? Irrelevant. Marketing was all about personality, and he was certain she could charm her way in.

There was just one problem with Lance's plan.

Daisy Donaldson wasn't charming.

Lance Delaney—handsome, blonde (though not naturally, but Daisy never told you that), brown-eyed, tall and slender with cheekbones to die for and an enviable sense of fashion—always looked seamlessly put together. He could talk his way out of a prison sentence. Daisy, on the other hand, couldn't sweet-talk her way into a free iced coffee from Pret, let alone an entirely new career.

Because while she could be witty and enticing, especially as a youngster, she was also now awkward, clumsy, and chaotic. And hopelessly overaware of how she came across to other people. Which, coincidentally, is how Daisy ended up in insurance in the first place: stable, safe, painfully boring. The confidence that was meant to arrive with adulthood had somehow gone missing—and with it, that bold little child she used to be.

More like Disaster Daisy.

Lance and Daisy had been best friends for years, complementing each other in all the right ways. They had the same taste in music, the same taste in movies, and sometimes—annoyingly—the same taste in men. But where Lance carried himself with effortless confidence, Daisy did not. And that was what worried her the most. Sure, he'd talked himself into his new marketing job with ease. For Daisy? Just thinking about it made her stomach knot. She knew it was going to be tough, and right now, the negative voice in her brain was winning.

The regret of not thinking things through before quitting the secure job she'd stuck with for six years was REAL.

Argh. What on earth had she been thinking that day? Clearly, she'd made a rash decision in a rare moment where she felt fearless and far more confident than she really was—two qualities she was severely lacking right now. Damn her bloody impulsiveness.

And now, three months later, she was stuck with the absurd idea that she could somehow talk her way into an entirely new career. Oh god. She wished she could get out of this.

Argh, adulting was hard.

At twenty-seven, Daisy's life was—well, fine. Not dazzling. Not dreadful. Just… fine. The real problem was that Daisy was living some sort of double life, and there were two versions of her:

Daisy Number One—Corporate Killer Daisy. She nailed every job. She was focused, productive, and the best damn insurance sales consultant for that company. Before they wore her down, that is. She was bubbly, outgoing, a social butterfly who could crush it in the corporate world and could probably crush it in marketing if she could pluck up a bit of courage.

Daisy Number Two—The real Daisy. The messy one. The chaotic, too-much, laugh-too-loud, talk-too-fast one. The one with slightly less bravado than the first. The job-quitting, phone-call-avoiding, anxiety-ridden recluse. The one who had been seeing a therapist since she was eleven and still hadn't quite figured herself out. The one who sometimes wanted nothing more than to sit with her dog and shut the world out.

And lately? The latter had been winning.

The fun of her early twenties had faded, and thirty was approaching far too quickly. What did she have to show for it? Six years at the same insurance company, climbing the ladder from junior sales assistant to senior sales consultant, only to wake up one morning three months ago and realise—she hated it. She hated her boss. She hated everyone there.

The final straw? A passive-aggressive email from HR titled *"Creating a Respectful Shared Space"*, which was really just a thinly veiled attack on whoever had left a Tupperware of Spaghetti Bolognese in the communal fridge for more than 24 hours. *"Let's all be mindful of smells that may linger, and remember—we're a team, not a student flat!"* it chirped, complete with a smiling emoji. Daisy had read it three times, each pass-through making her blood simmer. It wasn't just the email. It was the fact that she knew it was directed at her.

It was the fact that she was almost thirty and being scolded like a schoolchild over pasta.

Also that her boss, Clive, had replied to all with "Well said!" and a gif of Gordon Ramsay.

She'd stared at her screen, let out a laugh that came out a bit too high-pitched, stood up, and walked out—leaving behind her mug, her lanyard, and any semblance of a plan.

At the time, it felt like a power move.

Now? Daisy wasn't so sure.

Daisy Number One had made that decision three months ago. Now Daisy Number Two was left to deal with the fallout, desperately wishing she could retreat into her shell.

Thing is, she never knew which version of herself she'd wake up to in the mornings—and today, it was definitely Daisy Number Two. And she really, really didn't want to go to this interview.

Daisy sat, recounting her last conversation with Lance in her head.

"Dais, you're being dramatic. It's marketing, not brain surgery."

"I have zero experience, Lance. They're going to see right through me."

"Please, you've been faking your way through insurance paperwork for years. Same thing, but with more emojis."

"That is not reassuring."

"Just wear something smart and short, a bit of lippy, smile, and try not to insult anyone."

"Wow. High expectations."

"If all else fails, flirt your way in."

"Lance, I think you're confusing me with you."

As much as she hated to admit it, he had a point. She needed to snap out of this rut before she became a full-blown recluse. For the past few months, she'd barely left the house, ignored her friends—including her other fiercely confident best friend, Lydia—dodged her sister Prim's calls, and generally avoided the world. Her only accomplishment? Rewatching her holy trinity of comfort movies—*The Holiday*, *The Parent Trap*, and *10 Things I Hate About You*—so many times that even they were starting to annoy her.

Wait—no. That was sacrilege. She could never get tired of Dennis Quaid's exceedingly handsome face (an entirely age-appropriate crush now), Jude Law's Mr Napkin Head, and Lindsay Lohan, the absolute ethereal being that she was.

God, she already wanted to stay home and rewatch them all. Maybe throw in *Mean Girls* for good measure…

Daisy groaned, mindlessly scrolling through her phone, snoozing her alarm for the third time, clinging to the early morning haze before she had to shower, get dressed, and pretend to be a functioning adult.

Her French Bulldog, Tino, waddled into the room, huffing dramatically for breakfast. He'd already kept her up half the night licking his paws, so he could wait a little longer, she thought. He then sighed like his life was unbearable—like he didn't live here rent-free and sleep 20 hours a day.

She reached down to scratch his ears. "Do you ever feel like you've made a huge mistake, Tino?"

He huffed in response.

"Right. Thanks for that."

She doom-scrolled some more. A girl from school had just gotten engaged. Another had run a marathon. Someone else was on a beach in Bali, sipping a cocktail out of a pineapple. Fantastic. Everyone was thriving while Daisy was debating whether she could feasibly call in sick to an interview. What she would give to be sipping cocktails on a beach in Bali right now…

No. Enough. She needed to channel Daisy Number One.

So, she forced herself out of bed, putting her phone on charge and laying it to rest on the bedside table.

That's when she saw it. Accidentally clicked on it.

An Instagram post. Her heart stopped.

Matthew.

Chapter 2:
Manifesting Success

Daisy couldn't do anything but stare at her phone. Why today of all days? Why did she have to see that? As if mustering the strength to switch personality wasn't hard enough, life had to throw a major flipping curveball on top. Fantastic.

Her trance broke when a call flashed on the screen — *Prim.*

Prim — her overbearing, terrifyingly capable older sister. The complete opposite of Daisy. A radiant force of positivity. Prim was beautiful, confident, charming, and good at everything Daisy wasn't. Yet, despite their differences, Prim adored her. She always tried to lift Daisy, though her well-meant pep talks often had the opposite effect — reminding Daisy just how far she felt from her sister's light.

She hesitated. She didn't want to answer, but Prim being Prim, she'd just keep calling.

"Hello, Prim. What do you want?"

"Well, that's just *charming!* I haven't spoken to you for an entire day, and that's your greeting? Your best, most beautiful sister?"

"You're my only sister, Prim. What do you want?"

"What's got into you? Touchy."

"It's nothing."

"Look, I'm just calling to make sure you're going to that interview. Grant says he's not paying your rent for another month."

Grant — Prim's saintly fiancé. When he signed up for Prim, high-maintenance and all, he unknowingly signed up for her awkward, messy, and perpetually broke little sister, too. To his credit, he never complained. He'd been covering Daisy's rent ever since she quit her job — something she was endlessly grateful for. Prim, however, wasn't quite as generous; mostly because it meant less money spent on her.

"Yes, Prim, I'm going," Daisy replied, reluctant but resigned.

"Excellent! You'll smash it, baby sis. Think *positive vibes!*"

"You sound just like Mum."

"Well, at least she's positive. Come on, Dais. You'll be great! A career change will do you good — get you out of the house, maybe even meet a nice bloke."

"Right. Because nothing screams emotional stability like joblessness and dating apps. Thanks, Prim."

"Okay, okay! But you're not going to be this pretty and perky forever, Dais—"

"Oh, more stellar advice from Dr Phil in Louboutins. Keep it coming."

"What? I'm just saying what everyone thinks."

Before Daisy's head could explode, she cut in. "I have to go get ready, Prim, before I start Googling how to fake my own death."

Prim, completely unfazed, started singing down the phone. "Byeeeeee!"

Daisy hung up with a huff, resisting the urge to launch her phone into the bush outside.

Prim was two years older — successful, tall, and strikingly beautiful. At 5'7", she was effortlessly slim, with ocean-blue eyes and long, glossy light-brown hair. Daisy, on the other hand, stood at 5'2" with a softer, rounder frame, hazel eyes, and a dark bob she kept dyed just to avoid any resemblance to her sister. A faint dusting of freckles crossed her nose — her only feature she somewhat liked. No matter how much she loved Prim, she had always felt like the lesser version.

The sisters had grown up in Battersea, South West London, with their grandparents while their mum, Jessie, flitted between lovers, hobbies, and life crises. Jessie Donaldson — still technically married to their estranged father Malcolm Donaldson — was more of a free spirit than a mother. A self-proclaimed hippy, she was always chasing new passions. Last week, it was Goat Yoga with a bloke named Alejandro, who was about thirty-two — almost the same age as Prim.

Nanna Jean, though — she was the true matriarch of their little family. Steady, unshakable, the glue that held everything together. Grandad Bill had passed when Daisy and Prim were still in senior school, but Daisy remembered him vividly: a proper old-school Londoner, always cracking jokes, a cigarette in one hand and a beer in the other. More than that, she remembered the way he spoke to Nanna Jean — always calling her *love,* his voice warm with adoration. He absolutely worshipped her. It was real love — the kind Daisy rarely saw anywhere else.

Eventually, though, the cigarettes and booze caught up with him. When Grandad Bill passed, Nanna Jean was devastated. She was never quite the same, but she stayed strong. She didn't let it show; she just carried on—because that's what people of her generation did. Daisy admired that kind of quiet resilience. It was a stark contrast to her own parents' so-called relationship, which, frankly, had never made much sense.

Prim had naturally—though not necessarily with Daisy's blessing—stepped into the motherly role their mum Jessie had failed to fill. Grandad Bill used to call her "Prim and Proper," a nickname Daisy loathed, especially because it was obvious that Prim was his favourite. That was when Daisy's confidence first began to falter— around ten years old. And the older they grew, the harder it became for Daisy to ever step out of her sister's shadow.

She loved Prim, truly. Her sister was caring, dependable, and always there when needed. But standing beside her, Daisy couldn't help but feel plain. In school especially, all the boys fancied Prim, leaving Daisy feeling dull and invisible.

That's about when she started referring to her sister as *"Perfect Prim."* Behind her back, of course.

Daisy really hated school when Prim was still there.

Well—until she met Matthew Devan.

Tino let out a long, theatrical sigh from the bed, as if he could sense the emotional storm brewing. Daisy scrolled back up to the post on her phone. There it was again the photo, the name, that stupidly familiar face. Matthew bloody Devan, smiling like he hadn't wrecked her for every other man since.

At first, he'd just been her friend. They spent all their time together. He was an introvert like her—nerdy, funny, and into all the same things. He was her person.

Daisy rubbed her temples, trying to shake the memories loose like dust. This wasn't helping. It was an Instagram post, not a wormhole to 2009. And yet, there she was again mentally curled up next to him, as if no time had passed.

It wasn't until Prim left school that Daisy finally began to come out of her shell, and that's when she realised she liked Matthew more than just a friend.

When Matthew turned fifteen, he lost his puppy fat and gained a sharp jawline. He started calling himself *Matt* (though Daisy would always think of him as *Matthew*). Suddenly, other girls noticed him too. He was still the same lovable nerd—but now, an attractive one. Still, he was Daisy's nerd, and she wouldn't have it any other way.

Matthew was a good-looking boy—6'1", dark brown eyes, thick dark hair, and the most gorgeous olive skin. His parents were both from London, with Indian heritage on his dad's side and Irish on his mum's. He'd inherited the best of both. And that smile—God, that smile could melt her in a heartbeat.

The summer before Year 11, Matthew finally asked Daisy out. Their shift from friends to something more was seamless. The first time she kissed him, she couldn't believe they hadn't been doing it all along. From then on, they were inseparable.

Tino whined again. Daisy glanced at him. "Don't look at me like that. I'm not texting him."

She hadn't had many other friends at school. It was always just her and Matthew. He had his cricket mates, sure, but Daisy didn't need anyone else—she was happy with just him.

They both stayed on for sixth form, doing their A-Levels at the same school. They were solid. It worked. He preferred staying in with her—gaming, playing guitar—rather than partying or getting smashed. They got serious in every sense of the word. Daisy loved him. He was perfect.

But university loomed, and reality set in. Matthew's dad had big plans for him—plans that included a prestigious degree at a university Daisy had no chance of getting into. They both knew their relationship wouldn't survive the distance from Edinburgh to Bournemouth.

And it didn't.

Even after they broke up, Daisy thought about him constantly. She even hid his posts on social media while at university, unable to face seeing his life go on without her. When she returned home after graduating, she wanted to reach out. She'd dated since then, but nothing—nothing—had ever compared to what she had with Matthew.

She still loved him.

But she couldn't bring herself to reconnect. Fear held her back—fear that he had changed, moved on, or no longer felt the same. So, she pushed him out of her mind, hid him on social media, and tried to build a life without him.

And, for a while, it had sort of worked.

Until today.

He'd found his way back—somehow—in the worst possible way.

Daisy locked her phone and flung it onto the bed like it was radioactive. "Brilliant. Come on, Tino—walkies," she muttered, striding toward the hallway. "We're not spiralling. We're totally fine."

She needed to shift gears. Channel Daisy Number One. Focus. But first walk the dog. Then go nail this interview.

Chapter 3:
Charm. Innovate. Elevate

In the crisp spring air, Daisy chose a calming walk along the Thames instead of cramming herself onto the Tube, hoping it would clear her head. April in London was always hit or miss, but today was gloriously sunny—a good omen, she decided. She pressed play on her same old playlist, a mix of familiar favourites that made her feel vaguely like she had her life together. For a moment, it was bliss.

Daisy loved walking. It always helped—it put things into perspective. But today, no amount of fresh air or carefully curated background music could quiet the nerves buzzing in her stomach.

Then her phone pinged.

Lydia: *You're gonna smash this interview!*

The other bestie.

Daisy: *Or cry in the bathroom halfway through. 50/50 chance.*

Lydia: *Confidence, babe!*

Daisy: *The only thing I'm confident in is that I'll trip on the way in.*

Lydia: *Manifest success!*

Daisy: *Manifesting unemployment.*

Lydia: *Drinks after?*

Daisy: *Maybe.*

Daisy had met Lydia Allard at Bournemouth University. Becoming her perfect best friend, Lydia had pulled Daisy out of her depression—and Daisy hadn't been able to shake her since. Lydia had even moved to London after uni.

She was, much like Prim, the total opposite of Daisy. Things just *worked* for her. An extrovert, always ready for a night out. She was single-handedly responsible for "Party Daisy," who had thrived—right up until this year. Or, more accurately, the past two months, when Daisy had given in to her quieter, anxious counterpart.

Lydia Allard was adopted. Her birth mother was Korean—or so her passport said—but she'd never managed to trace her. Her adoptive mother, Miyoung—who now goes by Mary—was also Korean but had lived in Essex since childhood. Mary was strict, with firm expectations for how things should be done. Lydia's adoptive father, Tony, was British and far less intimidating. Mostly, he was scared of Mary, which made him useless whenever Lydia wanted to push against the rigid rules she had been set.

After years under that kind of roof, Lydia had thrown herself into freedom with full force. It was obvious from the moment Daisy met her—and she'd been making up for lost time ever since. Moving close to Daisy's corner of Southeast London, settling in Southwark, was her way of erasing every trace of her constrained upbringing. Pretty, eccentric, and effortlessly cool, Lydia fit right into the stylish chaos of the city.

Lydia: *Dais... You can't hide from meeeee.*

Daisy smiled at her phone. Lydia was a force of nature and Daisy was going to need all the support she could get today.

As she stepped into the sleek, modern office near Cannon Street a serious glow-up from the soul-sucking insurance company she'd escaped Daisy tugged at her slightly too-sensible blazer like it was armor. Underneath, she'd opted for a lace-trimmed crop top instead of a stiff button-up, because yes, she could be professional *and* chaotic. Her wide-leg trousers skimmed her heels—heels she absolutely did not want to wear but apparently needed if she wanted to look taller and vaguely "businesslike." Each click against the polished floor sounded either confident or terrified. Probably both.

Her hair… actually cooperated. Minor miracle.

God, she felt like Prim. The thought made her want to throw her iced latte across the lobby. Perfect hair, perfectly tailored clothes, perfectly adult-ish. Ugh. She hated it. Still, maybe—just maybe—she could channel a fraction of that confidence without losing herself completely.

The reception area was flooded with soft London light from floor-to-ceiling windows. Minimalist furniture filled the space, and the air hummed with the quiet energy of people doing important things. Adjusting her hair, Daisy approached the reception desk, trying not to feel like an imposter. She was early—because anxiety never let her be fashionably late.

Then her phone rang. Loudly.

Every head in the lobby turned. Daisy's stomach dropped as she fumbled for her phone, cheeks burning crimson.

Nanna Jean. Of course. No concept of time—probably calling to congratulate her, assuming the interview was already over.

She spun on her heel, heading for the exit to answer—

And smacked straight into someone.

A very tall, very well-dressed someone.

Hot coffee splashed everywhere—ridiculously expensive hipster coffee seeping into his sharp, undoubtedly just-as-expensive navy suit.

"Oh, shit! I'm s-so sorry!" Daisy stammered, eyes wide with horror. She looked up and met piercing blue eyes beneath slightly tousled dark-blonde hair. He did not look amused. More... seething.

The man exhaled slowly, as if summoning patience from the depths of his soul.

Daisy, meanwhile, was still stuck on the fact that he was— without question—the most ridiculously handsome man she'd ever crashed into.

"Please, let me replace the coffee. Or the suit... or—"

He shook out his jacket, flicking droplets onto the polished floor, and arched a brow. "Really?"

"Oh—shit—I actually have an interview, but maybe later—" she blurted, words tumbling out.

"Look, it's fine. Don't worry about it," he said, his tone dripping with the kind of exhaustion usually reserved for bad Wi-Fi and people who walk too slowly in front of him.

A blonde receptionist materialised with a box of tissues and began dabbing at his sleeve. Daisy tried to help, tossing a few tissues onto the floor in the process, but she was more of a hindrance than a help. In the end, she just stood there uselessly, resisting the urge to spontaneously combust from sheer embarrassment.

"Thanks, Arabella, it's fine," the man said to the receptionist, his tone softening slightly.

Daisy scowled at her. (Like *she* was the problem.) Which was unfair. But whatever.

"I really am sorry," Daisy tried again. "Do you want my number? You can send me the dry-cleaning bill."

He let out a short laugh—dry, amused, faintly sarcastic. "Honestly, it's fine. Don't worry about it."

And just as her humiliation reached new heights, her coffee-splattered phone blared again.

"You should answer that," he said, raising an eyebrow. "Must be important."

And with that, he strode past the security barriers and disappeared into the lift.

Daisy winced. Great start.

Outside, she answered the call.

"Nan, hi. Sorry I missed your call—I was busy making a royal twat of myself, as per usual."

"Why, what happened, love?"

"Oh, just classic me, Nan—the flipping klutz that I am. Knocked an entire coffee over some poor guy. A really bloody annoyingly gorgeous one, by the way. God, when I mess up, I do it spectacularly."

"Daisy, love, you're rambling." Trying not to laugh.

"You know what? Never mind. I'll probably never see him again. Even if I do, I bet he'll run a mile. Oh god, I'm so nervous, Nan. Please, help me."

"You're worrying about it too much, love. So you're off your game—just be yourself, Daisy."

"Myself? A complete disaster?" she scoffed.

"Then be someone else for the interview. I was someone else for thirty years working at Tesco. You think I actually cared about Mr. Whitmore's bloody lottery tickets?"

"…Valid point."

"Now go get 'em." Nanna Jean replied before ending the call.

With a deep breath, Daisy marched back inside—only to realise her next obstacle was *Arabella*. Fantastic.

"Daisy Donaldson. I have an interview with—"

"Rhoda Williams, yes," Arabella said, barely glancing up as she typed. "Let me print your pass and email her assistant."

Daisy exhaled slowly, counting to five in her head—an old therapy trick from when she was eleven. It almost worked.

Then Arabella, who was less a receptionist and more a celestial event—beautiful, blinding, and entirely orbiting her own importance—smirked.

"Rough morning, huh?"

Daisy tensed. "…Yep. You could say that."

Arabella laughed. "You know, the more I think about it, the

funnier it is."

Daisy fought the urge to throttle her.

"Of all the people you could bump into," Arabella added, "you had to pick *Sam Callaghan.*"

Daisy froze at the sound of the name.

Sam. Callaghan.

Her stomach did a small, unsettling flip. But before she could process it, a voice behind her spoke.

"Daisy Donaldson?"

She shook it off. Focus. You're here for the interview, not to psychoanalyse your feelings for some ridiculously good-looking man who thinks you're a walking disaster in a blazer.

Ugh. Why did this have to happen today?

Daisy stepped out of the lift and into the office, immediately feeling out of place. The space was sleek—glass walls, polished concrete, and a huge neon sign on the back wall that read:

Create. Innovate. Elevate.

A far cry from her last job, where the only sign on the wall was a laminated printout about fire exits.

She whispered, "Manifest success, Daisy," just as Lydia had told her earlier.

It helped—for a second. She breathed in deep, centering herself. But as her heels clicked across the polished floor, it became painfully obvious that she had no idea what she was doing here.

Before she could make a run for it, another perfectly polished receptionist—with a flawless bob and an even more flawless outfit— smiled at her.

"Daisy Donaldson? You can go through—second door on the right. She's expecting you."

Daisy swallowed hard. She could do this. She *had* to do this.

Exhaling with as much confidence as she could muster, she straightened her blazer, squared her shoulders, and pushed open the door—just a little too hard—and almost went with it.

She managed to style it out.

She hoped.

Rhoda stood to greet her with a firm handshake.

"Daisy. Hi. Thanks for coming in. Rhoda Williams."

"Hi. Daisy. Thank you for seeing me," she replied, somehow managing to sound confident.

Rhoda sat back down at the large meeting table and gestured for Daisy to take the seat opposite. Daisy did, making a conscious effort not to let her leg bounce under the table. Her anxiety always came with a nervous tap—one that loved to appear at the worst possible times. And after this morning's reception disaster, that tap was *dying* to break free.

Across from her sat a woman who radiated confidence. Late thirties, maybe early forties, dressed in an effortlessly chic rose-colored suit. She barely glanced up from Daisy's CV before saying, "You don't have a marketing background."

Daisy's stomach plummeted. *Oh God. She's onto me.*

But then something inside her shifted—the part of her that had once closed high-value insurance deals. The part that knew she was good at what she put her mind to.

She sat up straighter. "True," she said smoothly. "But I understand people—how they think, what they respond to. Insurance sales isn't that different from marketing. You have to be persuasive, tell a story, and make people believe they need what you're offering."

Rhoda raised an eyebrow. "Interesting take."

Daisy nodded, keeping her expression cool even as her heart

pounded. She had no idea where this sudden confidence was coming from, but she was rolling with it.

The rest of the interview passed in a blur. She answered every question with surprising composure, talked about problem-solving, adaptability, and her fascination with social media. She even cracked a joke that actually landed. And before she knew it, Rhoda was shaking her hand and offering to give her a tour of the office.

Wait—did she actually get the job?

She had no idea. And now, she was too scared—or possibly too mortified—to ask. It was like talking to someone for so long without knowing their name, even though they'd told you twice, and now it was way past the point where you could admit it. Except instead of a name, Daisy needed to ask if she was *employed.*

And she really, *really* wanted this job.

As it turned out, Rhoda was actually lovely. Definitely a career woman—Daisy could tell because, during the tour, she hadn't mentioned a husband or kids. She had, however, mentioned her dog, Bruce. Twice. When Daisy casually brought up Tino, it went down *very* well.

As they walked through the open-plan office, Daisy caught a flash of movement out of the corner of her eye—Lance. He popped up from his desk like a startled meerkat, whisper-shouting her name.

Everyone stared.

Subtlety? Not his forte.

Daisy grinned.

"Friend of yours?" Rhoda smirked.

"Yes. A good friend."

"I suppose we won't be sitting you at *that* end, then."

Daisy hesitated. "…So I got the job?"

Rhoda raised a brow. "Indeed. Anyone who can keep their cool after the ordeal you had in reception this morning and still nail an interview with no prior experience is a keeper in my eyes.”

Daisy’s mouth fell open. *How does she know what happened in reception ?*

But as they neared the check-in desk at the entrance to the floor, all became clear.

Standing there—looking somehow even more handsome than he had that morning (was that even possible?)—was *him.*

Blue suit (minus the jacket, thankfully). Ridiculously good hair. Victim of Daisy’s coffee attack.

Rhoda nodded toward him.

“Sam is my lead accountant in the finance department. He might have mentioned it.”

Daisy’s stomach dropped. She could feel sweat pooling in her palms. Of *course* he was here. Of course he’d mentioned it.

“He’s the one who signs off your expenses,” Rhoda added with a wink. “Probably best to stay on his good side.”

Fantastic. Shame she’d kicked things off by drenching him in his own coffee.

Sam smirked as he walked past but didn’t so much as glance at her. It hurt more than she wanted to admit.

Brilliant.

Just bloody brilliant.

Chapter 4:
A mix of curiosity and dread

Later, Daisy waited for Lydia in a bar near St Paul's, her mind replaying the day's events—both good and bad—as she stared solemnly into her half-drained pint glass. A glass half empty.

Now, don't get her wrong—Daisy wasn't being ungrateful. She was, of course, thrilled to have landed the job. But the realisation was beginning to sink in: she now had to *be* this version of herself every day. Daisy Number One. The confident, capable, high-performing professional. Could she actually pull that off long-term?

And, of course, there was *that* embarrassment—the coffee catastrophe—and the glaringly obvious fact that she might—just *might*—have a crush on one of her new colleagues.

Not that she wanted to call it that. And not that it mattered, because Sam Callaghan was most definitely *not* interested in her. He was more suited to the Arabellas of the world. After this morning's disaster, Daisy's chances with him were precisely zero.

One silver lining? She hadn't thought about the Matthew thing all day.

Except… now she was thinking about it.

"Sorry, sorry! I'm here—bloody traffic!" Lydia burst through the door, shoving her bag—and everything that *should* have been inside it—across the table. Chaotic as ever.

"My Uber was late, then it got stuck at bloody Piccadilly, and—well, I'm here now."

Daisy stood as Lydia pulled her into a hug, planting a kiss on her cheek.

"I've missed you, you bloody recluse loser." Lydia bopped

Daisy's nose affectionately.

"Thanks, Lyd. Missed you too."

"Why have you been hiding? You've missed so much."

Daisy hesitated. "I've been… well, busy?"

Lydia shot her a knowing look. "Daisy Donaldson, sitting at home in joggers and an Oodie, watching *The Holiday* for the eightieth time, is *not* busy. Your life isn't going to magically turn into a Cameron Diaz rom-com, and there is *definitely* no Jude Law waiting for you in the countryside."

Daisy scoffed, smiling as Lydia continued her tirade.

"And don't even get me started on the fact that it's a Christmas movie. Jesus."

Ironic.

"Hey, I didn't just watch that one. Look, I just haven't felt like partying, Lyd. I needed some me-time."

Lydia let out a loud, dramatic laugh. "Pathetic!" She slapped the table and waved over a waitress. "God, get me a drink."

Daisy grinned. There were many things to love about Lydia, but her brutal honesty was both her best and worst quality.

"So, what are we having? Did you get the job?"

"I did."

Lydia let out a delighted scream, clapping her hands. "Bottle of Moët it is! Actually… maybe just Prosecco." She turned to Daisy with a grin. "You can get this, right? I'm a bit strapped at the moment."

"Audition didn't pan out, then?" Daisy smiled sympathetically.

"No. It was *fucking awful*, Dais. But let's save that story for later. We're talking about you—tell me everything."

The waitress arrived, setting a bucket of ice on the table and pouring two glasses of Prosecco. Lydia immediately downed one, refilled, and flashed the waitress a grin.

Lydia Allard was always this energetic. A self-proclaimed "artist," she was a struggling actress with a few small theatre credits under her belt. Her most notable role had been playing Titania in *A Midsummer Night's Dream* at The Southwark Playhouse last summer. But right now, she was what people politely called an "out-of-work actor," surviving off last year's earnings and desperately in need of a new role. Daisy wanted success for her so badly it hurt—but there wasn't much she could do to help.

"So, come on," Lydia pressed. "Spill. How was the actual interview?"

"The interview went really, really well."

"Did you see Lance? Is he coming?"

"Yeah, he should be here soon. It went great—my new boss seems really nice. Scary, but nice. But actually… the morning was a disaster you would not believe."

Lydia's eyes narrowed. She knew that tone. Daisy had done a *Daisy.*

"Why? What happened?"

Daisy exhaled. "So, I walk into the building… and then my phone rings—on loud—so I turn to walk back out and ram straight into, probably, the hottest guy I've ever seen, spilling his coffee all over him."

Lydia's loud cackle turned heads from nearby tables. "You did *not!*"

"Oh, I did." Daisy groaned, dropping her head into her hands. "And it gets worse. He actually works for my new company."

Lydia slapped the table, absolutely delighted. "Dais! Mortifying!"

Daisy peeked up at her. "I know, right?"

"What's his name? What does he look like? Can we Insta-stalk him?" Lydia grinned, already fishing for her phone.

Daisy sighed. "No." Then paused. "Actually… yes. Shall we?"

Lydia squealed, grabbing her phone. "What's his name?"

"Sam Callaghan."

"How do I spell that?"

"I don't know." Daisy frowned. She'd only *heard* his name— never seen it written. They both leaned over the screen as Lydia typed and scrolled through the results.

"Nope. None of these are him," Daisy sighed.

"Well, what does he look like?" Lydia pressed.

"Dark-blonde hair, blue eyes, mid-twenties. Nice face?"

Lydia groaned dramatically. "Who doesn't have Instagram in this day and age? What about Facebook?"

"Well, that's more of an elder-millennial thing, Lyd," Daisy said.

Oh God. She immediately regretted this. Searching for him felt like an admission—like she was acknowledging something she wasn't ready to face. What if she didn't like what she found? What if he had a girlfriend? What if—

"I've bloody found him! It's Callaghan with a G." Lydia nudged Daisy, grinning triumphantly.

"Where? Show me." Daisy leaned in, feeling a mix of curiosity and dread. "Oh yeah… that's him."

"He's a footballer, Dais. Or was."

Daisy suddenly felt ridiculous for even looking. His profile was barely active—last post, 2019. Mostly football photos. Hardly anything to go on. Still, seeing his face again sent an unwelcome flutter through her stomach.

Lydia, however, was cackling. "Oh, Dais. I can't believe you poured coffee all over *this* guy. He is so fine.”

Daisy groaned. “Yeah, hilarious. But… not the worst news of the day.”

Something in her voice shifted, and Lydia immediately noticed.

“What?” Lydia frowned. “What’s happened?”

Daisy exhaled, staring at her glass. “It’s about Matthew.”

Lydia’s face fell. “Your ex, Matthew? Love-of-your-life Matthew?”

“He’s engaged,” Daisy said, the words tasting bitter as they left her mouth. “Saw the Instagram post this morning.”

“Matthew’s getting married, Lyd.”

There. It was out.

For a moment—silence.

Then—

“Noooo!” Lance’s voice cut through the noise as he arrived, looking utterly scandalised. He slid into the seat next to Daisy, eyes wide. “Matthew’s getting married? *Your* Matthew? Oh, babe.” His tone softened with pity.

Daisy barely nodded before Lance pulled her into a hug. Suddenly, the whole thing felt real. Too real. A lump rose in her throat. She swallowed it down.

“Are you okay?” he asked gently.

“I don’t think I am.” The words came out quieter than she expected. She rested her head on his shoulder, eyes stinging—but she refused to cry. Not here. Not now.

Lydia poured another drink, glancing at Lance before topping up his glass too. She didn’t say anything, but Daisy could tell she was holding back—probably torn between offering comfort and cracking an inappropriate joke.

In the end, Lydia did what she did best.

"So, want to hear something funny Daisy did today to a really fit bloke?" she smirked.

Daisy groaned. "Nooo, please."

But she was already laughing. Because that's what they did. They kept her afloat.

And tonight, she really needed it.

Chapter 5:
Cracking open a door you shouldn't have touched

Daisy awoke to the crushing weight of Tino sprawled across her stomach—his little furry body completely unbothered by the fact that she was on the verge of death. *Hangxiety* flooded her veins before she even opened her eyes.

How much alcohol had she consumed last night? Sure, they were celebrating her new job—but why did it feel like someone had taken a pneumatic drill to her skull? And why was her mouth as dry as— God, she couldn't even think of a comparison.

Somewhere in the distance—aka across the room—her phone was dinging. Far too distant for her to even *consider* getting up. The only water within reach was in a vase on the coffee table, and the flowers in it had been dead for at least a week.

Definitely not an option.

Life was hitting Daisy hard this morning.

And to top it all off, she had Prim and Grant's engagement party tonight.

Right now, Daisy could not think of anything worse. She'd rather stick pins in her eyes than go to *Perfect Prim's Perfect Engagement Party*. Alone.

It was at that exact moment she remembered. The memory returned like a bad smell lingering on the last train home.

Her stomach plummeted. Her heart shot into her throat.

She'd messaged Matthew last night. Slid into his DMs like an alcohol-fuelled squirrel on TikTok.

Yep. Daisy definitely wanted to die right now.

She groaned, squeezing her eyes shut as if that could somehow erase the memory. What had she even said? Was it bad? Did he reply?

Her phone dinged again.

Nope. She wasn't ready to face that yet. She'd rather throw herself out the window than deal with this. (Except she was on the ground floor, so she'd just land in the bushes—which, honestly, might be where she belonged.)

Then her phone rang—forcing her to move.

A little too fast, admittedly. The room tilted violently, and for a moment, she genuinely thought she might collapse *and* throw up at the same time.

She grabbed her phone off the table, blinking at the screen. Lydia.

Daisy took a deep breath and answered.

"Tell me you're alive," Lydia said dramatically. "Or are we holding a funeral for Daisy Donaldson's dignity?"

Daisy groaned. "Not now, Lyd."

"Uh-oh. That bad?"

"That bad."

"Talk to me."

Daisy flopped back onto the sofa, pushing Tino off her with a weak shove. "I might have messaged Matthew."

Silence. Then, in a hushed, horrified tone:

"Oh, babes. You *slid* into his DMs."

Daisy closed her eyes. "Yep. I blame Lance. He's such a bad influence—it was his bloody idea."

"Yeah, babe, you really shouldn't take guy-related advice from Lance."

"Bit late for that now, Lyd," Daisy huffed.

"Well, what did you say?"

"I—" She hesitated, forcing herself to open the chat. There it was: her own stupidity, preserved in plain text.

Daisy: *Congrats, Matthew. Really happy for you.*

Lydia gasped. "Oh. You were actually nice to him? I don't know if that's worse. It's polite. It's civilised. It's—"

"Exactly what a woman who's completely over her ex would say," Daisy groaned. "I hate myself."

Lydia sucked in a breath. "Did he reply?"

Daisy forced herself to check.

Matthew: *Hello Daisy. Thank you. It means a lot.*

She read it out loud.

"Okay, that's… bloody boring," Lydia decided. "Boring is good, right?"

"I don't know, Lyd." Daisy rubbed her temples. "Is that really something you say to someone you haven't spoken to in years? Someone you *loved*? For God's sake, I've been very carefully avoiding him for so long, and I've gone back on everything with just one message."

Daisy let out a strangled noise of despair.

Lydia sighed. "Okay, but closure. Just delete the chat and pretend it never happened. Yeah?"

"Easy for you to say," Daisy muttered.

"And you've got this party to get to. You might meet someone there! You know what they say—best way to get over someone is to get under someone," Lydia said, trying to sound supportive.

"Lyd. Nobody says that. Nobody in real life."

Daisy groaned.

"Oh, babe," Lydia said gently. "You're gonna need more Prosecco."

Daisy winced. "I never want to drink again."

A beat of silence.

"Sure, babes. Sure."

"Are you *sure* you can't come with me? I really don't want to go, but having you there would make it so much better," Daisy pleaded.

Lydia sighed. "Babe, you know I can't—I've got work. Otherwise, I would. Why don't you ask Lance?"

"Mr. Bad Influence?" Daisy paused. "Okay, fine."

"It'll be fun! You know I'm right. Shit, babe, I have to go. And make sure you delete that chat. Cut it off at the source so there are no more slip-ups tonight."

Then Lydia cackled.

"Yes, yes. I'll do it now. Bye, Lyd."

She did *not* do it.

Instead, she stared at the screen, feeling like she'd cracked open a door she never should've touched.

But it was fine. She didn't have to think about it anymore. She wouldn't be seeing him.

Right?

Daisy decided that a run was the best way to stamp out this vicious hangover. So she wrenched herself off the sofa, dragged herself into the shower, threw on her running gear, and headed out. Before leaving, she quickly texted Lance about the party. Lydia was right—she needed emotional support tonight, even if Lance was more of a liability than a help.

Daisy: *Morning sunshine. How's the head?*

Lance: *Dreadful, no thanks to you and that wiry minx Lyds.*

Bastards.

Daisy: *Are you free this evening? I need a date.*

Lance: *Oh babe, you know I don't do vaginas.*

Daisy: *Not that sort of date, you idiot. An emotional support date. Prim's engagement party. Free booze, free food. Her fiancé's parents are loaded.*

Lance: *I'm so in. WhatsApp me the deets.*

Daisy: *Love you. When I'm back from my run.*

Lance: *A run?!!! Bloody hell, Dais. Why are you going on a run, you savage?*

When Daisy returned from her run, she tried—and failed—to avoid her two upstairs neighbours, Viv and John, who were collecting their mail. She couldn't quite understand why they did this *together* at 10:28 a.m. on a Saturday, but she'd always found them a bit odd. Eccentric. The resident street busybodies.

She really didn't have the patience for whatever nonsense they'd come up with this morning, so she attempted to slip past quietly.

"Daisy! Hello, dear!" John beamed, leaning casually in the doorway. Daisy was about eighty-seven percent sure he was gay.

Not great for Viv.

"Hi, John. Hi, Viv. Got to dash—sister's engagement party to get ready for."

"Oh, how lovely!" Viv smiled brightly.

John didn't move.

"You should tell her, Viv."

"No, you tell her. You brought it up."

Daisy didn't have time for this pensioner back-and-forth. "Tell me what?" she asked, patience thinning.

"Well, Daisy, love," John began, "we think someone might be

stealing your mail."

What. The. Actual. *Fuck.*

Daisy blinked, trying to stay calm. "Really? I seem to get my mail just fine."

John persisted. "Well, we've been finding our mail in Rita's box—number twelve—and she swears she didn't put it there. So, we checked yours, and ours was in there—but not yours."

Holy mother of all things...

"Right. Could it just be the postman?" Daisy offered, desperate to escape. "Wouldn't hurt to check with him Monday."

"Oh! We never thought of that, did we, John?" Viv said, as if a lightbulb had just gone off.

"Sorry, I really have to go." Daisy squeezed past them and rushed inside, slamming the door behind her before letting out a muffled scream.

Tino gave her a long look.

"Don't you start," she muttered.

He grabbed the remains of his pink llama toy and began chewing.

They had eaten into so much of her *getting ready* time. Now she was going to be bloody late.

Chapter 6:
Prim has hit the jackpot

Surprisingly, after a shaky start, Daisy got ready in record time. She decided to take both Zara dresses she couldn't pick between and let Lance choose, rather than spend seven hours procrastinating.

Sometimes, she was just *so* productive.

She was channelling Daisy Number One today—even if it killed her.

After dropping Tino off with Nanna Jean's new neighbour, Sylvie—who seemed lovely but was still a potential dog thief in Daisy's mind—she jumped on the Tube like a packhorse and messaged Lance to say she'd be with him in fifteen minutes. A lie, obviously—it was closer to twenty-five.

They could grab an Uber from his place. The drive to Grant's parents' house (a severe understatement for the *mansion* it was) in Richmond upon Thames wasn't too far, so an Uber there and back seemed doable. Or maybe Daisy just didn't care anymore. She'd spent the entire morning running around like a madwoman, was now sweating it out on the Tube, and the thought of another train was bloody unbearable.

Technically, it hadn't been Prim's first choice for an engagement party. She'd had her eye on a grand manor with a hotel and spa attached, but some relatives had refused to travel too far.

"I don't like not sleeping in my own bed, Dais. You get it," Nanna Jean had said pleadingly—which meant Daisy had to be the one to tell Prim she wasn't coming if it wasn't closer.

Anything longer than an hour away was pushing it for Nanna Jean. Luckily, Grant's parents had swooped in with an offer: their enormous, luxurious house with a swimming pool. Crisis averted—

though Daisy was fairly sure Prim was still sulking.

Bonus for Daisy: she could escort Nanna Jean home in an Uber and still sleep in her own bed. Assuming she made it home. After last night's performance, she wasn't betting on it.

Bursting into Lance's flat in Camberwell, Daisy held up the two dresses dramatically.

"Help me. Which one? Bearing in mind it's *guaranteed* that my insufferable ex—Grant's dickhead brother Greg—will be at this party with a gorgeous blonde Barbie doll. And while I still hate him, I at least want to look somewhat gorgeous. Not like Prim's troll-like baby sister."

"Oh, I dunno, babe. Light blue is risky. What if you spill wine on it? Or, God forbid, ketchup?"

"Lance, please focus," Daisy pleaded. Time was of the essence. The Uber was waiting.

"The pink one—yes, the pink one. No, actually… blue."

FFS.

"I'm sorry, it's just… okay, the blue's too light. It's giving Easter Bunny vibes."

"Seriously? So pink?"

She ran to the bathroom and wriggled into the pink floral dress. It was figure-hugging, with soft ruffles that flattered her cleavage. She checked herself in the mirror.

"I think you're right—this is the one," she sang, stepping out.

"Yes. *YES.* You look amazing."

Lance and Daisy clapped like giddy idiots.

"Right, come on, trollop, let's get to this party—I'm parched."

As they arrived, Daisy already regretted it. Lance was gawking like he'd just stepped into Buckingham Palace.

"Wow, this place is amazing," he gasped. "Prim has hit the jackpot."

"Yeah," Daisy muttered, rolling her eyes. Yet another thing Prim had over her.

A waiter passed by with a tray of champagne. Daisy grabbed two, downed one, and handed the other to Lance before snatching a fresh glass for herself.

"You alright, babe?" he asked.

"You haven't met my family. You'll understand very shortly."

"DAISY!!"

Her blood ran cold. She looked at Lance.

"Auntie Sandra," she whispered.

"Run."

The party was spectacular. Inside, trays of exquisite food from London's finest caterers lined the walls—nothing but the best for their successful son. A pop-up bar took over the living room, while a cocktail station gleamed in the open-plan kitchen. Daisy couldn't help thinking that even though it was very *Prim and Proper*, it might be a little *too* perfect for Prim.

It was sweltering for April 19th. Daisy and Lance had spent the first twenty minutes hiding from Auntie Sandra, only to be ambushed by Uncle Graham—not Sandra's husband (since Sandra was the family cynic who despised men, marriage, and lived with forty-five cats), but another uncle entirely. He proceeded to inform Daisy that her biological clock was "tick, tick, ticking."

Her attempt to steer the conversation toward her exciting new job was met with a staggeringly sexist remark.

Luckily, Lance swooped in before Daisy could launch herself at the man. But even he wasn't spared.

"You married, then?" Graham asked him.

"No, haven't found the right fella yet," Lance replied casually.

Graham rolled his eyes. "Maybe you should marry Daisy."

Holy heavens. Daisy needed alcohol. A *lot* of alcohol.

They finally made it outside, where the setup was disgustingly sophisticated. A DJ played from a stage near the pool, beautifully decorated seating filled the garden, a dessert station stood under a gazebo, and—of course—a bloody champagne tower the size of Harrods sparkled beside the pool.

I'm sure they'll regret that later, Daisy thought.

They were soon cornered by Prim and their mum, Jessie—finally, two people Daisy actually wanted to talk to.

"You made it, Daisy, love!" Jessie pulled her into a tight hug. "And Lance! Hello, darling."

"Hello, gorgeous," Lance beamed, flashing one of his signature grins.

Jessie turned back to Daisy, eyes twinkling. "Still no fella yet, Daisy, love?"

"I'm enough trouble for the both of us," Lance cut in, nudging Daisy playfully.

Daisy shot him a grateful look.

Jessie gave Daisy a once-over, lips pursing ever so slightly. "You look beautiful, love. Bit much for an engagement party though, isn't it?" she added, nodding meaningfully at Daisy's cleavage.

"It's a summer dress, Mum," Daisy muttered, cheeks flushing as she subtly tried to adjust it.

Prim came to the rescue. "It's fine, Mum. If you've got it, flaunt it, eh, Dais?" She pulled Daisy into a hug. "I'm so glad you're here. Auntie Sandra's already pissed off Nanna Jean—something about how marriage is for shitheads—so we had to separate them. She's over there with Grant's nan now. Meanwhile, Grant's Uncle Bryan has already tried it on with Mum. It's meant to be a *civilised* bloody party."

"I actually thought he was quite alright," Jessie said with a laugh, nudging Lance before dragging him off to show him the dance floor beyond the pool.

Great. There went Daisy's moral support for the evening. Lance had always adored Jessie and her wild-child energy—it was inevitable.

"There are *so* many people here, Prim. Do you even know half of them?" Daisy asked, scanning the crowd.

"Well, Grant has a big family, and so do we—sort of—so I guess yeah. Plus, our friends. Have you bumped into Greg yet?"

"No, thank God. We were too busy dodging Auntie Sandra. Pretty sure she's still hunting me down. And if Uncle Graham tells me to freeze my eggs one more time, I'm going to freeze his bloody head."

"Daisy! You can't say that—it's a civilised party," Prim gasped, mock-shocked, leading Daisy toward the Pimm's cart.

"What, Prim? You're older than me, and he hasn't said that to you! I should've buried him in the tray of spring rolls."

"Nice," Prim giggled. "Anyway, Greg's over by the pool, so just… be aware."

"When am I *not* nice?" Daisy sighed, accepting a glass of Pimm's.

"You'd better stay away from Uncle Simon, then—he's only communicating in Dad jokes tonight."

"Oh, blimey. I'll steer clear, then." Daisy laughed, taking a sip. "This is beautiful, by the way. Grant's parents have really outdone themselves. You look gorgeous too. Can you at least give the rest of us a chance?"

"Thanks, baby sis," Prim chuckled. "It all came together really well."

"Have you heard from Dad?" Daisy asked, already bracing herself.

Prim sighed. "Yeah. He's not coming. Something about a work meeting in Lisbon. Because, obviously, that's more important than his daughter's engagement party. I told him he'd better show up to the wedding or I'm cutting him off."

Malcolm Donaldson strikes again—the eternal letdown. Daisy hadn't expected him to show, but still—there it was.

That little pang of disappointment. This time, for Prim.

"Harsh but fair," Daisy said gently. "But you really shouldn't get your hopes up with him, Prim. I stopped doing that years ago."

Their dad had been in and out of their lives since they were kids. A Scottish-born businessman forever jetting off somewhere, he always managed to show up for the big birthdays and glossy, photo-worthy occasions. But when it came to the moments that actually mattered—the hard ones—he was nowhere. His way of solving problems was to throw money at them, not himself. Daisy had stopped pretending that counted as love a long time ago. Prim, though, still gave him the benefit of the doubt.

"Oh right, Dais—because your life is all sunshine and roses?" Prim snapped. "I get that he's let you down, but I'm not ready to just shut the door on him. He's our dad. And I'm getting married. It matters."

She huffed, then added with an eye-roll, "He did send some outrageously expensive crystal thing as a gift, though. A duck. Or maybe a bird? Who even knows. Totally surreal."

"Classic Dad," Daisy muttered. "Can't show up, so he just throws money at it."

"Daisy, stop." Prim's voice softened—slightly. "Anyway, I have to tell you something. Not about Dad."

Daisy narrowed her eyes. "That sounded ominous."

Prim hesitated. "Well… there are a few warm-up speeches tonight. And as my maid of honour, you have to do a quick one."

She had to be joking.

Daisy's stomach dropped. It wasn't bad enough that she had to do a speech at the wedding—now she had to do a bloody *warm-up round*, too?

"Prim, you have got to be freaking kidding me. Why are you telling me this *now*? Surely this is information you could've shared with me, I don't know, yesterday? Or last week?"

"Nope." Prim grinned. "They'll call you up when they're ready."

"Oh look, there's my fiancé!" she added brightly before darting off, leaving Daisy fuming.

"Hey, babes," Grant greeted Prim, scooping her into a kiss. Then he turned to Daisy. "Hi, Dais. You look bloody gorgeous. Stay away from the rest of the blokes in my family, though, yeah? You've already got one on your tally."

Daisy laughed. "You're a dickhead."

She'd always liked Grant. He was perfect for her big sister—even if right now, Daisy wanted to drown Prim in the pool.

Then panic hit. Lance was off with Jessie, Prim had scarpered with Grant, and just when she thought things couldn't possibly get worse—Greg.

Grant's brother. Her ex. The delectable, arrogant twat himself— was striding toward her.

Daisy did *not* have the patience for this.

"Daisy, Daisy, Daisy," Greg drawled. "How's my beautiful girl?"

"I'm not your girl, Greg."

"What, not even a little kiss?" He leaned in far too close, and

Daisy swore he went to grab her ass—so she ducked, nearly losing her Pimm's in the process.

Now, Greg was *very* attractive. Somewhat tall—though not as tall as his brother, or as tall as Daisy usually preferred—light brown hair, hazel eyes, and annoyingly charming. She could see why plenty of women fancied him. (Even Prim had fancied him in sixth form— he'd been in her year—but they *never* mention that. Grant still doesn't know.)

Still, he was never Daisy's type. Too loud. Too smug. And she had no idea why they'd ever dated—let alone for so long. The breakup had been abrupt, but definitely for the better. Now, she merely tolerated him for the sake of keeping the peace—for Prim and Grant's sake.

"It's nice to see you," she said stiffly, giving him a quick hug. "But I really must go to the bathroom. Catch up later?"

Without waiting for a response, Daisy marched off toward the toilets, downing another glass of champagne on the way. *Damn, that was good stuff.*

She needed a moment—a full-blown, hide-in-the-loo moment.

The powder room was disgustingly perfect—powder blue walls, gold fixtures, and those fancy cloth hand towels that screamed *money*. Daisy gripped the sink and stared at her reflection in the mirror. Her cheeks were flushed, her eyeliner slightly smudged, and there was an unmistakable glint of panic in her eyes.

A speech. A *speech*. This was just typical of her life.

And of course, Prim had sprung it on her like it was nothing— like Daisy hadn't just spent the entire week holding herself together with dry shampoo and sheer willpower.

She exhaled shakily. "Come on, Daisy. You can handle this," she muttered to her reflection. "Channel Daisy Number One. You nailed that interview. You're charming. You're articulate. You are *not* going to cry and/or throw up in this fancy bathroom."

She blinked hard, straightened her shoulders. This wasn't about her—it was for Prim. And even though she wanted to murder her right now, she loved her too. Deeply. Infuriatingly.

She just about managed to calm herself down. Impressive.

Steadying herself, she walked back out, deciding she deserved a cocktail before tracking down Lance. The cocktail bar was incredible—so much so that she did a double take at the bartender. He looked suspiciously like the guy from *First Dates*. Surely not?

"Martini, please."

"Shaken, not stirred," an unnervingly familiar voice said behind her.

She turned, as if in slow motion.

It was bloody Matthew.

Bollocks.

Chapter 7:
Shaken not Stirred

What in the name of everything bloody sacred was Matthew Devan doing here?

At her sister's engagement party. Did Prim invite him? Did he invite himself? Was he here for *her*?

Why? Why? *Why?*

Daisy's brain was spiralling. She was far too stunned to form actual words, so all that came out was:

"Hi."

Awkward.

"Hi," he said back, smiling.

He laughed, looking impossibly handsome. For heaven's sake—why couldn't he have gone bald? Or gotten fat? This was just bloody great.

"So… you're here," she continued, painfully aware of how idiotic she sounded. Jesus Christ, Daisy—say literally anything else. She wanted the ground to swallow her whole. Preferably forever.

"Yeah, I'm actually here with my, um—"

"It's been a long time, eh?" she cut in nervously. "Do we shake hands? Hug? Too much?"

"Nah, a hug's fine." He smiled and pulled her into an embrace.

Oh God. He still smelled the same.

"You look wonderful," he said, eyes sweeping over her. "How've you been, Daze?"

"I'm good. Really good. Just got a new job. Marketing."

"Wow. That's not what you wanted to do though, was it?"

Is he serious? Piss off, Matthew. No one's doing what they dreamed of after uni. Through gritted teeth, she asked, "Yourself?"

"I'm a junior doctor now. St Thomas' A&E."

Of course he was.

Of course he was doing exactly what he—or more likely his father—had always planned.

Daisy realised she'd rather listen to Auntie Sandra list all fifty-two of her cats than stand here one second longer.

"That's fantastic, Matthew. I'm so happy for you. I'm really sorry—I need to grab my Nan. Needs her meds. Diabetes."

Was that dramatic? Maybe. She didn't care.

"No worries. It was good to see you, Daisy."

"Bye."

She made a beeline for Nanna Jean, dragging her outside.

"Oh, hello, love. Oops—where are we going?" Nanna Jean looked panicked, but Daisy wasn't stopping. She'd keep walking until she hit a border—or better yet, outer space.

"Nothing, Nan. We're just getting some air."

If it wasn't bad enough that she already had one ex at this party—the delightfully insufferable Greg Osborne, whom she'd successfully avoided—now Matthew bloody Devan was here too, and she felt physically sick.

It wasn't just the shock of seeing him—it was everything he represented. He wasn't just *an* ex. He was *the* ex. The one that had mattered. The one she'd imagined a future with, once upon a time. The one she had never quite managed to file under "youthful mistake" or "dodged bullet."

No, Matthew was the gold standard. The heartbreak benchmark. The one that made every relationship after him feel like a half-hearted imitation of something she'd already lost. The only one she had ever truly loved.

And now he was standing in the same room, smiling at her family, mingling like he belonged there. With his perfect fiancée. Like their history had never happened. Like he hadn't just disappeared into a different city and a different life, leaving her to unravel alone.

She hadn't seen him in years, and now here he was—older, handsomer, more put-together—while she was hiding in bathrooms and getting blindsided with maid of honour speeches she hadn't prepared.

It was like the universe had orchestrated the perfect humiliation cocktail—garnished with a smug ex and served ice-cold.

Daisy wasn't even sure why she still held him on a pedestal. She wasn't sure she wanted him back. She just knew she didn't want him marrying someone else. And now that he was... well, that sucked.

Outside, she gave Nanna Jean a reassuring hug and sat her down near the cake table. She seemed content enough, and thankfully Jessie and Lance were nearby.

Lance took one look at Daisy's face and knew something had gone down.

"Daisy, what's up with you, love? You look white as a sheet," Jessie said.

"I dunno what's up with her," Nanna Jean chimed in. "She dragged me out here so fast my bloody feet left the floor."

Daisy paced. "Sorry, Nan. I just... needed to get out. Matthew's here."

"Oh, lovely," Jessie chirped, not quite grasping the gravity. "Where?"

"Oh, Dais, are you okay?" Nanna Jean asked softly. See? Nan gets it.

"Yeah. It's Prim's party. I'm not going to ruin it or anything. I just need... a breather."

Daisy resumed pacing. Lance slung an arm around her shoulders.

"Babe. You look hot. You are a sensational career woman. Fuck them. All of them."

Daisy laughed. Jessie had absolutely no idea who or what was being fucked, but she shouted it anyway.

"Fuck 'em!"

A few of Grant's aunties looked over, scandalised. The four of them burst out laughing.

For the next thirty minutes, Daisy actually started to enjoy herself. She told Lance about the impromptu speech, and together they cobbled something half-decent. Maybe this wouldn't be a total disaster after all. Maybe she could even salvage her dignity.

The DJ had started his set, and as the afternoon light melted into a soft evening haze, a warm buzz filled the garden. People were laughing, chatting, sipping cocktails. Prim and Grant were dancing on the lawn, completely wrapped up in each other. They looked ridiculously sweet—utterly, annoyingly in love.

Daisy watched them, feeling a sharp pang of envy.

She wanted that. She really did.

Where had it all gone wrong?

She glanced across the lawn and spotted Matthew, laughing with who she assumed was his fiancée—a stunning woman with glossy black hair and unfairly good cheekbones.

Nope. Not today, Satan. Daisy did *not* want to meet her right now.

Thankfully, her thoughts were interrupted—albeit in the worst possible way.

"Well, that was a wonderful speech from the best man, Marcus!

Give it up, ladies and gents!"

Applause rippled through the crowd.

"Next up, we have the maid of honour, Daisy! Daisy, where are you, sweetheart?"

Shit.

Jessie, Nan, Auntie Sandra (when did she even get here?), Lance, and now Prim were all cheering her on. She gave a weak smile, thanked them for the "support," and stood up—heart pounding, palms slick with sweat. Totally shitting herself.

And then somehow, she was doing it. She was *actually nailing it.* The speech was going well, she was getting laughs, people were smiling—

Then her heel caught on the stupidly long microphone wire.

Time slowed.

Oh no.

She was going down.

And the only thing waiting to break her fall was the bloody champagne tower.

CRASH.

Daisy tumbled through it. Glass and champagne exploded everywhere, cascading into the pool. Splash casualties: Grant's mum, his nan, Matthew, and—of course—his fiancée. Probably.

Spectacular.

The DJ rushed to help her up, but Daisy couldn't meet anyone's eye. She couldn't even think. The embarrassment was off the charts—level three million.

So she did what any self-respecting disaster would do.

She ran.

Because this party?

This party *bloody sucked ass.*

And this is why she didn't wear fucking heels.

Later, Prim found Daisy upstairs, lying on the balcony floor, staring up at the stars with a bottle of champagne in hand.

"There you are."

"You found me." Daisy's voice oozed sarcasm.

"Are you okay? We're concerned, Dais." Prim lay down beside her.

"Peachy."

Daisy was very drunk now. She'd briefly contemplated diving off the balcony, but there was a gazebo below—so it wouldn't have had the desired effect.

"I'm sorry," Prim said softly. "I should've told you about the speech."

"I'm sorry I spoiled your party, Prim."

"*Spoiled?*" Prim cackled. "That was *stellar* entertainment, Dais. The party was getting bloody boring. You saved it. Well done."

"Fuck right off."

They both burst into hysterical laughter.

"Why am I marrying him, Dais? Is my life always going to be this dull if I do?" Prim sighed.

"Because you love him, and you guys are perfect." Daisy mock-gagged.

Prim laughed and reached over to hold her hand.

"What if I never meet my person, Prim?" Daisy murmured.

"What are you on about?"

"What if Matthew was my person? What if you only get one?"

"That's rubbish, and you know it. You're starting to sound like Auntie Sandra."

"Am not." Daisy swatted her playfully.

"You get more than one person, Dais. You'll meet someone one day when you least expect it, and he'll be *your* person. Jeez, some people get married more than once."

"Excuse me for being traditional and settling for just one."

Prim rolled her eyes and forced Daisy to sit up.

"Look, Dais, I know this whole thing with Matthew is rubbish. And I swear, I didn't know he was going to be here—I promise. I would've told you. His fiancée's a friend of Grant's family. Who knew?"

"So strange." Daisy smiled. "I know you didn't know. You wouldn't do that to me."

"Well, as I was saying, maybe he wasn't *the one.* You were just kids. It was only a couple of years. Your fella's out there—and it's not Matthew."

"Or Greg." Daisy smirked.

"Don't get me started on that one."

They both laughed, then sighed, gazing up at the stars.

"So, are you coming back to the party? Nan wants to go home soon."

"Do I have to?" Daisy groaned.

"Dais! Come on. Everyone's so pissed now they don't even remember."

"Fine."

They got up and headed downstairs.

"Oh, by the way," Prim added casually, "Greg's looking for you. I think he wants to rekindle."

"Nope." Daisy turned straight back toward the stairs, but Prim grabbed her arm, dragging her along.

"Like you have so many other options."

"I'd rather get with Podgy Porter," Daisy muttered. "Yeah, I've seen him here."

They burst out laughing as they made their way back to the garden. Jessie and Lance greeted them on the dance floor with open arms, pulling them into a hug-dance to *One Night*.

Daisy might've made an absolute arse of herself tonight (and wasted thousands of pounds' worth of champagne), but one thing she knew for certain—she had the best support network a girl could ask for.

And that made everything better.

Later that night, after the last of the confetti had been swept away and Daisy had finally stopped apologising for her monumental fuck-up, Prim stood barefoot in the kitchen wearing one of Grant's oversized T-shirts, her makeup smudged and hair pinned up messily. She looked like a woman in love—or at least a woman trying very hard to *feel* settled in love.

Grant came up behind her, wrapping his arms around her waist and resting his chin on her shoulder. "You smell like champagne and strawberries," he murmured into her neck.

"That's because I was drenched in it when Daisy tried to do that toast," she replied with a sleepy laugh.

He chuckled, lacing his fingers over her stomach. "You were amazing tonight, by the way."

She let out a soft breath, her fingers tracing over his. "You think?"

"My fiancée is a social butterfly. I barely got a word in."

Prim smiled, leaning her head against his shoulder. "My fiancé has a habit of telling the same joke in every speech."

He nudged her playfully. "It lands every time."

"Primrose Donaldson—soon to be Osborne—you worked the room like a queen. I swear my uncle even tried to flirt with you."

"Which one?" she asked, tilting her head slightly.

"The terrifying one with the cowboy boots."

She smiled, but the glow in her eyes flickered—just for a second. "Well, if you ever change your mind, I've clearly got options."

Grant turned her gently to face him. "Not a chance. You're it for me."

He said it so easily. So certainly. Like a man standing on solid ground—unaware of the tremors underneath.

Prim leaned into his chest, letting his warmth quiet the faint hum of unease that had followed her since she blew out the candles on the cake.

They stood there for a long moment, wrapped in the afterglow of the party. Everything felt perfect.

And yet…

Prim's gaze drifted to the framed photo on the mantelpiece—a holiday snap from three summers ago. They were tanned, sun-dazed, giddy with wine and youth. She remembered how certain she'd felt then. How sure everything had seemed.

Now there was a ring on her finger, and everything felt closer. More real. It was scary—but it was also life. Right?

"You okay?" Grant asked gently.

She hesitated, then nodded, not quite meeting his eye. "Yes. More than."

He kissed her temple. "In just three months, you'll be my wife. Can you believe that?"

Prim smiled faintly. "Yeah. Mad, isn't it?"

As he pulled her in and she rested her head against his chest, she felt it.A sudden, overwhelming *panic*.

Chapter 8:
Lydia is an absolute genius

The new and improved Daisy Number One was here—and she was here to stay.

Fast-forward three weeks, and Daisy knew she'd made the right choice. She actually loved marketing, was building great rapport with Rhoda, and working with Lance? It was the best thing ever.

There was just one problem.

Sam.

Why was he being so cold? Arrogant, even. Surely, he couldn't still be mad about the coffee incident?

Every morning, their interactions followed the same script, though lately, he'd been adding slightly more conversation—still with that ever-present undertone of disdain.

"Late again, Donaldson."

"Hmm, yeah. Bloody Jubilee Line."

Who did he think he was, my dad?

"Don't you live in the city? Like, walking distance?"

"Well… yeah, but it's still quite far. Like, twenty-six minutes."

The tube was usually quicker—fourteen minutes to be exact. Plus, Daisy had gotten up way too late to walk twenty-six minutes.

"Maybe you should get up earlier. Wouldn't be rushing all the time."

That was a dig. Definitely a dig.

Normally, she would've brushed it off, but today? Today, she was feeling daring. Narrowing her eyes at him, she said, "Oh, thanks for the unsolicited life advice, Callaghan. I'll be sure to file it under things I didn't ask for."

He tilted his head, smirking like she'd just delivered a killer punchline. "File it under reality check, maybe. Some people need it."

Daisy bristled. "Right. And some people need to mind their own business. Just saying."

His eyebrow quirked, dangerously amused. "Careful, Donaldson. That kind of attitude… could get you in trouble."

Flirtation? Definitely flirtation.

"Yeah? And what would you do, hmm?" she challenged, leaning slightly toward him.

"Depends," he said, his voice low and teasing. "Maybe I'd make you stay late just to watch you sprint for the tube. Or maybe… I'd pretend not to notice your little coffee incident from your first week."

Daisy flushed—half indignation, half because—fine—his grin was ridiculously distracting. "You mean your refusal to accept my apology? Charming."

"Terribly charming," he agreed. "But let's be honest, it wasn't that bad. You have a knack for drama, Donaldson. Makes life… interesting."

She snorted. "You're impossible."

"And yet," his eyes flicked to hers, glinting, "here you are. Still talking to me."

Daisy blinked, flustered. "Well… someone has to tolerate your arrogance."

"Exactly," he said, smirking again as he leaned casually against the pole. "Tolerating me. You're very good at it."

Her stomach did a little flip. She didn't need to admit it aloud. But yeah, fine—maybe she was starting to like him. Just a bit. And that was dangerous.

She returned to her desk, a shade of beetroot nobody had ever seen, and Lance slid over in his chair, grinning.

"What the hell was that?"

"I… don't know, okay? But I am so hot for him right now."

"Babe, the whole office is hot for you both. You could cut the sexual tension here with a knife."

Daisy tried to avoid eye contact with him all day and failed—especially when Sam appeared at the printer, leaning slightly forward with that impossible smirk.

"You know, Donaldson…" he drawled, "you're hogging the printer."

She choked on her coffee, nearly spilling it. "I-I'm… just… working."

"Sure," he said, eyebrows raised, clearly enjoying the flustered mess she'd become. "Keep telling yourself that."

Later, as Daisy walked past his desk to grab a file, Sam leaned back in his chair, eyes narrowing. "Try not to trip over yourself this time. I don't think I could handle the excitement."

Daisy's eyebrows shot up. "Excitement? Really, Callaghan? You've got a vivid imagination."

"And yet," he said smoothly, "you're still smiling at me."

Her cheeks warmed. "You're impossible."

"And yet," he murmured, voice low, "you keep coming back for more."

Her brain short-circuited. Her earlier boldness hadn't scared him off—it had opened a door. She liked it. Whatever it was.

The next morning, however, Sam was back to his usual grumpy self, arms crossed, eyes narrowed at his laptop. Daisy tried to catch his eye—any flicker of the mischievous, teasing guy from yesterday—but nope. Nothing. Just cold, efficient Sam.

She groaned inwardly. Great. The flirty Sam she'd been totally not thinking about all night was apparently a one-off. Imposter Sam.

Sam, on the other hand, was painfully aware of his slip. Normally, he kept his guard up—no cracks, no room for distraction. But yesterday? It had come too easily. She was too distracting. Maybe it was what she was wearing. Maybe it was just… her. Either way, it couldn't happen again. He didn't do relationships. Especially not at work. Mask back on.

Daisy, however, had other plans. As she passed his desk, she muttered, "You're very… cheerful this morning."

His jaw twitched, but his eyes stayed glued to the screen. "Yeah. I try not to be… too friendly."

Daisy blinked. "Too friendly? You're barely tolerable."

That earned the tiniest flicker of a smirk. "Exactly. Any more than that, and people might think I actually like you."

Her stomach flipped, heat prickling her cheeks. "Do you?" she shot back before she could stop herself.

Sam finally looked up, his gaze steady, unreadable. Then he shook his head with a quiet huff of laughter. "You ask too many questions."

And just like that, the walls were back in place.

But things were about to change. Daisy had just opened an email from Rhoda, sent late the night before. She wasn't coming into the office today—something had come up—and she wasn't going to make the May marketing mixer tonight either. Instead, she'd chosen two people to represent the company in her place:

Daisy Donaldson.

And Sam Callaghan.

Shit.

Daisy could understand why Rhoda had picked her—she was fast becoming one of her favorites, and with her newfound Daisy Number One confidence, she was more than capable of networking for Brandish.

But Sam Bloody Callaghan?

Was this about budget? Was Rhoda being funny? Or—God forbid—was she playing matchmaker? Rhoda had a lot to answer for when she got back.

Daisy later decided it was probably about budget… or more likely that Rhoda just didn't trust her with the company credit card. That, and Lance told her as much.

But mostly, Lance found the whole thing hilarious.

"I still cannot believe you threw coffee all over Sam Callaghan and expect him to jump into bed with you," he cackled, practically doubling over.

"Oh my God, Lance, shut up—people will hear you!" Daisy hissed, glancing around in panic. Lowering her voice to a whisper, she added, "I don't want to jump into bed with him. I just want him to be nice to me. Is that too much to ask?"

Lance smirked. "Daisy, babe, come on. It's so obvious you fancy him. And you're trying so hard to pretend you don't."

That bastard could always see right through her.

"It's not that," she huffed. "It's the principle. I apologised, and he didn't accept it. And it's annoying me. I don't fancy him."

Lance rolled his eyes. "Well, if you don't want him, I will." He tilted his head, glancing toward Sam. "God, he's so fit. What I'd give for him to be horrible to me." He let out a low, dramatic growl.

"Lance. Stop," Daisy groaned. "He's going to notice you staring."

But Sam didn't notice. He barely even looked up.

Well. Fine. If Sam wanted to keep barely acknowledging her and refusing to accept her (very sincere) coffee-spilling apology, tonight, he was going to acknowledge her.

Daisy was going to look absolutely, unignorably gorgeous.

She booked a last-minute salon blowout, threw on a fresh little black dress, and teamed it with silver heels that actually weren't murder on her feet. A sleek blazer finished the vibe—a whole "look at me, I run things" energy. She was ready.

Or at least, she thought she was.

Because, of course, things never went this smoothly for Daisy.

Walking down the aptly named Seething Lane, she heard her heels struggling on the uneven pavement, and then—

Crack.

One of her heels snapped clean off.

Bollocks.

Panic set in. It was 7 pm in central London. Nowhere that sold footwear was open. The event started in thirty minutes.

And then, she remembered a trick Lydia had taught her at uni.

Chewing gum.

Lydia, you absolute genius.

Daisy stood there, frantically chewing half a pack of Wrigley's, trying to get it as sticky as possible. It kind of worked… but there was no way she could walk all the way there.

She flagged down a black cab. It was going to be the shortest cab ride ever, but Daisy had to take drastic measures.

"Balls Brothers, Minster Court, please."

As she settled into the backseat, desperately holding the heel to her shoe, willing it to stick, she smirked to herself. She might just win this one.

Surprisingly, the event went swimmingly. Daisy was a

networking genius. Sam—shockingly—wasn't his usual arrogant self. In fact, he was actually… well, charming. He even complimented her outfit.

This behaviour was extremely dangerous for her growing crush.

After the event wound down, Daisy perched at the bar. To her surprise, Sam joined her.

At first, their conversation was formal, but then—slowly—it shifted into something deeper.

"I think I owe you an apology, Donaldson," he admitted, almost begrudgingly.

"Oh? And why's that, Callaghan?"

He smirked at the use of his surname.

"I don't think I've been as friendly as I could've been. To you. Over these last few weeks. And for that… I'm sorry."

Daisy blinked. She hadn't expected that.

She tried to play it cool, keeping her voice steady despite the fact that, for weeks, he'd been crushing her soul. "Maybe you've been a little cold. But I accept your apology, Callaghan."

"That is very gracious of you, Donaldson."

He smirked and edged his chair closer. Was he coming onto her?

No, Daisy. Don't get carried away.

But her brain was already halfway to a fantasy montage involving candlelight, shirt buttons, and his annoyingly perfect jawline. She tried to stay cool, but her pulse had shot up, and she was pretty sure her cheeks were doing that pink-tinged giveaway thing. He was just so… stupidly hot. And charming. And dangerously close to her personal space.

She needed to snap out of it. This was work, not some slow-burn, eye-contact-heavy romcom with lingering glances and a sex scene scored by Phoebe Bridgers. Focus, Daisy. Be normal.

She reached for her drink, trying to ignore the slight wobble in her hand—or the fact that Sam was now sitting just a little too close. Close enough that her brain was short-circuiting and her stomach had turned into a live wire.

"May I ask why you've been so off with me?" she said, aiming for casual but overshooting into vulnerable territory. "No? Too much?"

He winced. "I guess I didn't mean to come across as cold as I did. And please don't take it personally—I'm just like that with everyone."

Everyone. So it wasn't just her. She should have felt relieved, but weirdly, it stung. She'd spent weeks trying to crack the code of Sam: glimmers of warmth, then radio silence. Now she had to accept maybe she hadn't meant anything special after all.

"Huh." She was torn between pushing him further or dropping it altogether. This was the most he'd opened up, and she'd waited so long for an actual conversation. She didn't want to ruin it—but she also didn't want to leave things unsaid.

"My parents weren't exactly… affectionate," he continued, his voice low. "They never really showed emotion when I was growing up, so I think I struggle with empathy sometimes. I guess it rubbed off."

Daisy paused, trying to think about why he would be that way with anyone, let alone her. They had barely known each other, and yet there was this thing, this hum of something unspoken that always pulled at her when he was near.

"I don't think you're really like that, Sam," she said boldly, her voice softer now.

The way she said his first name—soft, almost flirtatious—made him pause. There was a flicker in his expression, something unreadable and electric.

"You don't?"

"No," she said. "You give off this cocky, slightly irritating alpha energy, sure. But I can tell… there's a decent guy under there. Someone who actually cares."

He looked at her, really looked, like he was trying to figure something out. His eyes held hers, and her heart thudded so loudly she was sure he could hear it.

"Thanks," he said quietly. "I try to be. I think I just… put up a wall with certain people. I don't know." He exhaled. "Anyway, I'm sorry if I upset you. Friends?"

Certain people. Her again?

She plastered on a smile and clinked her glass against his. "Sure. Friends."

But the word felt off. Wrong. Like calling a soulmate a pen pal.

"I'll try to be nicer, Daisy. I promise." He smiled again—warmer this time. More real.

"Thanks." She giggled, caught in that dizzy rush of being seen. He'd used her first name. Not Donaldson. That meant something, didn't it?

She grabbed her drink, fingers accidentally brushing his.

Static.

She stilled. So did he.

Then he stared at her—really stared. His face impossibly close, his breath warm against her cheek. Her pulse rocketed. She was sure—sure—he was going to kiss her. The tension was a live current now, crackling, intoxicating.

Then—he blinked. Frowned. Looked down.

"Daisy, why do you have no shoes on?"

She burst out laughing, the spell broken.

"Well," she began, clearing her throat, "one of the heels broke on my way here, and I had to—ahem—improvise. They barely made it through the event, so I chucked them.”

Sam’s face twisted in disbelief. “But how are you going to get home? Barefoot?”

“Uber.” She grinned.

He let out a low chuckle, shaking his head. “Daisy, I don’t think I’ve ever met anyone quite like you.”

She smirked. “One for the road?”

“Yes, go on then.”

And for the first time in weeks, Daisy felt… optimistic.

Maybe—just maybe—they could be friends.

At least it was a start. Because yes, Daisy did fancy Sam Callaghan a lot more than she realised.

Chapter 9:
Minor improvements

The next few days in the office went considerably better. Sam had stuck to his word and was being *slightly* nicer to Daisy—though there was still that cocky, arrogant undertone to nearly everything he said. And by "slightly," she meant the dialogue was pretty much the same… except now he occasionally used her first name.

Well—*sometimes.*

They'd managed to extend their conversations just enough for her to learn a few new things. He was twenty-seven—just a few months younger than her. He'd gone to a posh school in North London, which, Daisy suspected, was where he'd acquired that trademark arrogance.

He worked late most nights. Thought Arabella was *really* annoying—but he knew her boyfriend from school, which, according to Daisy's tactical deep dive (to determine whether he fancied Arabella, or was even capable of love at all), explained his politeness toward her.

He liked football—Arsenal, of course—and golf in his spare time.

"Boring!" Lance declared when Daisy shared this intel. "Can't get more cliché than that. Posh boy who likes golf."

Oh, and now Sam had apparently redirected his negative energy toward Lance. Go figure.

She still hadn't managed to find out if he was open to a relationship. She *did* know he was single—Lance had asked him several times (purely for research purposes, or so he claimed). He'd also asked if Sam was gay, to which Sam had simply smiled and replied, "Unfortunately not."

Daisy had to admit—that was actually kind of nice of him.

They'd exchanged numbers after the event, which Daisy was quietly thrilled about, but also potentially dangerous given her track record with drunk texting was… not great.

The next morning, Daisy pressed the button for the lift. Sam appeared behind her, leaning casually against the wall, coffee in hand.

"Morning," Daisy said, tilting her head.

"You're taking the stairs now, right?" he drawled, eyebrow raised.

"Not a chance. I like my knees," she shot back, folding her arms.

He scowled.

She smirked. "Ah, the grumpy charm is strong today."

He finally glanced over, one eyebrow arched. "And you… seem unusually chipper. Are you trying to annoy me?"

"Maybe," she admitted, leaning against the opposite wall. "Or maybe I just like seeing you scowl. It's… informative."

"Informative?" His lips twitched. "Oh, I see. You're studying me now. Dangerous hobby."

She gave a faint shrug, keeping her tone casual. "Someone has to keep the office interesting. And you're… predictably entertaining."

He smirked, that familiar spark of mischief flickering in his eyes. "Predictable, huh? Maybe you just haven't earned the full Sam Callaghan experience yet."

Daisy tilted her head, unimpressed but intrigued. "Oh, really? And what does that involve? More grumpiness or sudden bursts of charm?"

"Both," he said quietly, leaning slightly closer. "Depends how cooperative you are."

Her stomach did a little flip, despite herself. "Cooperative, huh? Sounds risky."

He took a slow sip of coffee, eyes lingering on her. "I like risky."

The lift pinged, doors sliding open. Daisy gave a dry smile. "See you at your desk, Mr. Risk-Taker."

He stepped out, voice low, teasing: "Donaldson… don't make me regret letting you survive this lift ride."

She caught his smirk over her shoulder and rolled her eyes—but inwardly, her pulse quickened.

Yep. Definitely starting to like him.

That was it—Daisy had to hatch a plan to get Sam Callaghan to open up more. With a little (okay, a lot) of encouragement, she decided to work late herself. Desperate times called for desperate measures. Maybe she could catch him off guard.

Then he appeared in the doorway, jacket slung over one shoulder, a football tucked under his arm.

"You're still here?" he asked, eyebrows raised, that cocky half-smile tugging at his lips.

"Yes," Daisy replied, eyes glued to her laptop. "Someone has to keep the office running. Plus, I like… tolerating you."

Shit. Too flirty. Reign it in, Daisy.

"Tolerating?" he echoed, mock-offended.

She looked up—clearly a mistake—because then she saw him. In shorts. And those legs… oh. My. God. She needed a moment to compose herself.

"You know," she said, glancing up with mock seriousness, "for a posh, golf-loving, Arsenal-supporting man-child who actually used to play football professionally, you're shockingly… agreeable."

He froze mid-step, then laughed low in disbelief. "Wait—what?"

"You heard me," she said, grinning. "You used to kick a ball around for a living. And now look at you—suit, spreadsheets, and this charmingly grumpy attitude."

He shook his head, smirking as he walked over and set the football on her desk. "Have you been stalking me on social media, Donaldson?"

Bollocks. Abort. Abort.

"No…" Daisy tried to hide the panic on her face—and failed miserably.

He just laughed. "Okay, yes," she admitted, "but it was totally by accident."

"Interesting," he said, leaning against her desk. "Well, I played a few seasons in the lower leagues. Not exactly Premier League glory, but it taught me discipline, teamwork… and how to survive office life with minimal groaning."

Daisy leaned back, raising a brow. "Teamwork, huh? Is that why you're so… annoyingly arrogant?"

"Depends who you ask," he countered, straightening up. "Anyway, I'm off to training—aka kicking a ball around with my mates before it gets dark. Don't tell anyone you know this about me. It ruins the mystique."

"Oh, don't worry," she said, smirking. "Your secret's safe. But I expect a full post-match debrief tomorrow. I want details on how this sarcastic side of you performs on the pitch."

He paused at the door, a genuine smile breaking through. "You're relentless, Donaldson. I like that."

For the first time, Daisy felt a spark of victory. If she could get him to open up about football, maybe she could get him to open up about… well, her.

Her mind wandered—as it always did when he left—imagining him on the pitch: shorts clinging to muscular legs, the ball at his feet, that smirk as he jinked past defenders and scored like it was nothing. She shivered. God, he probably made even *scoring goals* look devastatingly attractive.

And now she couldn't stop thinking about those legs. That smile. That whole maddening, impossible man.

Jesus. This crush was officially getting out of control.

The next day in the office, Daisy managed to only *occasionally* think about Sam Callaghan in a football kit last night.

And by "occasionally," she meant all night.

She'd even dreamt about it.

And of course, she ended up dissecting every single detail with Lance over lunch—despite promising herself (and him) that she wouldn't tell anyone. Because some secrets were just too good to keep.

"So, I worked late last night," she began, stabbing at her salad. "In an attempt to, you know… speak to him."

"Oh, Operation *Catch Sam Callaghan* is in force," Lance announced.

"Wait—you named it that? Seriously?" Daisy raised an eyebrow.

"Yes! Creative genius, right?" Lance nodded proudly.

"Jesus," Daisy muttered, rolling her eyes. "Well, he walked past my desk in… sportswear. Football kit."

"OMG," Lance nearly choked on his sandwich. "Please tell me you saw biceps. Or legs. Or—better still—p—"

"Just his legs," Daisy cut in quickly.

"I bet he has nice legs."

"Very." Daisy smirked, swirling her drink.

"So… please tell me you kissed him?" Lance leaned in, eyes wide like he'd just uncovered a murder mystery twist.

"Whoa, slow down," Daisy said, waving her hands. "I just… flirted. A lot."

"Bloody hell, Dais," Lance groaned. "Step it up before someone else does." He wiggled his eyebrows menacingly.

"I can't just walk up and kiss him! I don't even know if he likes me like that."

"I would have," Lance said with a shrug.

"Of course you would. I'm not you." Daisy groaned. "Why does he have to be so annoyingly—"

"Attractive, ridiculously confident and—" Lance fanned himself dramatically. "—I can't even!"

"Lance. Not helpful."

He chuckled, sipping his coffee.

"You're so dramatic." Daisy rolled her eyes, but smiled.

"You're welcome," he said with a grin. "Always happy to suffer vicariously through your love life."

"You better be," she said, smirking. "Because there's bound to be more."

"So… how did you leave it?"

"I told him I wanted a full post-match debrief today. And now I don't think I can do it."

Lance clapped his hands together. "Well, honey, you have to. Go get that debrief."

And before she could protest, he practically shoved her out of her chair.

Daisy's adrenaline spiked as they returned to the office. She was fully prepared to saunter over and flirt with Sam Callaghan.

But then her phone rang.

Prim.

"Hi, Prim!"

"Daisy, Daisy, Daisy!"

"Bloody hell, what now?"

"So, at the party, you said you wanted me to set you up," Prim said, way too cheerfully.

"Oh, for fuck's sake," Daisy muttered.

"Yes, but I'm *completely fine now*. I didn't mean it. I was just upset, but I'm totally over it. Like, fully," she replied quickly, already bracing for the worst.

"Too late, sunshine! I've already arranged a date. You're free tonight, right?"

Daisy scrambled for an excuse but came up empty. "Fine," she said finally. She mostly wanted to get her sister off the phone—and off her back—but also… what were her other options? Sam clearly just wanted to be friends. This new bloke could be nice, right? She trusted Prim's judgment. Mostly.

"Great! I'll send you the details," Prim chirped.

"Gee, thanks, Prim," Daisy said dryly.

"Gotta dash, I have a dress fitting. Don't be late. Let me know how it goes tomorrow. Love you, bye!"

Daisy threw her phone onto the desk and groaned. As if by magic, Lance appeared at her side.

"What was that about?" he asked, grinning.

"My bloody sister set me up on a blind date. Tonight," Daisy moaned, dropping her head onto the desk.

Lance tried—and failed—not to laugh. "Right, that's what I thought I heard."

"Argh, I sometimes fucking hate my life," she whined.

"Babe, this could be a good thing," Lance said brightly. "You know, get your head off—Sexy Sam." He mouthed the last words like they were classified information.

Daisy launched at him playfully, smacking his arm. "Stop it,

Lance! If he finds out, he'll probably stop talking to me altogether."

"Yeah, because you've made *so much* progress," he teased, deadpan.

Daisy burst out laughing, and so did Lance.

"Oh, Dais. I bloody love your life."

"What about you?" she shot back, desperate to change the subject. "Heard from Johnny Boy?"

"Nope. And it's for the best," Lance sighed. "We weren't going to work out anyway—not with his pregnant ex."

"Hmm, yeah. Bit of a curveball, that," Daisy muttered, immediately regretting bringing it up.

Just then, her phone buzzed.

Prim: *7 p.m. The Folly. Look for tall, blonde, glasses. His name's Joe. Good luck!!*

"Glasses? Hmm… okay," Lance said, peering over her shoulder.

"Seven p.m.? Shit, Lance—it's 5:45! How am I going to—"

Lance looked her up and down critically. "Well, you look presentable. Lose the jumper. That top is—" he broke into song *"sexy!"* He pointed to her lace bodysuit underneath.

He circled her like a stylist at Fashion Week. "Stand up. Can we make this skirt shorter? Those boots are not going to work." He gestured to her Dr. Martens. "Dais, do you even *own* shoes?"

"Under my desk," she said, crouching to grab a pair of tan heels she kept there for emergencies. No way was she repeating the last footwear disaster.

"How much makeup do you have?" he asked, eyes lighting up like a kid at Christmas.

Daisy opened her desk drawer, revealing a small *Boots* treasure trove.

"Loads," she said, grinning.

Lance gasped dramatically. "Daisy Donaldson! You've been hiding this from me, you bitch!"

"Well, I am always late," she chuckled.

"Right." He grabbed a handful of products and gave her a look. "Bathroom. Now."

They dashed toward the bathrooms, passing Sam's desk on the way. He looked up, frowning at the commotion, tugging out his AirPods. He could hear them giggling like schoolkids from the disabled loo.

Curiosity got the better of him. He stood, hovering just outside, listening.

When they finally emerged, he tried—and failed—to look like he hadn't been eavesdropping. He turned a shade of pink Daisy had never seen before. For once, *he* was the flustered one.

"What are you two up to?" Sam demanded, his tone sharp. "You sound like teenagers in there."

And just like that, he was back to his usual arrogant self.

Lance and Daisy froze like they were being scolded by their headteacher. Lance recovered first. "Daisy has a blind date," he said, glancing at his watch. "In, like—thirty minutes. Dais, you've got to go."

Sam's expression darkened instantly, his jaw tightening. He looked like someone had just spat in his cornflakes.

Why?

Lance noticed. He'd definitely be questioning Sam later. For now, he had one mission—get Daisy out the bloody door.

"Oh shit," Daisy said suddenly. She sprinted to her desk, grabbed her bag and jacket, and bolted for the exit, shouting over her shoulder, "Talk later!"

"Call me if you need an out!" Lance yelled after her, laughing.

Chapter 10:
Definitely a real date

Daisy arrived at the bar, late and desperately searching for—well, she didn't even know what he looked like. God, this was awful. She was going to flipping throttle Prim the next time she saw her. This was already so embarrassing.

She made her way to the bar, her anxiety through the roof. She needed a drink. Or five.

She scanned the room, heart thudding. Then she saw him: a guy with slightly-too-long, wavy blonde hair and glasses, sitting alone at a table. A glass of something dark rested in front of him, which he swirled lazily, eyes fixed on the rim as if weighing its contents. He looked familiar somehow, though she couldn't place why.

Oh God. Please don't be him.

He hadn't spotted her yet. She could turn. Run. Pretend she'd been hit by a bus.

Bollocks. He'd seen her.

Well, here goes. She had to give him a chance, right? Not everyone was—Sam Callaghan.

"Hi, Daisy, right?" His voice was soft, polite… but with a strange little edge.

"Hmm, yeah." Brilliant. Why didn't she just say no?

"I'm Joe." He extended a hand, weirdly formal.

"I've got us a table."

"Yeah, great," Daisy said, her laugh coming out far too nervous.

As they sat, she kept a tight grip on her glass. Best not to put it down. He could spike it.

Something about the way he sat—so unnervingly still, eyes flicking over the room like he was cataloguing potential victims—set her imagination sprinting. He's probably got a basement full of bodies.

Jesus, this was exactly why Daisy didn't do blind dates.

"Sorry, I've come straight from work," she blurted. "Just going to pop to the bathroom. Freshen up."

"Oh yeah, that's fine. Can I get you a drink?"

"Got one!" she said, far too brightly, before practically sprinting away.

She shoved open the bathroom door, fumbling for her phone. He was probably a perfectly nice guy. But the vibe was wrong. Very wrong.

Prim. Where the hell was Prim?

She scrolled. Ha. Got her.

She dialled.

"Daisy, what is it? Aren't you supposed to be on your date?"

"Prim, what the actual fuck? Are you trying to kill me off? What did I do? Please, tell me this is some sort of joke. Oh, this has to be a joke."

"What? No! He's a friend of Grant's. From work. Do you not like him—?"

"Have you even met him, Prim?"

"Well… no..?"

Daisy rubbed her temples. "Wait. Wait. You mean to tell me you don't even know what he looks like?"

"Well, it's a blind date, Dais?"

"He looks like Jeffrey Dahmer, Prim."

"Ah… The real one or Evan Peters?"

"How the fuck is that relevant? Oh Lord."

Daisy laughed, because what else could she do? If anything, this was typical of her poxy life.

"Grant said he was nice. Also, Evan Peters is alright."

Daisy was about to combust. But then it hit her.

She didn't have to stay. She just needed her fairy gay mother.

"You know what, Prim? Don't worry. It's fine."

"Okay… Dais? Are you okay?"

"Yes. Talk to you tomorrow. Bye."

She messaged Lance.

Daisy: *Help. Man looks like Jeffrey Dahmer. Not the Evan Peters version. Save me before it's too late. Pleeeeeeease.*

Lance: *Dying. Okay, en route.*

Right. She could handle this. Daisy Number One could handle this. She just had to stall.

She took a deep breath, then headed back out and plastered on a smile.

"Sorry to keep you waiting."

"It's fine," Joe Dahmer replied.

"Never been on a blind date before, have you?"

"No. I'm a blind date virgin."

Oh, for Pete's sake. Why was she like this? Do not tell the potential murderer you're a virgin, Daisy.

"So, you work with Grant?" she asked quickly, desperate to change the subject.

"Yeah. Well, briefly. I'm a contractor for his company…"

And off he went. About his job. As a surveyor, apparently. For ten whole minutes.

He seemed nice enough, but Daisy zoned out, wondering if she could get through Prim's wedding without ever seeing this man again.

Then someone approached.

Her heart stopped.

Sam.

Sam?

"Daisy, I'm so sorry I'm late, gorgeous," he said.

He bent down—and kissed her. On the side of her mouth.

Daisy completely malfunctioned.

"What's this?" Sam asked, eyebrows raised casually—as if he hadn't just kissed her on the mouth in public like it was just a Tuesday afternoon in their long-term relationship.

Dahmer looked like he might throw up. Daisy was still reeling from the kiss. Had she blacked out? Was this a dream? What the hell was going on? Where was Lance? Why was Sam here? And WHY, in the name of Jesus, Mary, and all the disciples, was he kissing her?

"I'm Sam," he said smoothly, extending a hand. "Daisy's boyfriend."

Boyfriend?

Boyfriend?!

Joe Dahmer hesitated before shaking it, eyes flicking between them like he was witnessing either a breakup or a sting operation.

Daisy's mouth dropped open, then closed, then opened again like a malfunctioning animatronic at a cursed Disney ride. Boyfriend?

What in the full-blown fever dream was going on? Had she missed a key plot twist in her own life? Was she in a coma? Was this some elaborate wish-fulfilment hallucination where hot men showed up uninvited and declared themselves hers?

She stared at Sam, eyes bugging out of her head, and mouthed: Where's Lance?

Sam leaned in. "I'll tell you later," he whispered, his voice a low rumble right against her ear.

The hairs on the back of her neck stood to attention like loyal soldiers. Her stomach did a weird gymnastic routine that would've made Simone Biles proud. But her brain was still very much in the Twilight Zone.

She nodded, slowly, trying to look casual. Totally normal. Everything's fine. Just sitting here with Geoffrey Dahmer and my surprise fake boyfriend who's kissed me into an identity crisis. Fine. All fine.

Meanwhile, Dahmer looked between them, shifting uncomfortably in his seat like he'd wandered into the wrong movie. Which, in fairness, he had. This was no longer Date Night. This was The Daisy Donaldson Shambles Show, now featuring unexpected snogging, mystery men, and possibly a public breakup, depending on how the next five minutes played out. Special guest appearance: sheer panic.

"Um, Daisy, you never mentioned a—boyfriend?" He cleared his throat, voice climbing several octaves like he was about to burst into a show tune.

"I'm so, so sorry, Jeffrey. Shit—Joe. Sorry. It's a very complicated situation that I probably should've told you about. At the start."

"It's fine. It's okay. I should probably—go though."

He left—possibly to write a long post about emotional trauma in his private Reddit group.

Daisy felt momentarily bad.

As soon as he was out of earshot, Sam muttered, completely deadpan, "Laters, Joe."

Then she lost it. She doubled over, clutching her stomach, tears of laughter streaking down her cheeks as Sam guided her toward the bar.

"That was awful," she wheezed. "But then bloody brilliant."

Sam smirked. "My first acting gig. Think I did alright."

"You went in hard," Daisy said, eyeing him. "Much better than Lance. Although Lance would've brought props. Or cried."

Sam shrugged modestly, clearly enjoying himself. "I actually had fun."

"I feel so bad," Daisy said to Sam, "but the vibe was definitely off with that bloke, right? It wasn't just me."

"Oh yeah, he was very odd."

They took a seat at the end of the bar. Daisy tried—tried—to act normal, sipping her drink, crossing her legs like someone who wasn't currently replaying that kiss on a ten-second loop. Her mind was under siege. It was like a Love Island recap, only more scandalous and with better lighting. Why did you kiss me? Why did you come instead of Lance? Please kiss me again.

"You got very much into the character," she teased, eyebrows raised.

Sam didn't answer immediately. Just kept looking at her. Held her gaze a second too long. The air around them fizzed.

And then she did what she did best: she shattered the moment like a clumsy waitress with a tray full of wine glasses.

"You still haven't told me why you showed up instead of Lance."

Sam smiled into his glass and—blushed. His whole face went a bit pink. Just when Daisy thought he couldn't get any cuter without violating several EU regulations.

"Lance had an offer he couldn't refuse," he said with a sigh, leaning back. "He now owes me."

"Oh, I bet you love that," Daisy laughed, full and loud—a proper belly laugh that made Sam look at her like she'd just hung the stars.

And he thought, quite genuinely, that her laugh might be the death of him.

"So," Daisy said, cocking her head, "you realise you have to come with me to my sister's wedding now. Because that guy might be there. And you told him you were my boyfriend."

Sam laughed. "Would we still be together if you keep going on blind dates behind my back?"

Touché. Touché. Damn it—she thought she had him.

"Depends how much you love me," she said, winking.

Bold. Too bold?

"When's your sister's wedding?" he asked, smirking.

"Sixteenth of August."

"Ah, that's actually my birthday."

Daisy gasped. "Is it actually?"

"Nope." He grinned. "Just messing with you. My birthday's in November."

"Oh, so you're a Scorpio." Daisy narrowed her eyes in mock suspicion. "That explains a lot."

Nice, Daisy. Freak him out with astrology. Maybe tell him you did a tarot pull before coming here. Really double down.

"I think I'm Sagittarius, actually. I think. Twenty-second of November."

"Well, that shut me up, didn't it?" she said, grinning.

"So when's yours?"

"Eighteenth of June."

"That soon? That's like, next month."

"Don't remind me," she groaned. "I'm a Gemini, by the way."

"Is that a good one? I don't really know star signs… other than mine."

Daisy blushed. "Erm, yeah. As a couple—the fake one we were tonight, obviously—we're apparently very compatible."

Sam raised an eyebrow and took a slow sip of his drink, eyes never leaving hers. Daisy was almost certain he caught the subtext she was trying to lay down.

"Well," he said, voice low, "let's review nearer the time, eh? About the wedding."

He clinked her glass with his, then downed the rest of his drink in one go.

"Another?" he asked.

"Hmm. Please." Daisy nodded, though her brain was short-circuiting. Did he just agree to come? Did he mean as a date? Did she accidentally skip a chapter of her own love life?

Is this a date?

She wasn't sure. But what she was sure of was that she wanted to kiss him so badly she might actually explode. Her skin tingled. Her heart pounded. It was like that scene from Alien, only less gross and with significantly more sexual tension.

He shifted his chair closer. His arm brushed hers. A shiver shot down her spine like a champagne cork in a pressure cooker. He rested his hand on the back of her chair. Their legs touched.

He was so close. Daisy swore he could hear her heartbeat. It was loud. Rhythmic. Like a drum. Or a stomach growl. Hopefully not a stomach growl. That would be mortifying.

His fingers tapped the bar. His leg bounced. He was nervous. He's nervous. He's going to do it.

He was actually going to "Daisy? Is that you?"

She turned.

Matthew.

For fuck's sake.Earlier at the office, after Daisy had left.

"So, Mr Callaghan. Spill it."

Lance turned to Sam, arms folded, an accusatory frown plastered across his face.

Sam cocked an eyebrow, feigning ignorance. "No idea what you're on about." He turned to walk away.

"Oh, don't you dare walk away from me." Lance trailed after him, lowering his voice. "Are you going to explain why Daisy going on a date made you look like someone just nicked your last bloody Oreo?"

Sam scoffed. "I don't even like Oreos."

"Oh, whatever," Lance waved a dismissive hand. "Are you going to explain or just admit you fancy my best friend?"

Sam sat down and let out a long exhale, rubbing a hand over his jaw. For a moment, he said nothing—just sat there, lost in thought.

Lance narrowed his eyes. "Well?"

"What?"

"I asked you a question, Callaghan, and you didn't answer. So?"

Sam exhaled sharply, then spun his chair to face Lance. "Fine. I fancy Daisy." He threw up his arms like he was taking a theatrical bow.

Lance fought the urge to squeal. He wanted to keep his cool, but knowing full well that Daisy had been harbouring a massive crush on Sam too? This was gold. Instead, he casually slid a Post-it across Sam's desk.

"Daisy's here," he said, tapping the note. "I'd bet my entire skincare collection that this date is going to be a disaster—because, well… it's Daisy."

Sam smirked. "Fair point."

Lance continued, lowering his voice. "Now, if she sends me the signal, I'm supposed to go rescue her."

Sam frowned. "Signal?"

"Oh, it's just a text. Just one word. Help."

Sam blinked. "That's it?"

"Yes, genius. And when it happens—and trust me, it will—I'll let you know so you can go save her instead."

Sam hesitated for a moment, then exhaled. "Okay…"

Lance clapped his hands together. "Excellent. My number's on the Post-it. Text me so I have yours, and I'll text you back when it's time for you to play knight in overpriced office-wear."

Sam shook his head with a reluctant smirk. Then realised Lance was grabbing his coat and bag, preparing to leave. "Wait, where are you going?"

"I," Lance said dramatically, grabbing his coat and bag, "have a Tinder date. Wish me luck." He winked. "Enjoy your night, Callaghan."

And with that, he flounced out, leaving Sam staring at the Post-it.

For a moment, Sam just sat there, tapping a pen and staring at Daisy's location, scribbled in Lance's messy handwriting. And then, before he could stop himself, he did something he hadn't done in a long time.

He smiled.

Not just any smile. A genuine one.

Because that's what Daisy made him feel like.

And for the first time, he finally admitted it to himself.

Chapter 11:
Sam Callaghan has lost his bottle

Daisy couldn't believe her eyes. She genuinely couldn't believe her luck. Like, really—the universe had it out for her.

Because, of course, Matthew Devan had to show up at this exact moment.

Sam Callaghan had been this close—this close—to kissing her again. She could feel it in the air, the tension crackling between them like the moment before a storm. And now? Now Matthew had gone and scared him off.

Brilliant. Just brilliant.

She flicked a glance at Sam, who had instantly shifted into his usual, infuriating, I'm-too-cool-to-care stance. His jaw tightened just slightly. His hands slipped back into his pockets. Yep. He was gone. The moment was dead.

Excellent timing, Matthew. As ever.

Daisy exhaled sharply, forcing a tight smile as she turned to face her ex.

"Matthew. Hi. What are you doing here?" she said through gritted teeth.

Because knowing Matthew Devan pretty well—and Daisy definitely did—he didn't like going out, and he didn't like lots of people. So this was just a cruel coincidence. A really bloody awful one.

Matthew hesitated for a fraction of a second, then gave a half-shrug, as if his presence was the most natural thing in the world. "Just a work thing. Some other doctors. I haven't seen you since... the party." His gaze lingered on her, searching her face for a reaction.

Daisy ignored the knot forming in her stomach. Instead, she gestured vaguely between them. "Right. Well, uh—this is my work colleague, Sam Callaghan."

The moment the words left her lips, Sam let out the softest scoff. Barely audible. But it was there.

Daisy frowned, confused.

"Colleague, sure. That's one way to put it."

What was he saying? What did he mean by that?

Daisy whipped her head towards him, narrowing her eyes. "You what?"

"Nothing," Sam said smoothly, the smirk still playing at his lips. "Just an interesting choice of words."

Daisy opened her mouth to respond, but before she could, Matthew—who had been watching this entire exchange with a slightly bemused expression—stepped forward, extending his hand.

"Matt Devan." His voice was polite but firm. "Nice to meet you."

Sam paused for a second before shaking his hand. His grip was strong—maybe a little too strong. Matthew didn't flinch.

Daisy watched the handshake, suddenly aware of the odd energy between them. Was this a thing? Was there some unspoken man-code happening right now?

She cleared her throat. "So, Matthew, do you come here often, or is this just a one-off?"

Matthew chuckled. "I didn't realise you were the resident gatekeeper, Daze."

Sam raised an eyebrow. "Daze?"

Oh, come on.

There was a faint commotion from the bar's entrance. Someone called out, "Devan, are you coming?"

Matthew exhaled and flashed a small smile. "Sorry, Daze. I've got to go. Catch up another time?"

"Yeah, sure," Daisy replied, her voice neutral, though her entire body screamed frustration.

"It was nice to meet you, Sam."

"You too." Sam forced a smile, though it didn't reach his eyes. Another firm handshake—too firm, actually. A silent battle of masculinity in the middle of a dimly lit bar.

Matthew disappeared through the door, leaving behind a thick, awkward silence. Daisy and Sam, still suspended in their almost-kiss, now didn't know what to do. The moment was dead, buried.

"So… that was your ex," Sam said through gritted teeth.

"That was my ex," Daisy confirmed, exhaling sharply.

Sam cleared his throat dismissively. "Look, I think we should go. It's late. Work tomorrow."

And just like that, Daisy's stomach plummeted. The shift in his tone, the way he was suddenly all business—it stung. She knew the moment was well and truly dead, and she didn't have the nerve to grab him and kiss him like she wanted to. Instead, she shrank into herself, slipping back into the version of Daisy who lets things go, who retreats instead of fighting for what she wants.

Sam, on the other hand, was kicking himself. Just when he was starting to let his guard down, it was back up. Seeing Daisy be warm with her ex had stirred something in him—something hot and possessive that he didn't quite know how to handle. Jealousy? Annoyance? Whatever it was, he hated it. And he really, really didn't like Matt Devan.

The taxi ride back to Daisy's was quiet. A few half-hearted words—"Thanks for saving me again." "See you tomorrow." And then she was gone, slipping out of the car before he could even process how much he didn't want her to leave.

As the taxi pulled away toward his flat, Sam found his mind looping back to the way Matt had looked at Daisy. The casual familiarity. The lingering tension. But most of all, that parting comment.

"Catch up another time?"

Sam's jaw clenched.

Because, no. No, that is absolutely not happening.

For someone who prides himself on being detached, on keeping things cool and casual, Sam was feeling anything but. He wanted Daisy. And for the first time in a long time, he was ready to try. He just had no bloody clue how.

Sam Callaghan has lost his bottle.

The next morning in the office, Sam was in an even worse mood than usual. His typical cocky arrogance had been replaced with something more out of sorts. He avoided feelings like this for this exact reason—because he hated feeling like this.

Daisy was late. As usual.

He snuck in, put his headphones in, and shut out the world. He just needed to focus on work and let the problem work itself out. That's how things normally went.

Except—why did he have this nagging feeling that this wasn't going to go away?

He sensed someone standing at his desk.

Lance.

"So, how did last night go? Were you gallant? Were you heroic? Has our girl been swept off her feet by the chivalrous Sam Callaghan?"

Oh, for God's sake. This really wasn't going to go away, was it?

Sam responded in the only way he knew how—arrogance.

"Shouldn't you be asking Daisy this kind of rubbish?"

"Daisy isn't here yet, so I'm asking you. Plus, does she know I know?"

"No, she doesn't. And no, it didn't go to plan."

"What? Why?" Lance asked, slightly crushed for his best friend, suddenly realising Daisy's lateness might have something to do with whatever went wrong.

"Her ex turned up."

"Matthew? Dr. Matthew?" Lance repeated in sheer confusion.

"Yep."

Sam turned back to his screen, shoving his headphones back in and scowling, signalling the end of the conversation.

Daisy arrived at the breakout floor in a blur of nerves and frustration, practically hurling herself into the booth opposite Lance. Her hair was wind-whipped, her cheeks flushed, and she looked like someone who'd just run from a ghost—and in a way, she had.

She'd barely paused at her desk, only long enough to throw down her bag and grab her cup, flashing Rhoda a breathless, apologetic wave. Coffee first. Sanity second.

She had also expertly, and very deliberately, avoided Sam.

Because she couldn't face him. Not yet.

She'd thought she could, but the moment she stepped into the office, her stomach had dropped to her shoes. The memory of that almost-kiss—so close she could still feel the brush of his breath—had been haunting her all night. It had been the kind of moment you only get once. Electric. Unexpected. Charged with everything unspoken between them.

Daisy could still picture the way Sam had pulled back the second Matthew appeared, like a flame being snuffed out by cold water. His whole energy had shifted—guarded, unreadable.

She didn't know what that meant. And the not-knowing was

torture.

Was he embarrassed? Regretful? Did he blame her?

And then there was Matthew.

Of course, he bloody showed up.

Why? Why did he want to catch up? Yes, they used to be best friends. But then they weren't. Then they were lovers. And now? After years of no contact? Now she had no idea what the hell he was. She was so confused.

When had her love life decided to get so bloody complicated? It was like she'd accidentally willed this chaos into existence.

Her brain, clearly unsatisfied with her usual problems, had gone, "Hey, you need more drama? Take some love problems. We were severely lacking in that department."

She groaned, slumping forward. Lance slid a coffee toward her without a word. Daisy wrapped her hands around it like it was life support.

"Oh my God, I need a gallon of these. Thank you," she moaned, taking a grateful sip.

"So, what's happening, princess?" Lance asked, all faux innocence. His eyes gleaming with anticipation.

Daisy sighed, leaning back against the booth. "Okay, where do I even start? First of all—you sending Sam last night? A surprise. A nice one, but still a surprise. And we'll circle back to that in a second. The blind date was a literal disaster—until Sam showed up. And then Dahmer left, and somehow… we had a kind of date? I think it was a date. And it was actually shaping up to be a really good night. Until bloody Matthew showed up."

Lance gasped with theatrical flair, though not convincingly enough to hide the fact that he already knew. Of course, Daisy didn't realise he'd been playing low-key matchmaker behind the scenes.

"No WAY," he said, hand on chest like a soap opera extra.

Daisy narrowed her eyes. "Yes, way. And not just showed up like, 'Oh, hi, fancy seeing you here.' No. He appeared at the worst possible moment. Because I'm about ninety-eight percent sure Sam was about to kiss me."

Lance's jaw dropped. "Oh my God, Dais. Are you serious?"

"I was about to kiss him," she said, softer now, almost like admitting it to herself. "I wanted him to kiss me."

Her throat tightened, and she gave a short, bitter laugh. "And then Matthew waltzed in like some kind of awful plot twist. Just killed the moment. Like—bam—emotional whiplash."

"Oh bloody hell, Dais. Matthew, of all people. So how did it end? What did Sam say?"

"Well… Sam actually did kiss me earlier in the night. When he first showed up."

Lance clutched his imaginary pearls. "Stop. This is better than I imagined."

Daisy groaned. "But it was in character. He was pretending to be my boyfriend, so I wasn't sure how real it was. But later, after the Dahmer drama, when we were just… us, the almost-kiss was about to happen. That felt different. Real. And then—bam—Matthew."

She exhaled loudly and slumped back. "And now? I have absolutely no idea where I stand. With either of them. I hate my life."

Lance blinked, trying to hide his smirk. "Okay. A lot of information to process. Let's rewind. Sam kissed you. In character?"

Daisy narrowed her eyes further. "Wait. Hang on a second. How did this even happen? You were supposed to be the one rescuing me. But somehow Sam ends up there instead?"

Lance froze. Shit. Caught.

"Right, so… I may have had a last-minute date. Tinder."

Daisy stared at him. "Lance."

"And, well… Sam sort of… stepped up."

She gave him a look that could peel paint. "That doesn't sound remotely like something Sam Callaghan would voluntarily do. Please tell me you didn't meddle."

"Oh, would you look at the time?" Lance said brightly, springing to his feet. "Daisy, we have a team meeting."

Daisy folded her arms, unimpressed. "Fine. But I'm not done with you, Mr. Delaney."

Sam spent the entire meeting desperately avoiding eye contact with Daisy, which only annoyed her more.

He didn't so much as glance in her direction—not once—and the more he retreated into himself, the more her frustration bubbled up inside her like a shaken can of Coke.

Because while Sam liked to hide from his feelings, Daisy had never mastered that particular skill. She didn't do bottling things up. She did blurting, overthinking, catastrophising. She felt everything, all at once, and tried to make sense of it in real time. Which was impossible when the person you needed answers from was pretending you didn't exist.

She could still feel the ghost of the almost-kiss—the tension between them so palpable she'd been convinced it was actually happening. And she'd wanted it. She hadn't misread it. She was sure of it. Until Matthew showed up like some kind of emotional wrecking ball, and Sam had instantly recoiled. Just… shut down.

And now? Now he was sitting two chairs away from her like a stranger. Taking notes. Talking to Rhoda. Not looking at her.

Fine.

If he didn't want to talk about it, she wasn't going to chase him. Not here. Not in front of their team. But her mind was doing laps around the track anyway.

Did I imagine it? Was it all in my head? Why didn't he say

anything after? Why is it always me feeling too much and him saying too little?

God, she was so tired of being the only one brave enough to admit when something mattered.

She blinked down at her notebook, where she'd written the word Strategy three times in a row and underlined it angrily.

This wasn't just about a missed kiss. It was about feeling something real—for once—and not knowing whether the other person was brave enough to meet her there.

Rhoda was running through details for the upcoming marketing events in Manchester and Edinburgh, smoothing out logistics even though both trips were still three weeks away. Daisy bit the inside of her cheek, trying to focus on what Rhoda was saying, but her thoughts were thick fog. She didn't need grand gestures or love confessions. She just needed something. A sign that she hadn't made it all up in her head.

Anything would've done.

A glance. A smile. A stupid joke.

But Sam said nothing. And somehow, that silence hurt more.

Daisy was trying so hard to stop the spiral, but her mind kept drifting—until she heard her name.

"Is that okay with you, Daisy?"

"Daisy?"

She snapped to attention. "Huh? Yep. Perfect."

She had no bloody idea what she'd just agreed to. She glanced at Lance, who was grinning.

"And you, Sam?" Rhoda continued.

Sam shifted uncomfortably. "Um, yeah. Fine."

It was so unlike his usual composed self that even Rhoda noticed.

"That's settled then. Daisy and Sam will handle Edinburgh, and Lance and Gerard will come with me to Manchester, since it's the bigger event. That should help with costs. Sheena, you'll have to hold down the fort the latter part of that week, okay? Penelope, note that down."

She nodded to her assistant—Penelope, a timid nineteen-year-old who Rhoda treated like a personal stress ball.

But Daisy's mind was reeling at the realisation that she'd just—

Agreed to a work trip on 10th June.

With Sam.

Just the two of them.

Shit.

She glanced at Lance again. He was practically glowing with delight, watching this drama unfold like it was his own personal EastEnders.

She sneaked a look at Sam. He was still avoiding her, now twisting a paperclip between his fingers like his life depended on it. But then—

He glanced up.

Just for a second.

Their eyes met.

And for the briefest, flickering moment, he smiled. It was barely there—hesitant, uncertain—but it was real. A flash of warmth that hit her square in the chest before he dropped his gaze again like he couldn't bear to hold it. Back to the paperclip. Back to the silence.

Her stomach flipped.

What was that?

An apology? A reassurance? Or just a reflex?

She had no idea.

And somehow, that was worse than if he'd just kept ignoring her altogether.

The smile had cracked something open, but the awkwardness had flooded right back in behind it, and now she was more confused than ever.

Rhoda frowned. "Honestly, what is going on with you lot today? The atmosphere is weird. Can we sort this out before the events, please?"

Daisy and Sam remained silent.

"Any other business?"

A collective no echoed around the room before everyone bolted for the door.

The rest of the day passed in a weird, stagnant silence. Normally, Daisy and Sam had their usual back-and-forth—snarky quips, inside jokes, subtle glances. But today? Nothing. Not even a passing comment. Just the clatter of keyboards and the low hum of the office aircon. The distance between them felt louder than any words.

Lance checked in before heading out. "I'll call you later, yeah?"

Daisy nodded, barely looking up from her screen. Her stomach was in knots, but she didn't trust herself to speak without sounding… needy. Angry. Both.

At 6:45 p.m., she finally looked around. The office was empty. Everyone had gone.

Everyone except Sam.

But she was still mad at him. More than mad—she felt dismissed. So she grabbed her bag, didn't say goodbye, and made a beeline for the lift.

Sam heard her chair scrape back and looked up just in time to see her walking away, her expression unreadable but her pace purposeful. He didn't say anything. Couldn't. The words caught in his throat.

He watched her go, his jaw tightening.

Because the truth was, he didn't know how to fix this. He wasn't good at conversations like this—raw, vulnerable ones that demanded you show up rather than retreat. And he was so used to retreating.

But then his thoughts took a ridiculous turn, generating faster than he could stop them.

What if she was going to meet him? The ex. Matthew.

His heart kicked in his chest.

What if she still had feelings for him? What if that's why the kiss hadn't happened? What if she'd changed her mind?

The fear came out of nowhere, cold and sudden, and it hit him square in the gut.

And it dawned on him—with sickening clarity—that if he didn't do something soon, if he kept hiding, kept pushing her away out of fear or pride or pure emotional cowardice… he was going to lose her.

To him.

To Matthew. A man he barely knew, except for the fact that he hated how Daisy looked when she talked about him—guarded, brittle, like she was reliving something she couldn't quite let go of.

And the worst part?

He couldn't blame her.

Because right now, he was giving her nothing to hold onto.

Daisy was too good. Too important. And Sam had no idea how to keep her without making a mess of it. But he couldn't let her go.

So he followed.

She had barely made it to the pavement when—

"Daisy! Wait!"

She stopped, turning just as he caught up.

"This is silly," Sam said, breathless. "Can we talk?"

She folded her arms. "Thought you were avoiding me."

"What? Daisy, no." He sighed. "Can we go somewhere? Not here."

She studied him for a moment, then pulled out her phone, quickly messaging **Nanna Jean:**

"Something's come up. Can you keep Tino one more night?"

Then she turned back to Sam. "Okay. Lead the way."

They settled into an intimate pub under the bridge, the kind with dim lighting, worn wooden tables, and the lingering scent of stale chips and ale. The hum of chatter mixed with the occasional clatter of a dropped glass, and a barman with a tea towel slung over his shoulder stood at the edge of the bar, moaning about the football match that was on.

Daisy initiated the conversation because she was coming to realise that Sam was a man of very few words when he had to be serious or talk about his feelings, and now he was already distracted by the match.

"So?" she said.

Sam exhaled, running a hand through his hair.

"I'm sorry. About last night. And today. If I made you feel uncomfortable in any way—"

Daisy tilted her head, smirking. "What exactly are you sorry for?"

She switched straight into flirtation mode. She could not be arsed with this back-and-forth—she just wanted to go back to how it was last night.

Sam relaxed slightly, grinning despite himself. "I don't actually know."

"I mean, the meeting was a little awkward." Daisy sipped her drink. "Why do you think that was?"

"Not sure. Something to do with me not talking to you. Or how last night ended." He rubbed his jaw. "I didn't want to leave it like that. It was just—awkward."

"Yeah. It was a bit." Daisy laughed. "I'd like it not to be awkward."

Sam smirked. "Me too. I just don't really know how."

Her stomach clenched. "What does that mean? What are you telling me, Sam?"

He exhaled, staring at his pint, spinning the glass nervously between his hands. Daisy watched him, the tension between them building.

She reached forward, placing her hand on the glass to stop it from spinning clean off the table—touching his hand in the process.

His eyes flickered to their hands. He didn't move. Didn't look at her.

"Talk to me, Sam. Please."

He sighed. Then—

He turned to her, cupped her face, pulling her in and smashing his lips against hers.

For a split second, Daisy's brain short-circuited.

Sam Callaghan is kissing her.

Then instinct kicked in.

She kissed him back.

Chapter 12:
What the hell was his deal?

Why had Sam Callaghan kissed her?

He liked her.

Daisy decided to shut off her mind and just enjoy the moment—because if there was one thing she knew about Sam Callaghan, it was that he had a habit of reverting back to cold, cocky, arrogant Sam at any given moment and acting like nothing had happened.

So she savoured it.

She could hardly believe it was happening. He liked her?

And because she was really, really enjoying it.

So was he, apparently, as he pulled her closer, running his hand up her thigh and deepening the kiss.

For ten blissful minutes, they lost themselves in each other—her hands tangled in the back of his hair, his hands on her waist, fingers tracing up the back of her jumper; her arms locked around his shoulders, pulling him in tighter.

"Do you think we should go somewhere more private?" she murmured breathlessly, trying not to break the kiss.

Sam nodded, drained the last of his pint, and kissed her again, like he couldn't bear to stop. They fumbled for their coats, trying to leave while still half-attached to each other.

He led her out by the hand, and Daisy felt her stomach flip. This couldn't be happening.

Oh, but it was.

And she wanted him—desperately.

Outside, they kissed again, pressed against the cold stone of the bridge—urgent, breathless, like two reckless teenagers who couldn't get enough. It teetered on the edge of romantic.

Until it wasn't.

Something shifted. A flicker of doubt appeared in his eyes. Like a lightbulb of insecurity had gone off in his head.

And then, Sam stopped.

Daisy let out a soft, involuntary whine as he pulled away, like a child being yanked from their favourite blanket.

She touched her lips, confused. "What the?"

He wouldn't meet her eyes. "I don't think we can do this."

Her stomach dropped. "What do you mean?"

He sighed. "Me and you. This. Us. We work together. It's not professional."

Daisy just stared at him.

But she also heard the words he didn't say.

I don't do relationships.

I don't want to get attached.

I don't want you to get attached to me.

The rejection felt real. It hurt.

But instead of fighting, instead of forcing him to admit that he wanted this too, she did something she never imagined she would.

She nodded.

Then she left.

"Daisy—" Sam called after her, but she kept walking.

Because she couldn't stand there pretending she was okay with this.

Because she was completely and utterly embarrassed.

And because she didn't trust herself not to turn around and kiss him all over again.

Daisy walked quickly, trying not to trip over her own feet, her breath catching in her throat.

Don't cry. Not here. Not over this.

She didn't even know where she was going. She just needed to move. To get away from the intensity of it all. From the look on his face—like he wanted her, but not enough.

Why did he kiss her if he was only going to push her away?

She wiped her cheek angrily, not sure if it was from the cold or what. Her chest ached, raw and tight, like her heart had been put through a shredder and then duct-taped back together by someone who had no clue what they were doing.

Back at the bridge, Sam stood frozen.

He hadn't meant for it to end like that.

But the panic had come out of nowhere. The second she smiled at him like he was something good—something safe—he'd felt the familiar weight press down on his chest.

He knew what this was. Daisy wasn't just a fling. She wasn't casual. She could ruin him in the best way possible. And that terrified him.

Sam ran a hand through his hair, muttering a curse under his breath.

He wanted to chase after her.

But what would he even say?

Sorry, I'm emotionally constipated? Sorry I kissed you like I meant it and then freaked out because I actually did?

Yeah. That would go down well.

He turned away from the bridge, dragging himself in the opposite direction.

Maybe this was for the best.

Maybe.

But as he shoved his hands in his pockets and walked into the night, all he could think was—

I've messed this up. And I don't know how to fix it. Daisy spent the next few days in a bubble—a blur. Her mind kept dragging her back to that moment—Sam kissing her. And the truth was, she wanted him so badly it felt like she might actually have a breakdown. The feelings were intrusive, overwhelming… and completely unwelcome.

How dare he come crashing into her life just when things were finally starting to feel normal?

Then her brain, in its usual unhelpful way, started whispering that maybe she wasn't craving him at all. Maybe she just wanted something familiar, something grounding. Like she still wanted Matthew.

Nope. Absolutely not. He was engaged. Firmly off-limits. She needed to file that one under *Bad Ideas I Will Definitely Regret Before Dessert.*

Thankfully, it was the weekend, which gave Daisy the perfect excuse to shut everyone out—Lydia, Lance, Prim. Everyone except Tino. Her loyal, delinquent pup curled up beside her like an emotional support loaf, occasionally thudding his head against her knee in search of a belly rub or a crisp.

She barely left the flat, cocooned in a sea of blankets, self-doubt, and mostly Netflix.

On Saturday night, she half-watched a true crime documentary while working her way through a tub of Ben & Jerry's, obsessively re-reading her messages with Sam. Not that there were many. And none of them were remotely romantic. Still, she analysed every single word for hidden meaning like she was the world's leading authority on passive-aggressive texting.

By Sunday, she hit rock bottom and started Googling Gemini and Sagittarius compatibility while Tino sat beside her, farting unapologetically and snoring like a tiny chainsaw. She considered pouring a glass of wine but opted for chamomile tea to avoid a full-on Bridget Jones "All By Myself" moment.

Then she drafted a message to Sam—seven different times—trying to strike the perfect tone. Not too needy. Not too breezy. Just… honest. One version simply said:

Daisy: *Hey. About the other night—I don't know where we stand and I hate feeling like this. Can we talk?*

Another read:

Daisy: *Hey, if you're avoiding me, could you just tell me? I'd honestly rather know than guess.*

She stared at that one the longest. Her thumb hovered over "Send" for a full thirty seconds before she hit delete. Because if she said it out loud, it would be real. And real was utterly shite.

Tino, ever unbothered, simply sighed and nudged her hand toward his chew toy. At least someone in the flat knew what they wanted.

But then came Monday. The comforting cocoon of the weekend was gone, and Daisy realised there was no way she could face work—or worse, face Sam Callaghan—so she called in sick for the first time ever.

She curled up with 10 Things I Hate About You, finding herself trying (and failing) not to relate her current emotional catastrophe to the film. At one point, during Heath Ledger's grandstand performance of I Love You, Baby, Daisy burst into tears, wondering why that kind of love was possible for them but not for her.

Jealous of a movie. Ridiculous, Daisy.

Why was big, messy, over-the-top romance possible for Patrick and Kat, yet completely unattainable for her? Then she remembered it was based on Shakespeare, so probably not the most reliable blueprint for love.

Then the buzzer rang.

Surely not?

No. Wishful thinking. Sam didn't even know where she lived.

Pausing the movie at the most crucial point and shoving Tino off her lap—to which he responded with a disgruntled growl—she answered.

"Hello?"

"Dais, open up. It's me. Lydia… and Lance."

Oh.

As Lydia and Lance stepped into her flat, it became immediately obvious that 'Recluse Daisy' was back. Lydia gave her a look of sheer disappointment.

"Dais, what's going on, babe? Why have you been shutting us out? What's happened?"

"And why are you not at work today?" Lance added, raising an eyebrow. "Who are you avoiding?"

"Why are you not at work?" she shot back, instantly on the defensive.

"Erm, lunch break," Lance replied smugly. "Plus, I needed to see this with my own eyes." He folded his arms and exchanged a look with Lydia.

"It's really stupid," Daisy said sheepishly. "Sam Callaghan kissed me."

"He what?" they both said in unison. "Is that not… good?"

Daisy shrugged. "Then he sort of… shut me down? Or shut me out. I don't know what it was. He's so unreadable."

Lance pulled her into a hug, his arms warm and grounding. "Oh, babe, when was this?"

"Friday night."

"Ah."

"I just can't face him. What am I going to do?" Daisy flopped onto her sofa, one arm flung dramatically over her eyes. "I'm background noise in my own life, Lyds. Like one of those sad montage songs that plays while the protagonist eats ice cream and sobs."

Lydia looked at Lance and raised an eyebrow. "Daisy."

"What?"

"You're supposed to be the leading lady of your own life, for God's sake."

Daisy peeked out from under her arm. "Did you just *Iris* me?"

Lydia grinned. "Absolutely. Now get up, have a shower, and put on something that doesn't look like you've given up on love and laundry."

She pulled Daisy up by the shoulders, looking her dead in the eye.

"Look, it's obvious you like him. And yeah, he's got issues. But you can't hide from this. You can't just shut yourself off because you're scared of what might happen. You need to talk to him. It's the only way you'll find out where you stand."

Lance chimed in, nudging her lightly. "Exactly. This isn't you. Not *new* you, anyway. We know you. You've got to be brave. You can't let it fizzle out."

"Yeah, but… I'm pretty sure he doesn't feel the same," Daisy whispered, her voice cracking.

Lance opened his mouth to respond but stopped, clearly hesitating.

"What? Lance, what is it?" Daisy asked. Lydia narrowed her eyes.

"Okay, fine," Lance admitted. "I have it on good authority that Sam fancies you." He tried to look nonchalant, but the smirk gave him away.

"How do you know that?"

"Because he told me."

Lydia exploded. "When was this? Why didn't you bloody tell her?"

"The night of the blind date," Lance said defensively. "It's why he showed up to rescue you, Dais. Don't you see?"

"Okay," Daisy said, holding up her hands. "But now he definitely doesn't. He said—and I quote—'We can't do this, because we work together.'"

"Then at least you know," Lydia said, her voice firm but kind. "And you can move on. But my advice? Find out what the hell his deal is first. Because it sounds like there's something he's not saying."

Lance nodded. "She's right. That sounds like a cop-out. There's more to this. You need to know."

"Don't let the fear stop you from taking the leap," Lydia added.

"We're always here for you, babe," Lance said. "But if you want advice on kissing someone who's emotionally confusing, I've got notes."

Daisy laughed, wiping her eyes. "Okay, okay, I get it."

"You've got this, Daisy," Lydia said, squeezing her hand. "Just be honest with him. And with yourself."

Meanwhile, Sam Callaghan was punishing himself.

He couldn't get the night out of his head. He hadn't stopped thinking about Daisy all day.

Why did he kiss her? Why did he give her false hope? Why did he make everything so—complicated?

Because he really likes her. And he needs to stop lying to himself.

He can't let his guard down. He can't fall for someone. Not now. Not ever.

God, why is he like this?

And why isn't she at work today? Is she avoiding him? Is that his fault?

Crap.

Sam couldn't focus. Not on work, not on anything. Rhoda had asked him about twenty-five questions that morning, and he hadn't answered a single one.

He pulled out his phone, thumbs hovering.

Sam: *Everything ok, Dais? Why aren't you in?*

Delete.

Sam: *I'm sorry if I hurt you.*

Pause. Hover. Delete.

Honestly, today could do one.

Then he heard her name—Daisy.

Lance.

Something about her being sick. Lance was going over at lunch to check in on her.

Should he go?

No. Way too much.

He officially decided: he'd screwed up, and now Daisy was avoiding him. The only thing left to do was bury himself in work and forget about it.

You made your bed, Sam. Now bloody lie in it. You didn't want a relationship—well, now you've got a non-relationship.

Deal with it.

Then his phone buzzed.

He grabbed it with an insane level of excitement.

Dad: *I haven't forgotten our conversation. Please come and see me tonight. I'll be at the office until 9.*

Brilliant.

Dad summons.

His dad—a lawyer and professional arsehole. Always had been, ever since Sam's football career went down the drain.

An accident. A lifelong injury. Not his fault, but little did he know, his dad would never forgive him for it.

His mum? Kind, but quiet. Suppressed. She loved him, sure, but it always felt… conditional. Forced. Since Sam's accident, she'd barely known what to say to him. Their relationship had faded into awkward silences and polite check-ins.

He was an only child. Most of his childhood memories were football-related. His parents loved him, but that love seemed tethered to his success. He was the kid with the golden feet. The ticket out. The pride of the family—until he wasn't.

The only person Sam had ever truly been close to was Lewis, his childhood best friend. Like a brother. They grew up next door, spent every moment together. Fought over football, teased each other about girls. But they loved each other in the way only boys growing up side by side can.

Then Sam got good. Really good. Signed at eleven, playing pro by fifteen.

Lewis's life went the other way. Gangs, trouble, drugs. Sam loved him, but he couldn't be around it—not with his future at stake.

His dad made the call: cut Lewis off, for your own good.

And Sam had no choice but to listen. For his career.

Lewis spiralled. Sam was haunted by it. He still felt like, maybe, if he'd stayed… he could've helped him, he could've saved him.

But survival, for Sam, meant more than just training and winning. It meant pleasing his parents.

And his parents were obsessed with money.

Luckily for them, Sam was earning it—serious money. Match bonuses, sponsorships, endorsements. His dad took control, telling him where to put it: property, investments, things Sam barely understood but happily signed off on. He didn't care. He was nineteen and living like every day was a highlight reel.

Until the accident.

Game over. Career over. And in the fallout, he lost Lewis too— the only person who had ever truly loved him without condition.

The only silver lining? His dad's financial manoeuvring had left him cushioned. The career was gone, but the money remained— enough to live comfortably, at least on paper. Though to Sam, it felt like cash he hadn't earned anymore. But somehow that was never enough for his father. Nothing ever was.

That evening, Sam walked reluctantly into his dad's office near Paddington. God, he hated this place. The glass, the chrome, the silence—it was miserable. Or maybe he was, knowing exactly what conversation was about to play out. The same one they'd had too many times before.

His father sat at the desk, not even looking up as Sam entered. No How are you, son? Just:

"Sit."

"I'll be with you in a moment."

Like Sam was a client. Like he was anyone but his son.

Cold and emotionless.

"So, Samuel, about this offer we discussed a few weeks ago. You haven't responded. It's a good offer. We pay good money here. It's worth it. Job security. Keep up with the mortgage on that flat of yours."

"I don't want to work here, Dad. I like my job. I like working for Rhoda."

His dad scoffs. "Rhoda Williams is a crook. Her breakout marketing firm is a vanity project. It's not a solid career path, Samuel."

Sam's face said it all. Rhoda isn't why he was still there.

There was another reason. She had freckles, a sharp tongue, and a French bulldog named Tino.

"What's wrong with you, boy? Have you gone soft? You haven't met a girl, have you? Last thing you need is a woman wasting your time when you haven't even got your future planned out properly."

"My future is just fine. And I just really like working there." He lied.

"Well, I really liked it when you had a football career, but you screwed that one up, didn't you? Took away that security. I think you maybe need to start listening to me."

Harsh.

"Dad, come on. I did everything you wanted me to do. After the accident. Please just let me continue my career. You put me on this path, I like it."

His dad had set him on the accountancy path not long after his accident. Mainly to drag him out of the depression he was in, stop him spiralling, and to give him something to focus on. And focus he did, passing all his exams in three years and carving out a decent city career. Sam did this, so his dad would leave him alone. But now, now it just wasn't good enough.

He looked at his dad. He was quiet. Thinking. Then all of a sudden, he gave in.

"Ok, fine. But if you're not any further in your career by this time next year, you're coming to work here. No arguments."

Fantastic. Now Sam has twelve months to magic up a promotion in a tiny office that runs on coffee, chaos, and the strength of Rhoda's eye rolls.

"Right, Samuel. I've got a meeting—with, uh… some other lawyers."

"At 9 pm?" Sam raised an eyebrow.

Sam was pretty sure his dad had a mistress. Whatever.

"I'll see you at the match Sunday? Arsenal. We can use the box."

Sam nodded. Bribery via football. Classic Dad.

"Sure, okay. Bye, Dad."

But he was already gone. No hug. No 'take care'. Just… gone.

Sam didn't go home. Not to his empty flat. Not when he felt this empty inside.

He headed to his local. At least the barman would be pleased to see him.

He nodded to a few regulars, muttering something half-friendly, and sat at the bar with a pint. Silent. Hollow.

His phone buzzed once in his pocket. He didn't look. It wasn't her. He knew that without checking.

But God, he wanted it to be.

He took a long sip, then unlocked his phone anyway. Scrolled to her name. Hovered.

One message. That's all it would take.

Just say something. Say you're sorry. Say you were scared. Say anything.

He opened the message thread and slowly typed:

Sam: *I'm sorry I left things the way I did.*

I should've said something. I just… I didn't know how to.

You caught me off guard. You always do.

I didn't mean to shut you out. I never mean to when it comes to you.

His thumb hovered over Send.

Then—he deleted the whole thing.

Too much. Too honest.

He tried again:

Sam: *Hey. Can we talk?*

He hovered over Send. Then—his mate Harry appeared. He put the phone back in his pocket.

"What's up with you, mate? You look like you've been dumped."

"Not quite," Sam muttered through gritted teeth.

"Maybe you should get yourself a bird. You look like you could use a good seeing to, mate."

"Shut up, you dickhead."

Harry grinned, slapping him on the back. "I'm just saying that whole brooding, arrogant, handsome thing? Not working for you anymore. Try being nice. Might get a second date."

Sam rolled his eyes. He hated how right Harry was. Like he could tell exactly what Sam had been up to.

"What, like your love life is so successful? You're hardly beating them off with a stick."

Harry laughed. "Yeah, well, that's because you're the better-looking one and it's deeply unfair. But at least I've got a personality."

Sam snorted. "Keep telling yourself that."

There was a pause, a flicker of something unspoken.

Harry nudged him lightly with his shoulder. "You alright though, mate?"

Sam didn't answer right away. He just stared ahead, jaw tight, heart heavier than he wanted to admit.

Then, quietly: "Yeah. I just need to send one quick message."

He pulled out his phone. The message was still there—waiting.

Half a sentence. Hanging in the space between bravery and retreat.

Sam: *Hey. Can we talk?*

It looked wrong. Too casual. Too vague.

Like it didn't come close to what he actually meant.

He hesitated, then typed more.

Sam: *I don't want to mess this up.*

He stared at the words. Then finally, sent it.

The second it went, his stomach dropped.

Because now it was real.

This was the root of it all, really.

Sam Callaghan—cold and closed-off on the outside.

But deep down?

Just a boy who wanted to be loved.

And for once, he'd found someone he actually wanted to love him.

Chapter 13:
Two pints and a packet of peanuts

Daisy returned to work the next day but didn't talk to Sam about the kiss. Instead, she buried it.

He had made her feel like she *had* to bury it—which wasn't like her at all.

Normally, she had to get things off her chest—especially when she felt this strongly about something. But with Sam, it felt… different. Like saying anything would somehow make it worse. Like she was chasing something he hadn't actually offered.

And then there was the cryptic text he'd sent late last night:

Sam: *Hey. Can we talk? I don't want to mess this up.*

What did that even mean?

Mess what up? There wasn't anything to mess up—he'd made sure of that. He'd kissed her, then pulled away. Looked at her like he wanted more, then said nothing.

Why did he always have to be so cryptic?

The whole thing made her feel like a lunatic.

Why couldn't he just say what he meant instead of leaving these vague emotional breadcrumbs for her to decode like some kind of romantic escape room?

What the hell was his deal?

So no, she didn't reply. And she didn't bring it up.

Because if he wasn't going to be clear about what he wanted, she wasn't going to do the heavy lifting for him.

Over the next few days, they slipped back into their old rhythm—

or rather, the awkward, clipped version of it that had existed before the amazing, life-altering kiss.

It wasn't how Daisy wanted things. Of course it wasn't. She still felt that quiet ache every time she saw him, still got that stupid flutter in her stomach every time his name came up or he walked past.

But if this weird, distant limbo was what he wanted, then fine. She had her pride.

He wasn't her boyfriend. He didn't owe her anything.

Still, his behaviour made her want to throw her stapler across the room.

She needed to focus.

In two weeks, she had the bloody Edinburgh work trip—and she was going to need every ounce of professionalism, caffeine, and emotional detachment she could muster to survive it.

With Sam Callaghan.

And his stupid, indecisive, maddeningly attractive self.

There was plenty to keep her busy to distract herself. Rhoda was definitely making sure she earned her wage this week. She had tasked Daisy with collecting the merchandise—wristbands, vouchers, buttons, pens, and promotional posters.

There had been a mix-up, and the items had been delivered to the wrong office—an office that refused to pay for postage to return them and would only send them back to the sender.

Rhoda, being Rhoda, had no time to waste. She wanted them collected that very day so she could start sending things out.

Daisy, ever the opportunist, gallantly volunteered to collect them—mainly to get out of the office and away from certain… situations.

The only problem? The office was quite a way down the road, and Daisy wasn't sure how she was going to manage. A taxi was, apparently, a ludicrous idea. So, she decided to just get on with it. She'd manage.

When she arrived, however, there were *three* large boxes and several poster tubes.

Shit.

Daisy decided to carry two boxes and a few poster tubes now, planning to return for the third later. That was a big mistake. Foolish Daisy.

She couldn't manage two. She had to keep stopping, dropping the tubes—and the whole thing was a disaster. She made it a few streets before one of the boxes slipped from her grasp, spilling pens and buttons everywhere.

"Fuck my life," she muttered.

And of course, right on cue, Sam Callaghan appeared—looking far too smug.

"Wow, you really ballsed this up," he said, clearly enjoying the spectacle.

Of course Sam would know she was doing this. He'd been cc'd on all the emails. But why did he have to come to her rescue? After *everything*.

"Thanks for stating the obvious," she shot back, wishing she could slap that annoying smirk off his face.

An annoying smirk that, damn him, made him look *incredibly* handsome today. And suddenly, Daisy's eyes were on his lips, her mind drifting traitorously back to their kiss—the warmth of it, the way her heart had thudded against her ribs like it was trying to break free.

"How did you know where I'd be?" she asked, raising an eyebrow, clinging desperately to her annoyance like a shield.

"Daisy, come on. I knew you wouldn't be able to handle this on your own."

The cheek.

Sometimes he was so bloody arrogant she wanted to punch him square in his gorgeous face. Or grab him and snog it off.

Instead, she settled for, "Fuck you, Callaghan."

And to her dismay, they both laughed.

That warm, familiar sound curled in her chest as they crouched down, collecting the scattered merch back into the box. Somewhere in the chaos, the tension between them softened—just enough.

As they scraped up the last of the leaflets off the floor, Sam spoke up, his voice quieter than before.

"I've missed this."

"Missed what?" Daisy asked, not looking at him. If she did, she wasn't sure what her face might give away.

"Hanging out." He shrugged, fiddling with a crumpled lanyard. "With you."

Daisy froze for a second, her breath catching. Why was he saying this now? It wasn't like Sam to be so... open. He usually specialised in brooding silences and vague texts at 11:47 p.m.

She bit back a hundred sarcastic replies and simply nodded, trying to keep her composure.

"Daisy," he said gently now. "Can we talk? Not right now—I know this isn't the moment. But soon. I'm really sorry for how I acted. I miss talking to you—about non-work stuff and that."

She rolled her eyes so hard it actually hurt—but it wasn't from annoyance anymore. It was self-preservation. Because he didn't even seem to realise *he* was the reason they weren't talking. He was the bloody problem.

And yet, here he was. Trying.

She exhaled slowly, nodding again. "Okay. Sure."

It wasn't forgiveness. Not yet. But it was something.

As she started to stand, Sam instinctively reached out a hand to help her up. His palm closed around hers, warm and familiar. She hesitated for a second—too long for it to be casual—before letting him pull her to her feet.

Their hands lingered.

Neither of them let go straight away.

And for one suspended, breathless moment, it felt like something might happen. Another kiss, maybe. The kind that had been hanging unspoken between them since that night.

But then Daisy stepped back, clearing her throat, breaking the spell.

Still, when she looked at him and caught the small, hopeful smile he gave her, something shifted. A tiny step forward.

And just like that, a small beacon of hope flickered in the sea of confusion Sam had created.

Later that evening, for the first time in a week, Daisy left work feeling optimistic.

That optimism would be short-lived, however, because as she stepped out of the office building, there he was—

Matthew Devan. Or *Matt* Devan, as he liked to call himself now, because he'd grown up into this super-cool doctor and was nothing like the mess Daisy had turned into.

Honestly. Her life.

He was leaning against one of those ridiculously large outdoor potted plants that were so popular in London these days. Daisy couldn't help but think how absurd it was that a tree or plant needed such a massive pot to sit in—*outside*. But, whatever. Architecture.

"What are you doing here?" Daisy asked, furrowing her brow.

"I really need to talk to you," Matthew said, looking strangely unsettled. "Are you free for a quick drink?"

Daisy hesitated. Every instinct told her to say no—to walk away before she got sucked into whatever this was. But curiosity, or something dangerously close to nostalgia, won out.

"Okay, sure," she replied, albeit reluctantly.

As she followed him to a nearby pub, she couldn't help but wonder—why now? Why, after all this time, did Matthew suddenly want to talk? And why, after everything with Sam, did her heart still skip—just a little—at the sight of him?

They slipped into a quiet pub near London Bridge. It was a Wednesday evening, so the place was nearly empty, the low hum of conversation blending with the occasional clink of glasses behind the bar.

Matthew returned with two pints and a packet of peanuts.

Jesus. Another reminder that he knew her so bloody well.

"Thanks." She gave him a small smile as he slid into the seat opposite. Daisy attacked the peanuts—*starving* didn't begin to cover it after the day she'd had.

He stared into his pint, brow furrowed as if trying to figure out how to start.

The suspense was killing her.

"Well?"

He let out a quiet laugh at her stroppy tone. "Still impatient, I see."

"Yep. Some things never change."

Matthew exhaled, shaking his head slightly. "I was just realising—the last time we were sat together like this was ten years ago, Daze."

She blinked. "Wow. That's gone horribly fast. And now I feel old. Thanks for that."

He chuckled. "Sorry. I'm old too, if that helps."

"Not by much."

"Still older." He took a sip of his pint, then hesitated. "It's just mad."

Another pause. *Why is this so awkward? It's Matthew, for heaven's sake.*

"You remember that day we spent in Hyde Park?" he asked, his voice quieter now. "The one where we sat on that bench—me with my skateboard, you with your sketchbook—half-drunk on Smirnoff Ice, just… talking about what we wanted to do with our lives?"

Daisy froze for a second, the memory flooding back like it was yesterday. It had been one of those lazy summer afternoons, the kind where the world felt like it was just theirs. She could almost hear Matthew's laugh again—that easy, carefree sound that used to make her feel like nothing else mattered.

"Yeah, I remember," she said softly, caught off guard despite herself. "We were so sure about everything back then."

Matthew's smile was gentle but tinged with something heavier. "I think that was the last time I really felt certain about anything."

Daisy swallowed. *Seriously? Why was he dropping this on her now—like some kind of emotional bath bomb, fizzing and expanding until she couldn't breathe?*

"So, Daze, what I wanted to say is—"

"Tell me about your fiancée," Daisy cut in quickly, her tone bright—almost too bright. "What's she like?"

Matthew frowned. He knew exactly what she was doing—putting distance between them, just like she had all those years ago. And it annoyed him.

Because this was what he wanted to talk about. It was all he'd wanted to talk about since she'd messaged him. Or maybe even before that. He just wanted some answers—to finally understand what he'd done to make her leave.

But he answered her question anyway. Begrudgingly.

"Oh. Right. Priyanka. Erm, well… she's great. She's a teacher. We met about eighteen months ago." He paused, running a hand through his hair. "Daze, I don't really want to talk about Pri. I wanted to talk about us. What happened?"

Daisy avoided his gaze, her fingers tracing the condensation on her glass.

Because the thing was—he hadn't really changed all that much. He was still as gorgeous as ever. Still Matthew. And yet… something was different.

And Daisy Donaldson, mess-up extraordinaire, had no idea how to put that into words. So she blurted out the first thing that came to mind.

"Why bring up the past, though? There isn't really an 'us' anymore, is there?"

Excellent. That went down like a lead balloon.

Matthew exhaled sharply, his jaw tightening. He looked… fuming.

Daisy had spent the last decade avoiding this exact conversation, and now here it was—happening in real time. And she was wildly unprepared. Because the truth was, she didn't even know what had happened back then. Not really. She'd shoved it into a mental drawer marked *deal with later*—and then slammed it shut.

Except "later" had stretched into ten years, with her thinking about him more than she'd ever admit.

And now he was here. In front of her.

She was terrified. Because she had no idea what she felt anymore.

The silence stretched too long, so she broke it.

"Look, I'm sorry, that came out wrong. But in truth, we ended it when we both left for uni. We both decided that. And we didn't make any effort to contact each other."

"I wanted to contact you, Daisy. *You* asked me not to."

Silence.

He continued, his voice softer now. "Did you not want to contact me?"

"I guess I presumed it was over. So… no." She bit back. A massive lie.

Matthew studied her, his expression unreadable. Then, quietly: "Did you stop loving me?"

Her stomach twisted.

"Matthew. Please don't make me answer that."

"Fine." He exhaled sharply. "Look, I can see you don't want to talk about this—even though I think we need to, because it's not going to just go away. Maybe this isn't the right time. I should just go."

"Wait." She reached out instinctively, grabbing his wrist before she could stop herself. "Why now? Why let ten years pass before asking me all these questions?"

There was a long pause. And then Daisy realised what was different.

He didn't feel like hers anymore.

Someone else had his heart. And that killed her.

And then he spoke.

"Because just hearing from you out of the blue the other week, and then seeing you at the engagement party—it made me realise I missed you. *Us.* The way we were."

Oh no.

He continued.

"Seeing you after all this time made everything come rushing back. And I should've reached out before. It was like, out of sight, out of mind—but now I can't ignore it anymore. You've always been in my heart, Daisy. I still love you."

Crap.

His words hit her like a tidal wave, pushing her emotions to the surface. She had waited so long—years—for him to say those words again. But now that they were here, spoken aloud, they felt… wrong.

Like they didn't belong to her anymore. Like she wanted to shove them back into his mouth and pretend she'd never heard them.

"Matthew," she said, anger rising in her chest. "You're engaged. You're getting married. You have no right to drop this love bomb on me."

His eyes darkened. "I know that. But, Daisy, my marriage—it's arranged. A marriage of convenience because, well, I'm twenty-eight. It's expected. I don't love her. I love you. I always have."

Daisy wasn't touched by this revelation. She was livid.

Because if he had loved her, why hadn't he told her years ago? Why not six years ago, when he came back? Why now? Why, when he was *unavailable*, did he think this was the right time?

She pushed back her chair and stood abruptly.

"I actually can't do this," she said, her voice shaking. "I don't want to. This is so—so shitty of you. Go back. Back to your fiancée, Matthew. And leave me alone."

And with that, she stormed out of the bar and into the busy London street.

Walking towards the tube station, she cried.

But she didn't look back.

Because she had no idea how to deal with it.

Chapter 14:
You can sleep on grass, right?

After the run-in with Dr. Matthew—as Lance had now decided he should be called—Daisy had spent the whole day in a funk, still reeling from Matthew and his bloody revelation, and right now she just couldn't face going home, alone.

So, naturally, she dragged Lance to the nearest pub.

As they left, there was no sign of Sam. Did he leave early today? Doesn't matter—Daisy had enough emotional baggage on her plate right now without adding him to the mix.

"Daisy Donaldson, you never drink on a school night!" Lance gasped, clutching his chest like she'd just confessed to murder.

"I know, but tonight I need to get shitfaced. It's the only way I'll cope."

Two bottles of white wine later, Lydia arrived, sliding into the booth with her usual dramatic flair.

"I couldn't hear you properly on the phone, but it sounds tragic. Dais, pleeeeease let me write a sitcom about your life—I need a job."

"Erm, no?" Daisy frowned… then genuinely considered it.

"Come on," Lydia pressed. "You've been single for so long you practically forgot what kissing is, and now—suddenly—you've got two gorgeous men in the mix. One ex, one colleague. This is prime-time material."

"Correction," Lance cut in, swirling his glass. "It's scandalous prime-time material. Like Love Island, but with fewer abs and more wine breath."

Daisy groaned, dropping her head onto the sticky table. "Exactly how do I choose between them? Eeny, meeny, miney… oh God, this is pathetic."

Because she didn't even know how she felt. Matthew had dropped the I still love you bomb and she hadn't stopped spinning since. Part of her wanted to believe him, because it meant those years hadn't been a lie. But another part—the louder part—kept dragging her back to Sam. To the stupid lift rides, to the smirks, to the way he made her feel alive and annoyed and seen, all at once.

She was torn between the past she'd never dealt with and the present she couldn't ignore.

"Luckily," Lydia said, topping up Daisy's glass, "Sam is basically shoving you away every time you so much as blink at him, and Matthew—well—he's engaged. So, honestly? It's not even a love triangle. It's just chaos with extra steps."

"Chaos with extra steps," Lance repeated, snorting. "That's going on your gravestone."

Because that's exactly what her life was. Chaos.

The three of them dissolved into cackles, sounding more like the Sanderson Sisters than functioning adults, until the pub finally kicked them out. They staggered toward the station, shrieking with laughter, somewhere along the way losing both Lydia and Lance to the London night.

Daisy, in her infinite wisdom, decided to take a detour. She had no idea what time it was, didn't care, and flopped onto the grass near Tower Bridge, stretching out as the world spun around her.

Her phone buzzed.

Sam: *Where are you?*

She squinted at the screen, struggling to focus. Shit. Did I message Sam? When? Her brain caught up just enough to recall sending him a voice note from the pub earlier, asking if he was okay.

If she weren't unceremoniously drunk right now, she'd be mortified. But she was, so it didn't matter.

She tried to send another voice note, but all that came out was an incomprehensible slur of nonsense.

Her phone rang. Oh, balls.

She blinked at the name flashing on the screen. Sam.

She answered, attempting to sound sober.

"Hey."

"Daisy, what the hell was that voice note?" He sighed heavily. "Where are you?" He sounded… worried?

"T'wer Bridge," she mumbled. "Jus'… chillin'."

Wow. She was so shit at this.

This was also the second time he'd been obliged to rescue her in recent weeks. He must have thought she was a complete liability. Which was the opposite of what she was trying to achieve when it came to Sam.

Daisy sighed dramatically and wondered if it was possible just to sleep there. Wouldn't be the worst idea. The grass was kind of nice actually, she thought as her brain lulled her into a dizzy dream. She blinked herself awake when she heard voices and realised there were two random guys crouched beside her, trying to help her sit up.

"Is she alright?"

"I dunno, mate. She's wrecked."

"D'you want some Monster, darlin'?"

"Think she needs water, mate."

The two guys started laughing. Daisy groaned.

Why is there always an audience when she hits rock bottom?

Before she could say anything, another voice cut in.

"Thanks, lads. I've got this."

Sam.

The two strangers frowned. "What is she, your bird or somethin'?"

Sam didn't even hesitate. "Something like that."

"Well, are you her bloke or not?"

"Yes," Sam said flatly. "And now, if you don't mind, I need to take my girlfriend home."

Daisy overheard and tried to process it, her foggy brain swimming in confusion.

"But you're no—" she slurred, her mouth barely forming the words, but Sam sighed and hoisted her up before she could finish. His arm wrapped securely around her waist, grounding her as she wobbled against him. She heard the lads mumbling something as they dispersed, the rattle of empty cans skittering across the pavement.

Sam's grip was steady but gentle. "I'm trying to help you, Daisy. Will you just bloody… let me?"

She didn't answer. Couldn't. Her mind was too busy replaying what he'd said.

Girlfriend.

That wasn't a word he threw around lightly, surely?

Her heart rate quickened as her brain spiralled, dissecting every possible meaning behind that one little word. Why would he call her that? Did he actually mean it, or was he just saying it to make the situation less awkward? Was he hoping to smooth things over, or was he really suggesting something more? She couldn't wrap her stupidly drunken mind around it.

Her thoughts raced as her eyes flicked to him, searching for a clue—some hint as to what he meant. But he was just standing there, watching her, and she had no idea what to do with all this. Was she supposed to feel flattered? Confused? Annoyed? The pressure of his gaze only made it worse. She wanted to look away but couldn't.

The wind picked up, and she shivered slightly in her outfit—a misguided choice for London's unreliable spring weather. She was wearing a vintage floral dress, creased now from hours of sitting, and a black leather jacket that did little to protect her legs from the chill. Her tights had a ladder up one side, and one of her Dr. Martens boots was slightly scuffed from where she'd tripped earlier. A perfect metaphor for how she felt—tired, a bit battered, and totally out of place.

She tugged her jacket tighter around her, wishing she could physically protect herself from everything—especially Sam's words. But no, she couldn't let herself feel this way. She was overthinking.

But if she didn't acknowledge it, then what? Was she supposed to pretend she hadn't heard him call her his girlfriend? A word that felt like it belonged to someone else. Someone less guarded. Someone who didn't feel like an emotional trainwreck.

The air felt thicker now, and Daisy couldn't shake the sense that the entire city might be listening to the chaos in her head. Her eyeliner had definitely migrated south, and her lipstick—originally bold and berry-toned—was now more of a faint smudge. She looked like heartbreak on legs, a walking disaster.

And yet, here was Sam Callaghan, steady and dependable, treating her like she was something precious. Like he hadn't pushed her away just days before. It made no sense. But her heart, damn it, her heart was still tethered to him, and no amount of rational thought could sever that bond.

"I didn't ask you to come," she mumbled.

"You didn't have to. I was worried about you. Dais, you sounded fucked."

That shut her up.

As they walked—well, as Sam half-carried her—towards the main road, Daisy leaned against his shoulder. Everything felt blurry. The city lights blurred into a mess of colours, the echo of footsteps fading in the distance, and yet there was this strange warmth in her chest that had nothing to do with the alcohol.

She didn't know what to say. She just didn't know anymore.

So instead, she closed her eyes and let herself rest against him, just for a moment longer.

The cab ride was quiet—Daisy slumped against the window, eyes half-closed, while Sam kept glancing at her, his expression a mix of frustration and concern. By the time they reached Sam's flat, almost an hour away in Shepherd's Bush, it was sometime after midnight, and Daisy was clinging to him like a sleepy koala. Sam thanked the driver, then carefully helped her out, shielding her from the rain with his coat.

Inside, the warm hush of his flat hit her like a lullaby. It smelled faintly of cedarwood, fresh laundry, and fresh coffee. Ironically. So much nicer than her one-bedroom. She stumbled slightly over the threshold, and Sam caught her by the waist, steadying her as he closed the front door behind them with a soft click.

"You're absolutely steaming," he said, with a slight chuckle.

"Nooo," Daisy protested, waving a finger at him, nearly tipping over in the process. "I'm charming."

"You're charming and steaming," he corrected, catching her before she swayed again. "Come on, shoes off," he muttered, crouching down to untie her boots as she wobbled above him.

She let out a sleepy laugh. "You always this bossy?"

He looked up, deadpan. "Only when I'm rescuing damsels in distress."

"Pfft. I am not a damsel."

"You're drunk in a ripped dress with one functional shoe and mascara halfway down your face."

"Okay, fine. Maybe slightly damselly."

She scanned the room, blinking slowly. "You live in a nice place," she mumbled, swaying a bit as she took in the tidy, open-plan living room. "Of course you do. Big windows. Moody lighting. Very

I read GQ for the articles."

"Come on," Sam said, his tone warm but firm, "let's get you to bed."

Her eyes lit up. "Oh? So it's that kind of night?"

He didn't bite. Instead, he gently guided her down the hallway with one arm wrapped securely around her waist. "You're staying in the bed. I'm staying out of trouble."

"You're no fun," she said, though the mischievous smile on her lips betrayed her.

He ignored it, pushing open his bedroom door. The room was simple—calm, even. White sheets, a minimalist lamp, the faint scent of his aftershave lingering in the air. Mmmmm, it smelled like Sam Callaghan. Daisy's stomach did a flip.

She clung to his hand, glancing around. "This is where you sleep?"

"Yep," he said, hands braced on his hips.

"Sexy."

Sam sighed, chuckling under his breath; she was persistent. He guided her toward the bed. She flopped onto it dramatically. "Ohhhh. This bed is outrageously comfortable. Are you rich?"

He laughed, sitting beside her cautiously. "I'm not rich, just... selective."

"You're very... heroic tonight," she said, her voice a little thick.

Sam raised an eyebrow, amused but still cautious. "Am I?"

She nodded slowly, her finger tracing absent patterns on his trousers. "The rescuing. The jacket-over-the-shoulders thing. Classic hero behaviour."

He smirked, his eyes sparkling. "I'll add it to my LinkedIn."

Her giggle was soft, but it made his chest tighten in a way that was both comforting and confusing. It wasn't just the alcohol—she was vulnerable, raw. And somehow, that made her even more stunning to him.

She shifted closer, her hand lightly resting on his thigh.

"Daisy," Sam said, trying not to laugh.

"What?"

"You need sleep."

She propped herself up on her elbows, eyes suddenly soft. "Can't I sleep with you?"

Sam froze. *In what way does she mean this now?*

"Daisy…"

"Not like that," she amended quickly, slurring slightly. "Okay, maybe a little like that. But mostly I just... I don't want to be alone."

Sam sighed, trying desperately not to crack. He hesitated, then spoke quietly, "You're not alone. But I'm not doing anything while you're like this. You'd hate me for it in the morning. And I'd hate myself."

Her hand shifted from his thigh to the collar of his shirt, gently pulling him closer. Her gaze was half-lidded, a teasing smirk playing on her lips.

He took a deep breath, trying to summon some shred of resolve. "Daisy…"

She tilted her head, their faces dangerously close. "I just... I don't want to think about anything right now. But you—"

Her fingers lingered on his shirt, tugging gently. "Can we just... stop thinking for a minute?"

Sam could feel the heat radiating from her skin, the weight of her gaze. Everything in him wanted to give in. But he knew—this wasn't the time. Not like this.

He pulled back slightly, his voice gentle but firm. "You don't want this. Not really."

Daisy looked at him, brow furrowed, her lips parted in confusion. "Yes, I do," she whispered, her breath warm against his face. "I want you."

Her kiss was sudden, bold—laced with wine and longing—her hands already fumbling at the buttons of her dress. Sam kissed her back instinctively, senses sparking to life the moment her lips touched his. When the fabric slipped from her shoulders and fell to the floor in a soft rustle, revealing her in nothing but her lingerie, his breath hitched.

He'd never seen her like this before. And God, was she sexy.

Fuck, he was in serious trouble.

Tentatively, his hands found her waist—reverent at first, then greedier. Gripping. Learning her.

She arched beneath his touch, her breath catching as his fingers slid over her hips, then up to her breasts. He grabbed them hungrily.

He groaned into her mouth, kissing her harder now, pressing her gently into the mattress as her legs curled around him.

Her skin was warm under his palms, soft and electric, and her moans lit something in him that had been dormant far too long.

A part of him—raw and reckless—was waking up.

She wanted this. She wanted him.

And God, he wanted her.

Her hands were in his hair, her body pressed close, and every part of him screamed to keep going.

But then—

A flicker of doubt. A cold thread of reality wound through the heat.

She was drunk. She was vulnerable. And this moment, as tempting and intoxicating as it was, wasn't grounded in clarity.

He stilled.

Pulled back.

His breath ragged, he sat up, shaking his head slowly, trying to come down from everything she'd just lit inside him.

"Nope," he murmured, voice hoarse with restraint. "Daisy, we can't."

She blinked, dazed, lips swollen, eyes wide.

"You're drunk," he said again, softer now. "You're still upset with me. And... this would be amazing. Believe me. But it wouldn't be right."

Her chest rose and fell as she stared at him, confusion flickering behind her eyes, her body still humming with want.

"I want you, Sam," she whispered.

"I know," he said, torn. "I want you too."

He reached out and tucked a strand of hair behind her ear, his hand lingering just a second too long.

"But not like this. Not tonight."

It took every ounce of willpower he had to pull away completely.

To get off the bed.

To put space between them.

Because if he stayed too close, he wasn't sure he'd stop again.

And she deserved more than regret in the morning.

She blinked, pulling back slightly, hurt flashing across her face.

"So, you're rejecting me?"

"Not rejecting you," he said softly. "I'm saying I want this to mean something. Not a drunk blur you wake up regretting."

She stared at him for a long moment, her chest rising and falling with quick breaths. "You're annoyingly noble, you know that?"

He chuckled, though it came out strained. "Yeah. It's

exhausting."

Daisy's bravado faltered, a softer look taking its place.

"You really like me, don't you?"

Sam nodded slowly. "Yeah. I do."

He shocked himself with the honesty.

She'd probably forget he said it come morning.

But it needed to be said.

She blinked back a tear, then tugged on his wrist like a child. "Okay. Just stay. Just for a bit?"

That, he could do.

He helped her into one of his t-shirts, averting his eyes like a gentleman—which was pointless, really, considering he'd just had his hands and mouth all over her.

But hey. He had reverted.

Once she was under the covers, looking small and fragile and extremely tired, he kissed her forehead softly.

He stood there for a moment, heart pounding, resisting the urge to kiss her again.

But he knew better.

"I'm just out there on the sofa, okay?" he said.

Daisy caught his hand before he could leave.

"Don't disappear."

His thumb brushed hers. "I won't."

As he walked toward the door, he muttered to himself, "Bloody hell, Callaghan…"

But as much as he wanted to cross that line with her, he knew one thing: he needed to get it right. Rushing wouldn't help.

Tomorrow, maybe they'd figure it out. For tonight, though, she just needed rest.

And he needed a cold shower. A really long one.

Daisy woke up in unfamiliar, wonderfully scented surroundings. She didn't remember getting there. But when she blinked again, she was definitely in a bed that wasn't hers.

Why is everything so… white? And nice?

Panic gripped her for a second—until she clocked the navy suit hanging on the back of the door. The faint smell of Sam's aftershave lingered in the air.

Oh. Sam's flat.

Daisy smiled as she glanced around at her surroundings, the soft light filtering through the blinds, casting a warm glow across the room. Sam's sheets, warm and fresh, tangled around her legs. The comfort of it all made her feel strangely safe, as if she could stay here forever and forget about everything else.

She felt a tiny sense of smugness settle in her chest. Despite everything—despite the tension and the confusing, tangled mess of emotions—she was here. With him. And that, in itself, felt oddly satisfying.

Then a new kind of panic set in as she did the obligatory check to prepare herself for the impending embarrassment.

Did I voluntarily get naked?

Did I sleep with him?

She was still mostly clothed—well, except for the oversized T-shirt, which was definitely not hers and smelled suspiciously like Sam. Her vintage floral dress was rumpled and strewn across the floor. But she still had her underwear on. Tights: gone.

Interesting. When did I lose those?

Sitting up groggily, her head pounding, she looked around. How was she going to get to work? Wait—Friday. She could work from home.

When she eventually got there.

Probably for the best, considering she was going to struggle to get up without puking. What on earth did she drink?

She spotted a cosy-looking robe hanging over a chair. She dragged herself up and grabbed it, wrapping it around herself, clutching her bag from the nightstand, and stumbling toward the en suite. She rinsed her face, attempted to tame her hair, and salvaged what remained of last night's makeup. She brushed her teeth with her finger and grimaced at her reflection.

Fantastic. I look like I've been dragged through a hedge. And why do I smell like wet grass?

Jesus, Daisy, this might be a new low.

She rifled through her bag for her phone. Nothing. Great. How was she supposed to face Sam like this? She glanced around for an escape route. There was none.

So, she shuffled sheepishly into the living room—and paused.

Sam was on the sofa, baseball cap on, controller in hand, playing a video game.

A video game.

She stared. "You're a gamer?" she blinked.

He glanced over, smirking. "Good morning to you too."

"Sorry. I just—" She frowned. "You always act so superior. I didn't think you did… normal lad things."

He laughed. "Nice to know you still think I'm an arrogant ass even when I'm saving yours."

She folded her arms. "I borrowed your dressing gown."

"That's okay," he said, eyes still on the screen. "Coffee?"

"Yes. God, yes."

She groaned and plonked down on the sofa.

"You're working from home today?"

Sam got up, heading into the kitchen. "Nah, I booked the last few days off."

Huh. So that's where he was.

Daisy looked around, taking in the details of his flat. Her eyes landed on a shelf displaying several old football trophies.

"You actually did play professionally, then?" she asked.

"You already knew that." He smirked.

"Why did you stop?" she asked.

He paused. "I got injured." His tone shifted—just slightly, like it was a difficult subject.

He returned with a mug. She took it gratefully, smiling sheepishly. He sat down in the armchair opposite her.

"Wait, seriously?" she asked.

He nodded. "Knee injury. Couldn't play anymore."

"How old were you when you stopped?"

"Nineteen." He looked down, uncomfortable.

For a moment, she just watched him.

No smirk. No sarcasm. Just… real.

Daisy didn't push. She just sipped her coffee and patted the seat next to her. "Sam. Can you sit here?"

He raised an eyebrow.

"I just—" she waved a hand, "you sitting over there makes me feel like you're my therapist."

He chuckled but moved to sit beside her, making her stomach do a backflip. How does he always look this good?

"To be fair, that's a lot tamer than what you said last night," he added, smirking.

And thus returns the cockiness.

"What?" Her stomach sank. "Oh god. I hope I wasn't too inappropriate."

"You were Daisy-level appropriate."

She choked on her coffee. "What does that mean?"

Sam grinned, clearly enjoying himself. "You might have tried to drag me into bed with you."

"Oh. Just to… cuddle, though?"

He made a face like he didn't want to say it—but also kind of loved this part, and that he remembered and she didn't.

"No, you wanted me to have sex with you. You were… quite clear about that."

Daisy died a little inside.

Of course, she did.

Daisy wanted out of this conversation. She debated going silent out of sheer mortification—but then something shifted. The way he'd been lately, the way he was now—it made her want to call his bluff.

If she was getting out of the friend zone again, if she wanted another kiss, she needed to summon that Daisy Number One confidence.

She tilted her head, sipping her coffee with a smirk. "And you turned me down? What's wrong with you?"

Sam raised his eyebrows, caught off guard.

She could swear there was a faint pink blush across his cheeks.

It was a start.

"I was being a gentleman," he said, suddenly very focused on tapping his fingers against his knee. "What kind of bloke sleeps with a girl when she's as intoxicated as you were?"

"Oh, so you wanted to? Interesting," she quipped.

Sam didn't correct her. He didn't answer, either. Just looked down, smiling slightly—like he had words he wasn't quite ready to say. Leaving out the part that they did kiss and almost went there.

A thought to spare her dignity.

Daisy decided not to press. She could wait.

Breaking the silence, she changed tack. "So… how do you go from football to accounting?"

Sam laughed, shaking his head.

They talked for a long while after that. He really opened up. For the first time, he was telling her about his life—and she wasn't pushing. Just laying the foundations. Slowly working on that wall he'd lowered once and then firmly put back up.

And Daisy realised—maybe she hadn't been seeing Sam properly at all.

Later, Daisy—now back in her flat, having achieved precisely zero work from home all day (oops)—was showered and feeling refreshed. She was happily cocooned in her little bubble again, anxiety well and truly gone, enjoying some quality time with Tino and Married at First Sight—another one of her weaknesses, along with Prosecco and, apparently, Sam Callaghan.

She was halfway through an episode, completely absorbed, when her phone buzzed faintly on the sofa beside her. With a sigh, she picked it up.

Lydia: *You mad that we lost you? You didn't reply earlier? And now it's 6pm!*

Another oops.

Daisy replied: *Oh sorry. I've been busy. It's fine. Not your fault—I wandered off. Classic Daisy. The night actually ended unexpectedly great. I'll fill you in tomorrow.*

Lydia: *Ooooh sounds interesting. Can't wait.*

She tossed the phone aside and settled back in. But just as she got comfortable, it buzzed again. She assumed it was Lydia or Lance and, fully in Daisy Number Two mode, chose to ignore it.

Then it buzzed again.

Jesus.

She groaned, grabbing it with an exaggerated sigh—but the second she saw the name on the screen, her heart did a backflip.

Sam: *I can't stop thinking about our conversation earlier. I'm sorry I didn't answer honestly—I shouldn't have left you hanging. But yes, Daisy, I did want to sleep with you. Just sober.*

What.

Is he drunk?

Before she could even process it, another message popped up.

Sam: *I'm not drunk.*

Well, that cleared that one up.

Daisy stared at the screen, pulse racing. She had prompted it out of him earlier, but she hadn't been sure if he really meant it. After the way he acted post-kiss—pulling away, shutting down—she wasn't convinced he even liked her like that.

But then, earlier today, he'd shown her a vulnerable side.

Still. Get real, Daisy. This could very well just be a booty call.

God, these mixed signals were driving her mad.

Another buzz.

Sam: *Can I come see you? I really think we should talk.*

Daisy exhaled slowly, fingers hovering over the keyboard.

Daisy: *I'm not really one for one-night stands or booty calls, Sam.*

The reply was instant.

Sam: *I know. I would never use you like that. I just want to see you. I like talking to you.*

Oh.

Oh?

Her heart was doing something ridiculous in her chest. She hesitated, then:

Daisy: *Okay.*

Sam: *Where?*

Daisy: *You can come to mine. 16 Fort Road. Ground floor.*

Sam: *Okay. Uber says 47 minutes?! See you then.*

Oh crap.

Why—why—did she just invite Sam Callaghan to her flat? What was she thinking?

She spent the next twenty-two minutes in a frenzied panic, frantically tidying, trying to make her mess of a flat look even remotely presentable. And then there was herself.

She wasn't even remotely presentable.

What if he wants to have sex? She was in no state for sex.

Not that she was expecting it. Obviously. But, just in case...

She still had twenty-five minutes. Result.

She jumped in the shower (again) and attempted a full-body shave. Just a precaution.

She also managed to dry her hair perfectly, a miracle. Found the most flattering underwear she owned (again, just precaution) and pulled on a slinky dark grey slip dress with delicate lace at the neckline and a hoodie to not make it completely obvious.

Halfway through fixing her makeup, the buzzer sounded.

She froze. Took a deep breath. Forced herself to walk—not run—to the intercom.

"Hello?" she answered, nonchalantly like she hadn't spent the last half an hour running around like a mad woman trying to ready herself for his arrival.

"It's me, Daisy. It's Sam."

Her stomach somersaulted.

"Come in," she replied, her voice unintentionally high-pitched. She made a mental note to calm down and not sound like an old lady.

She opened the door, and the second Sam stepped inside, Tino lost his mind. He barked furiously, launching himself at Sam like a tiny, wheezing demon.

Sam actually stepped back, visibly startled. "Jesus. Why is he so mental?"

Daisy shrugged, scooping Tino up and depositing him in the spare room—his room—with his toys and bed. "He's a Frenchie. They're renowned for being delinquents."

Sam laughed. "Not sure if that accurately describes him."

"Oi, stop insulting my dog. Do you want a drink?"

"Yeah. Whatever you're having." He took off his shoes and slung his jacket over the back of a chair near her breakfast bar.

Daisy poured two glasses of wine, trying not to overthink the fact that Sam Callaghan was in her flat. The adrenaline had worn off, and in its place: full-body nerves.

I mean, she wasn't this nervous yesterday, in his flat. The glaringly obvious fact she was missing was that yesterday she was hammered.

Yes, drink Daisy, drink. She discreetly necked a glass of wine.

Out of the corner of her eye, she saw Sam wandering around, casually inspecting her bookshelves and framed photos. The sight of him in her space felt surreal. If someone had told her this would happen after the infamous coffee incident when she first started at Brandish, she'd have laughed in their face.

He caught her staring, and her stomach flipped again. Why did he have to be just so incredibly handsome? So much so that she was panicking. About everything.

"Your place is nice," he said. Although she knew he was just being polite having seen his much nicer, much larger flat.

"Thanks. It's not—it's tiny. But I like it. And it's cheap rent for London."

"Yeah, I guess," he replied indistinctly.

She discreetly downed another half glass of wine for courage, then refilled before walking over to the living area to hand him his.

"Whoa, careful. I really like this jumper," he said, smirking.

She narrowed her eyes. "Did you just make a joke about the coffee incident?"

His smirk confirmed it.

In all the time she'd known Sam Callaghan, she wouldn't have pegged him as funny. But this—this was actually funny.

"One of my favourite memories of you, actually," he said, his eyes locking on hers with maddening intensity.

Her mouth fell open slightly. He was flirting.

Or was she overthinking again?

Why were they still standing?

She swallowed. "So… um, in your message—"

She didn't get to finish.

Because in that moment, Sam's hands slid around her waist, and his lips were on hers.

And God, she had missed this feeling.

Chapter 15:
Right now, she isn't thinking with her head

Sam Callaghan was kissing her again. This time, it was in her flat. This could escalate.

Daisy paused, hesitant, opening her eyes to gaze into his. Just to check that the moment was real.

It was, in fact, real. He was smiling.

This is definitely going to escalate.

"I have a confession. I didn't come here to talk," he murmured.

"You didn't come here to talk?" she repeated, almost to confirm it.

"I've been waiting all day to do that, Daisy. Since last night. In fact, all week."

She tilted her head, lips curving mischievously. "Hmm, okay. Then why did you stop?"

He frowned. "You stopped?"

"You're right. That was really stupid."

He laughed, and she took it as permission to move back in, pressing her lips to his again.

This time, she let herself melt into it—because, honestly, it was even better than the first time. Her hands slid around his neck, and he pulled her in, moulding her against him. Without thinking, she backed him into the bookcase—forgetting how tall he actually was—until thud.

"Shit."

"Sorry," she mumbled, stifling a laugh.

"It's fine. But maybe we should move… over there?" He nodded to the sofa, rubbing the back of his head.

She took his hand, leading him to the sofa. He sat down, and before she could talk herself out of it—before doubt could sneak in—he pulled her straight onto his lap.

She straddled him, wrapping her arms around his neck as she kissed him again, deeper this time. More certain. Her fingers tangled in his hair, tugging slightly, and he let out a low noise of approval. His hands moved instinctively—one sliding up her back, the other curving around her breast, thumb brushing over the fabric. She gasped softly, and the sound only seemed to encourage him.

He'd done this before.

The realisation hit her mid-kiss—last night. That feverish make-out session in his flat, before everything had paused. On his bed, in her underwear, his hands already familiar with the shape of her. The way he had pulled away too soon. For her sake.

Not this time.

He went lower.

His hands slid up under her dress, the roughness of his fingers a sharp contrast to the softness of her skin. He traced the back of her thighs, slow and deliberate, until he reached her hips. There, he paused—fingertips teasing along the waistband of her underwear, drawing slow, maddening circles on her skin that made her breath catch in her throat.

Oh god, this is really happening. The thought hit her like a wave, and she could hardly believe it. Every nerve in her body was on fire, but at the same time, she felt strangely weightless, as though she might float away if she didn't hold onto him.

"Daisy, can I touch you?" he whispered, his voice thick with desire, almost a moan. Her body responded before her mind could process it. "Oh god, yes," she breathed, barely managing the words. It felt unreal—like she'd waited forever for this moment, but now that it was happening, she wasn't sure she was ready.

Then he slipped inside, gently, his touch intimate and precise. Her breath hitched, and a quiet moan escaped her, caught between their lips as he kissed her deeper, his other hand anchoring her closer. He was slow, but sure—exploring her with aching patience, as though he wanted to memorise exactly how to unravel her.

Daisy's heart raced in a dizzying mix of excitement and disbelief. She couldn't stop thinking, this is really happening. He's finally touching me. It felt like a dream, like she might wake up at any second and find herself back in her ordinary, safe world.

But in this moment, she didn't want to wake up. She wanted this. Wanted him. Even if everything around it felt like a chaotic whirlwind of emotions she wasn't quite ready to face.

She felt the smile against her mouth—the self-satisfied kind that said he knew exactly what he was doing—and she couldn't even pretend she didn't love it. That bloody arrogance would be the death of her.

He kept going, the pressure building, until her head dropped against his shoulder, dizzy with how good it felt. She clutched at his jumper, eyes fluttering shut, breathing in the scent of him, the feel of him, the fact that he was finally here, really here.

"Oh, Sam…" she whispered, his name tumbling out of her on a breathless moan, barely audible but full of meaning.

That sound. That small surrender. It only spurred him on. His rhythm quickened, and then suddenly Daisy was gone—arching against him, clutching at his shoulders, moaning expletives into his neck as she came undone completely. Her whole body trembling from the inside out.

And then—his grip shifted.

Firm. Confident.

His hands cupped her arse and pulled her down onto him, drawing out the last flickers of pleasure until she whimpered again—

overstimulated but somehow still wanting more. He was making damn sure she could feel everything going on in that area.

Everything.

And still, through the haze of it, she managed to kiss him—sloppier now, desperate—until—

She reached down between them, one hand slipping into his waistband, tentative at first—then bolder when she felt the effect she had on him.

He groaned against her mouth, his hips jolting slightly at her touch.

"Jesus, Dais…" he whispered, his forehead pressed to hers, eyes dark and heavy-lidded. "You're going to kill me."

She grinned, fingers wrapping around him. God, he felt good. The sheer overwhelming want coursing through her wasn't just about touch; it was months of longing, confusion, missed moments, and words left unsaid—all rising to the surface now. A flicker of satisfaction bloomed in her chest at the way he reacted to her—his breath catching, his body tensing under her palm. He wanted her. Really wanted her.

Her voice was soft, teasing. "Seems only fair…"

He let out a breathless laugh eyes fluttering closed as if he were holding on by a thread. This man, who always seemed so calm, so composed, so maddeningly hard to read—now undone in her arms. Because of her.

Daisy whimpered into his kiss, her whole body lighting up from the inside. It wasn't just physical—it was electric. Raw. Like they'd both stopped pretending for once. No hesitation. No second-guessing.

And then—he paused.

"Wait. What is that noise?"

Daisy blinked, still a little dazed, looking around, trying to register the sound. And then she started to laugh.

"It's Tino."

Sam looked utterly baffled, as though he couldn't fathom that such an ungodly whining could come from anything living, let alone a dog.

"Tino?" he repeated, eyebrows raised. "I didn't know dogs made that noise."

They both laughed as the whining grew louder, escalating into something closer to an inhuman wail.

Sam stared at her. "Dais, is he okay? He sounds like a... chicken?"

"Yeah, he's fine. He just gets really bad separation anxiety. Just ignore him, he'll settle down."

Sam shook his head, looking horrified. "Ignore him? Daisy, I think we need to call someone. A priest, maybe?"

She smacked his arm playfully. He grinned and squeezed her waist, one hand stroking her back. For a moment, they just looked at each other—comfortable, despite the interruption. The heat still buzzed in the air between them, unmistakable.

Daisy shifted slightly in his lap, her voice low and teasing. "If it's bothering you... we could always move this to the bedroom?"

Sam's lips curled into a smirk. "Oh, it's bothering me. Extremely."

Before she could react, he stood, effortlessly lifting her, making her squeal.

"Okay—wait—bathroom, not bedroom—there, there—yep, that's it—"

"Right."

He dropped her gently onto the bed, immediately pressing kisses along her jaw as his fingers worked to pull her dress over her head. Daisy sighed into him, her hands sliding beneath his jumper, ready to tug it off—until he paused again.

"You know… this is probably the wrong time to ask, but… are you sure you want to do this?"

She groaned, nudging her forehead against his. "Sam. You're asking me this while I'm half-undressed and we're halfway there?"

He exhaled, his grip on her tightening. "Dais, I'm sorry, you were the one that said you didn't do one-night stands."

That made her pause.

"Is that what this is?"

He hesitated. "Well… no. Of course not. I told you I wouldn't do that to you. I'm just making sure you want to—"

She cut him off gently, sensing he was holding something back. Maybe it had to do with what he'd said earlier that morning—about his accident. Something about the way he carried himself, his reluctance to commit, made her think it was all connected. She didn't push him, but she wanted him to know he didn't have to hide anything.

"What do you want, Sam?"

Her fingers threaded through his hair, a tender stroke that made his eyes close for a moment, like that single touch undid him.

When he opened them again, his voice was hoarse. Honest.

"I want you, Daisy."

Her breath caught.

She swallowed hard, pulse racing. "Then you have me."

Right now, she wasn't thinking. Not with her head. All she knew was she wanted him—now, fully, completely.

She tugged his jumper over his head, fingertips grazing warm skin, muscle. She took in the sight of him—broad shoulders, lean strength, that hungry, undone look in his eyes that made heat pool low in her stomach. She'd imagined this for months. Craved it. But nothing—nothing—compared to the reality.

Sam Callaghan was here in her bedroom, stripped and ready.

And somehow, he looked just as undone as she felt. Like he couldn't believe they were here either. Like the last bit of resistance in both of them had finally shattered.

Sam's mouth found her neck, his lips trailing fire over her skin, nipping gently at the base of her throat before moving lower. His hands, confident and reverent, mapped her body like he'd been waiting to memorise her by touch alone.

When he stepped back to strip off the rest of his clothes, Daisy forgot how to breathe. Her heart pounded, wild and uneven, her body practically vibrating with anticipation. This was really happening.

And then he was back, pressing her into the mattress with a kiss that knocked the thoughts clean from her mind—hot, consuming, a silent promise. Everything else vanished. There was no past. No uncertainty. Just the weight of him and the desperate, glorious fact that she was finally his. And he was hers. At least for tonight.

"Dais," he murmured against her lips, his voice rough with need. "Shit. I don't have any condoms."

For a second, she almost laughed at how wrecked he sounded, how little he wanted to stop. Instead, she cupped his jaw and brought him back to her.

"You're in luck," she whispered. "I'm on the pill."

He exhaled hard, like the weight of the world had just slid off his shoulders. His forehead dropped to hers, and for a breathless second, they just stayed like that—skin to skin, suspended in something fragile and real.

Then—there was nothing but heat, breath, and movement.

The space between them disappeared.

His mouth found hers again, deeper this time, more urgent. Her hands slid into his hair, soft and damp with heat, and she caught a whiff of something unexpectedly floral. Wait—was that women's shampoo? Why did it smell so nice? God, even his hair was annoying.

And then he moved over her, settling between her thighs. She welcomed him with a soft sigh, and the thought vanished like smoke. The way her body responded, like it had been waiting for this exact moment. This exact man. He stilled, breathing ragged against her mouth, like he was holding something back. Like maybe he felt it too.

"You okay?" he whispered.

She nodded, pulling him closer, her fingers gripping his back. "More than." Making a mental note to personally thank that bloody coffee shop for merely existing.

He moved slowly, deliberately, like he wanted to make it last, to etch it into her. Every thrust built something tight and dangerous inside her, a tension that curled and clawed and demanded release. She was making sounds she couldn't control, couldn't even care to. Every time she breathed his name, it wrecked him a little more.

"God, Daisy," he murmured, the sound of it vibrating against her skin. "You feel… incredible."

She arched beneath him, nails dragging over his back, eyes clenched shut. It was too much. Too good. It felt like he was inside every part of her—not just her body but her bloodstream, her bones. She wasn't just falling hard. She was already his—and it was far, far too late to pretend otherwise.

And then it shifted—his rhythm deepening, his grip tightening as he pressed her closer, like he couldn't get enough of her. She met him every time, hips rising to match his, her heart pounding so hard it felt like it echoed through her whole body.

The pressure built—fierce, relentless—until it spilled over.

She shattered.

Not with fireworks, not with a scream, but with a breathless gasp that caught in her throat. Her body arched, her hands fisting in the sheets. The kind of release that stole her breath and blurred her vision and left her with nothing but the feeling of him.

Sam followed moments later, his face buried in her neck, his body trembling with the force of it. He stayed there, breathing hard, like he couldn't quite believe what had just happened either.

They lay tangled together, skin damp, limbs entwined, hearts thudding in sync.

For a long time, neither of them spoke.

She just kept running her fingers through his hair, eyes closed, her other hand tracing slow circles across his back.

Finally, Sam lifted his head and looked at her. His expression was so open, so wrecked in the best way, it made her heart twist.

"Hi," she whispered.

He smiled, that lazy, post-orgasm grin that made her stomach flip. "Hi."

She reached up, brushing a thumb along his cheekbone. "Still think this is just a one-night stand?"

His smile faded slightly, replaced by something softer. "Not even close."

Later, Daisy woke to the realisation that Sam Callaghan was still there.

In her flat.

In her bed.

Asleep.

A quiet thrill ran through her, curling around her ribs like a secret.

After what could only be described as pure, unfiltered euphoria—because yes, she had slept with men before, just not many, and never like that—she must've drifted off in his arms. Those muscular, ridiculously comfortable arms. Like human memory foam with an ego.

Obviously, Sam Callaghan—arrogant, gorgeous, infuriatingly sexy Sam Callaghan—would also happen to be incredible in bed.

Because of course he would.

She lay there, wrapped in the messy tangle of sheets and limbs, staring at him for way longer than was normal. Or legal. Probably both. His lashes were stupidly long. His jaw, even slack with sleep, somehow managed to look chiselled. His hair, slightly messy, made her want to kiss him all over again.

He stirred, shifting slightly, and his annoyingly perfect, prince-like face turned toward her.

"Stop staring at me, Daisy," he mumbled, eyes still closed.

She giggled. "Sorry—"

Before she could finish, he reached for her blindly, tugging her into his arms. He wrapped himself around her like she was his favourite blanket, and her body fitted perfectly against his warm, naked one.

And there goes her stomach again.

He sighed contentedly, pressing a soft kiss to her forehead before tilting her chin up, angling her face just right so he could kiss her properly. It was slow, lingering, so tender it made her toes curl.

She exhaled softly against his mouth, and he chuckled, his voice still sleep-rough and low.

"What time is it?" he murmured.

She reached for her phone, squinting at the screen. "3 am."

His eyes cracked open, brows lifting slightly. "So we have loads more time? I don't have to go right now?"

"You definitely don't have to go," she whispered, fingers combing through his hair, enjoying the weight of him, the calm in her chest that hadn't existed before tonight.

A slow, devilish grin spread across his face. "Good."

His hands slid down her back, fingers tracing the curve of her spine, before settling firmly on her arse and pulling her closer. Her legs wrapped around him instinctively, like her body remembered the rhythm of him already. His mouth found hers again, deeper this time, consuming, stealing the air right out of her lungs.

The kiss was so good—so intoxicating—that a small moan escaped her throat before she could stop it.

Sam groaned, his grip tightening like her sound had undone him completely. "Oh, Dais…" he muttered against her lips, voice frayed at the edges. "That moan is going to destroy me one day."

She smiled against his mouth, heart still hammering, her body already remembering every place he'd touched her, every way he'd made her fall apart.

Maybe she was already a little destroyed too.

He kissed her again—slow, teasing—and then another, lower, just beneath her jaw, his hand stroking lazily down her thigh.

"Can I tell you something?" he murmured, lips brushing her skin.

"Mm-hmm," she breathed, barely able to think with the way his thumb was circling just above her knee, coaxing goosebumps in its wake.

"I haven't been able to stop thinking about you since the minute you bumped into me, drenching me in coffee."

She laughed, the sound light and sleepy. "You mean when you glared at me like I'd ruined your life?"

"I did not glare."

"You totally glared. You looked like you wanted to report me."

"I wanted to kiss you," he said, matter-of-fact, his voice rough and low. "But I was soaked and irritated, and you were… I don't know. This blur of sarcasm, freckles, and chaos. And I panicked."

She tilted her head, eyes searching his. "You panicked?"

He nodded slowly, brushing his nose along her jaw. "You were too much."

Her brow lifted. "Wow, thanks."

He grinned against her skin. "Not like that. I mean—too much in the best way. Too alive. Too funny. Too distracting. Too… you."

Her chest tightened, all breath and heat and something deeper.

"Plus, it was highly inappropriate timing. But after that, I couldn't get you out of my head and then you were on the office floor with Rhoda. And I thought—"

"Thought what?"

He grinned against her neck. "You were sexy as hell."

"No, you didn't."

She rolled her eyes, playfully shoving his shoulder—but he caught her hand, kissed the inside of her wrist, and looked at her with that now-familiar mix of mischief and heat.

His voice dropped. "Dais… I'm still not done with you."

Her breath caught. "Oh?"

He nodded slowly, running a hand down her back, over her hip, and back again, eyes locked on hers. "I was trying to let you sleep. Trying to be good."

"How's that going?"

"Terribly," he said, flipping her gently onto her back.

And just like that, his lips found hers again, soft but sure, a kiss that tasted like confessions and promises wrapped in heat. Then his hand moved—slowly, deliberately—back up her thigh, settling where she was already aching for him.

Her breath hitched. "Oh god…"

"No," he whispered, lips curling into a smirk. "Just me."

She let out a soft laugh, equal parts exasperated and desperate.

"You're so annoying."

"You love it."

She did. She really did. And as his mouth met hers again, her hands pulled him closer, welcoming every inch of him like it was inevitable.

Because maybe it was.

And as they sank into the dark again, limbs tangled and hearts pounding, there was no mistaking it this time—

This wasn't just round two.

This was them possibly turning a corner.-

Saturday morning came, and Sam Callaghan was still there.

In her bed.

Daisy blinked against the soft morning light streaming through the blinds, her heart still racing from the intimacy of the night before. She wondered how long this would last?

Her insecurities flared up, whispering their ugly doubts. What was he doing with someone like her? What if he regretted it all? What if he only wanted a moment of escape, something that had nothing to do with her? God, she hated this side of her brain.

Deciding she couldn't bear the awkwardness of facing him too soon, she gently slipped out of bed, careful not to disturb him. Her feet hit the cool floor, and she pulled on the nearest pair of gym leggings before making her way to the kitchen. She let Tino out, watching the little dog stretch before he raced to the door, barking with joy as if he'd been starved for attention all night. She laughed quietly to herself before securing him in the hallway with the baby gate.

Sam wasn't ready for that type of awakening.

When Daisy returned to the bedroom, she half-expected Sam to still be asleep, untouched by the world. But when she slid back under the covers, Sam stirred. An arm crossed her stomach, pulling her back into his chest, his grip warm and possessive, even in his sleep.

"Hey," he muttered, his voice rough from sleep.

Daisy's heart skipped a beat, and she couldn't help the giggle that escaped her lips. How was this real? How is he real?

"Hey," she whispered back, feeling the warmth of his breath against her neck.

He pressed a kiss to her nose, soft and lingering, and Daisy's breath caught in her throat.

"Did you sleep okay?" she asked, his thumb absentmindedly tracing patterns on her skin.

"Like a baby," he answered with a slight laugh. "Which is surprising, considering your dog is proper loud."

Daisy's laughter bubbled up naturally at the memory of Tino's whining. "Sorry, you'll get used to him," she said quickly, but the words slipped out before she could stop them. And when they did, she felt her heart sink. Shit, why did she say that? That was an assumption that would surely make him run for the hills.

"Oh, will I?" Sam replied, voice playful, but there was an edge to it, the tone that let her know he was smirking. That his eyebrows were raised, a glint of mischief in his eyes.

Daisy panicked, her cheeks flushing with a mix of embarrassment and fear. "I mean, if you want to. I'm not trying to make you do anything—"

He cut her off gently, but firmly, his fingers brushing through her hair and cupping her face with a tenderness that stole her breath away. "Daisy. Shut up," he murmured, pulling her in for a kiss, deep and all-consuming, like he was trying to erase any doubt, any worry she might have.

When he pulled back, his forehead resting against hers, his eyes heavy with something soft, something real.

"You're not getting rid of me that easily, Dais," he said, his voice low and serious.

She pulled back, blinking up at him. "What do you mean?" she asked, trying to sound casual, but her voice came out a little too breathy.

Sam propped himself up on one elbow, the duvet slipping down to reveal the line of muscle along his torso, and Daisy had to concentrate very hard on not losing her train of thought entirely.

He looked at her, his gaze steady. "I mean," he said slowly, like he was choosing every word with care, "I'm not gonna pretend last night didn't happen. Or this morning. Or any of it."

Daisy swallowed, her heart hammering again—for a different reason now. A quieter, shakier one. She shifted slightly, curling her fingers under her cheek to keep herself steady. "Even if I'm sometimes… too much?"

There it was. Out loud. The fear that always hummed under her skin. That she was somehow too messy, too emotional, too chaotic. Too her.

He gave her a look—somewhere between affection and utter disbelief. "You are too much. And thank god for that."

She blinked, unsure she'd heard him right.

He grinned, soft but certain. "You think I need someone soft and easy to manage? Have you met me?"

A laugh escaped her before she could stop it, the tension breaking like a string pulled too tight. "Fair point."

He leaned in and kissed the corner of her mouth, then the tip of her nose like it was the most natural thing in the world. "You challenge me, Daisy Donaldson. You make me feel things I usually keep locked up. And yeah, it scares the shit out of me. But I also kind of like it."

She stared at him, genuinely speechless—which, for her, was

unheard of. Part of her wanted to say something light, make a joke, shift the mood—but another part just wanted to believe him.

"Also," he added, lips quirking, "I think your dog likes me."

She gasped. "You've known him for twelve hours!"

"Twelve intense hours," he said solemnly. "We've been through a lot together."

She dissolved into laughter, burying her face in his chest as he wrapped his arms around her, pulling her close like he didn't want her to go anywhere.

And in that moment, wrapped in warmth and tangled sheets and something terrifyingly close to hope, Daisy stopped wondering when the spell would break.

Because maybe it wasn't a spell at all. Maybe it was something real.

She was just there. With him. And maybe—just maybe—he was there with her, too.

They kissed again, slower this time, like they both knew what it meant now.

And Daisy couldn't help but wonder what on earth she had done to Sam Callaghan.

Chapter 16:
What has she done to Sam Callaghan

Sam left Daisy's flat around midday, as her presence was required at Prim's bridal shower that afternoon in the city.

Jesus, how many events do these weddings have? Daisy was fairly certain these sorts of gatherings were meant for pregnant women, but now brides had to get in on it too? And you were supposed to *shower* them with gifts? They were only getting married. They got wedding gifts, didn't they? Surely the wedding itself was the gift? A lifelong commitment to the man you love should be enough.

They hadn't even reached the hen do yet, and already Daisy's social battery was running on fumes.

When she arrived at Simmonds Bar in Liverpool Street—an event arranged by Prim's stuck-up friends—Daisy felt her anxiety creep in. Her eyes darted around the pavement outside, desperately scanning for Lydia. *Thank God Lydia was invited.* Luckily, Prim adored Lydia as much as Daisy did, and that had been confirmed when she'd asked Lydia to be a bridesmaid. A solid choice—and it meant Daisy had backup at these kinds of hellish events.

Then, her phone buzzed in her pocket.

Sam.

Her heart fluttered.

Sam: *Have fun tonight. Let me know if you need rescuing.*

Daisy hesitated. She wanted to be careful—say the right thing without coming across as clingy.

Daisy: *Thanks! I might have to take you up on that offer.*

Yes. Perfect. Leave it there, Daisy.

Her fingers hovered over the keyboard.

Daisy: *Missing you already…*

Her thumb hesitated above *send. No, Daisy. That's too much.* She started to delete it—

Suddenly, someone barrelled into her, scooping her into a suffocating hug.

"Hi, Dais!"

Lydia.

"Hi," Daisy managed, phone still in hand—only to realise, horror sinking in, that Lydia's over-enthusiastic ambush had caused her to hit send.

Daisy: *Missing yo*

Oh, for God's sake.

A fresh wave of panic crashed over her. *Why does this always happen to me?* Oh well. Maybe he'd like it. Maybe he'd find it funny. There was a chance he'd respond… right?

Nothing.

Still nothing.

Inside, Prim was already in the screeching phase of the afternoon, greeting everyone with open arms. Cocktails were everywhere, and two bottles of champagne chilled in silver buckets on the table. This was going to get messy.

Daisy, however, hesitated. She really liked Sam, and she wanted to at least *try* to behave herself. The last thing she needed was for him to actually have to rescue her again—this time from a drunken spectacle—leading him to think she was a raging alcoholic and ending their "situationship" before it had even begun.

She handed Prim a joint present from her and Lydia—a book titled *Marriage for Dummies.* They thought it was hilarious. Prim, not so much, but she was too tipsy to care.

At the bar, Daisy ordered a shandy—easing herself in. She needed a little alcohol just to tolerate the swarm of banshees that were Prim's friends.

She checked her phone again.

Still no reply from Sam.

Lydia, already eager for gossip after Daisy's mysterious disappearance the night before, wasted no time.

"So, catch me up, Dais. What happened Thursday night after we lost you to the night?"

Daisy laughed. "Well, I ended up at Sam's flat."

"Shut up! Sam Callaghan?!"

"Yeah. He rescued me. I was a right mess—lying on the grass near Tower Bridge. Lucky he did, otherwise I'd probably have ended up in the Thames. Or worse—committed to the Tower."

Lydia cackled. "Did you sleep with him?"

"Nooo."

"You're lying. Why have you gone red? Spill."

"Okay, well… not Thursday night—I was too drunk. But then last night, he texted me, I invited him round and… well, you get what I'm saying."

"Fucking hell, Dais. This is *massive.* Was he—? How was it? Was he good? Are you together? I have about a thousand questions."

"He was amazing," Daisy admitted, covering her face in embarrassment.

"Oh my God. Have you told Lance? Prim?"

"No, not yet. It was only last night. It's not anything serious."

The words stung a little as panic settled in—because she was still yet to get a reply after Lydia's little *fuck-up* earlier.

The night rolled on, and Daisy managed to stay relatively sober—

unlike Lydia, who was deep in conversation with Prim's friend Rachel, a woman who looked like an Iranian supermodel and had the personality of a Gucci handbag: flashy, exclusive, and completely hollow inside.

Daisy sat sipping a Pornstar Martini, subdued, when Prim plonked herself down next to her.

"What is up with you tonight, misery?"

"Nothing, I'm fine."

"You're not stumbling about or smashing into things. You're definitely not fine."

Prim was shouting in her ear—drunk beyond belief—but the concern was sweet.

"I just had a heavy night Thursday. Still feel a bit fragile," Daisy lied.

"Fine, well stop sitting there checking your phone and get up and dance."

"Okay, fine. I'm just going to the toilet, and then I'll dance. Promise."

Daisy escaped to the toilet, shutting the door behind her and exhaling a mountain of stress.

That unwelcome feeling—fear, dread, anxiety—crept into her chest.
Why hadn't he texted her back?

She was stuck now. She'd sent the last message. She couldn't double-text. She couldn't ask him to rescue her again. She came to the painful realisation and then—

Screw you, Sam Callaghan.

Daisy decided to let alcohol do its work.

She headed to the bar and ordered a round of Corky's shots. Lydia slid in beside her, grinning.

"Ooo, are we getting on it now, Mrs Reserved?"

"Yep," Daisy replied, downing three in a row and handing Lydia two.

"Yeah! Let's get Jägerbombs!" Lydia squealed, clapping her hands.

Sober Daisy was officially gone.At some point, the boys arrived—Grant, his best mate Marcus, Greg, Greg's best mate Liam, and a few others Daisy didn't recognise. Lydia was now entirely engrossed in a conversation with one of Grant's friends, Luca, who looked like a younger version of Mark Ruffalo. That left Daisy in the dangerous position of sitting next to Greg Osborne.

She decided to at least let him have *a bit* of a conversation this time.

"How've you been, Dais? You look really good lately. Don't know if I've told you that."

Daisy had a flicker of remembering why she'd ended up with him in the first place. He *was* quite cute.

"Thanks. You look as charming and handsome as ever."

Greg smirked. "Are you flirting with me, Donaldson?"

Oh.

"No. Just being polite. How have you been?" she said quickly, trying to steer the conversation back on track.

"Okay, fair. Yeah, really good. Work's the same old, but good. Getting more money at least."

As if that was possible.

Greg was a solicitor—he'd been earning good money since he was twenty-three, and he'd always loved flashing it about. That kind of money was dangerous for someone so young, but he seemed to have mellowed slightly with age.

"That's really good," Daisy said.

Greg shifted, his tone turning more serious. "Look, Dais, I'm really sorry for how we ended. I was a proper prick to you."

"Ahh, your apology is appreciated, Osborne. But that was ages ago. Do you think I'm bothered about that now?"

Greg actually looked hurt by her comment, and Daisy was surprised to see it—a flicker of vulnerability. She'd never seen that before.
And, well… he was still a very pretty man.

Nope. Daisy realised she'd had one too many Pornstar Martinis. She was starting to think Greg was an *option*.

Remember Sam, Daisy. You said screw him earlier, but he still might be waiting for you.

She snapped herself back.

"Sorry, I didn't mean to hurt your feelings. One too many martinis."

He laughed. "I'm not hurt. God, no. My pride maybe a little. I guess I'm just realising—the older I get, the more I see that the way I treated girls, or women… it needs to change."

Daisy nodded. "Tone down the flashy and laddish behaviour a bit, eh? That'd be a start."

They both laughed, then sighed, watching the dancefloor. After a pause, Greg's expression shifted again.

"I did really like you, Daisy. Still do."

He leaned in, and Daisy stopped him with her palm flat against his chest.

Oh no, no, no—you don't.

She spilled her drink slightly. "Oh. I wasn't expecting that."

"What—do you have a boyfriend or something?"

"Sort of."

"Ah. I'm not surprised. You're a catch."

"Thanks, Greg. You are too, just—"

"Not for you. Not anymore."

They stared at each other for longer than Daisy thought necessary, and then both burst out laughing.

"Probably for the best—for Grant and Prim's sake," he added.

"Yeah. That ship has sailed."

"All right, calm down," he laughed. "Can't believe you pied me off!"

"Sorry."

They both laughed.

It was quite impressive that Daisy had managed to shut that down as quickly as she did. She definitely didn't want to open that door again.

Just as she'd dodged that particular bullet, her phone buzzed with a message she wasn't entirely sure she should reply to. But of course, she was drunk—and weak.

Matthew: *Daze, please can we talk? Please can we meet up this week? I really hate how we left things and I just want to sort things out with you.*

Daisy, in her incredibly drunk state, replied with what she thought was in her head.

The message she *should* have sent would've gone something like this:

Daisy: *Matthew, you're engaged, and I have a semi-boyfriend. We've been broken up for longer than we were together, and this is just not what you think it is anymore. I wish you all the best, but I think it's better if you get on with your life and I get on with mine. All the best, Daisy.*

But, of course, she didn't send *that.*

Instead, she stared at her phone for a full five minutes, thumb hovering over the keyboard. She typed. Deleted. Typed again. Maybe she'd just wait until morning—sleep on it. Be rational.

Then her eyes flicked to the top of the screen. No new messages. Nothing from Sam. Not even a goodnight text.

Her stomach twisted.

Fuck it. It's fine.

And so she sent:

Daisy: *I hate how it was left too, I'm sorry I was mean. Sure we can meet up to talk about it. Message me when you're free.*

Daisy Donaldson—once again, self-sabotaging her own bloody life.

Daisy had no memory of the rest of the night, except being in a taxi with Lydia and Mark Ruffalo Jr.—at least that's what she thought it was, even though it felt more like the Nemesis ride at Alton Towers.

That, and the vague belief that she'd made it home at a *reasonable* hour. If 12:50 a.m. counted as reasonable.

She flopped onto her bed, and Tino immediately curled up beside her like a little bagel. The room tilted slightly—just enough to remind her she was several Jägerbombs past sober.

She picked up her phone—something she'd been deliberately avoiding for hours. Mostly because she was still low-key pissed, or maybe just pathetically sad, that Sam hadn't texted her back.

How hard was it to send one little message? Missing yo. Not even a full sentence. Didn't even mean anything. She scoffed to herself. *Typical. Afraid of a text, apparently.*

Then she saw it.

A message from Sam—sent ten minutes ago. She'd missed it.

Sam: *Sorry I didn't message back. Something came up. I'm missing yo?!*

Miss you too. Did you get home okay?

Oh. He was apologising.

And just like that, the fog of doubt lifted, and she was right back in the *I love Sam* bubble. That kind of reply that made her stomach flip and her face do that involuntary smile thing. Because for a brief, awful moment, she'd thought he was about to go full Sam Callaghan and ghost her. Again.

But he hadn't. He'd replied. And it was perfect.

She texted back instantly.

Daisy: *Is ok. Yeah, just got home.*

Sam: *Ok gorgeous. Are you awake?*

Daisy: *Just. Come round.*

Sam: *You sure?*

Daisy: *Yep.*

Sam: *Ok. See you soon.*

Why was he being so sweet? This was too much. A stark contrast to an hour ago, when she'd mentally condemned him. Daisy was too tired to overanalyse.

She was out.

She didn't know how long before her phone buzzed on the nightstand.

Daisy stirred, groaning softly as she reached out blindly, eyes squinting at the bright screen. 1:48 a.m.

Sam: *Daisy? I'm outside.*

She blinked, confusion fogging her sleep. Then—clarity.

Her heart gave an unhelpful lurch as she sat up slightly, the room dim and quiet except for the thudding in her chest.

She'd been so bold earlier.

Come round, I'm totally fine and totally not drunk again.

Oh, for God's sake, Daisy.

Still, her heart did that stupid little pitter-patter, because—well—she *did* want to see him. She wanted to cuddle him, smell him, bury her face in his chest and pretend things weren't complicated.

This was bad. So, *so* bad.

She had it really bad.

Daisy: *Sorry. Door's open.*

Daisy was fully awake now. Because she'd noticed something was slightly off—his words weren't flirty, weren't loaded with innuendo. They were quiet. Raw. Something in her stomach twisted.

There was a soft knock. Not the usual confident rap of Sam Callaghan. This was different. Hesitant.

She opened the door to find him standing there, hands buried in his coat pockets, hair slightly tousled like he'd run his hands through it one too many times.

He looked... wrecked. And not in the usual *just got back from the pub* kind of way. His eyes were bloodshot, his shoulders tense beneath his coat.

"Hey," she said softly.

"Hey," he echoed, and just the sound of his voice made something in her chest ache.

"Come in," she said gently, reaching for his arm.

He followed her inside, shrugging off his coat without a word. There was something heavy about him—like the air around him had thickened. She watched as he kicked off his shoes and headed straight for the sofa, sitting down like someone who'd been holding himself together all day and had finally let go.

Daisy hovered for a moment, then joined him, the cushion dipping between them. He didn't look at her—just stared at his hands, elbows on his knees, shoulders curved in as though he was trying to make himself smaller.

For a moment, she worried it was her. That maybe he'd changed his mind or regretted everything. But no—she knew that look. This wasn't about her. Whatever this was, it had roots somewhere else.

Her chest ached. She wanted to reach for him, wrap herself around him, tell him he didn't have to hold it all alone. But instead, she waited. Let him have the silence, the space. She would be here, ready, when he was.

Then, out of nowhere, he exhaled a shaky breath and whispered, "I missed you."

The way he said it—quiet, completely stripped of his usual bravado—like it had cost him something to admit. She didn't ask what was wrong. She didn't push.

And in that moment, all Daisy wanted was to make him feel safe. Safe and wanted and cared for.

She simply opened her arms. And Sam, without hesitation, folded into her, burying his face into her neck like it was the only place he felt safe.

His arms wrapped around her, and she held him tightly, stroking the back of his head, her heart pounding in a rhythm that wasn't quite fear, or love, or sadness—but something in between.

They stayed like that for a long time. No questions. No explanations. Just two people tangled in silence, breathing each other in.

Later, as his breathing slowed and his grip loosened, he murmured, "Thanks for letting me in."

Daisy kissed his temple softly. "Always."

He soon relaxed, the tension in his shoulders easing, and then he turned to kiss her properly.

"Hey, that's better," Daisy breathed.

He nodded, pushing her hair back with a kind of reverence, his fingertips brushing her cheek like she might vanish if he wasn't careful.

"I didn't come here for just that," he said quietly, eyes locked on hers. "I just… I didn't know where else to go."

Daisy swallowed, her fingers curling gently around his wrist. "It's okay. I didn't think you did."

They sat like that for a while, forehead to forehead, the warmth between them fragile but real. Sam's gaze lingered on her lips for a beat, and then he kissed her again—slower this time, more grateful than hungry. It wasn't about sex. It was about needing someone. Needing *her*.

Eventually, she led him to bed, both of them shedding only enough clothing to be comfortable, not exposed. When they curled into each other beneath the duvet, it felt natural—like this was something they'd done a hundred times, even if they hadn't.

Sam lay on his side facing her, one arm looped loosely around her waist, his breathing already more even. But his eyes stayed open, fixed somewhere beyond the room.

She pressed a hand to his chest, feeling the steady thrum of his heart. "You don't have to tell me what happened," she whispered. "But if you ever want to, I'm here."

"I know," he replied, voice barely audible. "Just… not tonight."

"Okay."

She kissed his shoulder and settled against him, feeling him finally begin to relax, his body sinking into the mattress with hers. And when he eventually drifted off, his hand stayed clenched in the fabric of her top, like some part of him was still afraid she might leave.

Earlier that night.

Sam was sitting in his living room, beer in hand, half-watching the football. But unlike most Saturday nights, he couldn't wipe the smile off his face. He also couldn't stop thinking about Daisy.

Yes, he'd let his guard down for a girl.

Yes, he'd slept with her.

And yes—he'd allowed himself to feel something.

Because, for once, he actually *wanted* to. And she wasn't just any girl.
She was infectious. In a way that slipped past all his usual defences.

He was going to text her. Too soon? Sam didn't care. He threw all his usual rules out the window.

Sam: *Have fun tonight. Let me know if you need "rescuing".*

Her reply was instant.

Daisy: *Thanks! I might have to take you up on that offer.*

God, he really hoped she did.

He was mid-daydream about her when his phone buzzed again. Another text from Daisy.

Daisy: *Missing yo*

What on earth? She couldn't be tipsy already—she'd only just got there. He grinned and started typing a reply, fully intending on 'rescuing' her later. He couldn't wait to see her again. Even if her dog mildly terrified him.

But that plan was about to change.

Sam's phone started ringing. He answered too quickly, thinking it was Daisy.

"Hi, Samuel."

"Mum? What's up?"

Odd. Sam usually avoided his parents where possible—seeing them was more chore than choice.

"Well, it's just that your father and I were wondering if you were free for dinner this evening. We haven't seen you for quite a while."

"It hasn't been that long. I saw Dad last week."

"Samuel. I would like to see you."

She sounded worried. His dad definitely wasn't. Sam was almost certain they wanted something. They were never this eager to spend time with him otherwise. *God, please don't let it be about that bloody job at Dad's firm again.* He thought he'd shut that conversation down last week.

Sam sighed. He couldn't think of a decent excuse, and there was a tone in his mum's voice that made him pause. He knew what it was like growing up under his father's thumb. Knew what it meant to constantly walk on eggshells. Now that Sam had left, his poor mum was probably catching the brunt of it.

"Erm, yeah. Okay. What time?"

"Excellent. Come to the house for 7:30."

"Okay, Mum. See you soon."

Sam chucked his phone onto the sofa and groaned.

Not the Saturday he'd planned.

Dinner with his mum and dad was tense.

Considering his dad supposedly wanted to see him, the man spent the first hour with his nose buried in the newspaper, barely saying a word. His mum fussed around him instead—asking about work, how he was getting on living alone, if he had any friends… if he had a girlfriend.

That part didn't bother him. He'd almost mentioned Daisy. But the second his dad's ears twitched at the word *girlfriend*, Sam bit it back. Now wasn't the time. Not here.

Then his dad folded the paper with a sharp snap, asked his mum to pour him a whisky and make herself scarce.

Here it was. The real reason he'd been summoned.

Sam's back went up before his dad even opened his mouth. He hated when he did this—used his mum to lure him over, pretending they cared. There was always a motive. Always a plan.

Any trace of the good mood Sam had been in had now completely vanished. His chest tightened. The walls of the house felt smaller. Like childhood closing in again. His thoughts flickered to the accident, then to Daisy—to how he'd managed to feel genuinely happy that morning.

And now this.

How could he ever bring her into his world when it was like this?

"So, Samuel," his dad said, tone clipped and businesslike. "I have some bad news."

Sam braced himself. *Here we go.*

"Your mother and I are getting a divorce."

…What?

That—he hadn't expected. At all.

"Why?"

"I've met someone else."

Sam scoffed. Typical. His dad had always been a bit shady, but divorce? That felt too final. Too real. *Why now?*

"Why now, though?" he asked through gritted teeth.

"Because it's not fair on your mother, Samuel, to go on like this."

"Come on, Dad. Tell the truth for once. The real reason."

His father hesitated. Just for a second.

"Because… Gabby, my partner, is expecting."

Shit.

Later, when Sam finally got home, the house felt quiet in the wrong kind of way.

He kicked off his shoes, dropped his keys, and sat on the edge of the bed, rubbing a hand over his face. Still in shock. A small part of him felt relieved—for his mum, at least. She deserved to be out of it. But that didn't mean this wasn't still a gut punch.

He picked up his phone. A few missed messages.

One from Harry, trying to get him out—which he ignored.

And one from Daisy.

The half-message she'd sent earlier. That tiny glimpse of light at the end of a long, horrible night.

Missing yo.

Sam smiled.

He opened the chat and typed:

Sam: *Sorry I didn't message back. Something came up. I'm missing yo?!*

I miss you too. Did you get home okay?

Daisy: *Is ok. Yeah, just got home.*

Sam: *Ok gorgeous. Are you awake?*

Daisy: *Just. Come round.*

Sam: *You sure?*

He hovered for a second before hitting send.

He wanted to say more. Wanted to tell her how awful the evening had been. How strange it felt to care this much.

Sam was trying—really trying—not to fall back into that old pattern. The one where he shut people out before they could get too close. Before they could hurt him.

He wanted to see her—*needed* to see her—though he knew he wouldn't be able to hide this mood. She'd notice in an instant. She always did.

But he sent the message anyway. No dramatic confessions. No heavy explanations. Just checking.

Then he stared at the screen, waiting, hoping she was still awake. Trying not to let the chill of that cold, familiar house ruin the warmth he was finally starting to believe in.

Daisy: *Yep.*

Sam: *Ok. See you soon.*

One thing was for sure—Sam's head was dealing with a lot right now.

But he needed someone.

Not just anyone.

He needed *her*.

Chapter 17:
Full procrastination mode

Sunlight poured softly through the curtains.

Daisy stirred first, her eyes fluttering open to find Sam still sound asleep, jaw slack, one hand stretched out across her side. She studied his face—he looked younger when he slept. Less guarded. Less complicated.

She eased out of bed carefully, not wanting to wake him, and padded into the kitchen in her sleep shirt to make coffee. As the kettle boiled, she replayed the night in her mind—the way he'd looked at her like she was the only person on the planet, the sadness in his voice, the way he'd held on.

Her phone lit up on the counter.

A message. From Matthew.

Shit.

Matthew: *I'm free Thursday evening? That work?*

Double shit.

Her stomach lurched as she scrolled back and saw the text she'd sent him the night before—when she'd been hammered. God, why had she agreed to meet him? She stared at the screen like she could will it to burst into flames.

"Morning."

Daisy nearly threw the phone in the sink.

Sam stood in the doorway, shirtless, hair a glorious mess. Gorgeous. Too gorgeous.

"Did I surprise you?" he asked with a quiet smile. It didn't quite reach his eyes, but it was something.

"No—hey." She forced a casual tone. "Coffee?"

"I'm not usually like that," he said, rubbing the back of his neck. "Sorry if I made things weird."

"You didn't," Daisy said quickly, sliding a mug toward him. "You just… needed someone. That's not weird, Sam."

He accepted the coffee, staring into it like it might spell out the answers. "I needed you. I still do."

Her chest tightened. She didn't trust her voice, so instead, she reached for his hand across the counter.

For a moment, it felt calm. Steady. Like maybe things didn't have to be so complicated.

She shoved Matthew's text to the farthest corner of her mind. Out of sight, out of reach. Probably where it should stay.

Sam stayed into the evening. Sunday stretched out like a warm blanket over them—slow and surprisingly easy. No tension, no unresolved drama. Just a day.

They made scrambled eggs for breakfast—Daisy burned the toast and swore at it like it was a personal attack, while Sam laughed and called her a *domestic liability.*

Later, Daisy took Tino out for a walk while Sam commandeered her living room floor, stretching out like he owned the place, watching some documentary about football scandals that he insisted was *"actually mad interesting."*

When she got back, he was still there—barefoot, lounging in one of her hoodies, and Tino curled up at his side like he'd always belonged. (Mostly, she reckoned, the dog liked the male energy.)

Daisy paused in the doorway, just watching them. The way the afternoon light spilled across the sofa. The quiet comfort of it all. Her flat had never felt so alive.

And then—like a cruel reflex—her mind flickered back to the text. *The one you're ignoring, Daisy. The one where Matthew asked*

She shuddered it off, forcing herself to focus on the here and now. But the bad feeling lingered—a low hum beneath the warmth.

They ordered Thai for dinner and ended up in a full-blown debate over who could handle more spice. (Spoiler: it wasn't Sam. One rogue chilli had him dramatically downing a whole glass of oat milk while Daisy cackled.)

"D'you mind if I stay again?" he asked as they sat entangled on her sofa.

"No, course not," she murmured, her lips brushing against his jaw. "I was hoping you would."

He was quieter than usual. Not distant, exactly—just… careful. Like he was trying not to let something slip. Not *full Sam Callaghan*, but close.

Then he kissed her—slow and deep—like he'd been thinking about it all day. Maybe he had. His hand cupped her jaw, thumb brushing along her cheek as he deepened it, his mouth moving over hers with a quiet urgency. Daisy's fingers slid into his hair, pulling him closer—the kind of kiss that said *stay* without ever needing words.

Passion sparked quickly, bubbling just under the surface. Their breath hitched in tandem.

"Shall we go to bed?" she whispered against his lips.

"Yes, please," he murmured, trying not to smile too wide as he swept her effortlessly into his arms, never quite breaking the kiss.

She laughed softly, arms circling his neck, as he carried her through the flat like it was the most natural thing in the world.

In the bedroom, everything slowed. The world narrowed to just the two of them—the low light, the warmth between them. They undressed slowly, not in haste or desperation, but through soft, reverent touches and kisses placed with care. His hands traced her curves as though trying to memorise them; her lips ghosted across his skin like a promise.

The duvet wrapped around them as they slipped into bed, warm and cocooning. Sam's arm slid around her waist with quiet confidence, pulling her close until their bodies aligned perfectly. She welcomed him in, wrapping her legs around his waist, a shiver running through her as he entered her slowly, a gentle pressure that made her exhale a shaky breath against his shoulder.

Their movements were unhurried, rhythmic. A soft, steady rhythm that matched the moment—less frantic than the night before, more like a whispered affirmation of everything that hadn't yet been spoken aloud. They moved together like they were made for it—for *this*—bodies learning each other in slow motion.

Sam's forehead rested against hers, eyes closed, his breath uneven. There was something raw in the way he held her—something almost broken in how tightly he clung. And Daisy felt it too. This wasn't just about desire. It was about needing to be close, to feel something real.

It didn't last long—he came quickly, as if he'd been holding something in all day, maybe longer. He whispered her name into the crook of her neck, a soft exhale that made her heart twist.

She held him close, brushing her fingers gently through the hair at the nape of his neck as his body finally stilled.

Afterwards, they lay tangled in silence, skin to skin, her head resting against his chest, his fingers idly tracing lazy circles on her back. The hum of the radiator, the slow rise and fall of their breathing—it was the sound of peace.

And in that small, sacred quiet, Daisy realised she wasn't afraid anymore. Not of what it meant. Not of what would come next.

She was just there. With him. And somehow, that was more than enough.

Daisy fell asleep with her back against his chest, his breath warm against her neck. Her body softened into his, and for the first time in a long time, she didn't dream of what could go wrong. Because right now, this—this quiet, utterly ordinary Sunday—was everything.

But Sam lay awake, eyes fixed on the ceiling, heart loud in the silence.

This was dangerous.

She felt too close. Too right. And that terrified him. Because Daisy didn't know the full story—how messy it really was inside his head. How sometimes he pushed people away just to prove they wouldn't stay. How much damage he still carried, damage he wasn't sure anyone should have to deal with.

She deserved someone uncomplicated. Easy. Someone who didn't wake up in cold sweats from things he didn't talk about.

His arm tightened slightly around her without meaning to, as if afraid she might slip away if he didn't hold on tight enough.

It felt like falling. Falling hard. And it scared the shit out of him.

But then she stirred in her sleep, murmured something half-formed and contented, and shifted closer. Her hand found his where it rested against her stomach, fingers curling gently around his.

And just like that, the spiral paused.

Maybe he didn't have to have it all figured out tonight.

Maybe—for now—this was enough.

Monday brought a whole new set of issues for Daisy.

How were they supposed to act at work? Was she allowed to kiss him in the hallway? Could she even tell people what they were?

Except… she didn't actually know what they *were*—because she hadn't asked.

He'd practically spent the entire weekend with her, woke up at her place that morning like it was the most normal thing in the world. But none of that answered the question spinning in her head on a relentless loop: *What are we doing?*

And there was something else niggling at her brain that she also hadn't addressed.

What the fuck was she supposed to do about Matthew?

She really didn't need this level of existential romantic panic before 9 a.m.

Her first obstacle: Lance. She had to tell him. She couldn't lie to her work bestie.

She cornered him near the printer. "Coffee. Now."

"Sure, babes," he said, already intrigued.

"Let's go."

They went to the café around the corner. As soon as the door swung shut behind them, she blurted it out. "I slept with Sam."

Lance stared. Then gasped. Then squealed. "Finally! God, I knew it! Honestly, I should start charging for my matchmaking services."

He was more shocked than Lydia had been—and, naturally, took full credit for the entire union.

Meanwhile, back at the office, Sam was… irritatingly normal. His behaviour barely changed, apart from the occasional knowing smirk or discreet wink when no one was watching.

He texted her small things he couldn't say aloud:

Sam: *You look very pretty today.*

Sam: *Have you told Lance yet?*

Sam: *I really want to kiss you.*

Sam: *I can't wait until we are alone.*

Their daily coffee runs were becoming more about stealing kisses than caffeine. The tension bubbled under the surface, simmering quietly behind boardroom doors and team meetings.

It went on like that for a few days. Stolen glances. Stolen touches. Life was busy—but Daisy was counting down the hours until she could drag him back into her bed. Judging by the way he'd kissed her in the stairwell that morning, Sam was just as eager.

And she had *completely* forgotten about the Matthew situation.

Then, one particular afternoon, Sam sent a message that made her stomach clench:

Sam: *Can we talk later?*

That one felt different. No kiss emoji. No cheeky tone.

More serious. More formal.

Now Daisy's head was in full procrastination mode.

She replied.

Daisy: *After work?*

Sam: *Yes, that works.*

Brilliant. Just when she thought things were finally going okay, the creeping dread returned with a vengeance.

And now she was bloody clock-watching.

By 7:30 p.m., the office was finally empty.

Heart pounding, Daisy approached his desk. "Where did you want to go for this… chat?"

He looked up and smiled—soft but unreadable. "Not here. Let's go in there."

He grabbed her hand—urgent, deliberate—guiding her into the small meeting room. The door clicked shut behind them. He twisted the blinds closed.

Daisy felt a quiet thrill. *What is he doing?*

He perched on the edge of the table and pulled her between his legs, crashing his lips against hers before she could ask another question.

Okay. This was *not* what she expected. But it was definitely something.

Minutes passed in a blur of hands and heat.

"We can't do this here," she gasped between kisses. "Someone might come in."

Sam raised an eyebrow, mischief flickering across his face. "What are you suggesting, Daisy Donaldson? I just wanted to steal a kiss—but now—"

That mischievous, devastating smirk hit her, and she was done for.

Still kissing her, he backed her towards the door, twisting the lock with a quiet click. His tie was undone in seconds. Her blouse followed. His shirt dropped from his shoulders. Her fingers skimmed across his chest, marvelling at how *real* he felt beneath her palms.

He was just… unreal.

And honestly? She wasn't sure how they were supposed to stop now.

He groaned as her lips found his collarbone. "Oh god, Daisy, I've been waiting all week to do this."

"It's only been three days. You could have just come to mine. We can go there now," she giggled, breathless.

"Hmm. I can't wait that long."

"Right. This is definitely more exciting."

He tugged her crop top over her head, eyes darkening as more of her skin was revealed. His mouth followed hungrily, kissing, tasting, claiming every inch he uncovered. One hand slid to the back of her head, drawing her into a deep, dizzying kiss, while the other found her breast, kneading it with a rough tenderness that made her gasp. His lips moved lower, kissing the soft space between, his breath hot against her skin.

Daisy's pulse was racing as she watched him unfasten his belt, each movement deliberate, loaded. Her gaze stayed locked on his, her teeth sinking into her lower lip without thinking.

"When you do that," he growled, voice low and thick with restraint, "it drives me mad."

Her breath hitched as he stepped closer, heat radiating off him as he pushed up her skirt, his hands firm on her thighs. She wrapped her legs around him instinctively, her body already aching for him.

A gasp slipped from her lips as he pushed into her—slow, controlled, deliberate. Like he was savouring every inch of her. But that careful rhythm didn't last. The need between them surged, unrelenting, and the pace shifted—urgent, messy, desperate.

They moved together like they couldn't get close enough, as if they were trying to dissolve into one another. Her name tumbled from his mouth like a prayer—reverent and raw—each breath catching with more need than the last.

And when the tension inside her finally snapped, it was electric—like a live wire had been cut. Sparks lit up behind her eyes, her whole body trembling as she came undone in his arms.

Sam followed moments after, his grip tightening, a low groan against her neck as he let go. His arms stayed locked around her, as if he never wanted to release her.

For a long, breathless moment, they stayed like that—still tangled, still shaking—foreheads pressed together, lost in the wreckage of what they'd just created.

Daisy exhaled a shaky laugh. "Well… that was—"

Sam cut her off with another kiss. "Yeah. It was."

"Didn't exactly have 'sex in a meeting room' on my bingo card for this year."

He chuckled. "Me either." He pressed a softer, more tender kiss to her lips.

But then her anxiety hit her like a bolt of lightning.

"Sam. What are we doing?"

Not quite understanding, he looked at her, brow slightly furrowed. "Well, Dais, we just had sex. At work. In a meeting room. Which, by the way, is never going to look the same to me now."

She pulled back slightly, the humour draining. "No. I mean… us. What do we *call* this?"

His face changed. That guarded look returned. "I don't know."

Her stomach dropped. "What do you mean, you don't know?"

"Daisy… I just… I don't think I can give you what you want right now."

She swallowed hard. "And what do I want, exactly?"

He looked pained. "A relationship. Something solid. And I just… I can't do that. Not right now."

"Why?" It came out small. Pleading. "Why are you being like this?"

He turned away, jaw clenched, wrestling with something she couldn't see.

"Can't you just be patient with me?" he said finally. "I still want you—so much—but I just… I don't want you getting in too deep when I might not be able to give you what you need."

She let out a short, angry laugh. "Patient? Sam, I *have* been so patient." Her voice cracked. "I don't understand why you can't just— why can't you tell me what the issue is?"

He clenched his jaw and turned away, like he was fighting an internal battle. Like there was something unsaid clawing at the back of his throat. Daisy watched him desperately, waiting, hoping he would just say it—whatever *it* was.

"Daisy, please, I just need time. I don't want to rush this. I don't want to make promises I can't keep. I don't want to hurt you."

She laughed—bitter, sharp. "Too late."

Daisy shoved past him, grabbing her clothes and dressing quickly. Her hands trembled as she buttoned up her blouse and adjusted her skirt.

"Daisy—please—don't leave." He reached out, but she flinched away.

"You just slept with me, and now you want to take a step back?" Her voice rose, thick with disbelief. "This is *fucking ridiculous* behaviour, Sam. You know that, right?"

"I never said that—Daisy, don't do this. Come on—"

She wasn't listening. She'd had enough of his shit. Enough of his half-truths and his walls. He wasn't doing this again.

"I'm done with this," she said. "Done waiting for you to decide if I'm good enough."

She stormed out, not looking back, even as he called her name.

That wasn't the Sam Callaghan who curled up in her bed and whispered that he missed her.

Not the man who, last weekend, had looked into her eyes so deeply she could *feel* his soul—the man who hesitated but still pulled her closer.

The man with his quiet struggles and unspoken wounds.

The one who'd said he needed her.

There was something he wasn't saying. Something keeping him from her.

And Daisy—idiot that she was—still wanted to know what it was. Still wanted to fix it.

But tonight, she couldn't. Tonight, she was done.

And tomorrow?

Well, she wasn't sure she'd want to see his face at all.

As she stormed out of the office and down the street, she did the unthinkable—a moment of pure self-sabotage.

She opened the chat with Matthew and typed:

Daisy: *Yes, sorry. Thursday evening sounds great. Send me a location and I'll meet you.*

Disaster Daisy strikes again.

Chapter 18:
Stop pretending I'm fine when I'm not

The following day at work was tough. Daisy was devastated—fuming, even—though she didn't let it show.

She couldn't.

She had to be professional. They had the work trip next week, and she'd be damned if Sam Callaghan ruined her career as well as her bloody heart.

So she ignored him. Cold. Professional. Arctic.

Besides, she had other things to occupy her. Like the small fact she'd arranged to meet Matthew tonight. She thought she'd already put that to bed weeks ago, but somehow, he just kept finding his way back in. Yesterday, it had seemed like an entirely great idea. Today? Not so much.

At least, according to Lance—who, upon hearing her plan, told her in no uncertain terms that she was "spiralling."

But Daisy was beyond making the right choices. She was in a hellish mood—courtesy of Sam *fuck-with-your-head* Callaghan—and she wanted to forget. Just for one night.

Too late to back out now.

Several cocktails later (thanks to Jenny from Sales—who Daisy had never drunk with before but who turned out to be absolutely hilarious for a millennial), she finally made it to the Samuel Pepys pub by the river. St Paul's side. Quaint. Charming. Impossible to actually get into.

She walked through a door that looked suspiciously like a function room and immediately backed out again. *Not crashing another engagement party today, thank you very much.*

Already tipsy. Already regretting this. Not a solid plan, Daisy.

She wandered towards the water, staring at the dark Thames below, vaguely wondering if it might be easier to just jump in and let the tide carry her away. Ridiculous. She was beyond help.

Then she heard it. A voice. *His* voice.

"Daisy, what are you doing, you nutter?"

She glanced up. Matthew. Leaning out of a window above.

"Oh, hi. I'll be right there."

Inside, he was slightly tipsy himself. He leaned down and kissed her on the cheek. Her stomach flipped—traitorous.

"I thought you weren't coming," he said, blushing. "After the other night."

Stop being cute, Matthew.

"Well, yeah," Daisy muttered, "but I thought I'd give you the benefit of the doubt."

He is not yours. Remember that, Daisy.

God, her mind was chaos. Also—why did he have to be engaged? The universe really did hate her.

"Pint?" he offered, eyebrow raised.

She stumbled slightly on the way to the bar, and he laughed. "Daze, you're steaming. Where have you been?"

"Never mind," she shot back. "Just… get me a drink."

They ended up in a booth by the window. He said his goodbyes to the two people he'd been with—risky, Daisy thought. *What if they told his fiancée?*—before sitting across from her.

"So—" he began.

"Look, I'm sorry for how angry I got the other night," she cut in quickly. "It was… out of line."

"It's okay," he said softly. "You weren't wrong. I was being a selfish prick. I just…"

He trailed off, sighed.

Just what?

She leaned forward without meaning to. He had that mesmerising way of reeling her back in—like muscle memory. Or maybe it was just the alcohol.

"I just…" He rubbed the back of his neck, then looked her dead in the eye. "I still have feelings for you. I miss you, Daze. I love you. And when I saw you with him—Sam—it did something to me. I hated it. I didn't want you with anyone else. So yeah, I got jealous. And I think I wanted to win you back just because…"

"Because you couldn't have me anymore," Daisy finished quietly.

He didn't argue.

"So what do you want now?" she asked, instantly regretting the words.

He smirked. "Well, I thought that was obvious."

His gaze lingered. He reached for her hand, leaned closer.

It was old. Familiar. And the heat of it almost made her lean in, too. Almost.

"Daze?" he murmured. "Tell me what to do here. Because I don't know."

"I don't know either," she whispered.

And she could have sworn—just for a second—that they were about to kiss.

Then a bell rang.

Last orders.

Saved—or cheated—by the universe.

Daisy shot up, heart pounding, knowing that this was wrong. "Matthew, I can't do this. I have to go."

"Daze, wait—" He scrambled after her, grabbing his jacket. "Let me walk you home."

"No."

She jumped into the first cab she could find, slamming the door behind her. Dramatic exit: achieved.

And then, inevitably, she cried. Again.

The cab driver definitely thought she was unhinged.

Which, to be fair, she almost certainly was. Because if her love life wasn't fucked up enough already, she'd just made it fifteen times worse.

And Matthew Devan was fast becoming the most complicated man that ever lived. More complicated than Sam Callaghan.

Friday morning arrived—unwelcome and aggressive.

Daisy cracked one eye open and immediately regretted it. Her head throbbed, her stomach turned, and the *hanxiety*—that special cocktail of hangover and existential dread—was already at a solid ten out of ten. She didn't even want to look at her phone.

So, for once, she tried something radical: a different approach.

No drinking.

No avoidance.

No self-destructive choices masquerading as *coping mechanisms.*

Instead, she called Rhoda, practically begging her to approve a last-minute holiday request. Miraculously, she got the day off.

She was going to see her therapist.

Well… *going back* was more accurate. Daisy hadn't seen Dr Nolan in five months. Not since she'd quit her last job. And even then, their final session had ended with Dr Nolan gently pointing out that before that, Daisy hadn't been in therapy for years—an observation that opened a whole new line of awkward, uncomfortable questioning Daisy had absolutely not been prepared for.

And she wasn't exactly prepared for it today either. But what choice did she have?

She needed to air some things.

Some Sam Callaghan–related things.

And—God help her—maybe, finally, she needed to talk about Matthew.

Standing outside Dr Nolan's office, Daisy hesitated. The building across town felt strangely untouched by time, as if stepping inside would transport her back to who she used to be. And that was the problem.

Going in meant going *back there.*

Back to being eleven years old and completely lost in the world.

Back to struggling to find a purpose.

Daisy had started therapy because, at eleven, she was diagnosed with anxiety and depression. Nobody knew exactly what caused it.They suspected hormones but weren't sure. Then one day at school, she'd had a panic attack, and Nanna Jean hadn't known how to help her. They kept happening for months. Prim had tried, but it only made Daisy feel worse—like she was a burden, a problem to be solved. Neither of her parents could help.

She needed someone to talk to. Someone professional.

And it worked.

She saw Dr Nolan every week, and things got better. Dr Nolan concluded that her dad's absence in her childhood had partly caused it—the uncertainty, the mixed emotions—all contributing factors. That was when Malcolm Donaldson vowed to try to be there for both girls as much as he could. He tried, and things did get a lot better.

Then, eventually, therapy became monthly catch-ups. And when she went to university, the visits stopped altogether. She told herself she was fine. That she was actually moving forward.

But then she came back. And she wasn't fine.

She struggled with her purpose. With the unresolved Matthew situation. So, she returned to therapy, seeing Dr Nolan regularly again.

Until she didn't.

Over the years, she gradually phased out the visits, convincing herself she was handling things on her own. Accepting herself—slowly.

This most recent spiral, however, started five months ago, when she quit her job. But Daisy had convinced herself she was dealing with it. She'd landed a new job. A fresh start. One that brought a whole new set of life-related problems—but nothing she couldn't handle. She was an adult, right?

But now…

Now, she wasn't so sure.

Come on, lift your head. Get out of your frozen state.

The lyric played in her mind—a line from one of her favourite songs.. A quiet push forward.

She took out her headphones.

And walked in.

The waiting room was exactly as she remembered it—calm, muted, too clean. Soft grey walls. Pale wooden floors. A faint scent of lavender from the essential oil diffuser on the small coffee table, right next to a neat stack of wellness magazines that no one ever actually read.

It was unsettling how nothing had changed. The same receptionist sat behind the curved desk, her hair in a severe bun, glasses perched on the edge of her nose. She barely glanced up as Daisy approached, typing something into the computer.

Daisy cleared her throat.

"Hi, I have an appointment with Dr Nolan."

The woman finally looked at her, expression neutral but vaguely knowing. Like she remembered Daisy. Like she remembered everyone who walked in here,carrying their baggage, looking for answers.

"Take a seat, Daisy. She'll be with you shortly."

Daisy nodded and turned toward the seating area. The chairs were still those weird modern ones—the kind that looked stylish but were secretly uncomfortable. She chose the one by the window, pulling out her phone, pretending to scroll, pretending she wasn't overthinking everything.

A message from Lance.

Lance: *Daisy, where are you?*

She had to reply to that.

Daisy: *An appointment. I'll explain later. I'll be back tomorrow.*

Then another—Prim.

Prim: *Daisy, why haven't you called me back? Call me when you get a chance. x*

Daisy felt a stab of guilt. She hadn't been ignoring Prim on purpose. She just didn't have the energy right now.

She returned to the mindless scroll. A low hum of voices filtered through from down the hall, the soundproofing not quite perfect. Somewhere, someone laughed—a therapist or a patient, who knew? The idea of laughing in here seemed strange. Daisy wasn't sure she'd ever done that before.

Before she could spiral any further, a familiar voice called her name.

"Daisy?"

She looked up.

Dr Nolan stood in the doorway, the same warm, professional smile, the same gentle curiosity in her eyes.

And just like that, Daisy felt eleven years old again.

She followed Dr Nolan down the short hallway and into her office, which—like the waiting room—was eerily unchanged.

The same beige walls.

The same bookshelf filled with psychology books she'd never read.
The same slightly-too-large armchair she used to sink into as a teenager, feeling like it might swallow her whole.

Even Dr Nolan looked the same: sharp bob, kind but no-nonsense eyes, and that slightly unnerving ability to see right through Daisy's bullshit.

"Make yourself comfortable," Dr Nolan said, gesturing to the chair opposite her own.

Comfortable. Right.

Daisy sat down, crossing one leg over the other, then uncrossing them. She placed her hands in her lap, then on the arms of the chair, then back in her lap again. Jesus Christ, why was she fidgeting so much?

Dr Nolan didn't say anything right away, just studied her like a puzzle she was about to solve.

"So, it's been a while," she said finally, her tone gentle but firm.

Daisy let out a small laugh. "Yeah… five months. Not too bad?"

Dr Nolan lifted an eyebrow. "Five months since your last visit, but if we're talking *regular* sessions, it's been, what… three years?"

Busted.

Daisy sighed, leaning back. "Fine. It's been a while."

Dr Nolan nodded, making a note in her leather-bound notebook. Daisy had always wondered what she wrote in there. Probably something like *Client still deflecting with humour. No signs of growth.*

"So," Dr Nolan said. "What's going on?"

Where should she even begin?

"I—" Daisy hesitated, suddenly aware of the lump in her throat. She swallowed hard, trying to push it down. "I don't know, really. Work stuff, I guess."

Dr Nolan didn't even blink. "Daisy."

Damn it. She was already onto her.

Daisy exhaled, looking up at the ceiling like maybe the words she needed were written up there somewhere. "It's… it's a lot of things, actually. But mainly—ugh, this is so cliché—I think I have a broken heart?"

It came out more like a question. Like she still wasn't sure she was allowed to claim that level of emotional devastation.

Dr Nolan leaned back in her chair. "Tell me about it."

And just like that, Daisy was talking.

About Sam. About how he infuriated her, challenged her, made her feel things she hadn't felt in years. About how they blurred every line between love and hate until she wasn't sure where they stood. About how he'd opened up to her and then shut her out just as quickly.

And then, somehow, she was talking about Matthew.

About how he was supposed to be the one—the safe choice—the person she could have built a life with if she hadn't sabotaged it. About how seeing him again had made her realise that what they had was over, and maybe had been for a long time.

About how, despite all of this, she still didn't know what she wanted. And how she really *wanted* to know. She was done with feeling lost.

Dr Nolan listened without interrupting, nodding occasionally, making those little "hmm" sounds that let Daisy know she was absorbing every word.

When Daisy finally stopped—drained from spilling months of pent-up emotions—Dr Nolan let the silence stretch for a moment before speaking.

"It sounds like you're dealing with two very different kinds of grief," she said. "One for something you lost a long time ago, and one for something you never really had in the first place."

Shit. That was harsh.

Harsh was what Daisy needed though, right?

Daisy blinked. "Jesus. When you say it like that, it sounds… depressing."

Dr Nolan smiled slightly. "Well, you *are* in therapy."

Daisy let out a short laugh, then sighed. "So what do I do?"

"What do you think you need to do?"

Ugh. Classic therapist move. Answer a question with a question.

"I mean… I think I need to stop pretending I'm fine when I'm not," Daisy admitted. "And maybe stop waiting for people to decide how they feel about me before I decide how I feel about them."

Dr Nolan nodded. "That sounds like a good place to start."

Daisy let that sink in. Maybe, just maybe, she was finally ready to start.

Daisy left Dr Nolan's office feeling… lighter. Optimistic, even. She headed home on the Tube, refreshed, feeling strong, getting her life straight in her head—a plan that didn't involve Sam Callaghan or Matthew Devan.

Then her phone rang, and she nearly threw it at the woman sitting opposite her.

Prim.

"Prim?"

"Daisy, why have you been ignoring me?"

"I'm sorry, I've been busy."

"Too busy to talk to your favourite sister? Nice."

"Prim, again, you are my *only* sister. And no, I haven't been—"

Daisy debated telling Prim about her visit to Dr Nolan. She decided against it. *This isn't growth, Daisy. Jesus, did you not learn anything from that last half hour?*

"I've had meetings at work. I'm on my way home now. What's up?"

"Was just wondering if you had a good night. Heard about you pieing off Greg—good work."

"Oh shit, he told you?"

"Grant, actually. But well done. Are we still on for Saturday?"

"Saturday?"

"Barbecue at ours. Bring a date. Actually, just bring Lydia or Lance—we don't need any more drama."

Daisy sighed. "Okay, Prim."

She hung up, somehow feeling more stressed than she had earlier.

And then her head turned on her. *Sam Callaghan.* He found his way back in—because she would love nothing more than to take him to that barbecue. Or just have him hold her.

For heaven's sake, she really wished she could shut him out.

Then her phone rang again, breaking the trance. She answered, thinking it was Prim, but instead—

"Matthew??"

"Bloody hell, I wasn't sure if you'd actually answer. Um, okay.

I was just wondering if you were free. Tonight? For a chat. Last night didn't go so well and—"

Daisy sighed. Mainly because it wasn't Sam.

"Erm, not really, Matthew. I'm just heading home after a really long arse day."

Seeing him right now was the *last* thing on her mind. But of course, he was persistent.

"I could pop over? Daze, I really need to see you. I want to make this right. Finally."

"Okay, fine. I'll be home in about fifteen minutes."

"Great, I'll meet you there."

Fuck's sake, Daisy, what are you doing? This is a mistake. A massive one.

Daisy returned home to find Matthew casually sitting on the wall outside her building. Her heart skipped a beat—taking her back ten years in an instant. She didn't care for that feeling. At all.

Walking straight into her flat suddenly felt like a terrible idea— probably one of the best decisions she'd made all year. So instead, she sat next to him on the wall.

"Hi."
"Hey."
"So, Matthew. Talk."

Harsh, Daisy—but this was growth. Well done.

"What, here? Can't we go inside?"

"No, Matthew. That's a terrible idea, and you know it. What if Priyanka finds out you've been in your ex-girlfriend's house? Or Sam—"

Shit. She stopped herself. Sam wasn't her boyfriend. But they were *something*—a situationship, whatever that meant—and she had feelings for him, so...?

It didn't go unnoticed by Matthew.

"Sam, yes of course. Is he your new fella, Daze?"

"Sort of."

"Well, is he or isn't he, Daisy? Because if he is, then it changes what I'm about to say dramatically."

Her pulse kicked. "What—what are you about to say?"

"Answer the question, Daisy. Is Sam your boyfriend or not?"

Daisy, ever terrible under pressure, blurted out the most inappropriate thing possible.

"We're sleeping together."

Great. Could've said *sort of dating*, could've said *it's complicated*, could've said *we're seeing each other*. But no—her brain went straight there. Twat.

"Right," Matthew said, looking down at his feet. "I see."

"Matthew, did you really not expect me to move on? Should I have just been waiting around, hoping you'd magically become *not engaged* to someone else? It's actually kind of ridiculous when you think about it."

"Not after what I said the other night, Daze." His voice softened. "I thought… maybe you felt the same. I thought we were—"

Daisy didn't answer. Across the street, she spotted Viv and John getting out of their car, already craning their necks in that nosy-neighbour way she hated. The last thing she needed was them seeing her talking—*again*—to Matthew Devan.

"Come on," she muttered, grabbing his arm and pulling him along.

"Daisy, what are you doing?"

"Nosey neighbours," she said over her shoulder. "Just trust me."

They ended up at the local park, sitting side by side on the swings, of all places. It was oddly fitting—though unintentionally sentimental.

Matthew looked around. "This brings back memories."

"Different park," Daisy replied flatly, unwilling to go waltzing down memory lane with him.

There was a pause before she turned to him. "I'm going to be honest—I don't really know what you want from me, or why you keep coming back into my life."

"Because, like I said before, I still love you, Daze."

Then it hit her—Dr Nolan's voice echoing in her head. *You decide how you feel about people, Daisy.*

She let out a breath. "You don't love me, Matthew. You love the version of me who loved you ten years ago. And now that I'm not that person anymore, you're chasing the idea of it."

They sat in silence, the chains of the swings creaking softly as they shifted.

"Do you love him?" he asked.

Daisy let out a dry laugh. "Who, Sam? I don't know. Maybe. I like him a lot. He's just… complicated."

"You don't do complicated," Matthew said. "You like steady. Simple. That's why we worked so well."

"We didn't work, Matthew. That's why it ended."

"It ended with the idea we'd eventually get back together."

She turned to him, incredulous. "Who made that plan? You? Because I don't remember agreeing to it."

Matthew looked away, jaw tensing. He knew she was right. He just didn't want her to be.

"What happened to us?" he asked, his voice softer now.

"Life happened," she replied. "And we grew up."

He reached over and linked his pinky with hers, like he used to. It hit her with a flicker of something—nostalgia, maybe—but it wasn't enough. Not anymore. And strangely, the guilt that followed wasn't for Matthew.

It was for Sam.

Because he was the one she was afraid to lose now. He was the one she was falling for.

"Matthew," she said gently, her voice steady but firm, "I'm going to say this once, and then I need you to let it go. It's over between us, and I don't think we can get it back. And me… I'm trying to move on."

She paused, letting the weight of her words hang between them.

"And you're getting married, Matthew," she added softly. "So maybe it's time you really moved on, too."

Matthew didn't respond right away. He just stared at her, as if the words hadn't fully registered—or maybe they didn't fit with the version of reality he was still clinging to.

"Okay. I'm sorry," he finally muttered, though it wasn't the kind of apology that meant anything. It was just a concession. He didn't want to lose this battle, but at least he was losing it on his own terms.

But Daisy could see it—the part of him that still didn't believe it. The part that only wanted her now that she was no longer his.

He stood up, stroppy and defensive. "I have to go."

Daisy stood too. "I'll walk you back."

"Please. It's fine." He scoffed.

"Fine. That's it, then."

She turned on her heel, but before she could walk away, Matthew grabbed her sleeve, pulling her back.

Oh shit. Please don't.

She turned—and before she could stop him, his lips were on hers.

Fuck. Fuck. Fuck.

What the hell was he doing?

Daisy tried to think of anything—anything—other than how the kiss felt. Her dad's dirty socks. Tino's farting. Anything that could distract her from the tingle running through her. But it was like the memories of who they'd been rushed back, taking her right to being eighteen again. She could almost taste the nostalgia.

It was bittersweet. Sad, even.

And before she could pull away, her body betrayed her. She kissed him back.

When she opened her eyes, she immediately regretted it. His gaze locked onto hers, filled with something she hadn't seen in years—love. It was too much. Way too much.

Panic set in. She pushed him away, shock and disbelief taking over.

"No, Matthew. What are you doing? This is so wrong."

He didn't speak straight away. Then his face softened, but his voice was quiet—and final.

"I'm sorry. Goodbye, Daisy."

And just like that, he was gone.

Shit. How dare he.

What the hell was that? A last-ditch attempt to win her over? A goodbye kiss?

That's it? That's *all* it was? Nothing more?

Her heart raced. She glanced around, but there was no one there. Not even herself, in a way.

What about Sam? Sam was going to be fine, right? She'd just kissed Matthew, but it wasn't like that meant anything. It was nothing.

And she definitely didn't need to tell Sam. A goodbye kiss didn't count. It didn't *mean* anything.

She was just going to push it to the back of her mind and forget it ever happened.

Yep. That's what she was going to do. She was going to bury it.

Very smart, Daisy.

She let out a shaky breath. She still didn't know what Matthew had really wanted to say. But maybe that was a door she finally needed to close.

For good.

Chapter 19:
Lydia Allard is hiding something

Lydia stumbled out of the cab laughing like a woman who'd just been released from a hostage situation—a very drunk, very flirty hostage situation. She yanked Luca towards the building like he was a particularly sexy carry-on bag.

"Why are there so many stairs?" he groaned.

Which, again, she found absolutely hilarious.

"Oh, come on, you lightweight," she cackled, nearly missing the step herself. Honestly, it was less of a flirtatious stumble and more of a near-death experience. But sure—cackling it is.

God, she was so drunk. Not her usual tipsy-dancing-to-Beyoncé drunk. No, this was *I-should-not-operate-heavy-machinery-and-might-vomit-in-my-plant* drunk. Normally she knew her limits—four drinks, then water. Maybe crisps. Responsible. Adult-ish.

But not tonight.

Tonight, Lydia was drinking with a mission: to forget. And apparently, that also included bringing home cute blokes named Luca who smelled like expensive aftershave and poor decisions.

Didn't matter, though. The flat was empty. Like her soul. And her fridge. But mostly her soul.

Because she'd left.

God, Lydia. Way to spiral at speed.

Here's the thing: Lydia had been hiding something for a while now. From her mum and dad (standard). From Lance (fine—he'd just make it about skincare). And, most painfully, from Daisy—her best friend in the whole damn world.

Lydia had a girlfriend. *Sort of.*

Well, not anymore.

Lydia had only realised this past year that she was bisexual. She'd always liked boys—sure. Had a type. Usually broody and emotionally unavailable. But there had been girls too. The odd flirty snog at uni. A weirdly intense moment with her Year 11 English teacher. Nothing she'd ever unpacked. Because why would she? Lydia was far too busy keeping everyone else emotionally comfortable.

Then came Emmy.

Her (now ex) roommate. The effortlessly cool artist with celestial hair and dark eyes that always seemed to be searching for something. She was the kind of person who could wear paint-splattered jeans and a simple T-shirt and still look like she'd just stepped out of *Vogue*. She painted like her soul was on fire and spoke about Kandinsky like he was an old mate. Lydia was gone for her by month four. Emmy noticed by month five. They kissed in the kitchen while boiling pasta and never looked back.

Except now, Lydia was doing nothing *but* looking back.

She'd put Emmy on a pedestal. Emmy was passionate, magnetic—she had that raw, creative energy that drew Lydia in like a tide. Even when she talked about abstract art (which Lydia still didn't fully understand), she moved with this kind of grace. And she never judged. She just radiated warmth. Lydia loved that warmth.

Of course, she never told anyone. Because Daisy would be hurt. Because her mother would probably faint, then deliver a monologue about grandchildren and the sanctity of womanhood.

Because Lydia was a coward. A *let's-not-make-this-weird* kind of coward.

Emmy didn't want to be a secret. She wanted brunches, parties, to meet Daisy. Lydia wanted… well, to not implode.

Spoiler: she imploded anyway.

The breakup was big. Loud. Emotional. And now Emmy was gone. Like, *moved-out, toothbrush-vanished* gone. Replaced by someone new. A flatmate who was nothing like her.

And Lydia—well, she was afraid.

Can you *imagine* Mary's reaction to Lydia having a girlfriend? God, she wished she wasn't such a wimp when it came to her bloody mother.

And then Daisy—how would Daisy react to Lydia hiding this from her for all this time, and not even telling her she was bisexual in the first place? The guilt was very, very real.

Lydia liked to live life happy. She hated confrontation, despite her brutal honesty, and she'd do anything to avoid falling out with people. She just wanted everyone to get along.

So Lydia buried her head in the sand. Denial sand.

And carried on.

She couldn't blame Emmy though. Who *would* put up with that? Being hidden like a secret shame? It was worse than the whole Daisy-and-Sam-Callaghan fiasco. At least Daisy wasn't forcing Sam to stay invisible.

This was worse. Self-loathingly worse.

Lydia couldn't handle the silence of her own flat tonight.

So, she was taking her own advice. The same advice Daisy had refused a few weeks ago—until she *hadn't.*

Get under someone to get over someone.

Lydia Allard = genius.

So here she was, dragging Luca into the fourth-floor sauna she called home. They were kissing sloppily, half-undressed, and barely made it to the sofa.

There was no romance. They were both so hammered Lydia could barely make out his face.

He kissed well. Smelled better. And told her she was funny—funny, which was basically foreplay for her.

Lydia didn't remember much else, other than convincing herself it felt like healing.

It didn't.

But it felt like *something*.

Until she passed out mid-snog.

Sexy.

Poor guy.

The next morning, Lydia woke up to a pounding headache, a dry mouth, and a niggling sense that something was off. That something was *wrong*.

The kind of regret that came with waking up to find a half-naked stranger in your bed.

She turned—and yep. There was.

Luca.

What? When did they move to the bed? She definitely remembered the sofa. There had been a *sofa*.

Jesus, her head was splitting. She needed to get out of this situation—fast. She poked him like he was a suspicious lasagne.

Luca stirred, stretching lazily before rubbing his face. "You alright?" he asked, voice still thick with sleep.

Lydia smiled the way one might if they were hiding a body. "Yeah, just—a bit of a headache. And I've got plans this morning."

Lies. The audition wasn't until later. But still—she needed him gone.

He gave her a look. Not quite annoyed, but definitely unimpressed. "Right. So, do I get coffee, or is this the part where you politely shove me out the door?"

Yikes. He wasn't wrong. And he *had* been nice—fun, even. But he wasn't Emmy. And he wasn't what she needed. Not really.

"Sorry, Luca," she muttered, grabbing her dressing gown from the floor. "Last night was… fun. But—"

"Yeah, yeah." He sighed, throwing back the covers and reaching for his jeans. "No hard feelings. Guess I misread the situation."

God, Lydia. You're a bitch. A bad bitch, but still.

She didn't argue. Just offered a small, apologetic shrug as he buttoned his shirt.

Then—just as he was fastening his jeans—something hit her like a slap to the face.

A memory.

The drunken fumbling. The heat of his mouth on her neck. Collapsing onto the sofa, hands everywhere. No hesitation. No second thoughts.

No condom.

Panic surged, nausea rising. She pressed a hand to her forehead and went white.

Fuck.

Luca caught the shift in her expression. "Hey—what's up?"

She swallowed hard. "Did we—?" She couldn't even say it. "We were careful, right?"

He hesitated, raking a hand through his hair. "I mean… I think so?"

"You *think* so?" Her voice rose.

"I mean… I was wasted, Lyd. I don't exactly remember every detail."

Neither did she. Which made it *so much worse*.

Luca frowned, rubbing the back of his neck. "Look, I'm clean, if that's what you're worried about. I can—if you want me to get tested or whatever, I will."

She nodded blankly, trying not to faint. Or scream. Or both.

As if that fixed it. The *other* thing. The thing she couldn't even bring herself to say.

"Okay," she mumbled, barely hearing his reassurances as he grabbed his jacket.

"Take care, yeah?" he said, lingering in the doorway for a second before she nodded stiffly, watching him leave.

As soon as the door clicked shut, Lydia sank onto the bed, head in her hands.

She'd been so desperate to forget Emmy—so desperate to *feel* something else—that she hadn't even thought about the consequences.

Now she had something else entirely to worry about.

Fuck her life. She'd wanted to feel something. Not… this.

Lydia sat staring at the wall for an unknowingly long time, her brain looping through the night like a bad film reel.

Then she snapped herself back to reality.

Nope. Not now. She couldn't spiral.

She had an audition. Her first in months. One that could actually pay her rent.

Bad bitch mode: *activated.*

She yanked her hair into a bun, slapped concealer under her eyes like it owed her money and blasted the top layer with dry shampoo until it looked like an intentional grunge aesthetic. That was still in, right?

Pulling on what was *definitely* a man's T-shirt (*definitely* not hers from M&S), she began the mad dash to get out of the house and across town.

She'd hit the pharmacy later. Probably. Hopefully. Google could tell her opening hours. On the bus. Which, miracle of miracles, she caught.

She even got a seat. Result.

All was semi-well.

And then—

Ding.

Daisy: *Bridesmaid duties number 362. Your presence is required at Prim and Grant's BBQ this Saturday. Pretty please. I also don't have a date either. Long story.*

Phew. Just Daisy.

Great. Mandatory joy. At least Daisy was dateless too. Misery loved company.

Lydia: *Sure babes. 100% there. You know it x*

So confident. So chill.

So definitely not screaming internally about a potential pregnancy.

Then it hit her.

Luca. Would. Be. There.

For heaven's sake. Why? Why? Why?

Why *wouldn't* the universe throw him at her again like a poorly written sequel?

She absolutely could not face him. But she couldn't let Daisy down either.

She briefly contemplated throwing herself off the bus.

Then her screen lit up again. Different name this time.

Emmy.

Lydia's breath caught. Because of course. Today wasn't done

yet.

Emmy: *Saw your Insta story. That bar looked familiar... made me think of you. Hope you're okay. x*

Lydia's stomach lurched.

Of course she'd posted an Insta story.

Of course Emmy had seen it.

Of course she'd messaged now—*now*—the morning after Lydia had slept with a man in a desperate, gin-soaked attempt to forget her.

What the hell was she doing?

She nearly missed her stop.

By the time she arrived at the theatre, she was flustered, under-caffeinated, and about 80% dry shampoo. She was also perilously close to vomiting. Not nerves—well, *some* nerves—but mostly gin-related.

Inside, the waiting room buzzed with actors who all looked better-rested, better-dressed, and definitely better-prepared.

Lydia smiled at the casting assistant like her life depended on it (because, frankly, it did), then sat down on a hard chair with a dog-eared script and a stomach full of regret.

And in the chaos of lines and nerves and trying not to burp gin mid-scene—

She forgot.

The pharmacy.

The pill.

The whole bloody situation.

She instead met up with Emmy.

Saturday arrived, and Prim and Grant's garden in Fulham looked like a Pinterest board had exploded.

Very *Prim.*

Fairy lights strung between overpriced olive trees, everything dipped in blush and sage, and a ridiculous grazing table boasting at least four types of hummus.

Lydia had arrived early—a mistake in hindsight. She was already trapped in a conversation with Grant's aunt, who was aggressively asking if she'd "met anyone nice yet."

And Luca—of course—had said hello the moment she arrived. Just a polite wave and an awkward smile that made her want to either vomit or run into traffic.

He was cute. Annoyingly cute. If Lydia wasn't totally and utterly smitten with Emmy, she might've liked him, like properly. But right now, she was firmly back in that emotional loop, having met up with Emmy several times.

And now, standing in this garden surrounded by coupled-up people and quinoa salads, she was regretting *everything.*

She could see him now, over by the BBQ with Grant, tongs in hand, flipping something vaguely chicken-shaped. He looked good. Of course he looked good. White T-shirt, navy shorts, tan skin catching the sunlight like he'd been personally blessed by the Greek gods. Those stupid forearms didn't help either.

And there she was alone, clinging to a glass of rosé. On her third, obviously.

Where the hell was Daisy?

Daisy arrived late—*fashionably,* she told herself. She wore a yellow sundress she'd panic-bought that morning from Zara and regretted the second she got into the Uber. Mostly because she was being attacked by bees. Constantly.

She spotted Lydia hovering near the world's largest charcuterie board and made a beeline (no pun intended).

"There you are," Daisy said, thrusting a glass into her hand. "You look like you're about to fake a phone call and climb the fence."

"I considered it," Lydia muttered, sipping gratefully. "You didn't tell me he'd be here."

"I thought it was obvious. He's basically Grant's BBQ sidekick. They've got a WhatsApp group about sausages."

"Oh god."

"Just breathe. It's fine. You're fine. You look fit. And he's been staring at you since you got here."

Lydia rolled her eyes, trying to act casual. She couldn't tell Daisy the truth—not here, not now. And fine, she *did* fancy Luca a bit. He was nice. Solidly nice. She owed him at least a conversation. She wasn't going to embarrass him in front of everyone.

"He probably thinks I'm going to throw up on his shoes," she muttered.

"You've done worse," Daisy grinned.

And then—because the universe was a petty little gremlin—Luca started walking towards them.

"Shit."

"Don't panic."

"*Don't panic?!*"

"Smile and sip," Daisy hissed. "Smile. And. Sip."

Lydia took a gulp—the kind that burned all the way down.

"I'll leave you to it." Daisy smirked, already backing away. Within seconds, she'd joined Prosecco Pong with Greg and Liam, leaving Lydia to face her fate alone.

"Hello," Luca said, leaning casually against a high table, bottle of beer in hand, curls slightly mussed, eyes crinkling when he smiled.

"Didn't think I'd see you again," he said.

"I live in London," Lydia replied dryly. "It's not like I moved to

Bolivia."

He laughed. "Fair. But still. You ghosted me."

"I didn't *ghost*," she said, lifting her chin. "I… faded."

"Oh, you *faded*," he echoed, mock-serious. "Cool, cool. That's much less brutal."

Despite herself, Lydia smiled. He was charming—ridiculously so. The kind of man who could talk a traffic warden out of a ticket on Cannon Street and probably get a free sandwich out of it too. And that night they'd slept together—well, it had been fun. Unexpected, messy fun.

Standing in front of him again, she remembered exactly why she'd agreed to it. He was sweet. And fit. And seemed to like her in that rare, genuine way that felt less about the chase and more about *her*.

They chatted easily about mutual friends, Grant's terrible playlist, Prim's hen trip to Amsterdam, the stag do in Portugal—normal, surface-level stuff. She was just about starting to relax when Luca's tone shifted.

"Hey, um… not to be *that* guy," he began, scratching the back of his neck, "but did you manage to, you know, sort the whole pill thing?"

Lydia blinked. Her stomach dropped like an elevator with its cables cut.

Oh God.

The pill.

She had *not* sorted the pill thing.

She'd meant to, of course. But then she'd got the part, had back-to-back rehearsals, bar shifts, a fight with her mum—and every time she remembered, it was the wrong time. The bus. The shower. The middle of the night.

Now it was too late, right?

She smiled when she said it, but it felt like swallowing glass. "Yeah, all fine. I took care of it."

Nice one, Lyds. You total fucking liar.

He looked visibly relieved. "Okay, cool. I just… I wasn't sure if I should text or what. Didn't want to be weird."

"You weren't," she said quickly, voice tight. "It's fine."

Luca smiled, warm and sincere. "Good. I just didn't want you thinking I was some arsehole who disappears after."

"You're not," she said quietly. "You're a decent one."

He grinned. "Don't ruin my image."

"Hey, *I* ghosted you, remember."

"Faded," he corrected, winking.

They both laughed. He offered to get her another drink; she politely declined. Then he drifted back to his mates, leaving Lydia standing there, heart pounding.

She turned to the table behind her, gripping the edge for balance, the other hand already fumbling for her phone. Her fingers shook as she typed.

What happens if you forget to take the morning after pill?

Can you still take it after 72 hours?

Chances of getting pregnant from one night?

Behind her, the music thumped on. Someone shouted about tequila shots.

But Lydia couldn't hear any of it.

She just kept thinking the same thing, over and over.

Please don't let this be a big deal. Please just let it be nothing.

Lydia Allard = total fucking mess.

Chapter 20:
If it helps with the budget, of course

After her visit to Dr Nolan last week, Daisy had been feeling… better.

Well, apart from the whole Matthew debacle—and that stupid, lingering *goodbye* kiss. But she'd firmly decided to put a pin in that. Pretend it never happened. Mentally yeeted into the bin. It was for the best.

And after those two minor life-shattering events, she'd made a decision: she was taking back control of her life. Properly. No more spiralling.

She'd spent some quality time with Prim and Grant—after an initial confrontation over her sudden radio silence, of course. Then came the Saturday barbecue, which she *thinks* she enjoyed, albeit through a haze of prosecco. She did end up crying in the Uber and trauma-dumping on the poor driver, but hey—at least she didn't text him. She'd stayed strong. Even though he *had* texted her.

And it took every ounce of willpower not to respond. Because he was so damn cute.

But she wasn't falling for it.

Progress, Daisy. Progress.

She'd visited Nanna Jean, even managed lunch with Jessie—fresh from yet another "spiritual path to find herself," this time in rural Ireland with a man named Alejandro. What Jessie expected to find there besides Guinness and potatoes was anyone's guess, but Daisy had long since stopped asking. She had enough problems of her own.

Lunch had been weirdly civil, mostly because Jessie had reinvented herself again. Her latest personality was built entirely around eating organic, which meant Daisy had to endure a fully plant-based menu in the quirkiest, dingiest vegan café in Chelsea. Ironic, really, given it was also the poshest postcode in London.

She'd barely had a moment to check her phone, or talk to anyone—especially not the one person she was actively avoiding.

And no, their initials did *not* begin with M this time.

Her strength was unwavering.

But all that was about to change.

Because today… the *work trip* had arrived.

Daisy had been dreading this all week, because it meant being alone—again—with Sam Callaghan.

She'd successfully avoided him since the compromising *event* in the meeting room last week.

Surprisingly, he'd been persistent. Not in an overbearing way—just... nice. Extra nice. Going out of his way to talk to her, slipping little comments into conversations, trying to bridge the distance she'd stubbornly built between them. Or that *he* had built—depending on the day.

And there had been moments—late at night, cocooned in her safe little bubble—when she'd almost caved.

When his texts popped up like landmines on her lock screen.

Please can I see you.

Please let me explain.

I miss you so much.

I just want to hold you.

But no.

She was Daisy Number One now. She was not weak.

And she would be damned if she let Sam Callaghan—with his stupidly perfect face and infuriatingly persuasive words—break her resolve.

Not this time.

At the airport, Daisy scanned the crowds—no sign of Sam. Good. She was putting off the inevitable, but she'd take every minute she could before being mentally and emotionally tortured.

She had an excellent idea. She hurried to the check-in desk, praying to whatever gods of air travel existed.

"Hi, I was wondering if there's *any* way I could change my seat?"

The woman shook her head. "Sorry, the flight's fully booked."

Daisy leaned in, hopeful. "Are you sure? Maybe someone could swap?"

"I'm afraid not. Sorry."

Balls.

She stormed off toward the nearest place that sold alcohol. Just one. She was going to need a bit of liquid encouragement to even *pretend* to smile.

Then she saw him.

And he saw her.

Of course. She knew he'd be here—going to the same poxy event—but somehow it still irritated her.

Sam crossed the space between them quickly, his fingers wrapping gently around her arm. He was warm—too warm—and her traitorous body reacted instantly, setting off a frenzy of emotions she'd worked so hard to bury.

"Daisy," he said, his voice softer than she'd ever heard it. "I'm glad I found you."

She swallowed hard. "Sam." Just his name. No warmth. No eye contact.

He looked wrecked—tired, troubled—and that was all it took to chip away at her resolve.

"Please," he murmured, his hand tightening gently around hers. "Can we just… be okay? We'll talk later, I swear. But right now, can we just—" He paused, eyes searching hers, his voice nearly breaking. "Can we just be together?"

Daisy exhaled shakily. Damn him and his soft eyes. His cracked voice. His bloody vulnerability.

"Fine," she whispered. "Okay."

His grip loosened, the tension in his shoulders easing instantly. When she finally looked up, he gave her a slow, lingering kiss on the cheek. The scent of him flooded her senses, and all her carefully built resolve vanished into thin air. Bollocks.

"I've missed you so much," he whispered against her ear.

Her breath caught, and before she could stop herself, she pulled him into a hug. His arms wrapped around her, his head tucked into the crook of her neck as he pressed soft kisses along her skin. She stroked his hair, letting them both stay there—just standing in the middle of the airport, holding on.

She felt him smile against her shoulder, and when he pulled back, those sea-blue eyes were full of something she couldn't quite name.

She melted. Kissed him—just a quick one—before reality snapped back like an elastic band.

"Don't think you've gotten away with this, Callaghan. I want answers later. I mean it."

His grin widened. "I promise I'll explain everything later. At the hotel."

"You'd better stick to your word, Sam. I mean it."

He chuckled—the sound of *Feisty Daisy* returning. "Let's get a drink."

He took her hand, and they headed for the nearest bar.

A few drinks later, Daisy was relaxed as they settled into their seats. The plane was small—just two across. She felt a pang of guilt about trying to switch earlier.

Sam shrugged off his jacket, placing it in the overhead locker, and she caught herself watching the way his shirt stretched across his shoulders and arms. Then her gaze drifted lower.

He caught her.

She looked away, blushing furiously.

Sam smirked as he sat down beside her, comfortably sprawling into his space. She didn't even mind.

"What are you blushing at?"

"Just… too much wine," she lied.

He took her hand, entwining their fingers, resting them on his thigh. Her pulse kicked up several notches.

"You know," she said quietly, "I actually tried to change seats earlier, when I was still mad at you."

He looked at her, mock-offended. "Harsh."

"I was *quite* mad."

"Well, I'm glad you didn't." His trademark smile flickered.

Oh, Daisy was done for.

"Are you still mad?" he asked softly, the playfulness gone. A flicker of regret passed across his face.

"A bit," she admitted.

"I'm sorry, Dais. For being… complicated. I am trying."

"Try harder. Please."

He rolled his eyes, smiling. "I will. Promise."

Before she could reply, the cabin crew began their safety checks, and the plane started to taxi.

That's when she noticed it.

Sam—who had spent the last half-hour being his usual cocky, confident self—suddenly went rigid. He gripped her hand tighter as the engines roared, eyes squeezed shut, jaw clenched.

Sam Callaghan was afraid of flying.

Daisy's heart softened instantly.

She lifted their joined hands to her lips, pressing a kiss to his knuckles. His eyes opened, meeting hers, and she gave him a reassuring smile. Slowly, he let out a breath.

She pulled him closer, resting his head against her shoulder, kissing the top of his soft, dark-blonde hair as her fingers brushed gently through it.

He sighed against her, eyes closing again, finally letting himself lean into her.

And in that quiet moment, he knew—he had to let the walls down.
He had to give her more.

Because this—her, them, right now—was exactly where he wanted to be.

They arrived at the hotel late. Too late for dinner, though thankfully the bar was still open.

Sam handled check-in while Daisy lingered a few steps behind, half-listening.

The receptionist looked up, eyes flicking between them before asking, "Would you like just the one room? You've got two booked. We can cancel one free of charge."

Sam hesitated. "There are two of us."

"Oh—apologies. I thought you were together. Just trying to save your budget. My mistake."

"Oh. Right." Sam paused again, momentarily glancing over his shoulder to gauge Daisy's reaction. Then he stopped himself.

Rhoda would ask questions if they only booked one. And Daisy—well, she might see it as presumptuous. Or worse—manipulative.

The last thing he wanted was to piss her off. Again.

But Daisy had heard every word.

He returned, handing her one of the key cards.

She hesitated. "Oh." realising that she didn't want to be in a room *on her own.*

"What's wrong?"

"Nothing."

Immediately, he caught it—the flicker of disappointment across her face. Smirking, he tilted his head. "She asked if we wanted just the one room. I figured you wouldn't like that, but I can go back if you'd rather share?"

Daisy's lips parted. "Well… if it helps with budget, I don't mind sharing."

What on earth was she saying?

His smirk widened. "Okay then."

He turned back to the desk. "Actually, we'll just take one room, if that's alright."

The receptionist smiled knowingly. "Of course, sir. Not a problem. I'll adjust the booking."

Sam nodded, feeling oddly warm under her gaze. As she finished updating the record, she paused.

"Room 405 might be more comfortable for two of you," she suggested, sliding across a different key card.

"Perfect," he said smoothly, flashing a grin before heading back to Daisy.

He took it without thinking, feeling one step behind the whole situation.

"Oh—and if you'd like to grab a drink before the bar closes," the receptionist added, "our concierge can take your bags up for you."

"That would be wonderful." His voice softened into that easy charm.. "You've been a great help."

"My pleasure."

He turned back to Daisy, dangling the new key between two fingers. "Sorted."

She arched a brow. "Indeed. Drink?"

He took her hand automatically.

"What about the—" She glanced back to see the concierge already whisking their luggage away. "Oh."

That was… convenient.

And then it hit her, all at once—she'd just agreed to share a room. With Sam.

He was going to see her without makeup, in pyjamas, probably with morning hair and a spot on her chin.

Too late now.

They perched at the sleek hotel bar, sipping two very nice, very overpriced cocktails. The tension between them had eased—shoulders relaxed, laughter flowing again—and Daisy had even started enjoying herself.

Sam, though, had grown quieter. Not absent, just thoughtful. The kind of silence that carried weight. She could tell he was fighting himself, running through the words he didn't quite know how to say.

"Sam," she said gently.

He looked up, wary.

"So… you said we'd talk."

He straightened, thumb brushing along his jaw again—a nervous tic she'd come to recognise. "Yeah. I know. I owe you that."

She hesitated. "I can tell it's hard for you. Whatever this is… it's not about me, is it?"

His eyes flicked up, startled. "No. Daisy. God, no."

Then, without another word, he reached into his pocket and pulled something out. A small, worn token.

She frowned slightly until he placed it in her hand. A St Christopher pendant. Old. Weathered. Familiar somehow.

"My best friend gave it to me," he said quietly. "Years ago."

Her lips parted. "Your best friend? You've never mentioned—"

"He's…" Sam swallowed hard, eyes darting away. "He's not here anymore."

Her breath caught. The simplicity of it made it worse—the way he said it, small and stripped bare. He didn't need to elaborate. The loss was written all over him.

He looked down at his drink. "I'll explain, I promise. Just… not here."

Suddenly, the bar felt too loud, too bright, too full of people who didn't belong in this moment.

She placed the pendant carefully on the table and rested a hand on his arm.

"Let's finish these and go upstairs," she said softly. "We can talk properly."

He blinked at her, almost surprised—but grateful. "You sure?"

"Yes." She smiled faintly, resting her chin in her hand. "I've actually really enjoyed today."

He reached for her, pulling her stool closer until their knees brushed. His hands found her thighs, warm and steady, but he didn't kiss her right away. Instead he studied her, something unreadable in his eyes.

"Have I told you..." his voice dropped, almost a whisper, "...how incredible you are, Daisy Donaldson?"

Daisy giggled. "Actually, no, I don't think you have."

"Well," he murmured, "you're one of the most incredible women I've ever met."

Her face flushed hot. She bit her lip. The words tumbled out before she could stop them.

"Have there been a lot?"

She instantly regretted it. Classic Daisy. Too intrusive. Too soon.

But to her surprise, his response was immediate.

"There haven't, actually." He smirked, that familiar cocky edge returning. "I don't normally do relationships, remember?"

Normally.

One word.

A single, tiny word that she clung to with everything she had.

Daisy leaned in and kissed him, tasting lime and rum on his lips, letting the thought settle somewhere deep inside her.

Several cocktails later, they stumbled into their hotel room—giddy, flushed, and far too giggly for two supposed professionals on a work trip.

They probably should have paced themselves. Luckily, the event wasn't until 2 p.m. tomorrow, and the earliest they were needed was midday.

Sam closed the door behind them, glancing around. The room was sleek, spacious, and dominated by a queen-sized bed. He immediately understood why the receptionist had suggested switching keys.

Daisy barely had time to process it before he was on her.

Their earlier conversation slipped into the background like mist.

She told herself it could wait. She'd get her explanation. But right now, she just wanted him—warm, real, *hers.*

One moment, they were standing across the dimly lit room, breathless and buzzed; the next, clothes were flying—her jumper over her head, his shirt half-unbuttoned before she gave up and yanked it open, buttons scattering like confetti.

"Erm, I really liked that shirt," he muttered between laughs.

Daisy giggled. "I'll buy you another."

Their mouths crashed together—messy, hot, all tongue and teeth and laughter. The kind of kiss that made thinking impossible. That made her forget the days of silence, the doubt gnawing at her chest.

Right now, there was only him—his hands in her hair, his lips at her throat, his body pressing hers down into the mattress like gravity itself had taken sides.

This was the first time they'd been drunk together, and it showed.

Everything was bolder. Sloppier. Louder. She squealed as he fumbled with her bra strap, swatted him when he nearly toppled off the bed trying to kick off his trousers. But the laughter dissolved into gasps when he finally entered her with a groan that sounded like surrender.

They moved together like they'd been waiting all week for this—for the heat, the release, the closeness.

It was fast. Frenzied. Raw.

Daisy clung to him, nails digging into his back, lips at his ear whispering his name like a secret only she was allowed to keep. Sam held her tight, his mouth everywhere—her neck, her shoulder, the hollow beneath her collarbone—as if he couldn't decide where to land, couldn't get enough of her skin.

And when it was over, they collapsed—a tangle of limbs, sweat-slicked skin, and breathless laughter.

She tucked her face into the crook of his neck, her heart still racing. Sam's hand drifted lazily down her spine, slow and reverent, as though he were trying to memorise her one stroke at a time. Every dip, every freckle, every soft curve he'd ached for.

Daisy's breathing evened out, her body melting into his.

He pressed a kiss to her forehead, exhaling deeply. Then it hit him—She was everything.

He couldn't wait another second. She had to know.

"So, Daisy," he said softly, stroking her shoulder. "Here's the thing…"

Oh God. Here it comes.

He was struggling, and now Daisy almost didn't want to know. She was so blissfully happy—wrapped in their little bubble of warmth—that she didn't want reality crashing in to ruin it.

But they couldn't stay here forever.

And she knew Sam Callaghan. Sooner or later, he'd go back to being cold, guarded, emotionally unreachable. She was on borrowed time.

But maybe now, if he did open up, she'd finally understand why.

She sat up, brushing her hair back and wrapping her arms gently around him. It seemed to help.

"When I was nineteen, I was in an accident," he said quietly. "But that wasn't the worst thing that happened that year."

He swallowed hard. "My best friend… Lewis. He was in the same accident. And he died."

"Oh God. Sam, I'm so sorry." Daisy's expression softened. "Was that the accident? The leg?"

He nodded, giving a half-smile. "Yeah. Quad bike. We were both on it—it hit a tree. I was injured, but Lewis… he was driving, drunk, and he died instantly."

She took his hand. He kept going.

"I really struggled with it," he admitted. "Watching my best friend die and not being able to help because I couldn't move. I just… had to watch him die." His voice cracked.

"I can't imagine," Daisy murmured, watching his eyes glisten. She squeezed his hand tighter without thinking.

"I guess you could say I never really got over it," he said quietly. "As if it wasn't bad enough that it ended my football career—it had to take my best mate too. We'd been inseparable since we were five. Losing him was… brutal."

He sighed, head resting against her shoulder, the silence heavy but intimate.

"I'm sorry you lost him, Sam," she said softly. "That must've been awful. If I lost Prim or Lyd… I can't even—just… I get it now."

He nodded slowly. "You see, that's why I struggle with my emotions—with love. The day Lewis died, my heart broke. I went off the rails. Hard. For two and a half years, actually. My whole future—everything I'd worked for—was gone in an instant. I'd just gone pro, Dais. I had other offers lined up. My dad was obsessed with it. He'd pushed me into football my entire life. And when it all disappeared overnight… he was furious. Not sad. Not worried. Just angry."

Daisy frowned. "Angry with you? But you were in an accident…"

"He needed someone to blame. And I was the easiest target," Sam said bitterly. "He told me I'd thrown it all away. That I shouldn't have been with Lewis. That Lewis was a bad influence. After that, he couldn't even look at me. And my mum—she just went quiet. Like we all had to pretend nothing happened.

"So yeah… we don't really talk anymore. Not unless it's Christmas or someone's birthday. Or they want something."

Daisy squeezed his hand, her chest tight.

"I made a promise to myself back then—no relationships. No close friendships. No falling in love. That way, I wouldn't get hurt again.”

“Sam, you were nineteen,” Daisy said gently. “That’s not a great plan to carry into adulthood.”

“I know, Daisy. But you don’t understand. You weren’t there. You didn’t feel that pain.”

“No, I suppose not.” She looked at him—*really* looked at him.

“But eventually,” she said softly, “you have to let your guard down. You deserve to be happy. And Lewis—if he was your best friend—he would’ve wanted that too, wouldn’t he?”

Sam exhaled, long and heavy. “He would have,” he admitted quietly. His eyes dropped to the floor for a moment before lifting back to hers. “But the headspace I was in… honestly, I just thought, what’s the point? I hadn’t met anyone who made me feel like that again. It’s hard to even let myself feel.”

Daisy’s heart twisted. Partly for herself and partly for him. Mostly for him.

He looked so raw in that moment—sad and broken and utterly unguarded. Like a boy still carrying the weight of something he’d never put down.

She’d always known there were walls with Sam. He was brilliant at pretending otherwise—with the jokes, the flirtation, the frustrating habit of disappearing emotionally just when things got too real.

But now it all made sense. The mixed signals. The retreating and returning. The way he could hold her so tightly and still somehow seem like he was somewhere else entirely.

It was because he was afraid—afraid of loving something, *someone*, and losing it again.

He looked at her then, eyes searching, something almost desperate in them.

“Does it make sense now?” he asked quietly. “Do I make sense?”

"A bit more," she whispered.

He gave a soft laugh, a lopsided smile tugging at his lips. "I'm glad I told you."

"I'm glad you told me too."

Daisy smiled, but her chest felt tight. She still wanted more—more clarity, more reassurance, more *him*—but she didn't dare push. Not now. Not when he'd just handed her the most fragile part of himself.

So instead, she stayed still. Let the silence say the things they couldn't.

What she didn't realise was that Sam was thinking the exact same thing.

He wanted to say it—that she was it for him. That he didn't know how he'd gone from locking the world out to suddenly *needing* her like air.

He wanted desperately to let her love him.

But the words stuck somewhere between his heart and his mouth, tangled in pride and fear and years of silence.

So instead, he kissed her.

And this time, it wasn't teasing or hurried or filled with heat. It was something else entirely.

It was slow. Anchored.

It felt like truth.

And as his lips pressed to hers, Sam realised—horribly, brilliantly, irrevocably—that he was vulnerable.

That she was everything.

And that he was absolutely, completely fucked.

The event itself went without a hitch. Daisy and Sam made a surprisingly good team, slipping into their roles with seamless ease.

From the outside, they looked every bit the polished pair—Sam in a crisp white shirt with his sleeves rolled just enough to show a hint of muscle, Daisy in high-waisted tailored trousers and a silk cami, her dark bob styled into effortless waves.

It was a good job they'd patched things up—well, mostly—otherwise it could have been a disaster.

Their chemistry didn't go unnoticed. If anything, it only enhanced their performance. The clients were charmed, engaged, hanging on every word.

And Daisy? She'd spent most of the evening subtly eye-fucking Sam across canapés and cocktails.

And he knew it.

He was cockier than usual, like a weight had been lifted. That familiar smirk tugged at the corner of his mouth every time their eyes met—which, infuriatingly, made him even hotter.

When he refilled her wine glass without asking, fingers brushing hers just a little too long, she had to look away to stop herself grinning like an idiot.

As the last client disappeared into the lift, Daisy sat at the bar waiting for him to settle the bill. Her phone buzzed.

Lance: *How did it go?*

Daisy: *Really good. Yours?*

Lance: *Yeah, good. Hold on—how was it fine? You and Sam were at loggerheads. No drama?*

Daisy: *No drama, soz. We might have made up last night. Twice.*

Lance: *Jesus, Dais. You don't hang about. I'm kind of gutted there's no drama—because I'm literally living for it. But happy you sorted it.*

Daisy: *Wait, I'll call you tomorrow. He's coming back.*

Lance: *You better, you hussy. I need details. Very intricate ones.*

Daisy laughed softly at her phone just as Sam returned.

"Ready?"

"Yep." She hopped off her stool, but before she could take a step, Sam grabbed her by the waist, his hand sliding down to her arse, pulling her into him and stealing her breath with another mind-melting kiss.

She would never get tired of that.

"Thought we might skip dinner and talk back at the hotel… room?" He raised an eyebrow, smirking.

"Oh, did you?" she teased. "Well, I am kind of hungry."

"Daisy, don't think I haven't noticed you've been trying to undress me with your eyes for the last two hours. It's been absolute torture."

"Okay, fine. But we eat after."

"It's a promise. I can be quick," he groaned, kissing her neck.

Daisy glanced around the room instinctively, still not entirely used to public displays of affection. She hadn't exactly had Sam Callaghan down as the PDA type.

"Can you?" she teased.

"Sounds like a challenge."

"Come on," she giggled, taking his hand as he held the door open for her, his fingers grazing her lower back as they walked out into the night.

Later, in their hotel room, they lay tangled in post-coital bliss, limbs intertwined beneath crumpled sheets. Sam held her close, fingers tracing lazy lines along her spine, while Daisy drew small circles on the back of his hand.

She was trying—really trying—not to let her feelings spiral, to keep her head clear. But he was making that impossible.

Then he spoke.

"I love this. Being here with you. And only you."

She turned towards him, brushing her lips softly against his before pulling back slightly, her gaze catching his.

Did he just say *love*? That was definitely something they'd be circling back to.

"Me too," she whispered.

She rested her head against his chest, the rhythm of his heartbeat syncing with her own. One of his hands slid slowly through her hair, the other warm and steady on her thigh. For a long time, neither of them spoke.

It felt quiet. Safe.

Too safe.

She shifted slightly, enough to see his face. "Hey," she murmured. "Can I ask you something?"

His eyes met hers—open, unafraid. "Of course."

"Last night… when you said you couldn't have a relationship— or didn't want one—was that just fear talking? Or did you mean it?"

Sam let out a long, heavy breath, as if he'd been holding it for hours.

"It was fear," he admitted. "And pride. And… maybe panic. Because I don't want to mess this up by wanting it too much."

She frowned. "Wanting what too much?"

"Us," he said simply.

Daisy sighed, thoughtful, still not quite getting the answers she needed.

Then he reached out, brushing his thumb along her cheek, his gaze steady.

"Last night, when I said I'd never met anyone who made me feel like that… I should've said more."

"Like what?"

He paused, then said quietly, "What I meant was—until I met you."

Her heart jolted, awful and wonderful all at once. The pieces were clicking.

He hadn't been pushing her away because he didn't care.

He'd been pushing her away because he *did*.

"So you *do* want me?" she whispered.

"Daisy, I wanted you—believe me, I wanted you. I just… when I met you, everything shifted. I couldn't explain it, and I didn't want to. I told myself I wasn't built for relationships, but you kept pulling me back in."

"Okay.." She laughed softly, and he smiled.

"I'm still figuring out how to… do this," he continued. "I've never had a proper relationship. I don't know the rules. I don't even know if I want the rules. But I do want you. I want something."

She drew in a shaky breath. "What are you saying?"

"I'm saying I want to be with you," he said. "Let's just… take it slow, yeah? No labels. Nothing too serious. Just… us. If you want that too."

He pulled her into his lap, bare skin to bare skin, warmth blooming between them.

Daisy hesitated. It wasn't the grand declaration she'd once imagined. It wasn't certainty.

But it was something—a start. A door slightly ajar.

And for now, that was enough.

"Okay," she said softly. "I think."

A hush settled between them again—not awkward, just charged. Intimate. Real.

"Yeah… so," he said after a moment, voice quieter now, "there's one more thing I should mention."

Daisy stilled. "That sounds ominous. You're not secretly married, are you?"

"God, no. Worse," he said with a dry smile. "My parents are getting divorced."

She blinked. "What? After all that?"

He glanced down. "My dad told me the night you were at Prim's bridal shower. They invited me to dinner,which they *never* do, so I should've known something was up. After the meal, he kicked Mum out of the room and just… dropped it."

Daisy's stomach turned. "Oh, Sam…" Then it clicked. "That's why you said something came up. Why you were the way you were when you came to mine."

"Yep. Sorry about that. I should've told you." He gave a disbelieving laugh. "Said he'd been seeing someone. And—well— she's pregnant."

"Wow." She reached for his hand. "That's… Jesus. That's a lot."

"Yeah," he said quietly, jaw tight. "They've never exactly been warm and fuzzy, but it still hit me sideways. My mum had no idea. And my dad just tossed it out there like a casual update—'by the way, your life is a lie.'"

Daisy squeezed his hand. "Is that why you've been so… distant? Cold? Bit of a prick?"

"Probably," he admitted. "I wanted to tell you that night. I nearly did. But I was *this* close to spiralling, and I didn't want to drag you into it. Not when I'm already really bloody complicated."

"You can always drag me into it," she said gently.

He looked at her then—really looked—and something in his expression softened. "I'm starting to get that," he murmured.

She rested her head on his shoulder. "You know, I hate that they pushed you into accounting. Not because you're not brilliant at it, but because you should've had a choice."

He gave a dry laugh. "Yeah. My dad was furious when football ended. Not that I'd been through hell or anything—no, he was just pissed I'd 'wasted potential.' Never quite forgave me. So the accounting? Just another compromise. Even now, he's trying to get me to join his firm." He rolled his eyes. "Which I have *zero* interest in doing."

Daisy lifted her head, meeting his gaze. "You deserved better."

His smile came slow this time, starting in his eyes. "Yeah, well… maybe I've finally found it."

Daisy smiled back, her heart softening. She reached to the bedside table and picked up the small St. Christopher pendant. "Here," she said, holding it out to him. "I think you should wear this. Lewis gave it to you. He'd want you to. Maybe he thought you needed a bit of extra protection."

Sam looked at the pendant, then back at her. His expression softened further as he chuckled. "You think he thought I needed protection from my own family?"

"I think you need protection from yourself," she teased.

He studied her for a moment, then smiled faintly. "You know, I think *you* should wear it."

Daisy blinked, surprised. "Me?"

"Yeah." He took the pendant from her and placed it gently in her palm. "I know it was his, but I think it might do you some good too. You've been protecting me for a while now. Maybe it's time it works both ways."

She stared at the pendant, then at him, her heart swelling with something deeper than words. Slowly, she nodded and slipped it around her neck. "Alright. I'll wear it. But only because you insist."

He smiled, watching her with a look that said everything he didn't. "Good. I think Lewis would approve."

They kissed, and this time it felt different—grounded, full of promise.

His hands slid up her back, drawing her closer, and she melted into him with a sigh. The warmth between them stirred again, quick and hungry—but just as it threatened to spiral, Daisy pulled back with a breathless laugh.

"I'm starving," she said. "Can we *please* eat now?"

Sam groaned, burying his face in her neck. "There's just one more urgent matter to attend to first." He grinned, pressing his hips against hers in a way that left no doubt what he meant.

Daisy smirked. "Well, you did bare your soul. I suppose it's the least I can do."

"Oh, is that so?" he murmured, arching a brow before flipping her effortlessly onto her back, pinning her with a playful growl.

She squealed, laughter bubbling from her chest.

God, she was in trouble with this man.

But for once, she didn't mind one bit.

They eventually peeled themselves out of bed, slipping into the hotel robes and raiding the overpriced mini-bar while waiting for room service. Daisy gathered snacks onto a tray—crisps, peanuts, chocolate bars—before collapsing beside Sam on the wide window ledge, where the city lights flickered below like a glittering sea.

Sam laughed. "I don't think I've ever seen a girl eat that much. Like a rabid animal."

She smirked, taking a sip of warm white wine from a tiny bottle.

"Okay, I'm officially human again. Now—where were we before I distracted you with my overwhelming sexual charisma?"

"Hmm… I think it was the other way around, but I'll let you have it."

"Cheeky." She winked. "Not my fault I don't have abs." She frowned lightly.

Sam let out a soft laugh and actually blushed, avoiding her gaze.

"Thank you, Daisy," he said quietly. "For being patient with me when I know you didn't want to be."

Before she could reply, a knock came at the door.

"Room service," Sam announced, like it was divine intervention.

Daisy watched as he padded over, collected the tray, and returned like a hero from a quest—with burgers, fries, a mini chocolate cake and two large glasses of chilled wine.

"You absolute legend," she grinned.

They dug in—bare-legged, cozy in their robes—food spread across the duvet like a royal feast.

"You're lucky I'm a sucker for emotionally repressed accountants," she mumbled through a mouthful of chips.

"And you're lucky I'm deeply obsessed with chaotic women with mental French Bulldogs," he replied, clinking his glass against hers.

And for once, the world outside didn't matter.

Chapter 21:
He was just 'A one' September 2015

Daisy stared into her teacup like it might offer her some sort of an answer. As if the swirling milk could somehow spell out a solution to the mess brewing in her head.

She hated it when she got stuck in her own thoughts, but this time, she was siding with them. Sensible Daisy had shown up for once.

She knew she had to do this. She couldn't carry on a relationship, keep pretending—not when they were in completely different places, physically, emotionally, in every possible way. As much as she really loved Matthew, it wasn't fair to him. And it wasn't fair to her either.

His parents had never truly wanted them together. Daisy had always sensed their disapproval—disguised as politeness, but unmistakable. They never encouraged the relationship. And after three years, it was clear: it wasn't really going anywhere.

Not that Daisy had minded. It's not like they were about to get married.

Still, she'd wanted to be with him. Always. Because she loved him.

And yet, something had always felt… off. She could never quite put her finger on it.

She nodded to herself. *Yes, I have to do this. Come on, Daisy. Set him free.*

"Daze, you okay? You sounded a bit weird on the phone."

Matthew slid into the booth beside her at the café, wrapping her in a hug and pressing kisses to her cheek and lips.

Okay. Bad start.

"It's nothing. Don't worry. Shall we eat?" She kissed him back anyway.

Nope. She definitely couldn't do it here. Not in a greasy spoon with Suspicious Sue and Dodgy Dave eavesdropping from the next table. She was definitely going to cry, and she didn't need an audience for that. Terrible idea, Daisy.

They ate in silence.

"So, Daze," Matthew said at last, nudging her, utterly oblivious. "Want to come back to mine? Parents are out." He winked.

And Daisy—traitor to her own plan—agreed.

Brilliant. You were supposed to break up with him, not shag him.

But the truth was, she wanted him. One last moment of closeness. One last memory before letting go. Just once more.

Back at his house, everything felt different. The urgency they'd always had was gone. Instead, it was slow, tender—loving. He undressed her gently, kissed her skin with care, and Daisy felt closer to him than she had in months. Maybe ever.

It was as if he knew. Somehow, deep down, he *knew* this was the last time.

He laid her down, kissing every part of her until she laughed in the spots it tickled. But deep inside, she was crying. Because she knew she was losing him.

Their bodies moved together, slow at first, then faster, breaths heavier, still wrapped in tenderness. And when they finally came together, a quiet sob escaped her. She tried to brush the tears away.

Matthew noticed.

"Daze? Are you… crying?"

She couldn't speak.

"It's just—"

He sat up, panic flickering. "We've done this a thousand times and you've never bloody cried. Have I lost my touch?" He tried to joke, but she didn't laugh.

She curled under the blanket, arms around her knees.

"Wait—have you cheated on me?"

"No, Matthew. I would never."

"Then what is it?" He paused. And then it hit him. "You're ending it, aren't you? Because of uni."

She nodded, tears sliding down her cheeks. "Yes, Matthew. We have to. You know this. I love you. I don't want to, but—"

He grabbed her hands. "No *buts*. You can't do this. I won't let you. I love you."

"Matthew, you know this is the right thing. I'm leaving Monday."

"Do you know how much I fucking love you, Daze? It's breaking my heart that you want to end this."

"Don't you think it's breaking mine too?" she snapped. "You're going to Edinburgh. I'm going to Bournemouth. That's practically opposite ends of the country. I just... I don't see how this can work."

He stilled. His face fell.

"Yeah. You're right. I don't either. But can't we at least try?"

Her tears came harder. "I don't think so. It's better this way. A clean start."

He didn't fight. Didn't argue. He just... accepted it. And that's when Daisy realised—maybe he didn't *want* to fight for it. Maybe he was okay with letting her go.

"Well," he said softly, "if this is what you want..." He hesitated. "But please—don't leave yet. Not right now."

He pulled her gently back into bed, holding her close.

"Just stay with me a bit longer."

They lay like that, wrapped around each other. Daisy didn't

remember how long. But she remembered that after that day, her heart never quite felt the same.

She never felt that way again.

Not until now.

Not until Sam.

When she held him on the plane.

When he told her he loved her.

When he looked broken—and she realised he needed her more than anyone ever had.

And in that moment, Daisy finally understood:

Matthew wasn't *the* one.

He was just *a* one.

Chapter 22:
A cause for celebration

Returning to work that Thursday felt oddly surreal. Not bad—just different, like someone had subtly rearranged the furniture in her brain. Everything looked the same, but nothing quite was.

Of course, Daisy knew that she and Sam were in *something*. A situationship. No labels.

Even Sam knew.

But nobody else did.

That was all about to change.

Lance was hovering. Lance *always* knew.

"Daisy Donaldson, you elusive minx," he hissed, dropping into the seat beside her. "Will you *please* tell me what the hell is going on between you and Sam already? I can't take it."

She feigned nonchalance, typing on her laptop. "How do you know something's going on?"

Lance scoffed. "Because you said you made up. Twice. And because of the way you two keep eye-fucking across the office. You're not subtle, babes. I need details."

Not the eye-fucking again.

She really needed to stop that. It was becoming a problem.

But she couldn't—not now. Not after finally opening Pandora's box and discovering exactly what lay beneath Sam Callaghan's crisp shirts and tailored suits. She'd spent months secretly fantasising, ogling, wondering what he was like underneath it all—his skin, his thoughts, the way he kissed when he wasn't holding back—and now she was expected to pretend he was just her arrogant work crush, nothing more?

Impossible.

The memories were still too fresh. His hands on her waist. That lazy smile. The way he looked at her when he thought she wasn't paying attention. The sound he made when she ran her fingers through his hair.

She shifted in her chair and tried not to combust.

"Okay," she muttered, keeping her voice low. "But not here. After work, we can have drinks."

"Oh god, you *best believe* we're having drinks." Lance clapped his hands, gleeful little gossip that he was. "I want *all* the filthy details."

Daisy rolled her eyes and grabbed her phone.

Daisy: *Lyds, are you free tonight for drinks? You, me, Lance. I have loads—like, LOADS—to catch you up on x*

No reply.

She stared at the screen for a second too long, then locked it. It had been a few weeks since the bridal shower. She'd spoken to Lydia here and there—texted about nonsense, replied to memes—but she hadn't *seen* her. Not properly. And if she was honest, she missed her.

She assumed Lydia had picked up another gig. But something felt… off. Lydia always replied straight away, even if it was a half-asleep voice note from the loo or a string of emojis that made zero sense.

She decided she'd call her at lunch. Maybe Lydia would laugh it off. Maybe she was hungover again or in another existential spiral about her career. Normal Lydia things.

Before she could spiral too far down that rabbit hole, someone cleared their throat.

Daisy looked up.

Sam.

Oh god. Okay. This was new. And bold.

He stood at her desk, hands in his pockets, looking infuriatingly attractive and far too pleased with himself. His hair was still damp from the rain outside, his tie loosened just enough to hint at mischief.

"Hey," he said casually. Like he wasn't completely upending her nervous system by existing.

"Hey," she echoed, forcing her expression into something neutral. She glanced around. So far, they were safe—no one was paying attention. Except maybe Lance, who was pretending to study a spreadsheet but was absolutely eavesdropping.

"I was wondering if you wanted to get lunch today?" Sam said. "Before the debrief this afternoon?"

The corners of her mouth twitched. She tried not to smile. Failed.

"Sure."

"12:30 okay?" he asked, tapping something absent-mindedly on the edge of her desk.

"Yes, Sam," she replied, voice deliberately calm as she bit her lip.

He smirked, leaning in just slightly to whisper, "You're going to give us away if you keep looking at me like that. You know I can't resist it."

Oh, for god's sake.

The hairs on the back of her neck stood up.

And then he was gone, striding away like he hadn't just detonated her entire morning.

Arrogant. Beautiful. Slightly flushed.

She stared at her screen, pretending to read a document while her pulse tried to regulate itself.

Lunchtime rolled around quicker than she expected.

Amazing how much work she could get done—and how fast the time went—when she was actively trying to distract herself.

Daisy had powered through two reports, replied to every email in her inbox (even the annoying one from Bina in HR), and colour-coded her calendar like she was some hyper-efficient corporate goddess instead of a woman trying not to think about sex in a hotel room.

For god's sake, Daisy. Get a grip.

Then her work chat pinged.

LD: *Any lunch plans, sweetness?*

DD: *Er... yes, actually. Sorry.*

LD: *You're ditching me for SC already? You dirty cow.*

DD: *How did you know?*

LD: *I know you, Dais. This better not become a regular thing or I'll have to murder him.*

DD: *It won't, I promise. It's just... needed today.*

LD: *If this wasn't a work chat, you KNOW what I'd be calling you...*

Daisy stifled a laugh.

Another ping.

SC: *Ready? Meet you by the lifts in two?*

DD: *Yep. Can't wait!*

Can't wait? Oh, Daisy—come on.

And the exclamation mark? Nothing screamed desperate like rogue punctuation.

She was on a roll today. If that roll was a wheel of cheese barreling down a hill in the Highlands.

She stood, grabbing her bag, already flustered—just as Sam

appeared, walking straight toward her.

He cleared his throat.

"Hi," he said, voice low.

Daisy turned slightly, arching a brow. "Hi? That's all I get after last night?"

Sam smirked, glancing sideways. "Well, I'd say more, but you—"

He cut off as Sheena joined them in the lift. She didn't say much—she never did—but you could practically *hear* the questions ticking behind her eyes.

They all settled into silence. The kind thick with unspoken things.

Daisy wanted to dive into his arms. Kiss that maddening, smug face. Kick Sheena out and press every single floor button just to buy them more time. Instead, she stood perfectly still beside him, clutching her bag like it might anchor her to reality.

They settled for smirks and stolen glances.

The second they were out of sight—through the doors, past reception, into the cool city air—Sam grabbed her hand and pulled her into an empty doorway.

And smashed his lips onto hers.

His hands slid beneath her coat, pulling her flush against him, fingers gripping her hips—desperate, like he'd been starving for her all morning.

"Oh god, that was torture," he groaned, resting his forehead against hers. "What have you done to me, Daisy?"

She laughed, breathless. "I'm not sure I can keep this up, honestly. You're just… too—well, *you*."

He raised an eyebrow. Smirked. "I think there's a compliment in there somewhere."

"Please don't do that."

"Do what?" He grinned, knowing exactly what he was doing.

"That look, argh."

She kissed him again.

They really needed to stop this.

"We should move," Sam murmured, lips still brushing hers. "Where shall we go?"

Daisy tilted her head, teasing. "How long do you have?"

"Daisy," he warned, voice low. "We have the debrief."

She sighed dramatically. "Fine. Boring lunch it is."

He laughed, leading her down the street.

At *All Bar One* on Cannon Street, Daisy slid into a booth while Sam returned with a pink gin and tonic for her and a pint for himself.

"We might need these if we're going to survive this meeting," he said, clinking his glass against hers.

She smirked. "What are you doing later?"

"Seeing you," he replied—far too cockily.

"Well, yes, but first I have drinks with Lance. You can join if you want."

Sam frowned. "Are you going to talk about me?"

"Of course."

He groaned. "Maybe I'll just meet you after."

Daisy grinned. "Scared?"

He didn't answer. Instead, he slid closer, wrapped an arm around her, cupped her face— and kissed her.

In the middle of a busy pub.

She'd said it before, but she really hadn't taken Sam Callaghan for a PDA man.

Right now? She was *living* for it.

Back in the office, it was straight into the meeting room and straight into *boring work mode*—when all Daisy wanted was to be back in the pub, kissing that impossibly smug, stupidly beautiful face.

Rhoda had called a post-marketing event debrief, and Daisy could already tell it was going to be hell.

She wasn't even a full day back, and she was already a hot, quivering mess.

Damn Sam Callaghan and his ridiculously fit body.

She could still feel the ghost of his hands on her skin, his lips at her neck. The weight of him. The way he had looked at her—like she was something he couldn't quite believe he finally had.

She shifted in her chair. *Nope. Not thinking about this now.*

Rhoda droned on about campaign performance metrics, brand engagement, and whatever the hell else marketing people liked to say. Daisy was barely listening.

Because Sam was sitting across from her. And she could *feel* his eyes on her.

She took a peek at him.

Big mistake.

He smirked.

And just like that, her brain was mush again.

Focus, Daisy. For the love of God, focus.

She forced herself to nod along, jot something—anything—down in her notebook. She could feel Lance watching her, eyes narrowed like he was seconds away from calling her out.

Then, because the universe was a cruel bitch, the conversation took a sharp left turn.

"Before we wrap up—any other business?" Rhoda asked, closing her laptop.

Daisy's heart sank. She knew that look.

Lance perked up immediately, beaming like an excitable child. "Oh! Yes, actually," he said, far too enthusiastically. "It's Daisy's birthday next week!"

Great.

Daisy groaned. "Lance."

"What? It's a cause for celebration!" He turned to Rhoda. "We should do something."

Rhoda looked intrigued. "A work night out?"

"Yes!" Lance agreed, a little too quickly. "It's team building. Excellent for morale."

Of course Rhoda loved this. The room hummed with agreement. Someone suggested drinks, someone else karaoke. And then bloody Sheena—who Daisy now vowed to hold a lifelong grudge against—suggested a *party*.

Daisy shrank into her chair. "No, really, it's fine—"

"Oh, don't be a misery, Daisy," Rhoda said, already pulling up her calendar. "Next Thursday, isn't it? That works."

Across the table, Sam tensed. It was subtle—no one else noticed—but Daisy did.

And so did Lance.

Her eyes flicked to Sam, catching the quick clench of his jaw, the slight curl of his fingers before he forced himself to look casual again.

Because Sam knew.

He'd remembered her birthday. He'd been planning something. Something just for her.

And now, this bloody work night out could ruin it before it even happened.

Which, to be fair, wasn't even his biggest problem.

Because somewhere, sitting on Rhoda's desk, was an invoice from Edinburgh.

With *one room* on it.

Lance, naturally, was watching Sam like a hawk.

His mouth curled into a smirk. "Ohhh," he whispered, just loud enough for Daisy and Sam to hear. "Something to say, Samuel?"

Sam rolled his eyes. "Shut up, Lance."

Lance grinned. Oh, this was going to be fun.

After the meeting, Sam cornered him near the kitchenette, making sure Daisy wasn't watching.

"What the hell do you think you're playing at?"

Lance smirked, clearly enjoying the drama. "Something you want to share, Callaghan?"

Sam sighed, rubbing the back of his neck. He hadn't planned on saying anything yet. "Well, yes… and no."

Lance folded his arms. "Oh, this should be good."

"I, uh… kind of had something planned for Daisy's birthday," Sam admitted.

Lance raised an eyebrow. "And why would you have something planned for just the two of you?"

Sam hesitated. Then exhaled. "Because—we're kind of together. She's my—she's important to me."

Lance gasped dramatically. "I *knew* it! Okay, fine, what plans have I ruined?"

"I had a private dinner booked at Seabird."

"The rooftop bar?"

Sam nodded.

Lance squealed quietly. "That's actually adorable. I'm sorry I spoiled it."

"Yeah, well."

"Actually, you can still do it. Just meet us after?"

Sam gave him a look. "How, Lance? No one knows about us. We weren't planning to announce anything yet. We just wanted to keep it… chill."

Lance's expression softened. "How much do you actually like my best friend, Callaghan? Because she's worth more than being your dirty little secret."

Sam exhaled. "It's not like that."

"Mm-hmm." Lance gave him a knowing look. "Look, you're going to have to tell people sooner or later. You can't hide forever—this office is way too small. Just… think about it."

With that, Lance walked off, leaving Sam standing there, shoulders tight with tension.

And he was right.

What the hell *was* he doing? He liked Daisy. A lot. More than a lot. So why was he acting like it was something to hide?

Before he could dwell on it, Rhoda's voice cut through his thoughts.

"You wanted to speak to me, Callaghan? I'm free now."

Shit. Time was up.

She'd seen the invoice.

He followed her into her office, tapping his leg anxiously as he sat down.

Rhoda studied him, then folded her hands on the desk. "So… is there something you need to tell me? About the Edinburgh trip?

Accommodation-wise?"

Sam could lie.

Actually, no—he couldn't. Not to Rhoda.

"Is this about the invoice?" he asked carefully.

"Yes, Sam. You only had one room." She paused. "Did—you and Daisy share?"

He swallowed. "Yes. The receptionist said she'd waive the cost of the second room, so I—"

"But why share?" Rhoda pressed. "Is there something going on between you two?"

He ran a hand through his hair. "Yes. I'm sorry. I should have told you."

Rhoda sighed—but her expression wasn't as stern as he'd expected. "How long?"

"It only recently became… something. But, I guess, a while."

"You should have mentioned it." She exhaled. "I get it, but you sharing a room on a work trip—it's not professional, Sam. I wouldn't normally allow it."

"I'm sorry. It was just to save costs—"

"Sam." She cut him off gently. "It's not about cost. It's about etiquette. I appreciate the honesty, though. And I'm not going to stop you from seeing each other. Just… be careful, okay?"

He nodded, shoulders loosening slightly.

"I like you both as part of this team," Rhoda added. "I'd hate for something to happen and, God forbid, I lose one of you. I don't want Brandish to be a casualty."

"Understood," he said quietly.

But as he left her office, one thing was crystal clear: he needed to figure out what he *really* wanted.

Because Daisy deserved better than secrecy.

The late evening sun bounced off the glass buildings as Daisy stepped out of the office, squinting slightly as she adjusted the strap of her tote bag. For the first time in a while, she felt *good.*

Her dark bob was slightly tousled from the day, freckles peeking out under a sweep of bronzer, a pair of tortoiseshell sunglasses perched on her head like a makeshift crown.

Lance caught up, looping his arm through hers. "Come on, babes. Still no word from Lydia?"

"No, it's weird," Daisy said, frowning. "I'll call her on the way to The Alice."

"Oh, and by the way—I know about you and Sam." Lance wiggled his eyebrows. "You *should* have told me."

Daisy groaned. "How? I'm so sorry, this week's been chaos. It all happened in Edinburgh, mostly."

Lance linked arms tighter. "I want *every* gory detail—starting with how big his penis is."

"Lance." Daisy gasped, loud enough for a few people in the lobby to turn.

They both cackled as they walked off.

At *The Alice*, Daisy called Lydia.

"Lyds, we're here! You coming?"

The Alice was their usual spot—cheap for London, with a ridiculous gin selection that suited Lydia perfectly.

"I'm so sorry, Dais. I can't make it tonight."

"Oh, but we miss you."

"I miss you too."

Lance snatched the phone.

"Daisy and Sam Callaghan have been shagging for weeks, and

now she's his girlfriend."

"You are *fucking joking!*" Lydia screeched through the speaker.

"I'm not his girlfriend," Daisy said quickly, nudging Lance and yanking the phone back. "We're not… labelling it yet."

"This is huge!" Lydia laughed. "Man, I wish I was coming now."

"Me too. I'll call you tomorrow, Lyds, okay?"

"Okay, babes. Love you."

"Love you too."

"Love you!" Lance shouted over Daisy's shoulder.

They hung up, both snorting with laughter.

They found a table in the corner, and Daisy texted Sam.

Daisy: *We're at The Alice.*

Sam: *Ok. I'll be over soon. Haven't left work yet. Rhoda. Explain later.*

Oh, shit.

Lance clocked her expression instantly. "What's wrong?"

Daisy hesitated. "It's… a long story."

"Don't care. Spill."

She took a deep breath. "Okay, so last week—remember when me and Sam weren't talking?"

Lance narrowed his eyes. "Yeah. What did he do?"

Daisy cringed. "This is going to sound bad… We sort of—um—slept together. In one of the meeting rooms."

Lance spat out his drink. "*Daisy Donaldson!* At work?! Which one?"

"The small one. The two-seater."

"Two-seater?!" Lance howled. "Continue."

"Nobody was there, it was like 8 p.m., I don't even know how it happened, but it did. Then we got into an argument and didn't talk."

Lance looked *thrilled*. "Already this is the best story I've ever heard."

"So we get to the airport, and he's all sad and apologetic, and I just... couldn't stay mad at him. On the plane, he was terrified of flying, and we just—connected again. Properly this time."

"Right, right. Now get to the part where you spent two days shagging. Hopefully not in meeting rooms—"

Daisy rolled her eyes. "I told him I wasn't going to put up with his crap unless he gave me a real reason for why he'd gone all cold."

Lance took a dramatic sip. "Typical man. Go on."

"Long story short—he opened up. Really opened up. And it was... valid. You could almost see the weight lift off him. He changed overnight."

She paused, swirling her drink. "But here's the catch—he said he couldn't do a relationship. Not yet. But he did say he wanted to be with me. Asked if we could take it slow."

"And you said yes?" Lance blinked.

"Erm... yeah. Was that bad?"

"Oh, babe." He clutched his chest dramatically. "If that's what you want..."

"I do. I just—he makes me feel so—ugh." She flopped back in her seat.

Lance smiled, softer this time. "Then I'm happy for you. Genuinely."

"That oozed sarcasm."

"No, no! I mean it." He grinned. "Now—onto the important stuff. How was the sex?"

Daisy groaned, half-laughing. "Obviously amazing. But

seriously—amazing.”

“And how big is his—”

Daisy shook her head laughing.

Lance narrowed his eyes. “Well?.”

They burst into laughter just as Sam walked in.

“Why do I feel like my ears are burning?” he said, sliding into the seat next to Daisy and kissing her softly on the lips.

“Oh god, get a room,” Lance muttered. “Oh wait—you did.” He stood, grabbing his glass. “My round.”

As he walked off, Sam turned to Daisy, his tone shifting.

“So… Rhoda knows. About us.”

Daisy groaned. “The invoice. Shit. What did she say?”

“She asked if we shared a room, and I told her the truth.”

Daisy winced. “So what do we do?”

“Well…” Sam leaned in, voice low. “I told her we were… seeing how things go.”

Daisy raised an eyebrow. “*Seeing how things go?* That’s very ‘high-school crush who sits behind me in maths’ energy.”

He grinned. “Better than ‘secret office shag with no future.’”

She let out a breathy laugh, though her stomach twisted a little. “True.”

He reached for her hand under the table, lacing their fingers together. “I meant it, you know. I want this. You. Even if I don’t have the right words for it yet.”

Her heart fluttered—ridiculous, dangerous, and impossible to stop. “You’re really bad at the whole ‘no labels’ thing.”

“I know.” He looked down at their hands, thumb brushing hers. “Turns out, I kind of like having something that’s just ours.”

Daisy smiled softly. "Well, now it's not just ours. Rhoda knows. Lance knows. And give it two days, the entire office will."

Sam groaned. "Yeah, and Bina from HR will probably corner me in the lift to ask if it's serious and make us sign something."

"God forbid. Then you'd actually have to define it."

They both laughed—but a beat lingered between them. A flicker of something unsaid. Something real.

"Okay, I'm back!" Lance plopped down with three cocktails. "You both looked dangerously close to having *feelings*, so I brought margaritas. You're welcome."

Daisy grinned, clinking her glass against his. "To feelings we're not labelling."

"To situationships!" Lance toasted dramatically.

Sam just smiled, quiet but content.

And as they drank, Daisy caught his gaze—warm, unguarded—and felt that small, traitorous hope rise in her chest.

Whatever this was… it was starting to feel dangerously close to *something*.

Even if neither of them was ready to call it that. Yet.

Chapter 23:
An actual proper date this time

The following evening, at Sam's place, Daisy was pacing.

She'd been trying to reach Lydia all day, and still—nothing. Every call went to voicemail. Every text sat unread.

And now, she was spiralling.

It wasn't like Lydia to vanish—not without a sarcastic one-liner or at least a passive-aggressive meme.

Today of all days, Daisy really didn't want to be stressed. Selfish, she knew—but tonight was meant to be a *big deal*. Sam was finally taking her on a proper date. A real one.

It had been his original plan for her birthday before the team hijacked everything with a spontaneous pub crawl.

Which felt... confusing. For a man who'd only recently declared he didn't want "labels," just *casual sex and cuddles,* this was starting to feel suspiciously like the opposite of casual.

Something about them never actually having a real, intentional date made tonight feel momentous. And who was Daisy to say no to that?

She'd just perfected her winged eyeliner—freckles still visible under glowy makeup—when her phone buzzed. Lydia. Finally.

Balancing it between her shoulder and ear, Daisy slipped on her boots and gave herself a last once-over in the mirror, a nod of approval at her slinky forest-green slip dress, layered with a cropped leather jacket for a touch of edge. Her dark bob tucked behind one ear, gold hoops catching the light.

She answered quickly. "Lyds?"

"Dais… I'm sorry. I really need to talk to you. It's important. Can you meet me? Like, now? It's kind of urgent."

Daisy's stomach dropped.

"What's going on? You're scaring me."

"I… I can't explain it over the phone. I just need to see you, okay?"

Daisy hesitated, guilt already bubbling up.

"Oh God, Lydia. Are you okay? I mean—look, I can't right now.. I'm at Sam's, we're about to head out. Our first proper date. I'm sorry. Can we talk later?"

A pause. Then Lydia's voice, small: "Oh. Yeah, sure. Don't worry about it. It's fine."

It definitely wasn't fine.

"Lyds, it's okay. I'll meet you. Sam will understand."

"No, babe, really. I'll talk to Lance or something. It's nothing. Forget I said anything. Go enjoy your date with Sam."

"Lydia. I'm not leaving you like this. Where are you?"

Another pause. "Dais, please don't. It's okay. I'll—"

"Send me your location."

"Argh. Okay. Love you."

"Love you too."

Daisy ended the call just as Sam walked into the room, fastening his watch, that effortless grin forming.

"Wow," he said, eyes sweeping over her. "You look… I mean, seriously. I need a minute."

She smiled faintly but didn't move. God, why did he have to be so *unfairly cute?* It made what she was about to say so much harder.

He clocked it instantly. "Everything okay?"

She took a breath. "That was Lydia. She's not okay. She wants to meet. Said it's important."

His brow furrowed. "Is she hurt?"

"I don't know. She wouldn't say. But her voice… it didn't sound good."

For a second, his jaw tightened—the barest flicker of frustration—before he exhaled and nodded.

"Okay. Then we go."

Her head snapped up. "Wait—you'd come with me?"

"Of course not," he said with a crooked smile. "She doesn't need both of us hovering. But you should go. I'll call the restaurant and push back our reservation. I'll wait for you outside."

"Sam, you don't have to—"

"Yes, I do. You love her. She needs you. That's more important than a table and a wine list."

Daisy's throat tightened. "You're not even a little bit mad?"

He hesitated, then gave a half-smile. "Mad at the universe, maybe. I wanted tonight to be special. But we'll still have our night, Daisy. Just not at eight o'clock sharp."

Relief and affection tangled in her chest, dangerously close to spilling over.

"God, you're annoyingly decent sometimes," she muttered, blinking back tears.

"Don't tell anyone. It'll ruin my reputation." He reached for her hand, squeezing gently.

She could feel the tension still humming beneath his calm.

"Sam… are you sure about this?"

He gave a small, sheepish shrug. "It's just… tonight, I had something important to ask."

Her heart thudded. "What?"

He sighed, raking a hand through his hair. "I—nothing. It can wait."

"Sam…"

He met her eyes.

The air between them shifted—soft, heavy, charged.

Then he leaned in, pulling her close, pushing his forehead against hers.

"Its fine Daisy. Really."

"Seriously though," she whispered. "I don't think I can keep doing this casually.."

"I know," he said quietly. "Neither can I."

She exhaled. "So… where does that leave us?"

A slow smile curved at his lips. "I think… maybe it's time for a label."

Later across town, Daisy and Sam arrived at the Camden bar Lydia had sent her location from.

It was, predictably, grim — the kind of place that smelled permanently of warm beer, sticky Jägerbomb residue, and the ghosts of bad decisions past. Sam looked painfully out of place, all sharp lines and expensive aftershave, as Daisy turned to him.

"You're waiting out here, right?"

He nodded with visible relief.

Daisy had barely stepped inside before Lance materialised from the opposite side, his coat flapping like he'd been reluctantly summoned to the scene.

They locked eyes. Mutual grimace.

"Oh great," Lance muttered, surveying the sticky floors and nicotine-stained walls. "Is it *Bring Your Emotional Baggage to a*

Health Hazard Day?"

Daisy wrinkled her nose. "Honestly, I think I got a staph infection just walking in."

They shared a brief nod of solidarity.

"But we're here for Lydia," Daisy said, pulling her coat tighter.

Lance raised a brow. "Aren't you supposed to be out with Sam?"

"We had a minor detour. Long story. He's outside." She waved him off. "Let's just find her."

They spotted Lydia tucked in the back with a group of people who looked suspiciously sober for a Camden bar on a Saturday night.

The second she saw them, Lydia stood and all but ran into Daisy's arms.

Daisy hugged her tightly. "I'm here. Now are you going to tell me what's going on?"

Lydia pulled back. "Where's Sam? I told you not to come—it's fine."

"He's outside. I couldn't leave you. You sounded awful."

"It's okay. Just a water infection," Lydia said quickly. "Nothing serious."

Daisy frowned. "Are you sure?"

"Yes! Lance is here, I'm fine. Please, just fuck off and enjoy your date. I'll call you tomorrow."

Lance glanced at Lydia, reading the lie instantly.

"You promise?" Daisy pressed.

"I swear, babes. Go." Lydia forced a grin, a flicker of her usual spark returning. "You look bloody gorgeous, by the way."

She slapped Daisy's ass and cackled.

Daisy smiled, uncertain but willing to let it go. She hugged her again. "Call me if anything changes."

"Go get laid!" Lydia shouted after her.

"Classy," Lance muttered.

"Always," Lydia said, sinking back into her seat.

Daisy stepped outside, the door thunked shut behind her. The bar noise replaced by the low hum of traffic and distant sirens.

Sam was leaning against the wall, hands in his coat pockets, head tilted, watching something on his phone.

She stopped in front of him. "She's okay."

He slipped his phone away, eyes searching hers. "Yeah?"

"She says it's nothing serious."

One eyebrow rose. "And you believe that?"

"I believe she doesn't want me to worry," Daisy admitted.

Sam's gaze softened. "And yet, here you are. Worrying anyway."

She exhaled. "I couldn't leave her. Not without seeing her. You get that, right?"

"I do," he said quietly. "You showed up for her. That's what you do." A pause. "It's one of the things I… really like about you."

Her heart gave a stupid little leap. "You're not annoyed?"

He shook his head, a faint smile tugging at his mouth. "Disappointed, maybe. But not annoyed. If it were me in there, you'd have done the same."

"Of course I would."

"Well then," he murmured, "you already know how I'd answer."

Something in her chest shifted—his words weren't loud, but they landed heavy.

She reached for his hand, warm and grounding in hers. "Still time to go to the restaurant?"

He studied her for a long moment, then broke into a grin. "Absolutely. Anything to get away from the smell of spilled tequila and broken dreams."

Daisy laughed, a real laugh this time, and tugged him down the street.
"Come on, Arsenal boy. Lead the way."

They finally arrived at the rooftop restaurant—an hour and a half late—but the receptionist, thankfully, was sympathetic to Sam's completely fabricated excuse. Shoutout to his imaginary niece.

And thank God, because it was *worth* it.

The place looked like something out of a dream: twinkling fairy lights strung overhead, candlelit tables casting soft pools of gold, and the London skyline glittering beyond the glass like a promise.

Daisy stared, wide-eyed, clutching Sam's hand like she might float away.

The low hum of a live band drifted through the air. Couples swayed on the small dance floor under the fairy lights, faces half-lit by candle glow.

It felt like a secret—like a place built for whispered confessions and almost-love.

The setting was perfect. It was *screaming* romance.

Daisy took it all in, heart fluttering.

She didn't do places like this. She did sticky pubs, takeaway pizza, and somehow spilling drinks on herself.

But tonight… this felt like a different chapter.

Sam handed her a glass of champagne, the bubbles rising like tiny exclamation marks. She took a sip, the fizz settling her nerves just enough.

He leaned in, voice low at her ear. "See? I told you. Important."

She turned to him, catching that smug, utterly pleased grin.

"Okay, Callaghan," she said, narrowing her eyes playfully. "You win this one."

The food was phenomenal. The wine even better. And the atmosphere—surreal. This was the kind of romance she'd never known. They laughed, talked, and with every passing minute, Daisy felt something unfamiliar creeping in.

Something dangerously close to joy.

For once, she wasn't sabotaging herself. She wasn't questioning or analysing—she was just *there*.

When dessert arrived, she heard it.

Her head snapped up.

"The night seems to fade, but the moonlight lingers on…"

She froze.

Her grandad Bill used to sing that song to her when she was little. She hadn't heard it in years—not like this.

Sam grinned at her. "What's wrong?"

"Nothing," she said quickly, blinking. "It's just… this is my favourite song."

"I know."

She blinked again. "You—what?"

"I requested it."

He stood and held out his hand, that same infuriating, heart-melting grin spreading.

"Sam—" she started, but her voice broke on a laugh.

Heart pounding, she took his hand, letting him lead her to the dance floor.

"Oh, Kingston Town, the place I long to be…"

She laughed, breathless. "I thought you hated dancing."

"I do," he said, pulling her closer. "But I'd do it for you."

Her chest ached in the best way.

"So earlier—during our, uh—heated discussion…"

"Heated discussion," he echoed with mock gravity.

"You said you wanted to label it?"

"I did." He nodded. "See, this is why tonight was so important. I was going to bring you here, ask you something—with all this cliché romantic nonsense. I actually had a plan."

"You had a plan?" she teased.

"Yes. I might not know what I'm doing, but I do know how to woo a woman. Sort of."

"So," she said, feigning nonchalance, "what was the question?"

He sighed dramatically. "Daisy Donaldson, will you… be my girlfriend?"

She gasped. "Hmm. I might have to think about it."

"*What?* Daisy—"

"What? I don't normally do relationships," she said, deadpan.

"Oh, you think you're funny?" He tickled her hip until she squealed. "How about I do this in the middle of the dance floor?"

"Okay! Stop! Yes, Sam—I'll be your girlfriend!"

"Finally."

"Erm, you were the one holding out, actually—"

He silenced her with a kiss.

They swayed until the next song bled in.

"When the night has come, and the land is dark…"

Stand By Me.

Daisy rested her head against his shoulder, smiling softly against the fabric of his shirt. This might just be the most romantic moment of her life.

Then—
The heavens opened.

A sudden downpour.

The one thing the restaurant hadn't planned for.

Staff scrambled with umbrellas, guests shrieked and dashed inside, clutching their glasses.

But Daisy and Sam?

Already soaked.

They stayed exactly where they were—laughing, drenched, still dancing.

Sam lifted an eyebrow. "You know… I think this might be *our song*. You know, should we ever need one."

Daisy froze. *Our song?*

Like a couple would have? Like a—like a *wedding* song?

Her breath caught, and all she could do was nod. "Yeah."

Because this—this moment—was the best, most impossibly romantic thing that had ever happened to her.

And she couldn't quite believe it was real life.

While Daisy's life was finally falling into place, across town, Lydia's was quietly unravelling.

She stood in a dingy bar bathroom, fluorescent lights buzzing overhead, breath shallow, eyes locked on the small plastic stick lying face-down on the counter. The test she'd just peed on—the one quietly deciding her fate.

Lance stood beside her, arms crossed, foot tapping impatiently.

"Well? It's been ages."

"The timer hasn't gone off yet," she muttered.

"I still can't believe you lied to Dais. She's going to be crushed you didn't tell her."

"You saw how happy she was, Lance. How *cute* she looked, all excited for her big date with him. I couldn't do it. I couldn't ruin her night." She exhaled shakily. "She needed a win. And hell, so do I… just a different kind."

"Fine," he said, sighing. "But I'm going to seriously struggle to keep my mouth shut. It's virtually impossible."

"You can, and you will, Delaney."

A beat of silence. The hum of the light filled the room. A fly buzzed lazily against the mirror.

Lance swatted at it half-heartedly. "Well? What does it say?"

"I can't." Lydia's voice cracked. She gripped the edge of the sink, knuckles white. "I can't turn it over."

"Babe, you have to. I'm here, okay? And Dais—when she comes back down from cloud nine—she'll be here too."

She swallowed hard, eyes fixed on the test. "Lance, please. Just… you do it."

He exhaled, muttering something under his breath. "Alright. Fine."

He picked up the stick, turned it over—and froze.

Her stomach dropped. "What?" she whispered.

Lance looked at her, all the snark drained from his face, eyes wide and soft with pity.

"Babe," he said quietly. "I'm so sorry. It's positive."

The air went out of the room.

Lydia's head spun. Her hands pressed against the cold porcelain sink, trying to anchor herself.

"Shit," she whispered. "Bloody hell."

She looked at Lance, eyes glassy. "What do I do?"

He took a long breath, voice gentle now. "Well, my love… telling Emmy—and the father—would be a start."

Lydia stared at her reflection—pale, stunned, mascara smudged.

The woman in the mirror didn't look like her.

She looked like someone whose life had just split cleanly in two.

Chapter 24:
Another mortifying chapter in Daisy's life is complete

Daisy woke up to her birthday the same way she did every year—with a quiet sense of dread.

She hated birthdays. Hated the attention. As a kid, she'd loved them, craved them even. But adulthood had changed that; now she just wanted the whole thing over with before it even began. Too many eyes on her made her skin itch.

Still—this year felt different. She'd reinvented herself. Daisy Number One. Or, actually, just *Daisy*. And she was bloody determined to enjoy it.

Besides, she had a boyfriend now. A proper, gorgeous, caring (if occasionally arrogant) real-life boyfriend. And a reluctantly planned team night out courtesy of Lance and Jenny. Fantastic. At least there'd be alcohol.

Maybe—just maybe—this birthday would be different.

Her phone buzzed.

Lydia: *Happy birthday bestie. Get up and out of bed, loser. Have fun tonight. Can't wait to celebrate with you!*

Daisy smiled. She missed Lydia—her brutal honesty, her chaos. Even if she'd been oddly distant lately. She still hadn't explained the panic call, or why Daisy had rushed to meet her only to find everything "fine." Lydia had even texted later to say the "water infection" was sorted and not to worry.

So Daisy had to believe her.

Another buzz.

Sam: *Happy birthday to my gorgeous girlfriend! Can't wait to see you today.*

That was almost *too* soppy for Sam. But see—this birthday was different. Good different.

By the time Daisy was on the tube, her phone was lighting up with messages. She felt momentarily overwhelmed until she reminded herself that none of it really mattered. Because now she had Sam. And she really, really missed him.

When she arrived at the office, her jaw dropped. Her desk looked like a pink explosion.

Lance.

Balloons. Everywhere. She looked like she was either turning ten or hosting a gender reveal. And that was a conversation she absolutely *did not* need to have with Sam yet.

She slid into her seat, trying to discreetly hide behind her monitor. The smell of latex filled the air—her least favourite thing after unsolicited attention.

The office was oddly quiet, a cluster of colleagues murmuring near the meeting room. Daisy enjoyed the peace while it lasted.

Then, a familiar hand touched her back—light but warm.

Sam.

She turned, grinning despite herself.

"Happy birthday, Dais," he murmured, pressing a quick kiss to her cheek before pulling her into a hug. "Thought I'd get in before everyone else."

"Thank you," she said, smiling. "And where, Sam Callaghan, is my present?"

He smirked. "Hmm. You'll have to wait for that."

"Oh no. Lunchtime?"

"More like tonight. After the over-elaborate office festivities."

Daisy groaned. "Wait, we're talking about an *actual* present and not, you know—because I want that too, but also something I can unwrap."

Sam's grin turned wolfish. "How about both?"

He leaned in for a quick kiss that turned decidedly *not* quick.

The clatter of the meeting room door made them jump apart like guilty teenagers.

Daisy stifled a laugh as Sam straightened his tie, pretending to inspect a nearby filing cabinet. Smooth.

The day dragged on with the occasional "Happy birthday!" and "Wow, that's a lot of balloons."

Jenny, who decided every time she walked past, was going to pop one, which was actually more of a help than a hindrance.

And if Simon from Accounting asked her one more time if she was "blowing up for the occasion," she was going to staple one to his head. Twat.

By 4:30 p.m., Daisy swapped her work clothes for her "special" birthday dress—a short silver slip paired with Docs and her cropped biker jacket. She looked hot. And Sam clearly agreed, judging by the number of times his hand mysteriously found her ass when he thought no one was looking.

The team's destination: a Chinese hot pot on Leman Street with attached karaoke rooms. It screamed Jenny and Lance.

They waited in the bar next door for Rhoda, who was—of course—late. In the meantime, Daisy and Sam endured the onslaught of nosy coworkers, now completely obsessed with their new status as the office's only couple.

"How long have you been together?"

"Did you know each other before work?"

"Are you getting married soon?"

Fucking Simon. Of course.

You can only answer so many questions before you start wondering if it was really worth it—letting the cat out of the bag.

Or so Lance had called it, right before telling Sheena the office gossip, knowing full well everyone would know by lunchtime.

But Daisy decided it was definitely worth it.

Looking at her man? One thousand percent worth it.

Especially when he kissed her cheek after every conversation, whispering, *"Have I mentioned how hot you look tonight?"*

Honestly. This man was not real.

She threw him a look. "Not so bad yourself, Callaghan."

That only seemed to spur him on.

And as she settled down into her seat she glanced down froze.

One—she'd never been here before.

Two—she had absolutely no idea how hot pot worked.

"You cook all your food in the broth!" Jenny shouted, as if this were common knowledge.

Daisy's stomach sank further. Only chopsticks. Of course.

Fantastic. Now her colleagues—and Sam—would think she was not only chaotic but also culturally ignorant.

She panicked, eyes darting around. Why did everyone else just *know* what to do? Even Lance. Even bloody Penelope.

Sam smirked. "Daisy, what's wrong?" he murmured.

She hesitated. "Why do they not give you knives and forks?" Her face went an alarming shade of pink.

His grin widened. "Do you want help?"

Before she could object, he demonstrated—smooth, effortless, maddeningly confident.

And just as she was about to thank him, Lance's voice cut through the table.

"Just when you thought these two couldn't get any cuter."

Daisy glared. *Lance, shut up.*

Halfway through the meal, Daisy's worst nightmare arrived.

Someone had bought a cake.

Of course they had.

Colin the bloody Caterpillar.

Daisy *hated* the attention. She buried her face in Sam's shoulder while he laughed, but Jenny and Rhoda dragged her up anyway for a full-volume, restaurant-wide rendition of *Happy Birthday*.

Unfortunately, half the restaurant was Chinese—including the staff—so it became the strangest, most wonderfully off-key version of the song ever performed.

Still, Daisy obliged. She wasn't about to be called a misery again. She leaned in to blow out the candles—

—and her bloody hair caught fire.

Hairspray. Of course.

Excellent. This was why she didn't *do* birthdays.

Jenny reacted first—by throwing a bottle of beer at her shoulder.

That was alcohol, Jenny.

Was she *trying* to set her alight?

Fortunately, it worked. The fire went out.

Her hair was slightly singed, her pride scorched beyond repair.

And her dress? Soaked.

Staff swarmed, fussing, and Daisy, crimson with embarrassment, assured everyone she was fine while mentally praying for a spicy hot-pot portal to Narnia to swallow her whole.

Lance and Penelope rushed her to the bathroom. Lance held her dress under the hand dryer while Daisy stood in her underwear in a cubicle, questioning every life decision that had led her here.

The toilet window was starting to look like an excellent exit strategy.

When they finally returned, it was *hilarious* to everyone else—especially Rhoda, who was laughing so hard she nearly cried.

At least the boss was happy.

Sam slipped an arm around Daisy, whispering, "Still the hottest girl in the room."

Daisy would very much like to keep this version of Sam, please and thank you.

As the drinks flowed and the noise rose, restaurant staff began gently herding them toward the karaoke suite—probably desperate to restore some peace to the other diners.

And just like that, dinner was over. Another mortifying chapter in the book of Daisy Donaldson.

A few smart people made their escape—Sheena, Gerard, Simon (thank God), Bina (the bore), and Rhoda (obviously).

Probably for the best.

Because karaoke? Was *wild.*

Drunk Daisy loved karaoke.

Sam?

Hated it.

As the chaos unfolded, he stood there, deeply uncomfortable. Singing in public? No thanks. Dancing? Even worse. If he had to rank ways he least wanted to spend an evening, karaoke sat neatly between tax audits and waterboarding.

But then he saw Daisy—her face flushed, eyes sparkling, utterly alive.

And, against his better judgement, he smiled.

Fine. He'd endure this particular brand of torture.

For her.

Before the night spiralled even further, Sam pulled her aside. "Because I had plans for your birthday—before this whole thing hijacked it—I sort of have a new surprise."

Daisy's heart squeezed. "Sam."

He smirked, brushing a strand of hair behind her ear. "Spend the weekend with me?"

She melted. He was impossible. Without hesitation, she grabbed him and kissed him, long and fierce, only pulling back to whisper, "Obviously."

Then someone called her name.

Song time.

Sam blinked. *Daisy?* Volunteering?

Lance grinned at him. "Oh, you're in for a treat, babe. She bloody loves karaoke."

And just like that, Daisy launched into *Valerie.*

Sam stared, floored. She could sing. Really sing.

He hadn't expected that. But then, Daisy was a woman full of surprises.

By the time she'd torn through Whitney Houston and Madonna—first with Lance, then with Jenny—Sam was in survival mode, doing everything short of faking a fainting spell to avoid being pulled up.

So he improvised. He grabbed Daisy and kissed her.

Lance, clocking the move and realising he'd lost, grabbed the mic instead.
"We don't have to take our clothes off—to have a good time—oh, naaaa…" he crooned, dragging a mortified Penelope into a duet.

Daisy collapsed against Sam, laughing so hard she nearly fell off her chair as Lance ad-libbed through the bridge. "Yes, I want your body, but we don't have to rush the affair…"

The image would be burned into Sam's brain forever. And not in a good way.

Then *Don't Cha* by the Pussycat Dolls hit the speakers.

Daisy froze. Smiled. And turned.

Sober Daisy? Sweet, composed, capable of blushing at eye contact.
Drunk Daisy Number One? A menace in lipstick.

Before Sam could stop her, she was dancing—on him.

"Daisy," he hissed, voice strangled. "What are you doing?"

She giggled. "Come on, loosen up."

"I don't know if you've met me, but this is not how I loosen up."

She leaned close, voice low. "Oh, I think it is."

His breath caught.

"Right. We're leaving."

She grinned. "Agreed."

Daisy barely had time to wink at Lance before Sam had her out the door.

They could hardly keep their hands off each other on the way home—if Daisy were sober, she might have been embarrassed. But she wasn't.

He was amazing. Gorgeous. And hers.

The rest blurred into a haze of laughter, urgency, and want.

They stumbled into Sam's flat—coats, shoes, and self-control abandoned in the hallway. Kissing like they couldn't remember how to stop, tripping over furniture, laughing between breaths.

It was her birthday, after all.

And that's exactly what Sam murmured against her skin as his hands slid under her dress. Then he disappeared beneath it.

Oh, her birthday had officially begun.

Later, the room was quiet.

The city hummed outside, a low, distant rhythm.

Daisy lay against his chest, still catching her breath, her pulse gradually finding his. His fingers threaded lazily through her hair, as if he couldn't quite stop touching her. Her skin still buzzed. Body humming but in a good way. A lovely, fizzy way.

She was still smiling when she spoke. "That was… unexpected."

"The birthday surprise?" he said, voice teasing.

She pinched his side. "You're disgusting."

"You loved it."

"I did *not* hate it."

He laughed softly, but when he looked down at her, his expression had changed. Softer. More careful.

"I meant it, you know," he said. "I wanted tonight to be good for you. All of it."

Her voice dropped. "It is."

There was a beat. The kind that felt heavier than silence.

Then, quietly: "You always do that."

She looked up. "Do what?"

"Act like you're not allowed to want things."

The words hit harder than she expected. "I don't—"

"It's okay," he murmured, kissing her forehead. "You don't have to explain. I just… I like when you let go. When you let yourself have good things."

Her heart went big and strange in her chest. "You're a good thing?"

He smiled—crooked, hopeful. "I'm trying to be."

And that—more than all the love making, all the teasing, everything before—was what undid her.

She didn't reply. Just curled closer, eyes closing as the warmth of him, of everything, wrapped around her.

For the first time in a long time, Daisy let herself believe she was allowed this— something good.

Chapter 25:
The luckiest little bean alive

Earlier that same evening Lydia fired off a quick message to Daisy:

I'm so, so sorry, can't make it. Something important came up. Call you tomorrow, babes. x

She'd planned to go. She wanted to go. It was Daisy's birthday, her best friend, and Lance had even said she could tag along to the work thing — *more the merrier*. But she hadn't been able to face them. Not properly. Not since everything changed.

Not since she found out she was pregnant.

Now she was living back at her parents' house, out of work, and clinging to optimism by her fingernails. Lydia always joked she was a walking disaster with good eyeliner — but this? This was next-level.

She'd been trying to reach Luca all week. He'd been busy, vague, or maybe just avoiding her. But tonight, he finally messaged: *Can meet tonight if you want?*

So here she was.

Sitting alone in a Covent Garden pub, staring at the door like it owed her money.

Maybe she should just go. Pretend she'd never sent that message. Pretend everything was still fixable.

But Lydia wasn't built that way. She was too honest — too direct for her own good. And besides, London had a cruel way of making the city feel small. He'd find out eventually.

She drummed her fingers on the table. Waited. Contemplated running again.

"Lydia, I'm so sorry — I came as soon as I finished work."

Maybe not.

She looked up. Luca stood there, slightly breathless, curls mussed, T-shirt and jeans rumpled from the day. Too casual for someone from an office — not that she'd ever figured out what he actually did. Maybe she should ask next time.

"Hi," she said, standing to hug him. It was awkward — too long for casual, too short for meaningful. "Thanks for coming."

"Yeah, well…" He rubbed the back of his neck. "I was surprised you texted. I thought you weren't interested?"

She exhaled. *Here we go.* "This isn't a date, Luca. I need to tell you something. Important."

His brow furrowed. "Right…"

"I'm not gonna beat around the bush. Remember that thing I said I sorted? I didn't. I forgot. And now…"

A beat.

"I'm pregnant."

His mouth opened. Closed. "Wait—what?"

"It's yours."

"You're sure?"

"One hundred percent. I don't usually sleep with guys. Lately it's been… girls."

"Oh." He blinked, recalibrating. "So…"

"And also," she added quickly, "I sort of have a girlfriend now."

Luca stared at the table like it might explain the situation for him. Panic flickered across his face.

"That is… a lot of information to absorb in ten minutes," he said finally.

“I know. I’m sorry. But I’m keeping it. The baby, I mean.”

“And I don’t get a say?”

“You can say whatever you want. But I’m not having an abortion. Not at twenty-eight. That’s non-negotiable. You can be involved, or not. Your choice.”

Silence stretched between them — heavy, waiting to snap. Lydia’s chest tightened. She braced for the worst.

Then Luca said quietly, almost like he was surprising himself,

“I want to be involved.”

She blinked. “You do?”

“I do. I’ve got a decent job, I live in the city — I can support you. I mean, I didn’t expect to have a kid with someone I barely know… someone who’s literally gay—but yeah. I want to be part of this.”

“You’re not bothered about the girlfriend thing?”

“No. It’s not about us. It’s about the baby. My kid. I’m in.”

Lydia couldn’t help it — she smiled. For the first time in weeks, the weight in her chest lifted.

“That’s… cool.”

“That’s cool,” Luca echoed, and they both started laughing. It wasn’t really funny, but somehow, maybe it was.

When Lydia got home, Emmy was sprawled on the sofa, flipping through *Vogue*, paint on her hands, elbows, and a bright streak across her cheek. Her half-finished canvas sat behind her, glowing in the lamplight.

“Hey,” Emmy said, glancing up. “How’d it go, babe?”

Lydia kicked off her boots, dropped her bag by the door, and exhaled. “Um… yeah. Surprisingly well, actually.”

Emmy sat up, eyebrows raised. “So?”

“He wants to be involved.” Lydia watched her carefully. “I’m sorry… is that going to make things weird for you?"

Emmy didn't even pause. "Oh, babe. Of course it bloody doesn't."

She crossed the room and cupped Lydia's face with paint-smeared fingers. "I love you. I'll support whatever you want."

Then she kissed her nose, leaving a smudge of yellow behind.

"As long as he's cool with this kid having three parents—one of them an occasionally chaotic, overly emotional artist—I'm all in."

Lydia exhaled, a smile breaking through the tension. "You're more than that. You're the best part of this."

"Yeah, yeah," Emmy grinned, waving her off. "Now tell me everything—and help me clean this paint off before I prime the sofa."

"Deal."

Lydia laughed and pulled her into a hug, not caring that she was now half-covered in blue paint.

"I mean it," Emmy murmured into her hair. "I know this isn't how you pictured it, but we'll figure it out. Me, you, and our chaotic extended cast."

"Yeah," Lydia said softly. "But it's scary. Letting people in. Letting *him* in. What if it all gets messy?"

"It *will* get messy," Emmy said, smirking. "It's us. Of course it will. But you've got me, and I've got you. And honestly? That baby's going to be the luckiest little bean alive."

Lydia smiled again—slower this time, warmer. "You're ridiculously good at this whole supportive-girlfriend thing."

"Right?" Emmy preened. "Tell your mum. Maybe she'll stop calling me 'that friend from art school.'"

"She likes you now."

"She called me *quirky* last week."

"She meant it as a compliment."

"She said it in the same tone she used when she found a mushroom growing in her bathroom."

Lydia burst out laughing. "Okay, fair."

They collapsed onto the sofa together, Lydia tucking her legs beneath her and resting her head on Emmy's shoulder.

After a beat, Emmy spoke again—softer this time. "You're doing amazing, you know. I'm proud of you."

Lydia blinked, caught off guard by the lump in her throat. "That means everything."

"Good." Emmy reached for the magazine with one hand and took Lydia's with the other. "Now let's eat before I get too sentimental and start crying into the rug. Again."

Chapter 26:
Daisy Donaldson is worth it

Daisy woke to sunlight bleeding through the slats of Sam's blinds — that soft, golden kind of morning light that made everything look like a dream. Her head was heavy on the pillow, limbs tangled in unfamiliar sheets: warm, soft, and draped over both of them like they'd been spun together.

Sam's arm was still slung around her waist, his chest rising steadily against her back. He was asleep, mouth slightly open in the way that would've made her laugh if she wasn't so absurdly content.

It took a few seconds to register it all. Her birthday. Last night. *All* of last night.

She closed her eyes briefly, letting out a silent breath. There hadn't been any overthinking, no spiral of what-ifs — just them, raw and reckless and completely lost in each other. It had been… a lot. Good. So good. But still, a lot.

Sam stirred behind her and groaned softly, tightening his hold. "You're awake."

"Barely," she mumbled.

"Happy birthday," he said, voice gravelly with sleep.

She smiled, even though he couldn't see it. "Pretty sure you already said that. Very enthusiastically."

"Yeah, well. You deserved it."

A pause. Then, "Also, I think I pulled something."

She turned, snorting. His hair was a mess, eyes half-open, grin pure mischief.

God, she liked this man.

"You pulled something? I've lost all motor function from the waist down."

"Worth it, though?"

"Oh, absolutely worth it."

They lay there for a moment — no jokes, no filters — just quiet, and that low hum of something real between them.

Then Sam reached out, brushing a strand of hair behind her ear, like he was holding a thought he wasn't ready to say.

"Right," he said suddenly, sitting up. "Actual birthday present. Give me fifteen minutes."

He disappeared out the door before she could ask what he meant.

Fifteen minutes later, Daisy wandered into the kitchen, wrapped in his dressing gown. Sam stood there — casual, maddeningly handsome in a T-shirt and cap — and tapped a box on the counter.

"Open."

Inside was a delicate daisy chain bracelet from that quirky little shop in Neal's Yard — the one she'd mentioned at least a hundred times. And underneath, an envelope.

A weekend getaway. The Cotswolds. A cottage straight out of *The Holiday*.

Her heart squeezed. He really had listened.

The boy did *very* good.

"Sam…"

He grinned. "Happy birthday, again."

She looked up at him, torn between laughing and crying. "You did good, Callaghan."

"Best part?" He leaned against the counter. "Neither of us are working today."

She blinked. "Wait—what?"

"I booked it off. Rhoda, Lance, Prim, your mum, even Nanna Jean — who, by the way, is dog-sitting Tino. It was a whole covert operation. We've got an hour before we hit the road."

It took her a second to process, her head pounding from all the information and the only response her brain could muster to this wonderfully thoughtful gesture was:

"For the Cotswolds?"

"Yes, Daisy. Where else?"

He laughed at her hungover confusion, pressing a kiss to her forehead. "Get ready. We still have to swing by yours to collect your stuff. Prim packed your overnight bag."

Of course she had. Trust Sam to plan a surprise *logistically.*

She was chaos; he was precision. And somehow, it worked.

By the time they'd collected her things and pulled out of London, Daisy was already in awe — and slightly intimidated. Sam's car was exactly him: polished, practical, just a touch arrogant. He drove with that easy focus she found maddeningly sexy, one hand on the wheel, the other occasionally brushing hers.

Forty minutes in, Daisy was already restless.

She leaned her head against the window, watching the motorway unfurl in streaks of grey and gold. "You know," she said, half-teasing, "for someone who claims he's not a romantic, this is dangerously close to a grand gesture."

Sam just smiled. "Maybe I'm full of surprises."

"So how long does it take to get there? That can't be right—what it's saying? That's *ages!* Are we stopping soon?"

"Dais… are you going to ask questions the entire way?"

"No," she lied, grinning. "I just—I'm not thrilled about long car journeys."

"The sooner we get there, the sooner you can have a drink." He reached over and kissed the back of her hand.

Bollocks. He already knew her too well.

"True."

They drove in comfortable silence for a while, Daisy staring out the window, then breaking it again—of course.

"So, have you secretly met Lydia, Prim, and Nanna Jean behind my back? Sneaky."

Sam smiled. "Haven't *met* them, exactly. I texted Prim—Lydia gave me her number. Lance's idea. Prim sorted Tino with Nanna Jean and said she left your stuff at yours. Did you know she had a key?"

"It's my spare. I keep it under the plant pot."

"Wow. That's dangerously trusting."

Daisy shrugged. "So who did you say you were?"

"Well, I'm your boyfriend, Dais." He laughed. "Have you not told them?"

"It's only been a week! Lydia knows. But Prim—"

"Pretty sure they know now." He smirked.

She smacked his arm, laughing. They fell into another quiet stretch, Sam tapping along to the radio. Daisy couldn't help sneaking glances—admiring him in that stealthy, *not staring but definitely staring* way.

He noticed.

"What are you looking at now?"

"How tall are you, actually? Your legs are… long. I like it."

He laughed. "I think six-four."

"Wow. That *is* tall."

"Yeah, I suppose it is. Especially to you, titch."

She slapped his arm again, grinning. Her thoughts, however,

spiralled somewhere much less innocent—specifically to what it would feel like if he picked her up. *Fantastic, probably.* She shifted in her seat. Of all the places to get turned on, Daisy. *In a car. On the motorway.*

"Want to play a game?" she blurted, desperate to distract herself. "Ooh! Let's do the alphabet game."

"The what game—wait, what is—oh for fuck's sake, this wasn't on Google Maps. What are they playing at?"

Traffic.

Hmm. Agitated Sam was… hot.

She bit her lip, trying not to laugh as he sighed dramatically. Definitely not helping her *earlier problem.*

"Stop laughing. I'm chill, okay."

She leaned over and brushed her hand along the back of his neck, fingers soft. "So chill," she teased. His shoulders dropped slightly, tension easing under her touch.

They reached **Cozy Cottage**—an Airbnb *Guest Favourite*—just before six, after a few strategic stops for essentials: wine, beer, snacks, and the kind of picky bits from M&S that scream "romantic weekend away."

The cottage was beautiful. Understated. Perfect.

Daisy almost cried when she saw it—then pretended she was about to sneeze to explain the tears.Inside, she poured wine while Sam collapsed onto the sofa, baseball cap tipped over his eyes, groaning softly. The drive—and probably the hangover—had caught up with him.

She set his beer and her glass on the coffee table, tossing a few logs onto the fire that was already crackling. It was June, technically summer, but rain pattered against the windows and a fire just *fit.*

Daisy sat on the floor, back resting against the sofa, and turned to press a kiss to his arm.

"You okay?"

He looped an arm around her and kissed the top of her head.

"I didn't say thank you," she said quietly. "For all of this. It's… really lovely. Nobody's ever done anything like this for me before."

He shifted, pulling her close. "Well, Daisy Donaldson. You're worth it."

Her heart actually hurt a little with how sweet he was.

Then he kissed her—properly. The kind of kiss that dissolves coherent thought, that makes the world feel like it's holding its breath.

And what came next could've been scripted straight from a film.

They started slow, the kind of slow that builds heat like a fuse. The firelight flickered over his face as he reached for her, his touch tentative at first, like he was asking a question without words. Daisy didn't answer—she didn't need to. She leaned in, meeting his mouth in a kiss that swallowed the rest of the world.

The crackle of the fire, the rain against the glass, the faint hum of crickets—everything melted away.

There was only them.

It was magical in the way some nights just are.

Every touch felt like an answer, every sigh a confession.

Her jumper came off in a soft tug, his shirt followed in an ungraceful heap. He kissed her like he was trying to relearn her — to memorise the shape of her, in case she slipped away again.

Daisy let herself fall into it. Into *him*. His hands were everywhere — warm on her back, sliding up her thighs, cradling her jaw like she might shatter if he held her wrong. She pulled him down with her onto the rug, fingers threading through his hair, tugging him closer.

It was messy — limbs tangling, laughter spilling between kisses when one of them knocked over a nearly empty glass of wine. But it didn't matter. Nothing did except the feel of his skin against hers, the way he whispered her name like it suddenly meant more.

And it was good.

Extremely good.

Not just in the physical sense — though yes, that was very good — but in the way it felt to be wanted like that. To *want* back. To be so completely wrapped up in someone that the world itself softened.

Afterwards, they lay tangled on the rug, cocooned in a throw blanket half-slipped off their legs. The fire had died down to embers, casting a sleepy amber glow across their skin. Sam kissed her bare shoulder, then her temple, then the corner of her mouth — like he couldn't stop.

Daisy didn't want him to.

She smiled, eyes closed. "This," she whispered, "might be my favourite movie."

"Even the part where I elbowed you in the ribs mid-manoeuvre?"

"*Especially* that part."

He chuckled, tightening his arm around her. "I'll try to be more graceful next time."

"Don't. I like you clumsy. Makes me feel better about myself."

And in that small, ridiculous, perfect moment — on a rug by a fire, with wine-stained socks and hearts full of *maybe* — they both knew they'd remember this night. Even after the fire burned out.

They woke tangled in crisp white sheets, sweating like sinners.

The fire was long dead, but the cottage had transformed into a sauna.

Daisy groaned, wrestling open the window. Cool morning air rushed in and she sighed, letting it wash over her skin.

Behind her, Sam stirred. He blinked blearily, hair a glorious mess. "Morning," he mumbled, smiling. "Why does it feel like a thousand degrees in here?"

Daisy burst out laughing. "When we— you know— got carried away by the fire, we forgot to put it out. And this place has underfloor heating. We've basically turned it into *Chernobyl*."

She climbed back into bed, curling against him as he laughed.

He kissed her. "Hmm. Last night was fun," he murmured against her mouth. "But it's far too hot in here for round two."

And yet, his fingers were already playing with the tie of her robe.

"Sam Callaghan," she teased, grinning, "was this your plan all along? Whisk me away and have your wicked way with me?"

"Yes and no." His smirk deepened. "I *do* have plans. But they can wait."

He rolled her onto her back and kissed her into the mattress — slow, deliberate, reverent.

And Daisy couldn't help but think, as the morning blurred back into heat and laughter, *this is too good to be true.*

Later, with the rain finally easing, they decided to go for a walk, just a short one, to the place Sam had booked for lunch.

Apparently, it was *very* special.

About an hour in, it became glaringly obvious they were lost.

Sam's brow was furrowed, his jaw clenched. Daisy, while mildly concerned, found his slow-burn meltdown... oddly endearing.

"Have you tried Google Maps?" she offered.

"Dais, I told you. No signal."

"Well, how about this way?"

"But it's meant to be *down here.*"

"Shall we just ask someone?"

"Ask who, exactly?"

She glanced around. "Well... that man with the dogs—wait.

Nope. That's sheep. Let's not ask him."

Sam huffed. Their *first argument.* How romantic.

"The instructions said, *take a left onto West Street and follow it down,* which we did. But it's not bloody here—argh!"

Daisy turned to find Sam standing in the middle of the path, exhaling sharply and dragging a hand through his hair. He did *not* look amused. More seething, like he was summoning patience from the depths of his soul.

She smiled. There he was — the Sam she'd met back in March, the one she'd drenched in coffee. And now he was hers. Flustered, frustrated, disgustingly thoughtful Sam — planning things for *her.*

She walked up to him and slipped her arms around his waist. He softened immediately.

"It's okay," she murmured. "We can find somewhere else. Maybe drive, or I don't know, get an Uber?"

"I don't think they *do* Uber up here, Dais," he sighed. "But yeah. You're right. I'm sorry."

"No need to apologise. I like just being with you."

He took her hand, still sulking slightly, clearly reluctant to admit defeat.

Wow, she thought. *He's so stubborn.*

Moments later, as they veered off the path (Sam swearing this "shortcut" was *completely legit*), Daisy's foot caught on a hidden root and — with a theatrical yelp — she vanished.

A loud thud. Followed by:

"Ow, ow, oh my God—shit."

Yep. She'd fallen into a ditch.

A *muddy* one.

Fantastic.

"Daisy?" Sam rushed over, peering down at her in a shallow ditch that only she would be able to find. "Are you okay? What the bloody hell happened?"

"Oh, you know," she said dryly, brushing a leaf from her hair. "Thought I'd have a lie down. I fell into a poxy ditch, Sam."

He tried not to laugh. And failed.

"Well, don't just stand there, you idiot! Help me!"

"Right, sorry." He climbed down, offering his hand and hauling her up — a smirk tugging at his mouth.

"Ow. I think I've sprained my ankle. And my pride," she groaned.

"Let me see." He crouched, gently examining her foot. "Yeah, it's already swelling. You're not walking anywhere on that."

"Well, unless you've got a wheelbarrow handy..."

"I've got something better." He turned and crouched in front of her. "Climb on."

"You're kidding."

"Daisy. Get on."

With a dramatic groan, she looped her arms around his neck and clambered onto his back, giggling as he hoisted her up — like a backpack full of sarcasm and wine.

"This isn't how I imagined being swept off my feet," she said, breath warm against his ear.

He huffed a laugh. "This isn't how I imagined this day going, full stop."

They trudged on — Daisy clinging to him like a loveable, mildly inconvenient sloth — while occasionally pointing out *helpful* landmarks like, "That tree looks like Alan Rickman."

Sam remained quiet, still stewing over the unexpected detour.

"Come on," she nudged. "You *have* to admit this is kind of funny."

He finally cracked, his mouth twitching into a reluctant smile.

And then, as they turned the next corner—

"This is it," he said, stopping dead. "This is the place. Fucking hell. Finally."

"See?" she said smugly. "A bit of patience."

His eyes narrowed. The anger made a brief cameo.

"Don't. Just don't."

That evening, after what was probably the most romantic meal of her life — easily trumping the chaotic rooftop attempt — not to mention the pub-based first-aid scenario (complete with a twisted ankle, a kind bartender, and borrowed crutches that spared them an embarrassing A&E trip), Daisy was reeling.

In the best possible way.

She cozied up to Sam in front of the fire, glass of wine in hand, feet tucked under his thigh. Outside, the wind howled like it had a personal vendetta against their little cottage, but inside was all golden light and warmth.

She'd made him sit through *The Holiday*, despite his loud, repeated objections that *no sane person watches Christmas films in June.*
She told him Jude Law in a jumper was seasonally appropriate. And he'd secretly loved it. She could tell — despite all the sighing and eye-rolling.

By the time the credits rolled, they were both tipsy. Sam had just performed a dramatic rendition of *Mr Brightside* into a corkscrew, which, Daisy suspected, was not his usual Friday-night routine.

She turned to him with a smirk.

"So come on then, Callaghan. Spill it."

He raised an eyebrow. "Spill what?" He grabbed her legs and pulled them onto his lap, casual as anything.

"I want to get to know you better," she said, poking him in the chest. "You already know everything about me. I'm basically an open book — a tragic, chaotic, wine-stained book. But you? You're like a mysterious hardback with no blurb. Possibly crime fiction."

He grinned. "Alright then, what do you want to know?"

"Let's play a game," she said suddenly. "The Deep-Question Drinking Game."

Sam narrowed his eyes. "That sounds fake and dangerous."

"It's real now. You have to answer a question honestly, or drink."

"What if I want to drink *and* answer?"

She clinked her glass against his. "Welcome to the advanced level."

He chuckled. "Go on then. Hit me."

"Okay. First question — tell me something you like or don't like. Something obscure. Not football, not golf, not me."

"Something obscure…" He stared into the fire, thoughtful. "I don't like… ice cream."

She blinked. "I'm sorry, *what?*"

"Ice cream. Meh. Never got the hype."

"Who hurt you? Seriously, who comes out publicly *against* ice cream?"

He shrugged. "It's cold, sticky, melts like it's in a rush to die. Tastes like sadness."

Daisy burst out laughing. "*Tastes like sadness?!* That's literally the opposite of what it is!"

He shrugged.

"I'm dating an anti-ice-cream sadist," she declared.

"Not sadist — *activist,*" he corrected smugly. "I'm fighting the dairy industrial complex."

"Right. Okay. You weirdo. Next question: what were you like at seventeen, eighteen? Full disclosure. What was baby Sam Callaghan like?"

He groaned, sinking further into the sofa. "Oh God. Seventeen-year-old me was… a bit of a cocky little shit, actually."

"Knew it!" she crowed, pointing at him. "Not that far off from now, then."

"Hey!" he clutched his chest in mock injury.

"I'm joking," she said sweetly. "Sort of. Still arrogant though, eh?"

"Never lost it," he said proudly, puffing his chest like an idiot.

"Great. My boyfriend is emotionally unavailable *and* full of himself."

"I am not emotionally unavailable."

"Oh really? Because you practically *glitched* when I told you I love that stupid freckle on your nose."

He frowned. "It's not stupid. It's rugged. Very charming, according to *Shout* magazine, 2012."

She nearly choked on her wine. "You were in *Shout*?!"

"Only in a group shot. U-17s pro team. But I looked fantastic."

Of course he did.

"Oh right, forgot I'm dating a footballer heart-throb. I bet you got loads of girls back then."

"I actually got fan mail. One girl made me a scrapbook — glitter-glued my name on the front. Terrifying, really."

Daisy was wheezing. "Please tell me you still have it."

"I might. In a box somewhere. Hidden. Deeply."

"It's in your bedside table, isn't it."

"...You got me."

She laughed so hard she had to put her wine down. When she finally caught her breath, she curled into him — warm, tipsy, stupidly happy.

He kissed the top of her head. Silence settled, soft and easy.

She liked that she could still learn new things about him — even if they were ridiculous things about dessert aversions and teenage ego. Somehow, it only made her love him more.

After a pause, she tilted her head, trying for casual. "So… how many girls are we talking, then?"

Sam groaned. "Daisy, no. We're not going down that road."

"Just a ballpark figure."

"Not that many, really. Football kept me busy."

She frowned, prompting him to go on.

"I've only ever had two proper girlfriends. Including you."

She blinked. "Really?"

He nodded. "Didn't date much in school. The odd fling. Dated a girl for a bit at seventeen. Then I turned eighteen, realised I liked freedom, and swore off anything serious."

"So you *were* emotionally unavailable."

He laughed. "No. I just liked being single. I've grown up now."

"Yeah, yeah," she said, thwacking him with a cushion. "Talk is cheap."

"More importantly," he said, catching the cushion and tossing it aside, "there's been no one as serious as you."

He pulled her close, kissed her forehead, then her mouth — slow, warm, disarming.

Daisy melted.

She'd ask more questions tomorrow.

Maybe.

Sunday morning at the cottage smelled like bacon, wood smoke, and whatever magic lived inside a Starbucks.

Daisy stirred beneath the thick duvet, blinking against the soft light creeping through the curtains. Outside, birds were singing, trees swayed, and—faintly—Sam was swearing at the stove again.

She smiled. She could get used to this.

Him. Cooking breakfast.

Or just… *him.*

It had been the best birthday weekend of her life. The dinner, the country walks (minus the ditch incident), the quiet, uninterrupted time with Sam. Her head still throbbed faintly from last night's antics and their highly competitive round of "Truth or Dare: Cottage Edition" — which had featured dares like doing your best cow impression from the porch, or confessing your most embarrassing teenage crush.

Sam had admitted he once wrote fan mail to a member of Girls Aloud.

Daisy had dared him to read it aloud, dramatically, by candlelight.

He'd done it. Shirtless.

They'd kissed under string lights, tipsy and breathless, before falling asleep tangled up by the fire.

Frankly, it should have been illegal levels of romance.

Her heart still hadn't recovered. She almost wished they could stay here forever, inside their little bubble.

Stretching lazily, she padded into the living room. Sam stood at the stove, shirtless, wearing joggers and a look of intense concentration as he tried to flip pancakes without incident.

"Morning, gorgeous," he said, glancing over his shoulder. "Don't judge my pancakes. They're more abstract art than food."

"I would *never* judge a man making carbs for me," she said, wrapping her arms around his waist from behind.

He kissed the top of her head. "Good. Because one of them looks like it's been through a war."

They ate by the crackling fire — pancakes drowning in syrup, coffee in mismatched mugs that read *Welcome to the Cotswolds* and *Text Santa.* Daisy rested her head on his shoulder while he scrolled through his phone, reading out useless celebrity trivia with the gravitas of breaking news.

It should have felt perfect.

And for a while, it did.

But then it crept in — that familiar, whispering dread.

This weekend was special. So was he.

And despite every effort not to, Daisy couldn't shake the feeling.

That maybe she'd lose him.

Nothing had happened. Nothing was wrong. But that didn't matter to the voice in her head — the one that had ruined perfectly good things before. It slipped in like a draft beneath the cottage door: quiet, cold, and impossible to ignore.

She hated it.

That sense of joy on borrowed time.

She could feel that other version of herself — Daisy Number Two — waking up. The one who second-guessed texts, built walls and called them "boundaries," told herself it was safer not to care too much.

Because things like this didn't happen to girls like her.

Not for long, anyway.

She was trying so hard not to self-sabotage. To stay present. To believe maybe, this time, she wouldn't break the good thing she'd found.

"You've gone quiet," Sam said suddenly.

She blinked. "Hmm?"

"You're doing your intense overthinking face. Should I stage an intervention?"

She smiled, trying to deflect. "Just wondering if it's too early for more pancakes."

"It's never too early," he said, nudging the plate toward her. But his eyes lingered. He wasn't fooled.

He knew her too well.

She leaned over and kissed his cheek to distract them both. "You're ridiculously nice to me, you know that?"

He raised a brow. "Only when you're not being weirdly moody."

"Charming."

But underneath the banter, the truth was pressing against her ribs.

How do you trust happiness when your brain keeps whispering you don't deserve it?

She hesitated. "It's nothing. I'm just... I'm really happy. With you."

He didn't respond right away. He just watched her, quietly — the kind of quiet that didn't demand, but didn't let her off the hook either.

Daisy took a breath. *Fuck it.* If she didn't say it now, she'd spiral later.

"Okay," she started softly. "It's just... I am happy. But I'm also scared. Because of how you were before — when you said you didn't want a relationship. I know you explained it, and I get it, I do. But sometimes I can't help feeling like... like the rug could be pulled at any second."

Sam scratched his jaw, expression unreadable — but not unkind. Not surprised, either. He *knew* this was coming.

Now was his chance to make it right.

"I think I'm really falling for you, Sam," she added, her voice trembling just slightly. "And I'm just… scared I'll lose you again. And I really don't want to."

He didn't answer immediately. Instead, he grabbed her hand, threading his fingers through hers and giving it a firm, grounding squeeze.

"You're not going to lose me, Daisy," he said quietly. "I promise. I meant what I said before — you challenge me, and I love that. When I'm not with you, I miss you. I crave you. I'm in this. With you. For the long haul."

Her chest rose with a shaky exhale. Relief and disbelief tangled in her throat.

"You are? You really mean that?" she asked, half laughing. "Even though you can be a bit of a twat sometimes?"

He pulled a face. "Wow." Then that familiar grin crept back — crooked, irresistible.

"Yes, Daisy. I really mean it. *Especially* then. That's when I need you the most." His tone softened. "And if I'm honest… I think I'm falling for you, too."

He tugged her closer, voice low now. "Come here."

She kissed him — softly, completely — like it was a thank you, a promise, and a prayer all at once.

And maybe it was for the best that they stopped there, lips still pressed together, foreheads touching, breaths mingling. Because three little words hovered on the edge of her tongue — dangerous, tender, *too soon.*

He wasn't ready. Not yet.

But she already knew.

She had fallen hard.

She was in love with him.

Chapter 27:
Prim doesn't want to be perfect

Prim had always wanted to get married. Since she was ten years old. And she'd been in love with Grant for even longer. Honestly, Prim had probably fallen for Grant before she even met him.

Despite her impressive career—Assistant Art Curator at The Tate, a job she adored—Prim really just wanted to be a stay-at-home wife. And she could. Because, as was often the case for her, things tended to fall neatly into place. Her life had always been effortless.

She met Grant eight years ago at a fundraiser, and from the moment he smiled at her, she'd known. He was tall, dark, handsome, rich, slightly older and devastatingly charming. A walking cliché. And she, a twenty-two-year-old brunette fresh out of university with stars in her eyes and a brand-new job, was completely swept off her feet. He promised her the world, and she believed him. She was utterly invested.

It had all the hallmarks of a bad romance novel, but somehow, it worked. For the past eight years, Grant had followed her around like a Labrador retriever with an Amex. Mostly because Prim wore the trousers. And Grant? He absolutely worshipped her.

But marriage—that had been a slower burn. Prim had been patient. She'd wanted to marry him after three weeks and jet off to the Maldives in a white bikini and a smug grin, but Grant, ever the sensible investment banker, insisted they wait. He wanted job security, a mortgage, and a solid foundation.

And now? Now her time had come. The proposal had finally happened—on a beach in Mexico—and it was the single most romantic moment of Prim's life. It was even better than she'd imagined. The Pinterest board was now a reality. But Prim was… scared.

Did she really want to get married? To the only man she'd ever loved? The only man she'd ever been with?

Sometimes—though she'd never admit it—Prim envied Daisy. Completely unaware, chaotic, freedom-at-all-costs Daisy. Prim had always been the role model, the dependable one. The perfect daughter. The eldest. The one who held everything together whilst their mum and dad were intermittent. Especially Malcolm. She'd grown up desperate to make him proud, even if he barely noticed. Everything had to be perfect—perfect grades, perfect degree, perfect job, perfect fiancé.

Perfect Prim.

And frankly, Prim was sick to death of being perfect.

She sat on the edge of the bed at Nanna Jean's, staring at the sage green bridesmaid dresses and her own wedding gown hanging beside them. The dress she'd chosen in a single afternoon. One trip. One fitting. Because, of course, Perfect Prim didn't need to um and ah. She just knew.

Every detail of this wedding had been mapped out since she was twelve. Grant had tried to contribute—tried to make it his too—but Prim had clung tightly to the reins. She'd let him have a few things. Small things. She laughed now, remembering the time he asked for an indie band at the reception because it reminded him of his teenage years. God, he was cute. But it had been a hard no.

"It's not an American prom, Grant, it's a bloody wedding. No."

He was so patient. Sometimes she wondered why. Why did he put up with her control-freak tendencies? Why did he never push back?

So why did she feel… sad?

Why the sudden jealousy? Of Daisy, of all people. Daisy, who couldn't commit to a toothpaste brand, let alone a man. Daisy, whose dating life was a whirlwind of terrible decisions and accidental entanglements.

But that was just it. Daisy had lived.

And Prim? Prim had Grant. That was it. One man. One relationship. One experience.

Grant, on the other hand, was older. He'd had other relationships. He knew things. Prim didn't even know what it was like to be heartbroken—not really.

Had she made a mistake?

The panic crept up, slick and cold and unwelcome.

Was this how Daisy felt all the time?

Oh no.

And then—she caught herself.

No. She was Perfect Prim. She didn't falter. She didn't spiral. She had control. She always had control.

It's just nerves, she told herself. Just cold feet.

Everyone got them. Didn't they?

"Are we going to get these dresses delivered then, Primmy? I haven't got all day, I've got to help Sylvie dye her hair later," Nanna Jean shouted from downstairs.

And just like that, reality snapped back in. This was her life. This was what she'd chosen. So she damn well better enjoy it.

Maybe… maybe she'd even let Grant have his bloody indie band.

Maybe.

After a quick trip to Perky Planet — not her usual haunt, but necessary given that Jessie worked there (when she felt like it) — Prim was almost out of the funk she'd been stewing in all morning. The coffee was decent enough, though Nanna Jean had already declared the place "too trendy for its own good." Still, it had become a family obligation and the only place Jessie deigned to drink from, since everything else apparently screamed *commercialism*.

Definitely something Alejandro used to say, but that relationship had cooled off in recent months. Jessie was back to being a free-spirited single woman—emphasis on *free*.

Now Prim had bridesmaid dresses to deliver and a schedule to keep.

Daisy, Lydia, Milly, Rachel, Eloise, and Grant's seventeen-year-old cousin Candy, who was full goth. Prim was thrilled with that late addition to her bridal party. Candy was beautiful, but goth didn't quite align with the sage green, romantic countryside aesthetic Prim had curated since she was twelve, but hey, compromise. And family politics.

First stop: Daisy. Nice and easy.

As they walked up to Daisy's building, Nanna Jean started muttering about the overgrown front garden, naturally blaming Daisy for its wild state.

"I'm pretty sure that's what she pays ground rent for, Nan," Prim offered, always ready to defend her scatterbrained little sister.

They buzzed. And buzzed. No answer.

Of course, Daisy was in. Where else would she be on a Saturday? She was practically nocturnal. Prim was convinced she hadn't seen daylight since the engagement party.

"I'm sure she still hides her key under—yep, here," Prim said, crouching to retrieve the familiar spare tucked beneath the plant pot, the one topped with a drunken ceramic gnome slumped like he'd passed out after one too many Negronis.

"I don't think we should just let ourselves in, Prim," Jessie said cautiously.

"What would she be doing besides sleeping, Mum?"

Jessie and Nanna Jean shrugged.

Prim proceeded to let herself, Nanna Jean, and Jessie into the flat like it was a perfectly normal thing to stage a family drop-in without warning.

"Dais?" Prim called, stepping inside.

"You better not still be in bed, it's half eleven—"

She stopped dead.

"Oh…" she gasped, immediately slapping a hand over her eyes like a kid stumbling into a horror film.

"Oh no."

Yes. Daisy was most definitely in.

As was Sam.

And they were very much on the sofa.

Entwined. Limbs everywhere. A tangle of bare skin and poor decisions.

"Prim—oh my god! Mum, Nan—what the actual *fuck*!?"

Daisy scrambled upright, face crimson, yanking her open robe around her body in a desperate attempt at damage control. Not that it mattered now. She'd just unintentionally flashed her entire maternal line within an inch of their lives.

Sam sat frozen for a beat, equally horrified, but with a kind of dazed resignation that only a man caught naked under a crochet blanket can muster. Bare-chested, flushed, and frantically scanning the room for the towel he swore he had earlier.

Ah.

There it was.

With Tino. Curled up on the floor, happily gnawing on it like it's a chew toy from heaven. Totally oblivious. Living his best life.

"Who do you think you are, just letting yourselves into my flat!?" Daisy demanded, face burning.

Silence.

Then—Jessie snorted.

Nanna Jean burst out laughing.

Prim groaned, still shielding her eyes, face screwed up like she'd seen unspeakable horrors.

"I knew it was a mistake to come early!"

"I warned you," Jessie said, wiping tears of laughter from her face.
"Well, I didn't expect full frontal sofa sex!" Prim shot back, eyes still closed. "I thought we'd find her watching *Call the Midwife* in her dressing gown!"

Daisy groaned and sank deeper into the cushions, dragging the blanket over her head like she could disappear entirely.

Sam, meanwhile, had the gall to smirk. Cool, calm, and entirely unbothered now that the worst was over. He stretched—and scratched the back of his head like they'd just walked in on him reading the paper, not cuddling Daisy like a heat source.

"Hi," he said smoothly, pushing his hair back like a shampoo commercial. "I'm Sam." A tiny wave. "Daisy's boyfriend."

Well. That's that, then.

They've been labelled. Defined. Announced.

In the most awkward, humiliating, semi-nude way possible.

Daisy, now buried under throw blankets and second-hand shame, poked her head out just enough to glare at him. He was grinning.

"Nice to meet you all," he added, utterly unrepentant.

"Well," Nanna Jean said, hands on her hips, grinning like the Cheshire Cat.

"It's about bloody time someone got a proper look at Daisy's bits, other than her gynaecologist."

"Mum!" Jessie yelped.

Sam choked on a laugh. Prim groaned louder.

Daisy wondered if you could legally disown your entire family.

And as mortifying as it all was—this total emotional car crash of a morning—she couldn't help it. She laughed too.

Because really, now that the worst has happened, what else was there to do?

At least it was out in the open now. Sam had met the family. They couldn't unsee it—but hey, they could only go up from here.

Probably.

Maybe.

God, she hoped so.

Prim had still not moved. She was standing frozen in the doorway like a traumatised Victorian child who had just witnessed ankles.

Jessie was now wheezing, tears streaming down her face.

And Nanna Jean? She'd already made herself at home in Daisy's kitchen and had started boiling the kettle.

"For god's sake," Daisy muttered, getting up, tying her robe tighter and chucking the towel back to Sam. "Why are you all here?"

Tino, annoyed, started snorting and darting around, suddenly delighted by all the attention.

Prim finally blinked. "We came to drop off the bridesmaid dress. And also, Nan wanted to see Tino. And Jessie was bored. And—well, not to walk in on you shagging on the sofa, if that helps."

"We weren't—!" Daisy started, then looked at Sam, who had casually pulled the towel around his waist like he was starring in a linen advert and not experiencing abject humiliation.

"Okay, we were, but—privacy is a thing! You can't just show up with a key like this is some mid-2000s sitcom!"

Jessie perked up from the hallway. "It does feel very *Friends.*

This whole vibe. You're totally a Monica, by the way."

Daisy glared at her. "I will throw you out of the window."

Prim's cheeks were still crimson. She hung the bridesmaid dress bag on the door and eye'd Sam, who—God love him—was now standing up, still half-naked, in the towel as if it would somehow improve the situation.

"Well," Nanna Jean called from the kitchen. "He's got nice legs, I'll give him that."

Sam smiled politely, like this was a normal Saturday morning and not the absolute worst meet-the-family scenario of all time.

"Tea?" Nanna Jean shouted.

"No!" Daisy and Sam replied in unison.

Daisy covered her face with her hands. "I hate all of you. Get out. Now."

But they didn't . Of course they didn't... Instead, Prim started asking questions—actual questions—about Sam's job, where he was from, and how long they'd been seeing each other. Jessie started taking mental notes because clearly, shewas already planning to discuss it privately with her daughter later.

And Nanna Jean was just pouring out cups of tea and handing one to Sam like they'd known each other forever.

Chapter 28:
I am never recovering from this

Somehow, by the time they did leave—two cups of tea later and with Sam having been quizzed within an inch of his life—it was almost… nice?

Well. Not *nice*. But it could've been worse. No one called an ambulance. Jessie didn't post anything on her midlife Insta-crisis. Nanna Jean didn't try to set Daisy up with someone else mid-conversation (*progress*). And only one person cried—briefly, and it was unclear whether it was from laughter or trauma.

And when the door finally shut, and Daisy collapsed face-first into a cushion, releasing a long, exhausted groan, Sam leaned over and kissed the top of her head.

"That went well," he says, his voice amused.

She groans louder. "I am never recovering from this."

He sits beside her, tracing slow circles on her back. "Still want this, though."

She peeks at him through her fingers, one eye squinting. "Even after seeing my nan in a Juicy tracksuit and my sister scream like she was walking in on a murder?"

He shrugs, totally deadpan. "Especially after that." He grins.

"Honestly, it was character-building."

She snorts. "For who? You? Me? Or my mum, who whispered, 'Is he a vegetarian?' like it was a diagnosis?"

He grins. "All of the above. You forget—I like a bit of chaos. Comes with the Daisy Donaldson package."

She turns her head just enough to meet his gaze. "You sure you can handle it?"

He leans down, his lips brushing her temple. "I don't want less of you, Dais. I want all of it."

And just like that, her mortification softened into something warmer.

Something solid. Maybe even… safe.

"Well," she murmured, "in that case… You'd better buckle up."

Not long after Sam left. Daisy is still reeling in shame.

Technically, he had an injury, but that hadn't stopped him from coaching a kids' football team with a mate on Saturday afternoons. He still loved football. Especially Arsenal.

She wasn't convinced. He was probably halfway to Peru by now, plotting a new life far, far away from the Donaldson family.

Daisy, still clinging to what little dignity she had left, curled in a booth at Caffè Nero with Lance, trying to debrief over a skinny latte.

She sipped it like it was some ancient elixir capable of erasing traumatic memories.

Sadly, it was not.

Lance sat opposite, arms folded, one perfectly arched brow raised in judgement—or maybe disbelief. He hadn't spoken since she finished recounting the sofa incident. Just stared.

"So," Daisy said eventually, voice muffled behind her cup, "that happened."

Lance blinked. "You mean to tell me your entire female bloodline walked in on you and Sam doing the horizontal tango on your sofa?"

"It wasn't a tango. It was more of a… nap. A very naked nap."

"Daisy."

Lance leaned forward, deadly serious. "Did Sam wink at your nan?"

"I don't know, okay?! Maybe. He was being charming, which made it so much worse."

Lance shook his head in disbelief, then broke into a grin. "God, I wish I'd been there. The drama. The nudity. The blanket modesty. It's like *Love Actually* meets *Shameless*."

"Don't." Daisy groaned, resting her forehead on the table. "I'm never showing my face at a family function again. I might move. To Norway. Or Swindon. Somewhere no one expects me to have sex or parents."
Lance patted her hand dramatically. "I'll visit you in your exile. Bring snacks. Maybe Sam, depending on how clothed he is." Daisy cracked a small smile. "I think he's traumatised. He pretended to be totally fine—made tea with Nan, flirted with my mum, chatted to Prim—and then immediately demanded a shower the second they left. I think he was exfoliating the experience off his body."

"Understandable," Lance said.

"He was basically emotionally waterboarded by the Donaldson women."

And with that, Lance burst into a fit of hysterics.

Daisy laughed softly, finally starting to feel that tight ball of horror in her chest loosen. Lance always had a way of doing that— wrapping her anxiety in sarcasm and glitter and reminding her that everything was survivable with enough caffeine and eye-rolling.

"Anyway," she said, sitting back up and poking at a flaky croissant, "I've decided I'm going to pretend it didn't happen. Like a mental Etch-a-Sketch."

"Great plan," Lance said. "Except Jessie will definitely be telling everyone."
"She's probably edited a TikTok by now," Daisy sighed.

"Oh, please. That woman had a title and soundtrack ready before she even walked in."

Daisy's phone buzzed on the table. It was a text from Sam.

Sam: *Still recovering. Might need another look at that robe later, though.*

She smiled, cheeks flushing slightly.

Lance leaned over, reading upside down. "Ugh. Gross. Also cute. But still gross. Are you two disgustingly in love now?"

"I think so," she said, surprised at how certain it felt.

"Well. Great. I'll start planning your couple's name embroidery. I'm thinking 'Saisy' or 'Dam'. Thoughts?"

"Lance—neither of those are good."

"No, no, let it simmer. Like a good stew. Or unresolved relationship trauma."

They toasted their coffees like survivors of war.

Because really, after this afternoon, Daisy figured she deserved a medal. Or at the very least, a loyalty card stamp and a day off.

"So where is Lyds then, Lance? It kind of feels like she's avoiding me," Daisy asked, her brow furrowed.

"No, babe, she's not. Definitely not."

"Is it because I couldn't meet with her? I still feel so bad, but it was important. It was our first proper date."

"She totally got that," Lance said quickly, reassuring. "She's just been flat-out with this new show." A half-truth, but one he delivered smoothly.

Because Lance knew everything. The pregnancy. The relationship with Emmy. He'd been sworn to secrecy, and it was killing him. Not telling Daisy felt awful—especially when she was trying so hard to stay connected. But it wasn't his news to share. Lydia hadn't told her yet, partly because of the show, and partly because… well, she was trying to squeeze in as much work as she could before she started to swell up like a balloon.

"Yeah, I'm so happy she got that part. It's amazing." Daisy

sighed. "Gutted she can't come to Amsterdam though. I really miss her."

"Let's do something after. The three of us. Even if I have to drag Lydia out in full costume. Bottomless brunch. We'll make it a thing."

That'll be a nice surprise for Lydia, Lance thought, trying not to smile too knowingly.

"Ooo, that would be amazing! Let's get a date in," Daisy clapped, suddenly lighter.

Then Daisy's phone rang.

Prim? God, hadn't she seen enough of Daisy today?

"Hey Prim, what's up?"

"Where are you? Can I meet you?"

"I'm at Caffè Nero—the one by London Bridge Station."

"Thanks. You sure it's okay? I really need to talk."

"Yes, of course."

Daisy hung up and pulled a face at Lance.

"Prim's coming here. She sounded... off."

Lance clapped his hands. "And who better to sort out drama? Me, of course."

Daisy laughed.

Prim arrived ten minutes later, flustered, cheeks pink, coat half falling off her shoulders.

"Hey," Daisy greeted, standing to help her with the chair. "Want a coffee?"

"No, it's okay. I've just ordered an oat milk latte—they're bringing it over."

Prim sat. Daisy followed suit.

"So... you okay?" Daisy asked gently.

"Yes. I'm sorry about this afternoon. I really am."

"Don't worry about it, Prim. It's already buried in the back of my mind. Forgotten."

It was not. It was still raw. Very much front and centre. Possibly etched into her soul.

"Okay, well... I need some advice."

"What kind of advice?"

"Relationship advice."

"Oh, I'd better sit this one out," Lance said, sipping his drink.

"I'm sorry—you, the one about to get married, are asking me, who was just caught mid-thrust with her boyfriend of two weeks, for relationship advice?"

"Well, yeah. When you put it like that, it does sound a bit silly."

Daisy scoffed into her latte.

"It's just... the sex." Prim hesitated. "How often do you and Sam... do it?"

Daisy spat out her coffee. Lance nearly choked. And, of course, that exact moment was when the barista arrived with Prim's latte and caught the question mid-air, eyes wide, visibly lingering.

"Prim—what the fuck?"

Prim was deadly serious. "Well?"

"Um, I don't know. Quite a lot?"

"Define quite a lot."

Lance smirked. "Yeah, come on, Dais. We all know you're at it like rabbits."

Daisy shot him a look. "I don't know, Prim, I wasn't exactly expecting to be put on the spot in the middle of a coffee shop on London Bridge." But Prim looks like her life depends on this answer.

"Okay—fine. When we're together, like staying over at each other's, two or three times a day?"

Prim looked appalled. "Three times!"

"Sometimes four." Daisy shrugged. Lance nodded like a proud coach.

"I'm sorry, have you seen him, Prim? He looks like he was carved by the gods. Hell, sometimes I initiate it, just to check he's bloody real."

"Fair play, Dais." Lance agreed, grinning.

Prim stared into her coffee, clearly searching for answers.

"Wait—are you and Grant having problems?"

"No!" she snapped, a little too quickly. "I mean... not problems. Just... issues. Bedroom stuff. And it's giving me doubts."

"How bad is it?" Lance asked.

Don't make it worse, Lance, please.

"I mean, you're getting married. And you've had, like, every event of the century to plan—he's probably just knackered," Lance added.

Prim sighed. "Yeah, maybe. It's just... You start thinking about these things when you're about to commit for life."

"Believe me," Lance said, "Daisy and Sam are not your comparison point to the lifelong commitment that you and Grant are about to share. They're still in the honeymoon phase."

"Hey," Daisy interjected, mock-offended.

"Oh, come on. You're like two horny teenagers—shagging one minute, avoiding each other the next."

Prim finally cracked a smile.

"It's normal to have freak-outs, Prim," Daisy said. "Or so I hear. What would I know? I basically—"

"Treat Sam as your personal sex gremlin?" Lance offered sweetly.

Both Daisy and Prim choked on their coffee, laughing.

"That's disgusting. Go wash your mouth out, you dirtbag. And for the record, he's not complaining." Daisy smirked into her coffee.

"Where is Sam, anyway? Recovering?" Lance asked.

"He's at football."

"Sam? In a football kit?" Lance raised an eyebrow. "Dais, why aren't you watching him?"

"Oh, I've been banned."

They both looked at her in unison. "Why?"

"Heckling. Apparently, when you're supporting the coach, you're not supposed to heckle from the sidelines. Something about it not being 'foul play'."

They all cracked up.

Then Daisy remembered. "Oh—Dad called me earlier."

"When?"

"Just before you got here."

"You didn't call him back? Dais." Prim looked mildly scandalised.

"I forgot!"

"He's coming to town. For the stag next weekend. Probably wants to meet Sam," Prim added.

"What? When?"

"Thursday. I think he wants to do dinner."

Daisy rolled her eyes. "Why?"

"Daisy, don't be like that. He's our dad. At least he's trying."

Daisy sighed dramatically. "Fine. I'll call him back."

"So," Lance said, raising an eyebrow, "what are the plans for the rest of the day, ladies?"

"Grant's at golf all day, so... not much until later, I guess." Prim sighed.

"Sam doesn't finish football until five-ish. Then I have to squeeze in sex sessions number two and three." Daisy said casually.

They all burst out laughing.

"Joking! I'm free this afternoon. What were you thinking, Delaney?"

"Well," Lance said, eyes twinkling, "I think we need to shake Primmy out of this mood. I'm thinking bottomless brunch at Urban Meadow. Look how sunny it is!"

Prim looked uncertain, but Lance was already grabbing her coat and pulling out his phone to make a reservation.

"You two are such a bad influence," she muttered.

"It's fine, Prim. Sam can meet us later—and you can grill him about our sex life yourself."

"Maybe invite Grant, too," Lance added. "He could pick up a few tips."

"Oh my god, this is not funny." Prim groaned.

They cackled their way out of the coffee shop, already halfway into brunch mode.

By the time Sam arrived at Urban Meadow, the bottomless part of brunch had truly lived up to its name. Daisy had a mimosa in each hand, Lance was dramatically recounting a story about his tragic love life to an entirely uninterested but delicious-looking Peruvian waiter, and Prim had that specific look of someone tipsy enough to be giggling but still sober enough to feel embarrassed by it.

"Look who it is," Daisy grinned, wobbling slightly as she stood to greet him. "Our football coach-slash-sex god."

Sam arched an eyebrow. "Do I want context?"

"Absolutely not," Prim muttered, cheeks already pink.

"Nice to see you again, Prim," Sam said cautiously as he leaned down and kissed Daisy, one hand slipping casually around her waist. "You lot look like trouble."

"We are trouble," Lance said proudly, raising his glass. "And you, darling, are late."

As Sam took the empty seat next to Daisy, Lance tilted his head and gave him a slow once-over.

"You sure you don't have any brothers?" he asked, sipping his mimosa. "Or cousins? Second cousins? I'll even take a step-relative at this point."

Sam laughed. "Sorry, I'm the only one. You'd have to marry into the family."

"Tragic," Lance sighed. "But not off the table."

Daisy nearly snorted her drink. "Please don't flirt with my boyfriend at bottomless brunch."

"I will flirt with whoever brings good bone structure and emotional stability to the table," Lance said matter-of-factly.

A few minutes later, Grant arrived, all tan chinos and golf-club charm. He kissed Prim on the cheek and nodded politely to the table. "Sorry to break up the party."

"Grant! Sit for a second," Daisy said, tapping the seat next to her. "This is Sam."

The two men shook hands, both giving that half-appraising look British men do when sizing each other up.

"Football, right?" Grant asked. "Prim mentioned."

"Yeah, well, ex-player. I still coach on Saturdays. Keeps me out of trouble," Sam replied.

"She also mentioned you play golf."

Daisy and Prim exchanged eye rolls.

Here we go.

Grant continued. "Me and a couple of mates are going early afternoon tomorrow. We've got a last-minute slot. Fancy it?"

Sam blinked. "Yeah, alright. I'm terrible, but I like shouting at trees, so it sounds ideal."

"Perfect. I'll text you the details." Grant turned to Prim. "Ready?"

Prim stood, still clutching the last dregs of her drink, slurring. "Bye, you terrible influences."

"Love you!" Daisy shouted after her, then turned to Sam with a smirk. "You golfing now?"

"Apparently."

"Well, wear something tight. Lance and I need new screensavers."

Sam laughed and kissed her again, slower this time. "You're a menace, you know that?"

"And you," she said, brushing a crumb off his shirt, "are brave. Also, my dad is in town. Wants to meet you."

He froze for just a second. "Does he now?"

"Thursday night dinner."

Sam nodded slowly. "Alright. Let's do it."

"Good. Just... try not to mention the incident from this afternoon."

"Oh, I plan to bring PowerPoint slides, Dais."

Daisy groaned, but she was laughing, and everything—for now—felt golden.

Sam emerged from the bedroom, looking unfairly hot for someone about to play golf.

Golf. A boyfriend who plays golf. Who the fuck even is she?

But yes, hot. Like, annoyingly so. He was wearing a polo shirt that fit just a bit too well, khaki shorts, and those ridiculous white trainers that somehow made his legs look even longer.

Daisy felt her stomach do a traitorous flip.

Sam adjusted his collar in the mirror, trying to work out whether he looked like a man ready for nine holes of golf or a bloke auditioning for a toothpaste commercial.

The answer was probably both. Damn these shorts.

He walked back into the living room, where Daisy was hungover, wrapped in a blanket like a burrito, sipping coffee, and giving him that look. The one that says, *I'm judging you, but also, I fancy you a bit, so you're allowed to live.*

"You're sure I can't bail?" he asked, tossing his keys from one hand to the other. "There's still time to fake a hamstring injury."

She smirked. "Coward. Given the way you met the rest of my family, this should be a walk in the park."

"Actually, you're right. Always better to meet people with clothes on."

Daisy laughed. "You'll be fine. Just nod when he talks about course strategy and act fascinated by his mustard collection."

Sam groaned. "Really? Mustard? You're kidding?"

"Nope. He's terrifyingly passionate about condiments."

Sam rolled his eyes. Daisy continued, "Oh, and he also supports Arsenal."

"What?! Why would you not open with that vital piece of information, Dais?" He frowned.

Of course, Grant would support the same football team that Sam fiercely worshipped.

"I'm sorry." She giggled. "You've got this. And don't let him rope you into joining a WhatsApp golf group. That's how they get you."

He leaned down and kissed her, slowly, gently, because even though he was only going to be gone a few hours, something about being with her made it hard to leave. She tasted like coffee and toothpaste and had that sleep-smudged sweetness that had become so familiar lately.

"Text me if you miss me," he said, trying to sound casual, breezy, unaffected.

She grinned. "You'll be lucky if I remember your name." Lifting the remote, she launched Netflix already.

He laughed, heading out the door with a backwards wave. "Bye, gorgeous."

Jogging down the stairs, wondering when he started using words like *gorgeous* unironically.

Probably around the time Daisy climbed into his life with her oversized jumpers, chaotic energy, and complete inability to hide how she felt.

His phone buzzed in his pocket as he got outside.

Grant*: I'm just down the street. White Merc. Remember good energy. Steady. See you soon.*

Sam chuckled to himself. Steady energy. Alright.

He had surprised himself. Everything was happening so quickly, and he would have almost certainly have checked out by now. Emotionally.
But weirdly, he found himself hoping this went well—not just for Daisy, but for him. Because the thought of being part of her world—sisters, dads, barbecues, eccentric mothers and all—didn't feel like pressure. It felt a whole lot better than the unemotional world of his

own family.

Like a door opening.

And for once, he wasn't running the other way.

As soon as the front door clicked shut, Daisy sank back into the cushions, grinning and groaning at the post-bottomless brunch hangover feeling. Tino was snoring loudly next to her, giving her side-eye as though he'd been thoroughly put out by her mere movement.

Daisy knew that Sam had fully accepted her into his life when he allowed her to bring Tino with her into his flat. His impeccably immaculate and clean flat. Daisy was, of course, on a constant level of paranoia when she was there, but he was part of her, and they came as a package. So, Sam had to just deal with it.

She grabbed her phone. The flat was quiet, and for the first time all morning, her brain wasn't screaming with panic. She felt… settled. Which was weird. But also, kind of nice.

She opened her messages and typed:

Daisy: *Sam has gone to meet Grant. What the actual hell. Golf! I think your fiancé might fancy my boyfriend. Also, how's the head?*

Three dots appeared almost instantly.

Prim: *Omg stop. Awful. You guys are terrible. Feel like I've been hit by a bus.*

Fifteen minutes later, her phone buzzed again.

Prim: *Grant just texted me saying "I like him. Very steady energy." ??? What does that even mean??*

Daisy*: It means he's passed the test. Your weirdo fiancé and my super hot man are now bonding over golf balls and flagsticks. I'm disturbed but also kind of proud.*

Prim*: You are in DEEP Dais. Admit it.*

Daisy stared at the screen, the bubble of truth rising before she could push it away.

Daisy: *Yeah. I really am.*

She put the phone down, heart weirdly full. And for once, it didn't terrify her.

The course was quiet, except for the steady thunk of iron meeting ball and the occasional distant shout of "Fore!"

Sam wasn't awful at golf—he wasn't about to win any trophies—but he was playing it safe. Mostly, he was focused on not humiliating himself in front of the man who'd soon be his girlfriend's brother-in-law. And his. Probably. Hopefully.

Nope, he was getting carried away here.

Grant lined up his shot like it was a military operation, paused just long enough to make it dramatic, then sent the ball flying straight down the fairway like it had personally offended him.

Sam whistled low. "Impressive."

Grant shrugged. "Therapy helps."

They laughed and started walking. The silence between them settled in surprisingly easily, like they'd passed some kind of unspoken test. Then Grant glanced over.

"So, listen… I've got my stag do next week."

"Yeah?"

He paused, then looked at Sam a little too directly. "You should come."

Sam blinked. "What, really?"

"Yeah, I know it's short notice, but I wasn't exactly expecting Dais to, you know, get a fella. She's—how do I put this without offending her boyfriend—chaotic?"

Sam laughed. "Yeah, she definitely kept me on my toes."

"It's in Portugal. Nothing too wild—just a few of the lads. Bit of beach, bit of golf, too much beer, probably an argument when someone loses a passport or does something idiotic after one too many pints. Standard stuff. So… you in?"

Sam nearly tripped over his own shoe.

"Oh—uh, seriously?"

Grant nodded. "Yeah. Dais speaks highly of you. That's rare, by the way."

Sam let out a half-laugh, half-sigh. "I'll take that as a glowing endorsement."

"You should. Besides, it'll be good for you to meet the rest of the circus before the wedding. If you can survive my mates, you can survive the Donaldson clan."

He meant it as a joke, but it landed with more weight than Sam expected. Not in a bad way. In *this might actually be a real* kind of way.

"Yeah, mate. Thanks. I'd be up for that."

And, to his own surprise, he really meant it.

Chapter 29:
Rescuing his ass this time

Sam hadn't been in the office all day. Which was very unlike him. Especially for a Wednesday. Daisy hadn't heard from him since yesterday lunchtime. It was strange considering they had been living out of each other's pockets for weeks. But she casually kept her distance, trying not to emotionally suffocate him. But she was a tad worried.

He hadn't messaged.

Hadn't replied to hers.

Not even one of his smug little voice notes or a meme captioned, "you: always late."

At first, Daisy tried to brush it off.

Maybe he was just swamped.

Maybe he'd gone golfing again with Grant. No, Prim would have said.

No, Daisy. Everything is fine.

Maybe he'd just lost his phone.

But by lunchtime, a full 24 hours later, her stomach was doing slow, dreadful somersaults, and her brain was circling through every worst-case scenario. He's changed his mind.

He's ghosting you.

He's realised you're too much.

She slammed her laptop shut.

Seriously. Please stop it.

She wasn't doing this again. She wasn't falling back into that anxious pit where one missed message felt like the beginning of the end.

They were fine. Better than fine. She had metaphorically melted into his arms on a rooftop while Ben E. King serenaded them from invisible speakers.

He had asked her out properly. This was not the same as before.

And yet.

That devil on her shoulder still whispered:

You always mess it up.

The rest of the day was intolerable. Daisy had achieved nothing and avoided everyone just in case they asked her where Sam was, because right now, how she felt, she would probably cry.

Embarrassingly so.

Fucking Sam Callaghan. Why did she have to go and catch feelings? Push him into a relationship? Open him up so that he could trample on her heart?

Daisy had had enough by 4.00 pm. She was going home. Fuck this.

She'd barely stepped through her front door when her phone buzzed.
Lance.

She answered immediately. "Please tell me you've heard from him."

"Babe," Lance said, his voice pitched with concern, "have you spoken to him? No one at work has."

She froze. "No. Not all day." Her voice cracked. "He's not been like this for a while. I'm not angry this time—I'm just… worried."

"Same." Lance sighed. "This doesn't feel like a flake-out. Something's up."

Daisy's breath quickened. She pressed a hand to her chest, as if she could physically push the rising panic back down. "I knew I shouldn't have forced him into this; it was too soon. I knew it."

"Dais," Lance cut in firmly. "Stop. That's not it. He was fine after that. You guys were good. Don't go down that road."

But she was already halfway down it. The part of her that had been waiting for the other shoe to drop was now screaming, *See, I told you so.*

And then—her phone buzzed again.

A different notification.

Sam Calling.

She nearly dropped it in her scramble to answer.

"Sam?" she breathed.

Nothing.

Daisy tried calling back.

Come on, Sam. Don't do this.

Voicemail.

She froze. Stared at it like it might explode. It rang again.

Unknown number.

Please don't be bad news. Please just be him.

"Hello?"
A voice crackled through. "Is that Daisy?"

Her heart stopped. "Yes… Who's this?"

"You Sam's bird?"

Jesus. Who was this?

"Yes," she said cautiously. "Where is he? Is he there?"

"Yeah, he's here. He gave me this number earlier and told me to call if he got too messy. Said you were his girlfriend." The voice softened slightly. "I'm Harry, by the way. Mate of his."

She blinked, stunned. "Messy?"

"Yeah. His phone's dead, and he's... well, a bit fucked."

Daisy pinched the bridge of her nose. "Where are you?"

"The Stag. East Finchley."

Of course. Finchley. Why wouldn't it be miles away?

"You should come get him. They're about to throw him out."

Fantastic. "Right. I'll be there."

She hung up and opened Google Maps. Fifty-two minutes on the train. Fifty-two minutes.

What the hell was he even doing in East Finchley? Was he just wandering the outer boroughs on a personal pub crawl?

Still—relief hit her like a wave. He wasn't ghosting her. He wasn't gone. He was drunk. Steaming.

Annoying, inconvenient, and utterly him.

She grabbed her bag. She did owe him. And she was grateful—ridiculously grateful—that he was okay.

But mostly? She hoped Sam Callaghan knew just how lucky he was that she was dragging herself halfway across London to rescue his drunk, gorgeous, stupid arse.

Daisy arrived at the pub Harry had given her the address for—The Stag—a rough-ish place, luckily just outside of the station. So there was less chance of her getting kidnapped before she could even get to Sam. She had so many questions, but now was not the time.

Now, Daisy knew she was no saint. She had her fair share of drunken escapades and rescues, and Sam had always been there for her. This time, she had to be there for him.

She took a deep breath and stepped inside, spotting him immediately. Slumped on the floor against the bar, his head lolling slightly, his eyes unfocused.

"Here she is," Sam slurred. "Daisy. My girlfriend. Come here." He took a swill of his beer.

Jesus, he was absolutely cooked. She was going to need help.

She crouched beside him. "What are you up to?" she asked softly, removing the beer from his hand.

"Well, Dais, I drank quite a lot of—I don't know what, but it was really bloody strong."

"Sam, why? Why didn't you call me? It's been over 24 hours. Is this why you weren't at work today?"

"Wait, what day is it?" He sighed heavily. "Today was the anniversary of my accident. Nine years."

Ah.
Daisy didn't push for more. Not here. She just needed to get him home. Instead, with the help of Harry and another guy—Mark, apparently another old schoolmate—she managed to get him outside. But then Daisy quickly realised no Uber or taxi was going to take him in this state.

Prim.

Daisy: *Prim. SOS. Sam is very drunk. Can't get Uber. Bring Grant.*

Bring black bags.

Prim: *WTF, Dais. Where are you?*

Daisy: *Finchley. I'll explain later. I'll send you my location. Thank you so much. You're the best.*

Prim: *Ok, fine.*

She waited. Sam sweetly tried to pull her in for a hug. She allowed it, even though, for once, he didn't smell like heaven.

"I'm so sorry," he murmured against her hair. "For getting into this state. For making you come pick me up. I love you, Dais."

Daisy froze.

He might be steaming, but he hadn't said that before. And just when she thought she'd imagined it, he pulled her tighter, pressing a sloppy kiss to her arm.

"Oi," he muttered. "I said I love you."

"I heard you."

"Do you love me?"

Daisy hesitated. She knew she did. She had known for a while, but should she say it? And here, of all places, when he probably won't even remember it. This is not how she pictured it in her head. Then—

"Yes, Sam. I love you."

He'd better not make her regret saying that.

"Sweet." His eyes rolled back, and he slumped, but she'd take it.

"I've never said that to anyone before," he murmured.

Before she could unpack that, Prim and Grant pulled up.

Getting Sam through her front door was a mission, near impossible, dragging his tall arse while batting away his multiple attempts to kiss her and get her attention. God, he was so needy when he was drunk.

She managed to get him into bed, handed him some water, which he accepted groggily, and watched as he sighed and promptly passed out. Tino hopped up between them like a tiny, furry chaperone, taking full advantage of the middle of the bed.

At around 3.00 am, the dog stirred, waking Daisy. She let him out, then secured him in his bedroom.

When she slipped back into bed, Sam shifted, considerably sobered up.

"Wait—how did I get here?" he mumbled.

"I had to rescue your arse this time."

He chuckled, then winced. "I reek of alcohol."

"Yeah, no shit."

"My mates are a bad influence."

"This time, I don't think it's their fault."

His expression sobered. "Ah. I told you, didn't I?"

"You did."

He downed the water she'd left on the nightstand and let out a long sigh. Finally, he met her gaze, eyes glazed with guilt. "I went to his grave yesterday. And today… I just… I got drunk. It was horrible. Everything came back. I'm so sorry I didn't message or call—I just didn't want to feel anything."

"It's okay." She pulled him in for a hug.

When he pulled away, Daisy studied him—raw, vulnerable, yet stronger than he gave himself credit for. He had been living in hell for years.

"I just dread this day every year," he admitted. "I don't know how to cope. I still feel so guilty."

Daisy sat up. "It wasn't your fault. It was an accident, Sam. At some point, you have to stop punishing yourself."

"I know… tell that to my dad."

She sighed. That man, despite having never met him, was fast becoming a supervillain in her mind.

"I lost so much that night. My best friend… gone. My football career… over. My leg… ruined. Felt like my whole life was over, Dais."

"And your dad didn't help," she muttered.

"No. But he was right. I fucked up."

Daisy shook her head and gently squeezed his hand. "No. Your dad had no right to make you feel that way—all these years."

"Yeah, I know that now. Now that I have you."

"You don't deserve the pain you've carried. It was an accident, Sam. Your dad was wrong. I just wish I'd been around sooner to tell you that."

His hand brushed the necklace around her neck—the one he'd given her in Edinburgh. The one Lewis had given him.

"You're still wearing it," he said quietly.

"Of course. You asked me to."

A small, broken laugh escaped him. "He would've liked you, you know. He'd have tried to chat you up… said you fancied him more—but that was just him."

Daisy smiled, tears pricking her eyes. "He sounds like he was a really good bloke."

"He was the best."

A quiet pause settled between them, the sadness filling the room like fog.

Then, slowly, Sam pressed his forehead to hers. "But… look at us now. We're still here. Still standing. Still laughing, somehow."

Daisy let out a shaky breath, a small smile tugging at her lips. "Yeah… we are."

He smiled, pulling her in. "I feel better now. Because of you."

She kissed him softly, murmuring against his lips, "You have me, always."

And he exhaled—finally allowing himself to believe it.

The next morning, hungover but still stupidly cute, he pulled her into his arms.

"Morning," he breathed, his voice rough with sleep as he kissed the side of her head.

"God, you stink," she groaned into the pillow. "Like a brewery and… something suspiciously citrus-adjacent."

"That's not very nice, Dais—especially when I told you I loved you last night."

He smirked, but his eyes searched hers, just to be sure.

Her head lifted slightly. "You remember?"

"Course I do."

His voice had gone soft now, tender. He reached to brush a strand of hair from her face, tucking it behind her ear like it mattered.

"I love you. So much."

She blinked, slow and full of something that felt like falling.

Not the scary kind, the good kind—the kind where your chest feels too full and too light at the same time.

"Say it again," she whispered.

"I love you."

He said it like it was simple. Like it was easy. Like it was the most obvious thing in the world.

She smiled, eyes a little misty.

"I love you too."

There it was. Out in the open. No backtracking, no panic, just… peace. The kind she hadn't felt in years.

She buried her face into the crook of his neck, and he tightened his hold around her, lips pressing to her hair.

Outside, the world was already moving—but in that bed, in his arms, everything stilled.

Maybe this wasn't the end of the chaos. But it felt like the beginning of something solid.

Something true.

She wrapped her arms around him, and he kissed her head.

"But seriously, you need a shower. We've got work. And then you're meeting my dad tonight."

Sam groaned dramatically. "The interrogation begins."

"You'll be fine. Just… maybe don't lead with the whole 'I got pissed up for two days' story."

He laughed, rubbing his eyes. "Right. Charm first, oversharing later."

She grinned. "Exactly. Win him over with your newfound golf chat. Save the emotional baggage for round two."

"Got it. Smooth operator this evening, broken man tomorrow."

"Perfect. Just how my dad likes his future sons-in-law."

Shit. Her mouth. Why did she say that?

Abort. Abort.

Daisy could feel the heat rising in her cheeks as Sam's eyebrows lifted, just slightly. Not judging—just amused. That was worse.

Can she breeze past it? Yes. Yes, she can.

She rolled her eyes with exaggerated flair. "Right. Shower."

Sam leaned closer, his voice low and teasing. "I'll shower… if you join me."

Daisy sighed, like it was a massive inconvenience. "Fine."

Like she'd ever say no.

He kissed her again, this time on the mouth—slower, sweeter—and she allowed it. And for a moment, her panic melted away, replaced by the quiet certainty that somehow, this thing between them… it was real.

In that moment—with his arms around her and sunlight sneaking through the curtains—she knew.

There was nowhere else she'd rather be.

Chapter 30:
Meeting Malcolm Donaldson

The restaurant was the type of place that didn't have menus—they simply told you what you'd be eating, as though you were lucky to be there at all. Sam adjusted his shirt collar for the third time as Daisy fixed her lipstick in the mirrored wall beside their table.

"Stop fidgeting," she whispered.

"I'm not fidgeting. I'm mentally preparing."

"For battle?"

"For Malcolm Donaldson. Is he as chaotic as you, because I think that might work in my favour."

"No, unfortunately, the chaos is all Jessie."

"Balls."

"Sam. Please, just chill," Daisy said gently, pressing a kiss to the back of his hand.

"I'm trying," he muttered. "I really am. I'm also very hungover."

"Oh, really?" she said, raising an eyebrow. "Maybe next time, don't disappear without telling me where you're going, and I could've stopped you—or at least made you eat some carbs first."

He groaned. "Don't. I already hate myself enough."

She softened, threading her fingers through his. "Hey, I'm not mad. I was just… scared."

His eyes flicked to hers, guilt simmering just beneath the surface.

"I didn't mean to worry you."

"I know," she said quietly. "But you did. Because I care. And I need to know you're okay—even when you don't feel like talking."

He let out a long breath and nodded, squeezing her hand.

"I'll try. I promise."

She gave a crooked smile. "Good. Now drink your soda water, tragic man."

He looked at her, open-mouthed and laughing.

Prim and Grant were already there, sipping something wildly overpriced and pretending not to watch them. Grant winked and gave Sam a discreet thumbs-up under the table. Prim just smiled sweetly—terrifyingly.

Then the arrival.

Malcolm Donaldson swept into the restaurant precisely three minutes late, like he owned it. Which, judging by the maître d's reaction, he might have. Tailored dark grey suit, salt-and-pepper hair slicked back, and a presence that screamed old-school banker energy.

Or Bond villain.

"Sweetheart," he beamed, sweeping Prim into a hug and planting a kiss on her cheek. Scottish accent thick. "You look radiant. Honestly, are you glowing or is that just the serotonin of being better than your siblings?"

"Hi Dad," she laughed, hugging him back. "You know Daisy's here, right?" Prim added.

Malcolm turned, grinning. "Of course. I clocked the dramatic eye-roll from across the room. Good to see you, Button."

"Don't call me that," Daisy muttered, standing to greet him. He kissed her on the cheek, and she endured it with the air of someone being knighted against their will.

"You look nice, Dad, smart. Like Alan Sugar," Daisy added dryly.

"Well, I knew I'd be surrounded by women of style tonight." He nodded warmly at Grant. "And men of… reasonable taste."

Grant grinned. "Evening, Malcolm."

"And this must be the mysterious Sam," Malcolm said, turning to him with a calculating glint. "I've heard… well, actually, I've heard nothing. Daisy keeps her cards close."

Then Malcolm turned to Sam with an evaluating glance that could've peeled wallpaper.

Sam stood. Extended a hand. "Nice to meet you, sir."

"Oh Malcolm, please." Malcolm shook it, firm and cool. "We're all adults here. Even if my youngest still insists on dressing like she's raided the stockroom at Urban Outfitters."

Daisy opened her mouth, probably to tell him exactly where he could shove his commentary, but Sam gently nudged her knee under the table.

"Hmm. Strong grip. Decent watch. Good shoes." He looked him up and down. "You'll do."

Daisy buried her face in her napkin.

Sam laughed, a bit too loudly. "Thanks—I think?"

They all sat. Malcolm ordered a bottle of wine with a price tag that could've covered Sam's monthly salary, then launched into a story about buying a vineyard "for the tax break." Meanwhile, Sam focused on not looking like a man who had just wandered into a live performance of *Succession*.

Daisy leaned over and murmured, "You're doing great. He hasn't asked your net worth yet."

"Yet," Sam said, smiling tightly.

But then something shifted. Between the wine and the starters, Malcolm turned his attention properly to Sam. Asked about his work, where he grew up, his intentions with his youngest daughter. Sam answered honestly—no embellishments, no bravado.

"Sam used to play football professionally," Prim offered

helpfully halfway through mains.

"Really, that's impressive. Who for?"

Sam froze for a fraction of a second. "I did, yeah. Luton Town. Had to stop at nineteen, got quite a serious injury," he answered, suddenly wishing that the room had air.

Daisy glared at Prim for putting Sam on the spot, although she didn't actually know the full extent and just looked confused.

"Ah. That's too bad," Malcolm said, not pressing further—he could sense the lad's discomfort. Instead, he simply nodded and took a sip of wine. "Injuries will do it, though. Especially when you're young and think your body's indestructible."

There was a beat. Sam's shoulders eased a little.

"So, you like football then? Who do you support?" Malcolm asked casually, slicing into his scallops.

"Arsenal."

Malcolm pulled a face, like someone had handed him a pint of warm lager. "Huh. Nobody's perfect. Isn't that right, Grant?"

Grant laughed. "Pity Man U can't quite meet their standards though, eh Malc?"

The table chuckled, and Sam found himself smiling—an actual, genuine smile.

"Ah, see Sam," Malcolm continued, gesturing with his fork. "I know I sound like a Glaswegian, and you're thinking, why does this old Scottish man support an English team and not Rangers? The answer is: English football is fantastic, I've lived here most of my life… but also—" he nodded at Grant, "—Sir Alex Ferguson. The man was a genius. And let's be honest—historically, United are far superior to Arsenal."

Sam and Grant exchanged a look, then in perfect unison muttered, "Rubbish."

Malcolm chuckled to himself.

Daisy watched this with narrowed eyes. Was Sam… enjoying himself?

"I like you, Sam," Malcolm declared. "You've got a good head on you. Calm energy. Very un-footballer."

"Thanks?" Sam chuckled.

Daisy's nerves prickled. She felt a weird twist in her stomach, watching the two of them get on. It was… unexpected. But then again, Malcolm had only met Matthew maybe once before. Maybe that was why this felt so different.

Malcolm leaned back, swirling his wine. "Just promise me one thing—if this thing with Daisy gets serious, don't let her pick the music at your wedding. Without being rude, her taste is… eclectic."

"Eclectic?" Daisy spluttered. "You bought me a Girls Aloud CD for Christmas when I was fifteen."

"Exactly. Charity begins at home."

Sam leaned in to whisper, grinning. "You really do come from chaos."

She kicked him under the table, but she was smiling too.

And as the wine flowed, and the waitress collected empty plates, Sam realised something surprising: he actually liked Malcolm. The man was a bit flash, a bit theatrical, sure—but he was warm, funny, and without the cold-blooded judgement Sam was used to from his own dad. And when Malcolm raised a toast "to family—however dysfunctional," Sam quietly clinked his glass and meant it.

It was the first time in a long while that the word *family* didn't sound like a warning.

When dessert arrived—some architectural lemon tart that looked more like a modern art installation—Malcolm actually smiled.

"So," he said, swirling his wine. "You're coming to Portugal tomorrow, are you?"

Sam nodded. "Looking forward to it. I appreciate the invite."

Malcolm raised his glass. "Grant told me you handled the golf like a gentleman. No ego, no tantrums. That goes a long way in this family."

Daisy blinked. "Is this… a compliment?"

"Don't get used to it," her dad said. "But yes. I like him. Don't mess it up."

Sam looked at Daisy, who was trying not to choke on her tart. He reached under the table and squeezed her hand.

"I'll do my best," he said.

And for once, Malcolm Donaldson just nodded. No smirk. No lecture. Just… approval.

Which, from him, was basically a standing ovation.

They spilled out onto the quiet Mayfair pavement, the air still warm for a London evening in August.

"Right, Sam will see you in the morning. Daisy, try not to keep him up too late." Malcolm shook his hand and actually winked.

Daisy internally cringed. Sam laughed.

"See you tomorrow, mate," Grant said to Sam, patting him on the back and then whispering, "Worst part's over. You did good," before slapping him on the back. Daisy and Prim hugged.

Malcolm waved down a sleek black cab like he was royalty, sweeping Prim and Grant inside with a final, "Don't do anything I wouldn't do!" which, coming from him, left far too much wiggle room.

Sam slipped his hand into Daisy's as they walked toward the corner, his thumb brushing lazy circles on her skin.

"Well," Daisy said, exhaling. "That went... suspiciously well."

"I was braced for a personality quiz and a blood test," Sam said. "Instead, I got... compliments? And scallops?"

"He must like you," she said, sounding almost put out by it.

Sam grinned. "Is that a problem?"

"No. Yes. Maybe." She paused. "In fairness, he hasn't met anyone, well, not anyone I actually like."

Sam gave her a look. "Wait, you like me?"

"Oh shut up."

They crossed a side street, Sam still holding her hand like it was the most natural thing in the world.

"He's a character, your dad," Sam said finally. "But he's also kind of a legend."

"God, don't tell him that. He'll have it printed on a t-shirt."

Sam laughed. "He reminds me of absolutely no one in my family, which is probably why I liked him. He didn't once make me feel like I needed to prove something."

Daisy looked over at him. "You don't."

He stopped walking, tugging her to face him. "I know that now. You helped with that."

Daisy's stomach flipped in a way that had nothing to do with the wine or the terrifyingly tiny lemon tart.

"You're soft," she teased, just to steady herself.

Sam leaned in, brushing his lips against hers with a smile. "Only for you."

Daisy melted, just a bit.

They stood like that for a moment, the low buzz of the city around them, everything slightly too lovely for real life.

And just before she could ruin it with another sarcastic quip, Sam spoke again, softer this time.

"Your dad said not to let you choose the wedding playlist."

Daisy raised an eyebrow. "Already planning the wedding, are we?"

"I'm just saying… if 'Sound of the Underground' comes on, I'm not responsible for what happens."

She laughed, tipping her head against his shoulder. "You're an idiot."

"Your idiot."

And somehow, that felt truer than anything either of them had said all night.

Chapter 31:
Han Solo is actually gorgeous in real life

Daisy stood in the hallway at stupidly early o'clock, watching Sam throw his things together for his weekend with Grant and the lads. Oh, and her dad. Great.

She was happy, really—he was getting involved with her family, bonding with them. It was all coming together quite nicely. But Daisy couldn't help but feel selfish. She quite enjoyed having him all to herself, and now, well, everyone else wanted a piece of him.

And then there was that devil on her shoulder. What if someone—Greg, for instance—said the wrong thing, and Sam decided this relationship wasn't for him? What if he came back and ended it with her?

God, Daisy really wished she could actually punch that devil in the face.

"Are you sure you'll be okay without me?" Daisy asked, the words slipping out before she could stop them.

Sam raised an eyebrow, his half-packed bag slung over his shoulder. "Dais, I think I'll survive." He said it with a laugh, but there was a trace of humour in his voice. "It's just golf and a few pints. Nothing too crazy."

"Right." She nodded, trying to hide the small smile creeping across her face. "Just—don't get completely trashed again, okay? I'm not coming all the way to Portugal to bloody rescue you."

"Oh my god, Dais, that was one time." He laughed. "I should be more worried about you. You're a liability."

"I'm your liability though," she joked.

"True." Sam grinned. "I'll be a good boy, promise. You've got your hands full with Prim's hen anyway."

Daisy rolled her eyes. "Let's just hope I don't end up in a canal or something."

"You're going to have a sick time. Just—don't get high, Dais." Sam winked.

"Please. You know I'm no good with booze at the best of times, let alone that," Daisy teased. Then she added, "But I will definitely take a few 'wild' pictures for you."

"That's what I'm afraid of," he chuckled, leaning in to plant a soft kiss on her forehead.

Daisy felt a flutter in her chest. He was leaving, but something about this felt different. Like something was shifting. She swallowed, forcing herself to smile.

"Have a good time. Don't forget to send me a text so I know you haven't gotten stuck in a random field or died of alcohol poisoning."

"You got it. Have fun with Prim. I love you."

"I love you too." She kissed him again, and for a split second, she wondered if he'd notice how badly she didn't want him to leave. But no, he didn't.

With a quick wave, Sam disappeared down the stairs, leaving Daisy standing in the hallway. Her mind wandered back to the idea of a quiet weekend in Amsterdam with Prim and her friends. Lydia wasn't even bloody coming. It was just her and Prim's other friends. Daisy was already dreading it.

But hey, it was for Prim.

She grabbed her phone and sent a quick text to Prim.

Daisy: *On my way! Prepare yourself for the chaos!*

Okay, so maybe she was a bit more upbeat than she was actually feeling. But it had to sound convincing, right? She couldn't tell Prim that she was contemplating faking a leg injury or—albeit a little desperate—throwing herself off Sam's balcony.

And yes, Daisy was feeling slightly territorial over Sam.

Looking around Sam's flat, now empty and still in his absence, Daisy realised she was going to miss him more than she cared to admit. But for now, there was no time for second-guessing.

Prim's hen do awaited. And despite the whirlwind of emotions buzzing around her, Daisy knew this weekend would be something she wouldn't forget. Whether she wanted to or not.

She headed to St. Pancras for the 11:27 train.

As she stepped onto the platform, she was met with giggles and cackles. A sea of pink cowboy hats and feather boas. Jesus. So original. Daisy rolled her eyes.

"Want a Pink G&T in a can?"

Milly asked her, grinning like a madwoman, her ridiculously long, bedazzled nails tapping against the side of the can as she handed it over.

God, her friends were wankers. Daisy knew she was going to need all the alcohol she could get to survive five hours on a train with them, let alone an entire weekend.

They arrived in Amsterdam just before 6:30 pm. The hotel was conveniently close to the station, so it was a drop-and-run situation. Straight out the door. Daisy was surprisingly sober. Gin just didn't have the same effect as Prosecco, and she needed something stronger.

Rachel dragged Daisy to the bar for shots, and god, she needed them. Prim was already on her way, so they left her slumped in an armchair near a fire, while Milly and Eloise were doing some stupid video for TikTok.

"You okay, Daisy?" Rachel asked.

"Yeah, just a bit sober," Daisy lied. The truth was, she was missing Sam, but she wasn't about to sound pathetic.

"It's a real shame Lydia couldn't make it. She's a blast," Rachel said, blinking her ridiculously beautiful lashes at Daisy.

"Yeah, I miss her. But she's got this new role—a play. She couldn't get the time off."

"A play? Wow, she's so cool." Rachel blinked again. Daisy was momentarily jealous of her beauty. Even her blinking looked rehearsed. Like she'd had lash extensions blessed by angels.

"So, Prim tells me you've got a new boyfriend and that he's really fit," Rachel continued, sipping her Aperol like it was laced with secrets.

"Um, yeah." Daisy sighed, trying not to sound defensive. Why the hell was Prim telling people about Sam?

"He's actually on the stag," she added casually, like it wasn't a huge, relationship-defining thing she hadn't even mentally processed yet.

"Oh, so he's a keeper then. Must be serious if he's on the stag."

Yeah, must be, Daisy thought. But her reply was less than confident.

"Oh yeah." She fake-laughed, hoping it passed as normal human enthusiasm rather than 'existential spiral in progress.'

They moved from the bar to a surprisingly modern club—not at all as shady as the first couple of bars they'd almost wandered into, one of which looked like it doubled as a tattoo parlour and possibly a money laundering front.

As they settled into the bar area, drinks started flowing more freely. They'd commandeered a low velvet booth in the corner—very *Sex and the City* does Amsterdam, if Carrie Bradshaw wore vintage Zara and was avoiding her therapist.

Someone had ordered another round of espresso martinis, which were already going down way too easily, and Daisy finally unclenched her jaw.

Prim was up from her armchair episode now, revived with a second wind, and dancing in the middle of the booth while Eloise attempted to reconnect her veil to her cowboy hat using what looked like chewing gum and sheer willpower.

Daisy had accidentally lost her own hat in the last bar. Oh, what a shame.

Milly had invited over a group of cute, bleach-blonde German lads—each one clearly under twenty-one and radiating horny Erasmus energy. Daisy decided to go full ninja and hide from them as much as possible.

She'd resisted the urge to text Sam up until now, not wanting to embarrass him on the stag. Instead, she perched on the edge of the booth beside a tall, willowy bloke—Taavi from Finland, who was clutching a bong in one hand, a harmonica in the other, and was passionately trying to convince her that the sex museum was a far more culturally significant experience than the Van Gogh Museum.

"The artists there—pioneers," he said seriously, his eyes wide with conviction.

"Erm, no, mate. I don't think so," Daisy replied politely. She couldn't wait for Prim to hear this. Her head would explode.

Still, he was actually really nice. He asked if she had a boyfriend. She showed him her lock screen—a photo of her and Sam, taken outside a coffee shop in The Cotswolds, her head tucked into his chest.

He studied it, nodding. "He looks Scandinavian."

"I don't think he is? I think he has Irish heritage?"

"He must be. Swedish or Norwegian. I can tell."

Daisy made a mental note to ask Sam if he was secretly Nordic.

Rachel and Prim appeared beside her just as Taavi moved on to chat up Rachel—naturally. She did look like someone who'd just stepped out of a music video. He offered out his bong, which they all declined with awkward, overly grateful smiles.

Don't get high, Daisy. Not in a booth. Not in public.

Taavi was just about to play them a song on his harmonica when his mate Patrik showed up and announced they had to "bounce." Probably to bless some other booth with bong-and-blues energy.

Prim's friend Lena returned after a thirty-minute disappearance with some bloke named Ansel—glossy hair windswept, lipstick slightly smudged, looking like someone who'd just had a time. She slid in beside Daisy like she was gliding into a scene from a Lana Del Rey music video.

"Anyone want a muffin?" she asked, breathlessly, holding up two slightly squashed but very appetising-looking muffins.

"Where the hell have you been?" Prim laughed, shifting to make room.

"With that Ansel lad," Lena grinned, waggling her eyebrows. "Proper nice boy. Terrible shoes."

"Where did you get muffins?" Daisy asked, already accepting the offering like it was a peace treaty.

"There's this weird 24-hour café down the road. The guy behind the counter gave me three for the price of two because Ansel told him I looked like Dua Lipa. I don't, obviously, but I'll take the carbs."

Daisy crammed a big chunk into her mouth like she hadn't eaten in a decade. Her stomach immediately thanked her. Little did she know that would come back to bite her in about 45 minutes.

"God, this is heavenly," she said, mid-chew.

Lena grinned. "Right? Dangerously good. Oh—and I've made Ansel promise to find us a boat party for tomorrow. So, you're welcome."

Daisy gave a muffled thumbs-up, already wondering how she'd survive a boat party without hurling muffin into a canal.

Prim leaned in, mischief in her eyes. "Lena, Rachel was just saying how fit Daisy's boyfriend is."

"Oh—the ex-footballer!" Lena perked up, reaching for her phone. "I googled him."

Daisy almost choked.

"You what?"

In all the time she'd been with Sam, it had never occurred to her to Google him. Probably because it felt... wrong. Like peeking behind a curtain that wasn't meant for her. Besides, she'd already done enough low-level stalking back when Lydia first showed her his Instagram.

Lena shoved her phone in front of her face. "Look."

"Why are you Googling my boyfriend?" Daisy asked with a frown—but curiosity got the better of her.

There he was. A handful of photos from his early career—one of him at nineteen, absurdly handsome and even more baby-faced. She spotted an article headline about the accident and immediately looked away.

Nope. Not tonight. Too intrusive.

She handed the phone back.

Lena shrugged. "Curiosity. Plus, Prim said his name and that he was a footballer. He's hot. You did well."

"He's got his own Wikipedia page!" Rachel declared like this was simply a fact, not a compliment.

Daisy, still coughing, took a large sip of her drink to save herself from further interrogation.

Then—

"Daisy, is this your fella?" Eloise piped up, suddenly appearing with her phone, holding out a photo of four lads. When the hell did she get here?

Of course, Eloise had intel—she was Marcus's girlfriend, and Marcus was Grant's best man. So obviously, she had access to the group chat of doom.

Interrogation: ongoing.

Milly lunged for a closer look at the screen. It was a snap of the lads in Portugal. And there was Sam, smiling and shirtless. He looked criminally hot.

Daisy's stomach fluttered. Great. Now her internal organs were joining in.

"Oh God. You're all going to turn into Sam fans, and I'm just going to be the girlfriend that dies mysteriously halfway through the documentary," she muttered.

"No offence," Lena said, patting her knee. "But you'd be the main character. The girl who gets justice. Maybe a podcast."

"Thanks. I always wanted to be a posthumous feminist icon."

They all laughed, and the tension in Daisy's chest eased. Maybe this weekend wouldn't be so bad.

Unless the cocktail-muffin combo betrayed her. Which—judging by the ominous gurgle in her stomach—it was already plotting.

"I need food," she mumbled.

"Just have more muffin," Lena urged. "I'm done. Too sweet for me."

"You're sweet enough." Came a very European voice behind them. Ansel.

He reappeared like a walking cologne ad, whisking Lena and Prim up for a dance. The girls squealed and disappeared into the crowd.

Eloise and Rachel slid into the booth beside Daisy. She looked at the picture again. "Yeah, that's my Sam," she gushed, before realising what she'd just said.

My Sam? Fuck, what the hell?

The girls kept scrolling through Marcus's pictures, but Daisy… Daisy just felt light. Weirdly light. Like she was floating a few inches above herself.

Really fucking weird.

Like she's on a cloud.

Her phone buzzed, pulling her out of her daze. She grabbed it.

Sam: *Hey gorgeous. Hope you are having a good time. I miss you.*

Daisy: *How's it? It's good here, really chill.*

Sam: *Daisy? Are you hammered. Already?*

Daisy: *You're really hot.*

Yep, she's gone.

Sam: *You are too, where are my pictures at?*

Daisy sent him a selfie of her, Eloise, and Rachel.

Sam circled her face and sent it back with the caption: *"You're gorgeous."*

Daisy stared at the message. She missed him.

Something shifted. That funny, fizzy feeling in her chest returned—then suddenly, she was on her feet with an overwhelming need to drink a gallon of water and eat fifty-six burgers.

Her legs felt like jelly. Walking was a challenge.

But she left the club.

She ate McDonald's.

She drank water.

Then somehow, she was at the train station. It was enormous. Looming. Like the Labyrinth.

She suddenly wanted to go home.

She blinked. *Why is that clock stopped? Wait—why is it going backwards?*

Before she could process any of it, she was on a train. The carriage swayed gently. The lighting was alien. The people didn't look real. They sounded like *The Sims*. It felt like a spaceship. *Where the hell was she going?*

Space?

Star Wars. *IT FEELS LIKE STAR WARS.*

Chewy, you're here?

Nice.

Darth—nah mate, you can fuck off.

Wow. Han Solo is actually gorgeous in real life.

Stay away, Han. I have a boyfriend.

Chapter 32:
A trip on the millennium falcon

Daisy woke up in her front garden.

Outside her flat. Birds chirping. Sun shining.

With no idea how the fuck she'd gotten there.

Oh god.

She was supposed to be in Amsterdam. Somehow, she was back home, with no keys, no luggage, but, surprisingly, her phone and passport were still in her bag. She checked the receipt in her bag—348 euros for a train ticket. Bloody hell, Daisy, you got the train home...

High.

Yep, she got high.

Even though Sam told her not to. God, he was going to be so mad. At least she was home safe.

She checked the receipt hoping that it had miraculously changed into something less insane. That train was 4:48 am. What was she doing all that time? Lying on the platform?

She had no recollection of the night. How long had she been lying in her front garden? She checked the time on her phone—midday. And there were fifteen missed calls from Prim, eleven from Sam.

Shit.

She called him.

"Daisy, babe, fucking hell! Why haven't you been answering? Are you okay? Prim's been worried sick."

Double shit.

"Yes, I'm fine. I'll call her in a sec. I'm at home, Sam."

"What? Why?"

"I don't know. I just know I'm back in London, outside my building."

"You got high, didn't you?"

He started to laugh.

"Not voluntarily. Fuck's sake, I don't even remember taking anything. Probably that muffin. Oh, God. That poxy Lena girl."

Sam was in hysterics now.

"Fucking hell, Dais. How the hell did you get home?"

"Oh, you're enjoying this, aren't you?"

"Enjoying it? Dais, this is fucking gold. I can't believe you got high and instead of enjoying Amsterdam, you came home." He was laughing so much. Daisy wanted to throttle him through the phone. "At least you're safe. Brilliant."

"Yeah, I feel terrible. I think I need to throw up."

"Go get some breakfast, Dais. And a shit-ton of water. Call Prim, though. Now. She's been calling me nonstop."

"Okay, I love you."

"Love you too, Dais. See you Sunday night, yeah?"

Daisy sighed. God, she bloody loved that man, even if he had just spent the last ten minutes laughing at her and offering no help whatsoever.

She hesitated before calling Prim because she knew she was about to get an earful. Instead, she opted for a quick text.

Daisy: *Prim, I'm alive. Somehow made it home. High. I'm so sorry, I hope I haven't ruined your hen.*

Her phone rang instantly.

"Daisy, what the hell? How? When? Why? I've been calling you!"

"Prim, it's not my finest hour, okay? Last thing I remember was you slumped in that armchair and Clare force-feeding you water, and then Lena gave me some of her muffin. That Lena... she's dodgy, Prim."

"Oh shit. Really? Well, you didn't have to eat it, you knobhead. And how the hell did you get home?"

"I bought a train ticket for 348 euros, Prim. Not the best decision, but considering I thought I was buying a ticket for the Millennium Falcon, I'd say it was a fair trade-off just to get home."

"Okay..." Prim tried to control her laughter. "Well, I'm glad you're safe. I take it you're not coming back?"

"Not much point, is there? You're back tomorrow morning. You go enjoy yourself and bring my bag home."

"Okay, I will. Love you, baby sis."

"Love you too, Prim. Enjoy yourself."

"Bye."

Daisy tried to get up, and her head spun, forcing her to immediately lie back down. She realised she was in for the most mammoth hangover of her life.

Then, she heard her name.

"Daze, what are you doing in a bush?"

Please don't be Viv or John. Jesus.

Wait. They said "Daze." She squinted up at the sun.

Matthew.

Oh god, why?

What the actual hell was he doing here?

He helped her up.

"Matthew, what are you doing here?"

"Um, okay, this is awkward, but you actually texted me last night saying you were going to space...?"

Of course, she fucking did.

"And, well, I thought I'd come check if you were okay."

"Well, I'm sorry you wasted your journey. I was supposed to text my boyfriend, Sam, not you."

"Hmm, okay. Well, at least let me help you inside," he said as she stumbled.

"It's fine, honestly," she said, struggling to get her key from under the plant pot.

Of course, it's not there. She removed it after the whole Prim-letting-herself-in incident, where her entire maternal line caught her and Sam 'at it' on her sofa. She wasn't ready for that to happen again anytime soon. Once was mortifying enough.

Bollocks. Now, when she actually needed her spare key, it wasn't there.

Seriously, fuck her life.

"Okay, Matthew, don't go. I might need your help. My key isn't there, so I'm locked out."

"Why don't you have keys, Daze?"

"It's a really long fucking story. Can you take me to Nanna Jean's? She has a spare, but she lives in Battersea. It will take forever on the tube."

"Of course."

Just as they were leaving, John appeared. No Viv this time.

"Oh, Daisy, you're awake. Why on earth would you sleep outside, dear?"

"Erm, because I locked myself out, John. That's why."

"Oh, you should have said. You could've come into ours. Viv wouldn't have minded."

Like fuck she would. She'd rather boil her own head.

"That's a really kind offer, John, but my friend here—he's come to the rescue now."

"Oh? What's happened to your boyfriend? Samuel, is it? The really tall, gorgeous young lad?"

Daisy can feel Matthew rolling his eyes.

"Sam, he's in Portugal. Stag do. He'll be back Sunday. This is, um, Matthew, my friend."

"Right."

She mouths "go" to Matthew.

"See you later, John."

They ran and jumped into Matthew's car.

Later, Daisy had managed to get back into her flat after collecting her spare key from Nanna Jean. She offered Matthew a coffee. It's the least she could do after he'd been running her around all morning.

"So, I wanted to apologise, Daisy, for kissing you the other week. It was well out of order."

"Okay…"

Daisy wasn't sure she wanted to do this dance with him again. She didn't have the patience.

"Look, it was stupid, intrusive, and I don't know why I did it. It was selfish of me to try and mess with your life like that. To do it in my, um, situation. Please, can we just… Can we be friends?"

Daisy felt a smile stretch across her face. Because yes, it was stupid. Yes, she loved Matthew. She always would. But she also loved Sam, and it was in two very different ways because Sam had her whole heart.

"Yes, Matthew, we can be friends."

Later that evening, Daisy decided she had to see Lydia. This was ridiculous. She wasn't sure why she was avoiding her, but she was no longer allowing it. And she had to fill Lydia in on the latest drama. It had been ages since she'd seen her, what with Sam becoming her boyfriend and everything else, and in all honesty, she just missed her best friend.

She fired a quick text message, and Lydia replied instantly.

Daisy: *Hey Lyd, you free for a drink?*

Lydia: *What—yes. Hold on. Why aren't you in Dam?*

Daisy: *Long story. I'll tell you when I see you. It's a classic.*

Lydia: *Yesssss classic Daisy drama. OMG, I can't wait to see you.*

She got ready and headed into town to meet Lydia at a Korean restaurant on Carnaby Street. As she sat down, she noticed Lydia hadn't ordered their usual bottle of Prosecco—probably for the best after last night's events, Daisy was still absolutely hanging.

Instead, Lydia was drinking some kind of weird milk-based drink. Daisy opted for a Bloody Mary. An attempt at recovery.

Lydia leapt up to hug her. She looked… different.

"Hey, baby girl. I've missed you." She shrieked.

"I've missed you too, Lyd. How have you been?"

Lydia paused, her eyes suddenly welling with tears.

"Lyd, are you okay? Why are you upset?"

Daisy moved around to sit beside her, a sinking feeling forming in her stomach. Guilt creeping in. She had been so wrapped up in her own drama—and Sam—that she had clearly missed something huge in her best friend's life. She suddenly felt awful.

"Daisy, it's not you, okay? I haven't been completely honest."

"Okay…"

"A lot has happened these last few weeks. I have a few things to tell you. First—I'm pregnant."

Daisy had taken the worst possible moment to sip her drink, which ended up splattered tomato juice all over the table—and Lydia.

"Oh my God, sorry! Shit. Lyd, are you okay?"

"Yeah, I'm fine. I'm keeping it." quickly wiping herself "Oh, and Lance knows."

"Wait—what? Lance knows?"

"I needed help. I had to tell him. We weren't deliberately hiding it from you. I made him swear to secrecy. I'm sorry."

Daisy blinked, still reeling. "Right… and who's the father?" making a mental note to return to Lance later.

"It's Luca."

Another ill-timed sip. Fantastic.

"Luca? As in Grant's mate Luca? You know he's going to be at the wedding, right? You're a bridesmaid!"

"Daisy. I don't need judgment right now."

"Sorry. That came out wrong. It's just... a shock. Quite a big one."

"It's okay. He knows. He was actually really sweet about it. Wants to be involved as much as possible, wants to support the baby financially and I'm happy with that."

"Okay. So are you and him... together?"

"Well—this brings me to the other thing."

An intentional pause as the waitress arrived to take their order. Once she was gone, Daisy leaned in, desperate for answers.

"So?"

"I've been seeing a girl, Dais. I'm bisexual."

Daisy sat stunned. She had barely wrapped her head around the pregnancy—now this?

"You're... bisexual? Since when? Why didn't you tell me, Lyd?"

"I didn't know. Not until about six months ago. When I met Emmy."

"Emmy? Your roommate Emmy?"

Lydia nods.

Daisy fell silent, processing. Then, she shifted beside her and wrapped Lydia in the biggest hug, tears stinging her eyes.

"I'm so sorry you felt like you couldn't tell me. That I wasn't there for you. That you had to go through this without me. I've been such a crap friend."

"Daisy, stop. This isn't your fault. It's my mess."

"But I wanted to be there for you. I hate that I wasn't. God, I was so wrapped up with Sam and my own life. I'm so sorry, Lyd."

"You were happy. You and Sam were finally together. I get it."

"I should have been there though."

"You're here now. That's all that matters."

They ugly cried for about fifteen minutes, and for once, Daisy didn't care about the extra attention from the rest of the restaurant.

"So are you and Emmy—are you together?" she asks, wiping her nose.

"We are. And she knows everything. She can't wait to meet you properly. And Sam, of course."

Daisy grins, a little overwhelmed but genuinely happy. "That's amazing, Lyd. I'm still in shock, but I'm so happy for you. I mean it."

"Thanks, Dais."

"When can I meet her? Properly. I mean, I know she was your roommate, but I don't really know that much about her. Tell me?"

Lydia smiles at the thought of Emmy. "Emmy's great. She's petite, cute, beautiful, she's twenty-six, an artist."

"Wow, amazing. Prim would love her. Can I see any of her work?"

"Well actually, there's a gallery in Southwark showing some of her stuff. The opening is next weekend. You and Sam should come."

"We definitely will. Send me the details."

For the first time in weeks, Lydia looked lighter, like a weight had been lifted.

"So... Amsterdam. What the hell actually happened?"

Daisy winces. "Let's just say—if someone offers you a muffin in Amsterdam… don't eat it."

Lydia burst into laughter, and Daisy joined her.

When Sam walked through the door to Daisy's flat that evening, she was sitting on the sofa in a trance—half processing, half watching The Great British Bake Off. Lydia's revelations had been a lot, and now she was grappling with the uncomfortable truth that she'd become so distant from her best friend's life, she didn't see any of it coming. She missed all of it.

But there was one thing that was becoming all too clear: Sam was fast becoming her other best friend—and she needed to find a way to make space for both of them, without either feeling forgotten. There was definitely room for both.

"Hey," Sam says, voice croaky, as Tino immediately lost his mind with excitement.

"Oh, hey Tino. Hey, hey." He gave the Frenchie some much-needed attention.

"I am so glad you're back. I've had... an interesting weekend."

"Oh really? More interesting than your little 'accidental getting high' episode on Friday?"

"Yeah." She playfully swiped at him. "I met up with Lydia yesterday. She's pregnant. And bisexual."

"Wait, what?" Sam blinked, clearly trying to process both pieces of information at once.

"Yep. She has a girlfriend. Her name's Emmy." She then adds casually, "We're going to her gallery opening next weekend to meet her."

"Right..." Sam looked like his brain had given up— he was far too hungover to deal with this conversation.

Daisy kneeled up and kissed him softly. God, she had missed his smell.

"Sorry—how was your weekend?"

He dropped onto the sofa beside her, resting his head on her chest with a groan.

"I feel like death, Dais. But it was really good."

"That's good." She smiled, fingers stroking gently through his hair.

"I missed you. A hell of a lot."

"You did?"

"Yep. I wouldn't say I was pining, exactly, but it was something close. Grant's started calling me Romeo."

"Why?"

"Apparently because I couldn't stop talking about you, messaging you..." She laughed, leaning in to kiss him. "That's actually kind of adorable."

Sam grinned wickedly, grabbing her and flipping her underneath him.

"Oh yeah—I can do better than adorable."

"One thing's for sure—you're never leaving me again," she warned, eyes narrowing in mock-seriousness.

Sam chuckled. "Okay, that's a promise."

Then he kissed her—one of those brain-altering, breath-stealing, everything-melting kisses—and in that moment, she didn't want him to ever stop.

The kiss deepened, his hands already slipping beneath the hem of her top.

"Did I mention I missed you?" he growled, dragging her shirt up and over her head in one swift movement, his mouth immediately trailing down the curve of her collarbone.

"Once or twice," she giggled, breath catching as his lips found her skin again—and then she stopped giggling altogether when she heard him undo his belt.

He kissed lower, slower, his stubble scratching deliciously against her chest as he worked his way down. "You smell the same," he murmured, lips brushing the underside of her breast. "Like vanilla and chaos."

"Excuse me?" she gasped, laughing breathlessly as he unhooked her bra with maddening ease.

"I stand by it," he said, trailing kisses across her now-bare skin. "Sweet but absolutely unhinged."

"Oh, please," she whispered, tangling her fingers in his hair, tugging just enough to make him groan. "You love it."

"Yeah," he said, voice thick. "I really fucking do."

His hands skimmed down her sides, hooking into the waistband of her pyjama shorts. He tugged them down slowly, like he had all the time in the world—despite the fact that Tino, asleep in his bed, could require attention at any moment.

She writhed beneath him, half-laughing, half-desperate. "We've got, like, eight minutes max before he starts pawing at the door like a furry pervert."

"Then I'd better make them count," Sam murmured, eyes dark as he kissed her hip, then lower.

He dipped between her thighs with a certainty that made her head fall back instantly. He knew exactly how to unravel her.

And that he did.

Her fingers clenched the edges of the sofa, hips lifting instinctively as she moaned out his name.

"Oh my God—Sam," she gasped, already close. "I—don't stop—"

He didn't. Not until she came undone beneath him, shattering apart in waves.

He kissed his way back up her body, slow and smug, his smile wicked. "Best sound in the world," he whispered, lips brushing her jaw as he settled between her legs.

Daisy thought back to the first, and only night, of the Hen, how the other girls were giddy over his pictures. Her man. All hers. She felt satisfyingly smug.

She reached down, guiding him with a soft touch and they both groaned like they'd been starving for it. Moving slow and controlled at first, every movement driving the breath from her lungs. She clung to him, nails digging into his back, gasping his name between kisses. As the rhythm built fast, she dug her heels into the small of his back, urging him faster.

"Christ, you feel—" he broke off with a growl, biting her shoulder lightly, hips stuttering.

"Don't you dare stop," she moaned, pulling him closer, breath catching.

"I'm not going anywhere," he panted, kissing her hard, swallowing her moans as the second wave tore through her. He kept going, breath ragged, forehead pressed to hers until he came undone.

Collapsing together, sweaty and tangled and utterly spent, limbs a mess across the sofa.

Somewhere in the hallway, there was a faint scratch-scratch against the door.

Daisy laughed, chest still heaving. "There's the pervert."

Sam groaned. "I'll walk him later. I physically cannot move."

She rolled into his side, grinning. "Worth the risk of emotional damage?"

"Every time." he murmured, kissing the top of her head.

Chapter 33:
Delicious and functional

After a hellish weekend, Daisy wanted nothing more than to curl up in bed with Tino and Sam and shut the world out.

But instead, she dragged herself up.

Well—Sam did. Because despite being annoyingly cute, he was also annoyingly efficient. And an early riser. How does he do this with a hangover?

Anxious and quietly furious at the world, Daisy got in the shower.

And by *got in the shower*, she meant stood under the water for twenty minutes questioning every life decision she'd ever made. Did she really need a job? Could she just… not?

But as she stood there, face half-melted against the tile, a little voice started nagging at her. That uneasy, back-of-the-brain kind of itch.

There was one small issue with the weekend.

One minor detail she hadn't mentioned to Sam.

Matthew.

Bloody Matthew.

She had failed to tell him that Matthew had come over. And, to be fair… she probably should have. But what with the muffin comedown from hell, Lydia's revelations, and the sofa sex, it just—it slipped her mind.

Then again, Daisy also hadn't mentioned that Matthew kissed her a few weeks ago. She and Sam weren't technically together at the time—but still. Maybe she should have brought that up too.

She planned to. She really did.

But things were going so well right now, and with the wedding just around the corner, Daisy wanted to stay in the bubble.

Just a little while longer.

And hide from it.

Classic *Daisy Number Two* behaviour.

And as we all know, with Daisy Number Two, it never ends well.

Daisy thought that behaviour was behind her.

And that fact was about to become painfully obvious as she and Sam left for work together.

Bloody John and Viv.

"Well, good morning to you both."

"Morning," Daisy said, far too brightly.

Sam just nodded, non-committal. He barely talked to his own neighbours—he wasn't about to start with Daisy's.

"So, Sam's returned then," John said, like he was narrating an episode of Coronation Street.

"He has," Daisy replied, voice uncertain—because it hit her. Like a dropkick to the chest.

John had spoken to them both, to her *and* Matthew that night. He'd asked where Sam was. Oh God.

Don't say it, John. Just don't.

"So, your friend Matthew—the one who popped by the other night—is he a mate of yours, Sam?"

Shit. Shit. Shit. Shit.

Daisy was absolutely screwed.

Sam frowned, pulling out the AirPod he'd just put in.

"Sorry, what was that?"

Daisy jumped in fast. Desperate, almost.

"Oh—it's nothing! We've got to get to work, John. Have a lovely day!"

She grabbed Sam's hand and practically dragged him down the street.
"What was that about?" He looked at her, puzzled—but it seemed he didn't really hear.

Daisy had gotten away with it.

For now.

But she was on borrowed time. She *had* to tell him. She had to explain it was innocent. That there was nothing for him to worry about. That Matthew knew—and, more importantly, she now knew.

She was in love with Sam.

And Matthew wasn't anything to her—anymore.

"Can we have lunch? Just the two of us today?"

"Of course, gorgeous." He lifted her hand and kissed her knuckles, like always.

And Daisy felt her stomach flip. Just in the bad way this time.

Daisy was halfway through pretending to read an email when Lance wheeled his chair over with all the subtlety of a drag queen entering a funeral.

"Right," he said, placing a Tupperware container dramatically on her desk. "Emergency. I've brought you one of my probiotic gut-healing brownies."

She blinked at him. "That sounds like a contradiction in terms."

"They're delicious *and* functional, thank you very much. Plus, I know you were drinking this weekend. Your skin is screaming."

Daisy glanced at her reflection in the black screen of her monitor.

She did, admittedly, look like someone who had eaten a questionable muffin in Amsterdam and cried through a Korean dinner.

"I love you, but I might throw that at you." She reached for a brownie. "These haven't got pot in them, right?"

Lance ignored her, scanning her face like a concerned mum. "Something's off. You've got that guilty, slightly hungover energy."

"That's just my personality."

"No, no, this is different." He leaned closer. "What did you do?"

Daisy narrowed her eyes. "Why would you assume I did something?"

Lance sat back with a smug smile. "Because you always do something. And when you do, you get twitchy. Like now, with your foot doing that little tap-tap-tap under the desk."

She stopped her foot mid-tap.

"I hate you," she muttered.

"I know. Now spill."

She sighed, opening the Tupperware despite herself. "I may or may not have forgotten to tell Sam something about Saturday night."

Lance's eyes lit up like a teenager catching wind of scandal in the group chat. "Go on."

"Matthew came over. On Saturday. Completely uninvited— because, in theory, I was still in Amsterdam. Sam was still on the stag. And John, our nosy neighbour, decided to casually drop it into conversation this morning."

Lance practically clutched his invisible pearls. "You are chaotic evil, my love."

"I know. I panicked, changed the subject, and now we're doing lunch and I have to actually… tell him. Properly. The whole thing."

"Shit, Dais."

"It gets worse." She lowered her voice. "A while ago. Before Sam and I were official… Matthew kissed me."

"Holy crap. Why am I only just hearing about this now, you absolute trollop?"

"Because it was after I had decided I wanted to be with Sam. Because I didn't want to relive it. I wanted to bleach it from my brain, Lance."

Lance's tone softened. "Dais… you do need to tell him. All of it. I love you, but if this comes out later, it's going to wreck him."

"I know," she said quietly.

He gave her a small, sincere smile. "You've got this. Just be honest. You've changed—you're not the old Daisy who runs from stuff anymore."

She nodded, biting into the brownie. It was weirdly good.

"And also," he added, "if it all goes horribly wrong, you can come live with me, and we'll run away and open a boutique skincare café in Brighton."

Daisy laughed. "Deal. But only if I get to name it."

"Only if it's pun-based."

"Obviously."

Her phone buzzed.

Sam: *You've officially ruined my concentration. Hope you're happy.*

She stared at it for a second too long.

"I've really got to tell him," she said, more to herself than to Lance.

Lance nodded solemnly. "At lunch. Full honesty. And maybe don't start with the part where your ex kissed you. Ease him in. Like a gentle serum."

Daisy met Sam at a cute but slightly dingy Italian place on the corner—the one with terrible acoustics and an aggressively romantic playlist that always seemed to be playing That's Amore at a wildly inappropriate volume. But the food? Incredible. Not that Daisy could even think about eating. Or thinking, really. Not with what she had to confess.

Sam was already seated at a table outside, sunglasses on, scrolling through his phone like he hadn't spent the entire morning melting Daisy's insides. He looked up as she slid into the chair opposite. That bloody smile. It made her momentarily consider keeping her mouth shut forever and never telling him anything ever again.

"Hey," she said, a little too brightly.

"Hey," he replied, reaching across the table and catching her hand. "You okay? You seemed a bit… distracted this morning."

There it was—too casual. Too careful. He was fishing.

Damn it. Of course, he knew something.

"Yeah," she said quickly, fidgeting with her napkin. "Just… tired. It's been a bit of a whirlwind lately."

They ordered—him: pasta and a beer; her: a salad and a creeping sense of dread.

The silence that followed wasn't easy, companionable silence. It was tight, weighted. Sam sipped his drink like he was giving her one last chance to speak. Daisy stared at the condensation on her water glass like it might provide a script.

"Okay," she blurted. "I have to tell you something."

Sam set his glass down, watching her closely. Too closely. "Go on."

She hesitated, pulse roaring. "While you were away… Matthew came over."

Sam didn't flinch. Not really. Just the smallest shift in his eyes, like he'd been waiting for her to say it. "Right. And?"

Her stomach dropped. Of course. The neighbour. He already knew.

"I didn't invite him," she rushed out. "He just turned up. Said he wanted to talk."

She told a half-truth—she had texted him, high and in a haze, thinking it was Sam. But still. The end result was the same: Matthew had turned up uninvited.

"He took me to Nanna Jean's to get my spare key, dropped me back, stayed for about ten minutes. Nothing happened. It was awkward. I just wanted him gone."

Sam's jaw tightened. His voice was even, but too even. "And you didn't mention this yesterday because…?"

"I don't know," she admitted, voice small. "Because it didn't mean anything. And you'd just come home and everything felt so good and I didn't want to ruin it. I panicked."

He leaned back, studying her with a look she couldn't quite read—half hurt, half calculation. Like he was deciding whether this was just Daisy being Daisy, or something he really needed to worry about.

"Anything else I should know?" he asked quietly.

Daisy froze.

This was it. The bit she still didn't know how to say. The part that knotted her stomach.

She met his gaze. "A few months ago… before we were properly us… he kissed me."

Sam blinked. Once. Twice. Then his jaw locked. "He bloody what?"

"I pulled away," she said quickly. "Told him it was a mistake. But I didn't tell you then because I didn't know how I felt—about you, about us. I didn't want to mess it up before it even started."

He leaned back, looking away, shoulders rigid. The muscle in his jaw ticked.

Oh God. Was this the old Sam Callaghan again? The cold one. The guarded one.

Panic spread through Daisy's chest like wildfire.

She took a shaky breath and reached across the table, desperate. "I know how this sounds. But I need you to know it meant nothing. He's not the one I want. You are. I love you, Sam. I only love you."

That word—love—landed. His eyes flicked back to hers, and something shifted. For a split second, she saw the wall crack.

But then—just as quickly—he shuttered himself again.

Because the truth was, it wasn't her he was furious with. It was Matthew. But anger was easier than vulnerability. And he had never been good at untangling the two.

He exhaled slowly, unclasping her hand from his, his knee bouncing under the table. His silence pressed down on her until she felt like she might choke.

Finally, he muttered, "We should get back." Rising from his seat.

Her heart dropped. "Sam… wait. Please."

He paused, not quite meeting her eyes. "Look, I'm glad you told me. I just… I need some time to process this."

The words were calm, but his tone wasn't. Not really. It was clipped, controlled. Wrong.

Daisy's panic surged, high-level, chest-tightening panic. He said he needed time, but all she could hear was distance.

Back at the office, they walked in like storm clouds—Stone Cold Sam Callaghan and a very sheepish, very guilty Daisy trailing behind.

Lance, of course, clocked it immediately. He mouthed: Did it go okay?

Daisy replied with frantic hand gestures and an expression that said it all.

No. It did not.

They returned to their desks. Sam was unusually quiet. Cold. Distant. That wall was back with a vengeance.

Lance messaged her on work chat.

LD: *So he didn't take it well?*

DD: *Nope.*

LD: *Oh babe. I'm sorry. At least you were honest.*

DD: *Right. I'm basically Spencer Hastings at this point.*

The tension hung heavy in the office. No texts. No casual glances. Nothing.

And then—

LD: *Sam has left the building.*

DD: *WDYM?*

LD: *He just grabbed his coat and bag. Gone. Vanished. Like David bloody Blaine.*

Shit.

Daisy's heart dropped. She quickly texted him.

Daisy: *Where did you go? Sam?*

Read. No reply.

She banged her forehead against her desk with a groan.

Why does she always ruin things?

Chapter 34:
The confrontation

That night, Daisy spiralled. Proper spiral. The kind where she ended up lying on her bed surrounded by empty wine glasses, half a packet of crisps, and Tino giving her the kind of side-eye that screamed: Pull yourself together, woman.

Her thoughts looped on repeat: she'd ruined it, lost him, destroyed the one good thing in her life. Every time she tried to reassure herself—he said he needed time, he didn't dump me—another wave of panic smothered it.

Then came the mental slideshow of all the stupid things she'd ever done. Quitting jobs. Texting exes. Crying in Ubers. Classic Daisy Donaldson: self-sabotage – the best bits.

In a moment of weakness, okay, three moments, she texted him.

Daisy: *I'm really sorry. Can we talk?*

Daisy: *Or… not. Just tell me you're okay.*

Daisy: *Please.*

Read. No reply.

Her chest tightened. She sent another. Then another. Eventually, three little blue ticks just sat there, mocking her. He was definitely ignoring her now.

When she finally fell asleep, it was more like passing out from exhaustion.

The next morning, she couldn't face it. She avoided Sam like the plague.

Mainly because she had very unhingedly cried on the tube on the way to work; the look was unmistakable. No fillers here, just regular heartbreak.

She needed to get a grip.

She took the long way round to the kitchen, ducked into meeting rooms that weren't hers, even faked an urgent phone call just to escape walking past his desk.

But by mid-morning, she couldn't avoid noticing it: Sam's lip.

Split. Red. Suspiciously swollen.

He looked like he'd walked straight out of a boxing match, except he was just… sitting there typing. Calm. Professional. Like nothing had happened.

Daisy froze by the printer, eyes glued to his face.

What the actual hell?

Lance swivelled in his chair, whisper-hissing: "Oh my God. Why does Sam look like he lost a fight with Conor McGregor?"

Daisy's pulse thundered.

What the hell has happened?

She waited patiently until the afternoon for most people to leave the office before she had made up her mind to try, she had to. Heart pounding, palms clammy, she headed towards his desk, and he was already leaving. Jacket on, headphones in. Head down as he passed with barely even a look.

It wasn't rejection. But it wasn't what she needed either. Her throat closed up as she carried on walking past to god knows where. "Another time then," she muttered to herself. Briefly pretending to look out the window and then returning to her desk feeling deflated. Defeated. Like her insides had turned to stone.

By the time she got home that night, she collapsed onto the sofa, exhaustion crashing over her until sleep finally won.

Because little did she know, Sam hadn't gone to clear his head yesterday.

He'd actually taken himself to St Thomas' Hospital.

To find Matthew.

To look him in the eye. To confront him.

Sam left work in a foul mood. One part frustration, one part guilt. He'd avoided talking to Daisy all day, desperate to sort things out, yet still simmering with anger. Why had she lied? Or withheld the truth?

A fleeting thought of taking responsibility for his own behaviour crossed his mind—maybe he owed her an explanation—but his pride wouldn't allow it.

He wanted to sulk. So instead of resolving things when he could, he chose to stew.

Sam headed to the pub, seeking the comfort of a pint and the permission to wallow, staring at the dregs of his drink while his mind replayed yesterday: storming into St Thomas' Hospital, blind rage coursing through him, utterly unprepared for reality.

He had gone in fully prepared to punch Matthew square in the face the moment he saw him—right there, in the middle of his workplace. But eventually, the rational part of his brain kicked in, and he realised it was a terrible idea.

For one, he had no clue where to find Matthew or even what he was going to say. For two, it was wildly inappropriate—it was a hospital, after all. And three, there was a very real possibility he could get arrested. Definitely not the kind of confrontation his dad would approve of.

But he needed to find Matthew and speak to him properly. Get him to agree to talk this out.

And also politely ask him to stay the hell away from his girlfriend.

Sam had boldly walked up to the reception desk.

"Yes, sir, name please."

Oh, right. It's Accident & Emergency.

"Sir, hello, what is your name? What's the issue?"

"Erm, I'm not sick. I'm actually looking for someone—a doctor. Dr. Devan?"

"Doctors won't see anyone who's not sick, love. This area is for urgent medical needs."

"I know that. I just need to know where he works."

"I can't give you that information, sir. Now, could you please step aside? There are other patients waiting."

"Wait—hold on. Please—where can I get that information?"

"It's a busy afternoon, sir. You'll need to head to the main hospital if you want to arrange an appointment with a doctor. Right now, you're holding up the queue."

"But I don't need an appointment." Sam huffed in defeat, stepping aside. Another passing staff member noticed his anguish and spoke up quietly.

"Dr. Devan works in Children's A&E. You might want to head through those doors to find him. But he is really busy today."

"Right. Thank you."

Sam walked into the children's department, feeling suddenly guilty. Sick and injured kids were everywhere, and Daisy's heroic ex was out there saving lives. How the hell was Sam supposed to compete with that?

Maybe she was better off with him.

He stood at the reception desk, debating whether he should even go up. This was wrong. He turned to leave—but then he saw a face he recognised in the back of the reception.

Dr. Matt Devan.

Matthew was laughing and joking with the receptionist and a staff nurse, flashing his signature smile. Smug prick.

Sam forgot all those morals he had before, and he was now seething. He wanted to wipe that smile off his bloody face.

He marched up to the desk, a mental battle with himself to stay calm. Remember, Sam. This is a hospital, not your local.

"Sam Callaghan," Matthew said, recognition sinking in. "What are you doing here? In children's A&E? Do you have secret children?"

"No. Look, I need to speak to you. Briefly. After your shift."

Matthew hesitated, then agreed. "I have a break in forty-five minutes."

"Pub. Slug & Lettuce," Sam instructed. Matthew smirked but didn't argue.

Sam turned and walked out, making his way to the pub. He sat in the dim light of the Slug near Waterloo Station, staring at his pint. What was he doing? What would Daisy think?

But no. He had to do this. He had to know why the hell Matthew couldn't stay the hell away from Daisy.

God, this situation was complicated. Sam had never been in a relationship before, and he was in way over his head.

The thought of the kiss between Daisy and Matthew gnawed at him. He hadn't seen it, but he couldn't stop imagining it. How dare Matthew touch her? His hands, his lips... on his girlfriend. On his Daisy.

Before he could work himself into a frenzy, he heard a voice behind him.

"Sam."

Matthew had arrived, still in scrubs. A tactical move to make this look even worse than it was, Sam thought. He stood, his anger returning like a moth to a flame. Visibly taller than Matthew but surprisingly not as bulky.

"Outside. Beer garden." Sam said, his voice low.

Matthew laughed. "Are you joking?"

Sam scoffed. "No, mate, I'm not joking." He started walking toward the beer garden.

"Well, can I at least get a drink first?" Matthew asked, following.

Luckily, the beer garden was fairly empty. They settled at the bottom, the tension thick between them.

"So, can you explain what the hell is going on?" Matthew asked, frowning as Sam began pacing.

"You know what's going on. I know about the kiss. The meet-ups. The messages. All of it."

"Ah." Matthew raised an eyebrow.

"Who do you think you are, pestering my girlfriend like that? I've got to admire your persistence, mate."

"Technically, she wasn't your girlfriend. She told me you were complicated?"

That set Sam off like a firework. He stepped forward, voice low and dangerous.

"You don't know me, mate. You don't know our relationship, and yet you tried to force yourself back into her life. When you're engaged. You should be ashamed."

"Mate, calm down. This is a public place." Matthew smirked.

Big mistake.

"I should rip that little smirk off your face, you smug bastard." Sam grabbed Matthew by the collar.

"Now hold on—she is my ex. And she was replying to me. If she didn't want to, she wouldn't have," Matthew said, holding out his hand to try and put some distance between them.

"Because she's a good person. You were taking advantage."

"I was not."

"You kissed her, mate. We were involved. Do you have any idea how inappropriate that is?"

"Maybe she wanted to kiss me. Did you ever think about that?"

Sam's temper flared. One swift movement, and Matthew crashed into a wooden table.

Matthew got up, throwing a punch at Sam's mouth. Words escalated into punches—one, two, three—until they both realised they were fighting in the beer garden.

This was ridiculous.

Matthew collapsed onto a bench, exhaling heavily, dabbing at his nose.

"Okay," he said finally, "I guess I deserved that."

Sam sat opposite, still seething, not making eye contact as he wiped his busted lip with a serviette. Blood stains on his grey suit.

Matthew continued, "Look, let's just calm down and hear me out. Yeah?"

Sam stayed silent for a moment before replying.

"We were happy. She's not interested in you anymore, mate. You're in the past. Go back to your bloody wife."

"Fiancée."

Sam shook his fist at the correction. He was just starting to calm down.

"Okay, look, I'm sorry," Matthew said, his tone shifting. "Let's just calm down, I was out of line. I know," Matthew tried a gentler tone. "She's with you. She loves you. Last time I saw her… it was clear."

Sam listened, silent. The tension didn't fully fade. Beating Matthew hadn't fixed anything.

He wanted to believe it—that she loved him—but the truth he refused to admit, even to himself, gnawed at him: he couldn't imagine life without Daisy.

With a heavy exhale, Sam stood. "I have to go."

He left Matthew in the beer garden, bloodied and speechless, and headed home. To wallow. To stew. To sit with the fact that, right now, he didn't know how to fix this. Too proud to admit it, too stubborn to stop thinking about her.

And now here he was alone in another pub. No better off than yesterday.

He checked his phone briefly.

Flicking back to her messages he had read but left on read. Fingers hovering over the keyboard. Mentally replying.

He couldn't. He just ordered another drink. And another, then staggered home.

It had been two days of emotional turmoil for Daisy. Sam had asked for space, and she'd 'withheld information'—okay, lied, but in her defence, it wasn't malicious. She could sort of understand why he was upset. If the shoe were on the other foot… she'd probably be furious too.

And Sam Callaghan wasn't like other men. He could flip, just like that, back into the old, guarded Sam. She had to let him come to her.

Although, truthfully, she was getting a bit impatient.

"You sorted it out yet?" Lance asked, leaning against the kitchen counter.

"Nope. I really think I might have completely screwed this up."

"Oh babe," Lance said, pitying. "For once, I actually don't have any advice."

Daisy laughed. Rare. Very rare. Lance always had advice.

Always.

She let herself sink back into the seat. The tension simmered, relentless.

"Should I be angry?" she asked finally.

"I mean, I don't know… you did kiss your ex. And…"

Daisy cut him off, exasperated. "I mean the ignoring—the complete refusal to let me explain myself."

Lance nodded thoughtfully. "I think he asked for space, and this time, you actually need to give it, babes. If you want him, you let him come back to you."

"But what if he doesn't?"

Lance grinned. "Babe. You're basically his Lorelai Gilmore. He can't stay away."

Finally, that Friday afternoon, Sam as usual stayed at his desk, arms crossed, eyes on his laptop—as Daisy walked past on her way back from Rhoda's office, she could feel him watching her out of the corner of her eye.

She hesitated, then took a deep breath to approach him because Daisy hated not being able to speak to him, not sorting things out, not having her say.

And it was now virtually impossible to bear.

She didn't like it that it was her in trouble, she much preferred it when Sam was causing the trouble.

She had to try. Heart pounding, palms clammy, she hovered by his desk before blurting: "Sam, can we talk?" Glancing down at his bruised lip. She really needed to know what that was about.

"I know you said to need to have space and time to process but I—I really feel like you need to at least give me a chance to explain—"

He didn't look up immediately. Finally, he gave her a slow,

measured glance. "I agree," he said quietly, almost too casual, "we can… talk. Just not here. Later after work. When I've figured out how not to bite your head off." He smirked.

Another small beacon of hope. Her stomach did a little flip. "Later? You mean… actually talk?"

"Yes," he said, a faint twitch at the corner of his mouth—half smirk, half warning. "It's been long enough, I guess."

Daisy exhaled, relief flooding through her. "Okay… good."

"Good," he murmured, turning back to his screen, though his eyes lingered on her for a heartbeat longer. "And Dais… don't do anything drastic before that, yeah?"

She rolled her eyes but smiled. "No promises."

She returned to her desk, triumphant. Lance wheeled over.

"So…"

"After work."

"Yes," he said a little too loudly.

"Lance, stop. He'll hear you."

"I told you though, didn't I? Lorelai Gilmore."

They laughed.

Daisy watched the clock all afternoon, and eventually, Sam approached her desk sheepishly, ready to leave.

"Where shall we go?" Daisy said brightly.

"Don't mind."

"Sam?" she frowned.

"Let's just go to yours. It's closer."

Once inside her flat, the air shifted, and they sat facing each other. Daisy swallowed hard, her chest tight.

"Sam… I'm really sorry. I didn't tell you about Matthew right away. I… should have. I didn't want to hurt you, or make things messy, mostly I didn't want to ruin the wonderful bubble that we were in, but I realise now I just made it worse by—" Daisy choked back a tear.

Sam's jaw softened, and a small, almost imperceptible smile touched his lips before pulling her into a hug.

"Daisy… I've already forgiven you."

"You have?"

"The moment you told me, it was fine. I just struggled to process it. And… I'm sorry it took me so long to get here, to actually face this properly. I guess I was scared. But I've thought it through and I'm not—anymore."

Relief flooded through Daisy, and without thinking, she leaned up and kissed him. Sam winced, rubbing his lip lightly.

"Oh," she said, a grin breaking through. "Can you please explain what the hell happened with your lip?"

"Um, okay— I kind of might have gotten into a bit of a scuffle with—"

"With who?"

"Matt Devan?"

Daisy looked at him, frowning—until she clocked just how annoyingly cute he looked.

"Why, Sam? Why?"

He gave a shrug, trying to look as charming as possible. "He came off far worse than me."

"Sam. And why were you fighting with bloody Matthew?"

"Because of you, Daisy. I'm not letting him treat you like that. He's engaged and still playing games—messing with your head behind his fiancée's back. And mine. It's not okay. Someone had to call him out."

"For once, I agree with you." she smiled.

Sam grinned and pulled her in by the waist, kissing her.

"Ow," he winced. "Okay—yep. That still hurts."

"Oh no, do you need a nurse?"

He scoffed. "You can be my nurse. Maybe even wear the outfit…"

She rolled her eyes. "You're impossible."

"But irresistible," he added with a wink.

She hit him playfully.

"So, I'm forgiven?" she asked sheepishly.

"Just about," he said. She frowned. He kissed her. "I love you, Daisy Donaldson. You've got me trapped."

Daisy's heart felt like it could burst.

She was no longer focused on her double life, the two Daisies. They'd merged into one. The confident, smart, intelligent Daisy. The one who is great at her job and supportive to her family and friends. The one who loves Sam Callaghan with her whole heart.

All this time she'd spent thinking about Matthew—what could've been, what should've been—when, really, walking out of that dead-end insurance job, getting this new one, meeting Sam, and loving Sam... that was the original plan.

She just didn't know it at the time.

"Then we're both doomed," she whispered.

This crazy girl, her over-complicated life. She was the one thing he'd been missing all along, in his lonely one.

Chapter 35:
The Unfathomable Power of Chaos Walking

Things had finally settled into something resembling normal. Prim's wedding was fast approaching, but for once, Daisy and Sam had a weekend to themselves—no chaos, no drama, just quality time. Just them.

Well, almost.

Daisy had completely forgotten about the gallery opening she'd promised Lydia she'd attend. The one where she'd meet Emmy—Lydia's girlfriend. Who, by the way, Lydia was not only dating but also pregnant. By Luca. Not at all complicated.

Daisy wasn't sure what to say. Or how to act. Was it weird? Was it fine? It wasn't even her situation, and yet she was spiralling like it was. Typical. And Sam—he didn't know anyone. She didn't know anyone, not really. Why did she always agree to things when she was feeling social, only to regret them completely when the day arrived?

Yep, Daisy was extremely nervous because she didn't want to make the situation awkward. When it wasn't even her situation in the first place. Damn her stupid brain.

Her anxiety was on a rampage. All she wanted was to enjoy a night out with her boyfriend without the internal drama.

But then Sam walked in, instantly grounding her with just a smile.

"You ready to go?" he said, that half-smile working overtime.

The gallery in Southwark was small but buzzing, filled with artsy types sipping wine from plastic cups and pretending not to eavesdrop on each other's conversations. Daisy tugged at the hem of her jacket, already regretting her choice to "dress the part" in a floaty dress and boots.

Sam, meanwhile, looked unfairly edible in a charcoal grey shirt with the sleeves rolled just enough to show off his forearms. He caught her staring and winked.

Right. Focus.

She turned to the nearest canvas—a giant square painted entirely blue. "So… what do you think?" she whispered.

Sam tilted his head, frowning. "Honestly? Looks like someone spilled Dulux and got paid for it."

Daisy snorted into her wine. "Thank God. I was worried you were about to launch into some deep analysis about 'the void of modern existence' or something."

He smirked. "Sorry to disappoint. My art knowledge stops at doodles on my maths homework."

"Same," Daisy admitted, glancing around at people nodding gravely at sculptures that looked like broken furniture. "We're frauds."

"Completely," he said, clinking his plastic cup against hers. "But at least we're frauds together."

She laughed, the knot in her stomach loosening just a little.

And then they spotted Lydia by the window—glowing, genuinely glowing, like someone who had finally started breathing again after holding it in for years.

"You came!" Lydia beamed, pulling Daisy into a hug that lingered a little longer than usual.

"Wouldn't miss it," Daisy smiled. "You look incredible. Actually glowing. Is that pregnancy or being-in-love?"

"Bit of both," Lydia laughed. "Come on. Emmy's just over here—she's dying to meet you."

Daisy laced her fingers through Sam's and followed Lydia to

Emmy. She was petite, with cropped curls, expressive brown eyes, and smudges of paint still on her fingers. She looked like someone who lived entirely in colour—even her clashing clothes felt like part of a palette.

"Daisy!" Emmy grinned. "Finally. Lydia never shuts up about you."

"All lies," Daisy said. "Nice ones, I hope."

"The nicest. And you must be Sam?"

"That's me." Sam said, shaking her hand. "Love your work. I know absolutely nothing about art, but Daisy's been educating me."

"Daisy knows nothing about art." Lydia scoffed. "She once called a Monet 'blurry flowers' and genuinely thought it was a compliment."

Daisy rolled her eyes. Everyone laughed, and Emmy's smile only grew.

"Come on, I'll show you the piece Lydia helped inspire. It's in the back."

As they wandered deeper into the gallery, past bold canvases and half-finished sculptures, Daisy felt something shift inside her—not just pride for Lydia or admiration for Emmy's bold, emotional art— but something else. A sense of beginnings. Of hope. Of finally stepping into something real and alive.

She nudged Sam and whispered, "By the way, if anyone asks me what I think of the composition, I'm just going to say 'haunting use of negative space' and hope they don't realise I'm talking about the fire extinguisher."

"Here we are," Emmy said proudly. "I call it The Unfathomable Power of Unseen Talent."

The three of them stared at the piece, squinting slightly—trying to figure out exactly how it was Lydia, and if she was, in fact, actually in it.

Daisy glanced at Sam, who mouthed What the hell? behind his hand. She stifled a snort.

"What do you think?" Lydia beamed. "Isn't it beautiful?"

"Um… yeah, it's very… original," Daisy added despite having no clue. "Lucky you."

"It's just such a compliment," Lydia gushed, squeezing Emmy's hand like it might anchor her to the moment.

Daisy nodded, but her awkwardness was rapidly catching up with her. Sam looked like he was mentally searching for the nearest exit, doing everything in his power not to burst out laughing.

The whole moment was too much.

"You know what?" Daisy said quickly. "I'm absolutely parched. How about you, Sam?"

"Extremely," he agreed, a little too eagerly.

"We'll catch up with you both in a bit," Daisy said quickly. "Need to check out the—buffet."

Lydia laughed, utterly oblivious.

Daisy spun on her heel—and immediately tripped over the base of a sculpture. A very expensive-looking, precariously placed sculpture.

It wobbled. Dangerously.

Sam lunged, catching her just in time, yanking her away before she collided with it. But not before Daisy let out a sound somewhere between a gasp and a dying seal.

"Sorry! Sorry!" she winced, face burning as a few people turned to stare. "I'm just… admiring the floor. Very… textured."

Sam gently redirected her by the shoulders. "Why don't we just get a drink, yeah?" he whispered. "Before you accidentally bankrupt me."

"I'm not saying no," Daisy muttered, mortified. "But I swear that sculpture moved.”

“As did your dignity, briefly,” Sam added laughing. “Jesus, what have I signed myself up for with you.”

Daisy scowled at him.

They reached the drinks table.

“Next time I’ll just wear bubble wrap,” Daisy hissed, snatching a glass of wine.

“So that painting?” Sam said, trying—and failing—not to laugh.

“It was really something, wasn’t it.” Daisy smirked. “I’m pretty sure it was a bit of a dig at Lydia, but I didn’t really want to say.”

“Unseen talent. Yeah, it absolutely was.” He started laughing.

“Oh god, please don’t laugh. She will see.”

“But Dais, come on—” They both cracked up, trying to smother their laughter behind their wine glasses.

“You know what? I’m inspired,” Sam added with a playful tone. “I’m going to create a piece for you. I’ll call it The Unfathomable Power of Chaos Walking.”

Sam was already in hysterics, laughing at his own joke.

She smacked his arm, laughing too. “You, Callaghan, are an uncultured swine.”

“Yes, but I’m your uncultured swine.”

Later, Emmy and Lydia rejoined them.

“So Daisy, your sister works at the Tate?” Emmy asked.

“Yes, she’s a curator.”

“That’s amazing. I’d love to get my work into the Tate one day.”

Daisy heard Sam cough slightly. She didn’t dare look in his direction because she knew—absolutely knew—she wouldn’t be able to keep a straight face.

She knew that drastic times called for drastic measures.

"Sam," she said sweetly, "could you get me another drink? I really hurt my leg earlier. On that bloody sculpture."

Sam gave her a look that said Really? but nodded. "Sure. Anything to stop you from causing further injury to yourself or priceless art."

He left to refill their wine, and Emmy, blissfully unaware, waved excitedly to a group of collectors and wandered off to speak to them.

Lydia leaned in beside Daisy.

"Thanks for coming."

"Of course, Lyd," Daisy said. "I wouldn't have missed this for the world. I'm so proud of you."

"Thank you. And thanks for not saying her painting of me was absolute shite." Lydia winked.

Daisy snorted. "It was okay."

They both burst out laughing.

"It doesn't even resemble me. Or a person, for that matter. But I admire her creativity so much. Because I love her."

"Probably has a good chance of getting into the Tate. They normally love stuff that's different—"

"Please do not say that. Not today."

"So, at what point do they ask you to buy a painting though, Lyd? Because I really don't want to be put in that position." Daisy grinned. "Although, it might be extremely hilarious to approach Sam and watch him squirm."

Lydia laughed. "That's a brilliant idea."

They stood laughing.

"So, how are you feeling? With the baby and everything?"

"Yeah, not bad. Had a scan last week—me, Emmy, and Luca.

Total comedy skit.”

“Oh god, I bet.”

“No, actually, it was fine once we got over the awkwardness. The doctors couldn’t get their heads around it. Clearly living in the past.”

“What about you? Have you had sickness?”

“I’m not gonna sugar-coat it, Dais. The first trimester is rough. Be warned. You know… when you and Sam eventually procreate.”

Daisy spat her drink back into the cup.

“Lydia! What are you saying? Shush—he’ll hear you!”

Lydia laughed.

“What, you don’t see kids with him? Liar. You’ve thought about it at least eighteen times.”

“Of course, I have—but I could never say that to him, Lyd. He’d run a marathon in the opposite direction.”

“He would not. He loves you. Adores you, you idiot. You can see it by the way he looks at you.”

Daisy paused, her thoughts drifting. Kids with Sam. They would be downright gorgeous. And he was so supportive. Bringing up children with him would be… kind of a dream. They could have two. Call them… what even goes with Callaghan? Hallie and Annie, obviously.

And suddenly, it didn’t feel as scary as it once had. She stared across the room at him, looking awkward and annoyingly handsome. He spotted her and smirked.

Nope. Way too soon to be thinking about this. Actually, she was royally freaking herself out now. He could probably tell. She needed to snap out of this before he came back.

Daisy turned her attention back to Lydia and sighed.

“I’ve said it before, Lyd, but I’ll say it again. I’m really happy for you. You and Emmy look genuinely happy.”

"You know what, Dais," Lydia said softly, her eyes on Emmy. "I am happy. And for the first time… I'm not pretending."

Daisy reached for her hand and gave it a gentle squeeze.

"You don't have to anymore."

They stood in companionable silence for a moment.

Then Sam returned, two glasses of wine in hand and an expression that screamed suspicion.

"Your drink, madam," he said, handing it to Daisy. "Procured with only mild trauma and a solid five-minute explanation about why the lady limps."

Daisy batted her lashes. "Thank you, kind sir. You've saved me from further embarrassment."

"I don't know," he said. "I've seen the way you handle liquids. I give it five minutes before this ends up on someone's shoe."

Lydia snorted into her diet coke.

"Have some faith," Daisy muttered, taking a sip.

"I do," he said smoothly. "Just not in your coordination."

Lydia raised her glass. "To enduring art, dramatic soul sisters, and Daisy's miraculous recovery."

"To my Oscar-worthy performance," Daisy added, clinking glasses.

Sam just shook his head. "You two are menaces."

Daisy smiled, looking between them. "But we're your menaces."

He groaned. "God help me."

Outside, the air hit them like a splash of clarity—cool, quiet, and deliciously free of modern art and small talk. Daisy tugged her coat tighter and leaned into Sam's side as they strolled away from the gallery.

"I genuinely think I came within inches of becoming

performance art," she muttered.

Sam laughed. "You very nearly took down an entire installation."

"Well, someone put it right in the middle of the walkway like it wasn't just begging to be destroyed."

"It was in the corner."

"Semantics."

He grinned, nudging her shoulder. "You know, I don't want to be dramatic, but I think I saved your life tonight."

"You did. I saw it all—my obituary was going to be Daisy Donaldson: tragically flattened by abstract modernism."

"You'd have gone down in history. Literally."

She snorted. "And the worst part is, I still don't understand what that painting was supposed to be."

Sam gave her a sideways glance. "Are we definitely sure Lydia was even in it?"

Daisy laughed. "I think she was the blue bit near the corner. Or the negative space. Honestly, I've had to stop thinking about it."

They walked for a while in comfortable silence, their steps echoing on the pavement.

Sam finally said, "You know, I like her."

"Which one?"

"Lydia. Though Emmy was nice too."

Daisy smiled. "Yeah, she's something. Messy. Complicated. But something."

He nodded. "Reminds me of someone else I know."

She raised an eyebrow. "Are you comparing me to my pregnant, chaos-vortex bestie?"

"Only the good parts."

She rolled her eyes, but she was smiling.

Then, softer: "She asked me if I'd ever thought about kids. With you."

Oh crap. Why, Daisy. Why?

Sam paused for a second, not surprised. "She asked me the same thing."

Daisy blinked, shocked. "Really?"

He nodded. "I said I wouldn't run."

"You wouldn't?"

"Nope. I mean, I'd probably panic internally. Maybe hyperventilate into a paper bag. But I wouldn't run."

Daisy stared at him, half-horrified, half-warm. "Are we actually having the baby conversation outside an art gallery?"

He shrugged. "It's either that or talk about the fire extinguisher you mistook for sculpture."

"That was one time. And it had a label, Sam."

They both burst out laughing. Sam pulled her close and kissed the top of her head.

"One day, maybe," he said. "Tiny Callaghans. Wreaking havoc. Tripping over everything like their mum."

"Terrifying," Daisy said, grinning into his jacket. "But weirdly… not so terrifying?"

He took her hand again. "Come on. Let's get you something fried and covered in salt."

"God, I knew I kept you around for a reason."

Chapter 36:
Heat off a freshly microwaved lasagna

The days after the gallery opening passed in a hazy blur of early starts, late-night texts, impromptu sleepovers and a strange new lightness Daisy hadn't felt in years.

It wasn't just Sam—although yes, he had everything to do with it. The way he touched her lower back when he passed her at the printer. The way his voice dropped when he whispered stupid jokes in meetings. The way she felt when she caught him watching her with that look—the one that said, how the hell did I get so lucky? (Answer: probably witchcraft. Or her boobs.)

But it was more than that.

It was waking up and feeling… right.

Settled.

For once, not performing or scrambling or second-guessing herself (okay, only a little bit).

She felt seen. Known. And—bloody hell—loved.

Prim's wedding was around the corner, work was piling up, and Jessie had just messaged her for the fifth time that morning about flower arrangements.

"Daisy, you must have an opinion on daisies!"

Lord knows why Prim had put their mum in charge of flowers. The woman thought "eucalyptus" was a type of mint. Jessie, meanwhile, was deep into her vegan, eco-warrior phase and insisted on compostable petals, which Daisy was fairly certain weren't a thing.

And yet, somehow, through all the chaos—with the Matthew stuff firmly behind her—life didn't feel like a mess anymore.

Later that week in the office, Sam wandered over to Daisy's desk with that familiar crooked smile and the swagger of a man who absolutely knew he looked good in navy.

"Can't I take you to lunch today? I know we're practically joined at the hip these days, but there's something I want to give you."

"In the middle of a restaurant? Sam Callaghan, you have zero shame."

"Funny. But it's not that. Although—there are a few meeting rooms vacant around 8.00 pm." He winked.

Daisy laughed. "Of course I'll have lunch with you. Where are we going?"

"I'll ping you."

As he walked off, she let her eyes linger a bit too long on his shoulders. That man—her man now. Officially.

Even met the parents and survived. Well, hers. She wasn't quite ready for Mr. Callaghan Sr. yet. From what Sam had said, the man once made a woman cry during a pub quiz.

Before she could get back to her emails, Lance slid into the empty chair beside her desk with a smoothie the colour of algae and judgement in his eyes.

"Oh God," Daisy groaned. "You saw that, didn't you?"

"Saw it? Darling, I felt it. Your flirty lunchtime vibes practically wafted across the floor like heat off a freshly microwaved lasagna."

"I'm in love, not in heat."

"Tell that to your pupils. They dilated so fast I thought you were about to seize."

She rolled her eyes. "We're just having lunch."

"You said that last week. And then I walked in on you two making out by the printer like teenagers who'd just discovered toner was an aphrodisiac."

"That was one kiss—it wasn't even that bad."

"Please, you had your hand on his belt. I'm not judging, I'm impressed. It's usually such a faff to undo those."

"Lance!"

He sipped his green goop serenely. "What can I say? I support love. I just don't want to get caught in the crossfire of your sexual tension. Get a room. Or at least go to his place."

She threw a pen at him, which he dodged effortlessly.

"Oh, and FYI," he added, standing. "If you're going to sneak off into a meeting room later, may I recommend Meeting Room five? It has the comfiest chairs and zero camera coverage."

"Noted." Daisy laughed but also turned a ridiculous shade of beetroot and spent the rest of the morning thinking about what they could get up to in meeting room five.

Over lunch, Daisy noticed Sam's knee bouncing. He hadn't done that in a while. Why was he so nervous? What was he about to tell her? She didn't like this feeling at all. She thought this was a fun lunch date with her boyfriend that would possibly lead into a hot make-out session.

But this wasn't it. The vibe was off and suddenly she was right back there.

Uneasy. Unsure. Uncomfortable.

The voice in her head was telling her to run. She ignored it.

"So," he began. "I have good news and bad news."

Daisy swallowed a lump down.

"Oh god. That sounds ominous."

"Bad first?" he offered.

She nodded.

"The bad news is... I got a new job. I'm leaving."

"Brandish? Or the country?"

"Brandish." He smiled.

Daisy blinked. Her stomach flipped. How would she survive not seeing his face every day?

"But why?"

"My dad's been on my back to join his firm. I've said no for years. But eventually, the pressure got to me."

"Sam, no. You don't want to work with your dad. That would be miserable."

"I'm not. I spoke to Rhoda—she couldn't offer more money at Brandish, but she put me in touch with her old friend at Vanta Collective. I interviewed for their Finance Director role. And… I got it."

"Why didn't you tell me any of this?" she frowned.

"I'm telling you now. Plus, you had all the wedding stuff going on, and I didn't want to add more chaos. Honestly, I should've told you. But I got the job. I got more money. And more importantly—I got to tell my dad to stick it."

She folded her arms, sulking a bit, despite herself.

"Vanta Collective? They're big."

"Yep. I'll have my own office. It's kind of cool." He smirked. "Daisy, please don't sulk. This is a good thing."

"I'm happy for you. I really am. But I'm going to miss you. No sneaky kisses. No meeting rooms—"

"Which brings me to the good news."

He slid a key across the table. Not in a box. Very intentionally. An attempt at avoiding a full Daisy meltdown. But it did have a little Kawaii keyring of a capybara attached.

"Look, I know you love the community in Bermondsey—"

Daisy snorted.

"But this is just… to show you how serious I am about you, Dais."

"A key?"

"To my flat. Yes."

"Why?" she asked softly.

"Will you move in with me?"

"But what about my flat?"

"Daisy, give your notice. I don't care. I just know I want to live with you. I want you in my future, Daisy. I love you."

"You want to live with me?" she double-checked.

"Yes."

"And Tino?"

"Yes." he sighed, resigned.

She beamed. This was it. He was it. Someone who loved her through all the chaos—flaws, anxiety spirals, and all. And the fact Sam also accepted Tino? That was a bloody bonus.

"I'd love to move in with you."

She squealed, leapt up to kiss him, and several people turned to stare like they'd just gotten engaged. Sam turned a spectacular shade of crimson.

"Right, sit back down," he muttered.

"So when?" she asked, practically clapping.

"I thought this weekend?" he said. "It's just a temporary fix though, my flat, because eventually I'd like to sell it, and we buy one together. One we both choose. That we both own."

"Okay. Um… this is big," she said, blinking.

"Only if you want to."

"You want to buy a place together. Seriously. Sam Callaghan, are you sure that you're not trying to wife me off?" she teased.

"Not yet. But eventually, yeah, I will."

She hadn't expected that answer. She sat with her mouth open. He continued.

"Let's try living together first. And if you haven't killed me by this time next year…"

Oh my God. That was practically a marriage proposal.

Who had she become?! Who had he become?!

"That's if you don't kill me first. Or Tino," she teased.

"I mean, you still have to survive meeting the Callaghans. Mum, Dad, Dad's bit on the side, my baby sibling. What a treat."

Daisy's face sank. She was already afraid of Sam's dad. Now she'd unlocked a brand-new fear: Not being good enough for Sam Callaghan in his father's eyes.

Brilliant.

She needed to change the subject. Fast.

"So… you'll have your own office?" she asked, raising a brow. "Do I get to visit if you're working late?"

"Oh yes. We'll definitely have to christen it at some point."

Great swerve, Daisy. Nothing distracts from a spiralling existential dread quite like the promise of desk-based sex.

Sam smirked like he'd just read her mind. "I'll even bring a 'Do Not Disturb' sign. Very official."

"Better make it two," she replied sweetly. "One for the door. One for me."

He choked on his coffee. Victory.

Let her spiral later. For now—she was winning.

Back at the office, Daisy could hardly contain her excitement. She was practically buzzing—grinning at her screen like it had just proposed to her.

Naturally, Lance appeared within seconds, armed with an oat milk latte and instinctive nosiness.

"Okay, spill," he said, narrowing his eyes. "You're glowing. Not like 'I just had a desperate make-out in the lift' glowing, but something happened. Why are you so hot and flustered—in a different way?"

Daisy spun slightly in her chair, beaming. "Well… Sam just asked me to move in with him."

Lance's jaw dropped. "Shut. Up."

"This weekend," she added, practically squealing.

He gasped dramatically, placing a hand over his heart like she'd just told him Beyoncé was doing admin in the break room. "Daisy Donaldson, you tart! You've been holding out on me. This is huge."

"I know! I still can't quite believe it. I said yes, obviously. So— bring your boxes and your A-game Delaney. You're helping me pack."

"Only if Sam's there. Shirtless."

"Duh. Of course." Daisy grinned.

Lance clapped his hands together. "Perfect. I'll bring wine, bubble wrap, and absolutely no emotional stability. This is going to be so fun."

"Also," Daisy added, "please stop me from packing six different kinds of moisturiser. I need to make space for the important things."

"Like what? Your vibrator and a bottle of emergency gin."

Daisy gasped. "Forget it. I'm asking Lydia."

Lance raised his latte in salute. "To love. And to living with a ridiculously hot man who, let's be honest, probably folds his towels in perfect thirds."

She sighed dreamily. "He really does."

"God, I hate you. Let's get sushi tonight to celebrate."

"Done. But you're paying."

"Fine. But only because you're now officially living every rom-com fantasy I've ever had."

They high-fived like two teenagers who'd just won a dance battle.

Daisy floated through the rest of the day. A new chapter was starting—and for once, it didn't feel terrifying. It felt right.

The moving day approached quickly.

It was happening. It was actually happening. Daisy Donaldson—serial overthinker, commitment-phobe, owner of seventeen mugs and only one working corkscrew—was moving in with a man.

And not just any man.

Sam Callaghan.

Ex-footballer. Emotional support sex god. The one who loved her even if she drenched him in coffee, had over-emotional outbursts, and knew when she was about to cry even before she did.

Seriously, how had this happened?

How was this her life?

Was she secretly a witch?

She stood outside his flat in Shepherd's Bush, hair scraped up into a claw clip Southeast London life crammed into two suitcases, three IKEA bags, and a suspiciously heavy tote labelled "misc" which was mostly skincare and one half-dead plant called Derek.

"Are you sure you don't want me to help carry something heavier?" Sam asked, taking the largest suitcase like it was a handbag.

"No, I'm helping," Daisy replied, adjusting the tote. "This bag contains my entire emotional support system—"

"And her vibrator," Lance cut in smoothly, appearing out of absolutely nowhere, wearing oversized sunglasses and a printed kimono, holding two bottles of Prosecco like offerings to the gods.

Daisy nearly dropped her tote. "Lance!"

Sam smirked. "Good to know your priorities are in order."

Daisy was mortified.

Lance feigned innocence. "Good morning to you too, lovebirds! I come bearing bubbles, bad advice, and an allergy to manual labour. Let's move some shit!"

"Lance, when I said bubbles, I meant wrap, not prosecco."

"All the more for me and Sam," he winked, and Sam looked like he might back out at any minute.

The flat was an old Victorian townhouse, a top-floor dream—light-filled, sloped ceilings, exposed brick, massive windows, and a balcony just about big enough for two chairs and a couple of glasses of wine. The kind of place that made people on Rightmove cry and start looking at flats in Zone 6 instead.

Daisy had always imagined herself living somewhere like this.

Just… not with a boyfriend.

Not yet. Not ever actually.

And yet here she was. Stomach fizzing, eyes bright, fully prepared to argue over shelf space and who did the bins.

Inside, the flat was already warm with sunlight and that comforting smell of Sam—clean laundry, aftershave, and just a hint of smugness.

"I cleared out two drawers for you," he said, nudging open the bedroom door.

"Two whole drawers?" Daisy gasped. "Generous king."

"And half the wardrobe."

"Oh wow. Next you'll be letting me pick a side of the bed."

"You already have. It's the one closest to the window because—quote—'airflow is important to your nighttime skin barrier.'"

She paused, smiling. "God, I love you."

She kissed him.

"Are you two shagging?" Lance called from the living room, already sprawled across the sofa reading Grazia. "At least wait until I leave. Or let me put music on first."

They broke apart laughing.

"Come on," Sam said. "I made you a welcome breakfast."

To Daisy's absolute shock, there was a full spread in the kitchen—avocado toast, eggs, berries, juice, and actual proper coffee that didn't taste like burnt resentment.

"Is this what living together is going to be like?" she asked, grabbing a berry and kissing his cheek. "Because I could really get used to this."

"Well, enjoy it now. By next weekend we'll be arguing over whether or not you left the bathroom light on."

"I always leave the bathroom light on."

"I know. That's why I'm mentally preparing."

Just then, a knock.

"Oh God," Daisy muttered. "Please don't let that be my mum with surprise banana bread and her signature brand of passive-aggression."

Sam peeked through the spyhole. "Worse."

He opened the door.

Lydia.

Pregnant. Sweating. Holding a Tesco bag and a grudge.

"I couldn't miss this," she announced, barging in. "Had to see it for myself. Any excuse for entertainment now that I'm off the booze. Ooh—are those croissants?"

She grabbed one before anyone could answer, lowered herself onto their sofa with a dramatic sigh, and propped her feet up on the coffee table like she lived there.

Sam blinked.

Daisy grinned, whispering behind her hand, "Welcome to the chaos."

He shook his head, equal parts baffled and amused. He liked solitude. He used to like solitude.

But now he had Daisy.

And Daisy came with chaos.

French Bulldogs, flaky friends, surprise family members, and inappropriate things in IKEA bags.

Eventually, when Lance left—after inspecting the fridge, giving unsolicited opinions on shelf organisation, and promising to sage the hallway "for balance"—Daisy and Sam finally had the place to themselves.

A calm settled over the flat. But it wasn't silence. It was something heavier. Thicker. Expectant.

"God, I thought he'd never leave," Sam murmured, voice lower now, eyes darker—something in him shifted. He stepped closer, hands slipping around her waist as he guided her into his lap on the sofa.

She let herself sink into him, straddling his legs, palms pressed flat against the solid comfort of his chest. But beneath the warmth and pull of him, a flicker of nerves stirred low in her belly. Not fear. Just… awareness.

Because this was real now.

She lived here. Her old life still trailed behind her like a ghost in worn-out heels, but it wasn't centre stage anymore.

Sam, however, had no time for ghosts. He tucked a strand of hair behind her ear and kissed her with a hunger that said he was all in. But when she didn't immediately meet him with the same intensity, he slowed, pulling back just enough to look at her—really look at her—like she was a mystery he never wanted to solve.

"You okay, Dais?" he asked gently, his fingertips tracing lazy circles at the small of her back.

She nodded. "Yeah. It just… feels strange. Good strange, though."

"We did it," he said softly. "I'm here. With you."

"Feels a bit like I'm dreaming," she whispered, breath catching as his lips brushed her jaw.

"Then let's make sure you remember it," he murmured, kissing down her neck and giving her a cheeky squeeze.

"Oh, so that's your plan?" she said with a breathy laugh, eyebrows raised.

Sam grinned, hands already sneaking beneath the hem of her T-shirt, fingers warm as they slid up the curve of her spine. "Hell yeah. We should make the most of the alone time. Before Tino arrives and demands emotional attention."

"We've got… Fifty-six minutes," she said, glancing at the clock.

"Better not waste a second, then."

He kissed her—slow at first, teasing, tasting—but it deepened fast. His mouth moved over hers with a hunger that lit a fire under her skin. He tilted his head, nipping her lower lip and drawing a gasp from her as her hips instinctively rolled forward.

He groaned into her mouth, hands tightening on her hips as he pulled her closer, pressing her deeper into his lap. She moved her hand slowly, deliberately, feeling the heat of him through the denim, the twitch of his reaction against her palm.

"Jesus, Daisy," he whispered, voice strained, reverent. His lips trailed down her throat, finding that spot just beneath her ear that made her shiver. Her free hand tangled in the back of his hair, pulling him closer.

"You drive me mad," he muttered, voice low and hoarse. "Completely fucking mad."

Her fingers teased at his waistband, tugging the button open with a confidence she didn't quite feel—but she needed to show him she wanted him.

He helped her, shoving his jeans down just enough and she didn't hesitate—as their mouths collided. The kiss turned messier, more urgent, teeth and tongue and breathless need.

"You're going to kill me," he groaned, his body tensing beneath her touch, head falling back.

She smirked against his mouth. "I hope not. I need you."

In one smooth motion, he tugged off her top, letting it fall behind the sofa. Her skin prickled as his hands skimmed up her ribs, thumbs brushing under the soft lace of her bra. The way he looked at her— like she was the only thing that mattered—was enough to undo her.

She tugged at his T-shirt, breathless. "Off."

He peeled it away, tossed it aside, then leaned in to kiss down her chest. Her bra came undone, slipping down her arms until she was bare. His hands traced her body like a map he already knew by heart.

Then he caught her beneath the thighs, flipping her onto her back with a breathless laugh. He hovered above her, forehead against hers, eyes dark and serious.

"I love you," he said quietly, firmly. "You know that, right?"

Her heart thudded. "I love you too," she whispered—just as his hand slid beneath the waistband of her leggings.

He paused, smirking. "No underwear?"

"Laundry day."

"Best day of the week," he muttered, pressing a kiss to her hip as he slowly peeled them off. She writhed beneath him, impatient now, her fingers tangled in his hair as he kissed along the inside of her thigh.

"Sam," she moaned, voice fraying. "Please."

"You've got me," he murmured, rough and low. "I'm right here."

Daisy felt the moment like a heartbeat. Yes, she had her fears and doubts, even now, when he was completely hers, but she would take this over anything else.

He pressed against her, skin to skin, every inch of him burning. When they finally joined, they both gasped, as if they had come home.

Their bodies tangled, mouths finding each other between gasps and half-laughed moans. The sofa creaked beneath them, the world shrinking to the rhythm of their bodies and the urgency in every touch.

They collapsed into each other, breathless, tangled, glowing with the aftershock.

"Still think I'm going to kill you?" she murmured, brushing his sweaty hair from his forehead.

He smiled, eyes half-lidded. "Only if you keep doing that."

She laughed, content, warm, entirely his, for now, at least.

"I don't want to move," he mumbled.

"You have twelve minutes," she said, snuggling into his chest. "Before Tino charges in here and starts judging us."

Sam groaned, flopping onto his back, an arm over his eyes. "Cockblock in fur form."

She laughed, pulling a blanket over them. "Worth it though."

He turned his head and kissed her shoulder, soft and certain. "Always."

Chapter 37:
Domestic bliss? Domestic chaos

Settling into domestic bliss might be a stretch, but Daisy was definitely dipping her toes in it.

Mornings now involved bleary-eyed kisses over coffee, passive-aggressive battles over who used the last of the toothpaste (always Sam), and full-blown diplomatic negotiations over the final slice of sourdough. Evenings were reserved for bingeing appallingly bad TV like it was high art, synchronized skincare rituals, sex in increasingly questionable locations, and Daisy secretly watching Sam sleep like some sort of unhinged Elizabethan ghost wife.

She was, despite her instincts, happy. Surprisingly.

Even Derek the plant seemed to be reviving in the new flat, and that had to be some kind of omen.

But then came the day Daisy was really trying to ignore—Sam's last day at Brandish. And Daisy? Daisy was freaking the hell out.

She tried not to show it. She really did.

"So," she said casually that morning, sipping her coffee and failing to sound casual, "your last day. Big deal. Exciting. Terrifying. Possibly life-ruining. No pressure."

Sam glanced up from tying his shoelaces. "Mostly exciting. Why, are you terrified?"

"What? No. Nooo." She waved a hand too vigorously and spilled oat milk down her dressing gown. "I'm super chill. Look at me. Just—chillin'. Like yoghurt."

He smiled. "You sure? Because your 'chill' voice is two octaves higher than usual, and you've been stress-hoovering since 7 a.m. Tino doesn't know if he's coming or going."

"It's called tidying for clarity," Daisy snapped, aggressively folding a throw blanket that had never once been folded before. "And maybe I'm allowed to be a tiny bit anxious that you're leaving your slightly unstable job with a few nice benefits and a Christmas bonus and that weird beanbag room—for the big, scary corporate world of high-rises, blue sky thinking, ergonomic chairs, and people who call each other 'partner' and use words like 'synergy' without flinching."

Sam raised an eyebrow, one shoe still half-off. "Technically... they call each other captains. It's a whole theme."

She stopped mid-fold. "I'm sorry, captains? Like... on a ship?"

"Yup."

"Oh great. So now you work on the HMS Wankery. Can't wait for your uniform."

Sam grinned, walking over and gently taking the blanket from her clenched hands. "I get it. Change is scary."

"It's not that I'm scared," Daisy said, already spiraling. "I mean I am, obviously, because that's my brand—but it's not just that. You're stepping into this whole new world. With, like, ambitious people. With goals and LinkedIn Premium. And I'm just... me. Working at Brandish and you won't be there."

He tilted her chin up with a smile. "You're the best part of my day. No title, corner office, or Captain of the Month award is going to change that."

Daisy blinked. "They have a Captain of the Month award?"

"Plaque and everything."

"I hate it there already."

"You haven't even been."

"I know. But I feel it in my spleen." She groaned.

He wrapped his arms around her, laughing, warm and reassuring and smelling of that stupid aftershave that made her knees feel like soup.

"Hey," he said gently. "You know why I'm doing this, right?"

She nodded, pressing her cheek against his chest. "Because you're brave. And brilliant. And slightly masochistic. Or you don't want to work with your dad?"

Sam laughed again. "All that and because I want to build something. Not just for me. For us."

Her heart did something wildly embarrassing in her chest—like a puppy chasing its tail inside a tumble dryer.

"Okay," she whispered. "But just promise me—no kombucha kegs. And no calling your new boss chief unironically."

"Done."

"And if this new place turns out to be a cult, you will text me a pineapple emoji immediately. That's our safe word."

He laughed. "You got it. One rogue pineapple coming your way."

They walked to the door, their usual commute bags slung over their shoulders—hers stuffed with lip balm, stress snacks, and inexplicably, a single slipper.

He turned back to look at her. "You ready?"

"No," she sulked, which only made him cuter, obviously, because he kissed her on the head. "Come on, Donaldson."

She stood in the doorway for a moment watching him—laptop bag slung over one shoulder, tie tucked into his pocket—still looking irritatingly hot for someone about to clear out a desk drawer and hand in a branded lanyard.

A knot of pride and panic twisted in her stomach. He was choosing a new path. A huge one. And she wasn't losing him—she knew that. But for the first time in a long time, the future was shifting. Real, scary, grown-up things were happening.

They were becoming one of those couples. With shoe racks and joint calendars. With plans.

That didn't mean she wouldn't also secretly spend the day googling "how to support your partner's scary life decision without spiraling and/or crying in a Tesco meal deal aisle." Because growth.

Daisy sat at her desk, glaring at her inbox like it had personally betrayed her. Which, to be fair, it kind of had. No urgent briefs. No PR emergencies. Just Sam Callaghan's last day and everyone acting like it was a good thing.

She was sulking. Quietly. Elegantly. With her headphones in and a facial expression that said, "Do not speak to me unless you're offering a biscuit or a time machine."

Lance clocked it by 9:13am.

"Are you really going to do the whole moody Desperate Housewives routine all day?" Lance whispered, spinning in his desk chair from the neighboring pod. "Because it's giving 'he died in the war' rather than 'he got a fancy new job with a view.'"

Daisy scowled. "He's abandoning us. You. Me. The beanbag room. For blue skies and a cappuccino bar and—ugh."

"You do know you're allowed to be happy for him and an emotional basket case, right?" Lance said, leaning across the desk divider like a gossipy meerkat. "It's called duality."

"I'm not an emotional basket case," Daisy snapped, dragging her email window around just for something to do. "I'm just... cold."

"It's twenty degrees in here."

"Well, then I'm internally cold."

Lance gave her a pitying look and tossed a packet of Percy Pigs onto her desk. "For your mood. And your blood sugar."

Across the office, Sam was deep in conversation with Angela— his replacement—both laughing about something that made Daisy irrationally annoyed. Probably one of those inside jokes she wouldn't be part of anymore. Soon, he'd be off to the big new job with ergonomic chairs and unlimited milk, and she'd be stuck here trying to remember how to use the printer without him.

Hmm. Yes. The printer. She remembered the last time he caught her in the printer room, struggling, and somehow, she'd ended up against it with his tongue down her throat. That was never going to happen again.

Sure, he was at home now. They lived together. But she couldn't exactly feel him up spontaneously against their fridge—it wasn't the same.

God, this day sucked ass.

Her phone buzzed.

Sam: *I know you're sulking. There's a cupcake on your desk. Eat it or I'm filing a formal grievance.*

She glanced over at him. He was already looking at her with that smug, affectionate expression that somehow made her want to both kiss and punch him.

She took a bite of the cupcake, trying not to cry.

Probably the first sad reaction to anyone ever eating a cupcake.

At 4.00 pm, there was an awkwardly cheerful leaving speech from Rhoda—of course—who compared Sam to "a loyal labrador who had unexpectedly learned magic with Excel." Everyone clapped. Daisy tried not to cry.

Then Sam stood up to say a few words, and Daisy was actually shocked.

What the bloody hell was going on?

Sam hated public speaking.

Who even was he?

She pretended she was rubbing mascara from her eye, but still, those pesky little wet balls you call tears were trying to break through.

"Oh great," Sam started. "I hate speeches, but I think Rhoda's warrants a response. I've loved working here," he said, scanning the room. "Not just because of the coffee machine and the surprisingly solid dental plan, but because of the people. You lot. And more so in the last year because of one person in particular…"

His eyes flicked briefly to Daisy.

"You've made the chaos worth it."

She blinked. Her heart was doing something tight and fluttery that felt like it needed a medic.

She didn't even realise that everyone was now staring at her.

If she had, she probably would've gone full raspberry.

But she was just looking at him.

Proud.

Later, back at his desk pod, Daisy leaned against the divider, watching as he packed up the few things that actually belonged to him—his mug, a stress ball shaped like an avocado, a pen she'd accidentally stolen and insisted was hers.

"This is so weird," he muttered. "I've sat in this chair for three years."

She didn't trust herself to speak.

He turned to her, gently tugging her into a hug, right there in the middle of the open plan office. "Hey. It's not goodbye. It's just… see you at home."

She pressed her face to his shoulder. "You're really leaving."

"Only to a building ten minutes away. Just one tube ride if you're lazy."

"Still." She scoffed.

"I'll miss you too, you know."

She looked up at him. "Even my annoying habits?"

"Especially those."

Her mouth quirked. "Okay. But if your new office has a cider tap or those beanbags shaped like avocados, I'm calling HR."

"I'd expect nothing less."

It went from Sam's last day to Sam's first day real quick after a supposedly chilled weekend—and by chilled, Daisy meant an "interesting" dinner with Prim and Grant that ended with Prim storming off and Grant looking utterly flabbergasted, having no clue what he'd done wrong.

Apparently, all he'd done was invite Sam to an American football game a few weeks after their wedding. American football. Prim didn't even like regular football, let alone the shoulder-padded, helmet-wearing version—so why was she being so cagey?

When they got home to their (this still felt surreal) flat, Daisy texted Prim to ask what was going on.

Prim replied with a classic: I'm fine.

Daisy knew her. She was not fine. And the wedding was coming up next weekend.

Still, Daisy didn't have time to worry about that because she had her own neurotic spiral to stage.

Sam was starting his new job.

She was pleased for him. She loved living with him. But one thing was for sure—she missed him being at Brandish. A lot.

There was no one to ogle anymore.

Lance, obviously, felt the same.

But now she had to go the whole day without calling or texting him.

She had to maintain some composure.

Let him settle in.

Give his new colleagues at least a full day before they realized his girlfriend was an unhinged woman-child with abandonment issues and a very low tolerance for change.

She could do this.

She was an adult. A grown-up. A composed, put-together woman who absolutely did not feel the sudden urge to fake a minor medical emergency just to get him to call.

Instead, she opened her work chat to message Lance.

DD: *Do you think it would be weird if I casually walked past his new office building at lunch?*

LD: *Only if you're wearing a trench coat and sunglasses.*

DD: *Shit.*

LD: *DAIS. NO.*

She spent the morning being casually fine.

Fine like, "Oops, I just opened his Instagram again for the third time in an hour."

Lance tried to confiscate her phone twice before 11am. By noon, she'd turned off WhatsApp previews to avoid the temptation. By two, she'd almost typed "Missing you like an idiot misses the point" before deleting it and slamming her laptop shut for dramatic effect.

She could feel the hours dragging, her brain inventing fresh reasons to be concerned—what if the building didn't have proper ventilation? What if he didn't eat lunch? What if he met a tall, glowy woman with incredible hair and a power suit who actually understood blockchain?

She even checked their Ring camera to see if he had come home for lunch. It was mainly for Tino, but still, it made a noise or recorded when someone went into the living room, even if it was on the balcony.

Daisy. Please, this is desperate even by your standards.

By 3:00pm, she was pacing the office like a war widow waiting for news from the front.

She messaged Lance again.

DD: *I can't concentrate. Want to come to mine and we can drink wine while we work?*

LD: *Is the pope catholic?!! Let's go.*

At 4:30pm, Daisy and Lance had set up in her flat.

She had made it nearly seven hours without texting Sam. A personal best.

But surely one little "How's it going, hotshot?" wasn't needy.

It was supportive.

Girlfriend-y.

Encouraging. Right?

Except she was not sitting on the sofa, staring at her phone like it was an emotional grenade.

She picked it up. Shoving Tino off her lap in the process, who then proceeded to bark at Lance until he picked him up.

Then she put it back down like it was radioactive.

Then picked it up again and dialed.

Two rings.

Three.

"Sam Callaghan's phone," a perky voice chirped. Female. Professional. With an accent that said Pilates before breakfast and absolutely no time for your nonsense.

Daisy blinked. "Oh. Hi. Sorry—um—where's Sam?"

"He's in a meeting," the voice replied, already bored. "Can I take a message?"

"Sure, just let him know his girlfriend called."

A pause.

Then: "Okay. And your name, please?"

"Daisy."

A beat. Then another.

"Okay…" the mystery voice said, like she was filing that under delusional women Sam once met at Pret.

"Wait—sorry," Daisy said quickly. "Who are you?"

"I'm Luisa."

"And why are you answering Sam's phone?"

"Because I'm his PA."

PA?! Since when did Sam have a PA? How was there already a glamorous-sounding assistant answering his phone?

"Right. Great. Okay. Just—tell him— Do you know what actually it's fine I'll talk to him at home." Daisy hung up before she could sound even more unhinged.

And then promptly threw her phone onto the sofa like it had insulted her shoes.

Lance looked up from his laptop, where he was working from Daisy's kitchen because he claimed the space had *better vibes and closer to the snacks.*

"Wow," he said, arching an eyebrow. "That sounded healthy and totally not mental."

"She answered his phone."

"Was it his parole officer?"

"His PA. Luisa."

"Oooh. Did we know he had a PA?" Lance's eyes gleamed. "Is she hot?"

"She sounded hot. The kind of hot that wears trousers with pleats and knows her way around a spreadsheet. I said I was his girlfriend and she acted like I told her I was his dog groomer."

Lance sipped his tea. "Or maybe she just didn't realise you exist yet because it's his first day and she's literally just met him."

Daisy narrowed her eyes. "You're supposed to be on my side."

"I am! I'm just saying—maybe don't burn down his new office over a woman who probably has Bluetooth headset trauma and hasn't had lunch yet."

"But Daisy was already gone. She flopped onto the sofa, one arm dramatically over her eyes. 'Why does he have to have a Luisa? What if she is extremely pretty and not at all chaotic?'"Babe," Lance said, gently prising the cushion she was now faceplanting. "If he wanted 'a Luisa', he wouldn't have asked you to move in. Now—how about I make you a distracting snack and you resist the urge to call her back pretending to be from HR?"

"…Fine. But I'm not deleting the email I drafted."

An hour and a half later, Daisy was hunched over her laptop like a woman possessed.

The spiral was fully spiralling. Daisy number two had returned— unstable, wine-fuelled, and clutching onto reason with a single chipped nail.

This was exactly what she'd been afraid of when Sam said he was leaving. New job, new office, new people. People she didn't know. Luisas.

And okay, yes—it was irrational. She knew that. But in her head, this was exactly how it went.

She wanted to keep him at Brandish where she could see him.

God Daisy. This—this obsessive-stalking behaviour? Not healthy. Not right.

"Got her," she muttered, sipping her wine like it was mission fuel. "Luisa Tavares. Twenty-four. Graduate of Bristol. Fluent in

Portuguese and probably the language of seduction. Her LinkedIn profile pic is just her… laughing on a beach. Who laughs on a beach professionally?"

Lance leaned over her shoulder, munching popcorn like it was a live broadcast. "Ugh, she's got the bone structure of someone who drinks chlorophyll. And look—'passionate about productivity'? That's code for 'uses pivot tables and breaks up marriages.'"

Daisy stared at him, wide-eyed.

He blinked. "Sorry. My bad."

"Look at her. She's calm. Together. Her last post was about how reading Atomic Habits changed her workflow. I cried yesterday because I thought I'd killed the basil plant."

"That basil was on life support anyway," Lance said gently. "And she doesn't have your sparkle. Your flair. Your… unusually deep knowledge of Love Island."

Daisy laughed. "Do I need to become this kind of woman now? Like, mature and minimalistic and with real opinions on passive income?"

Lance rolled his eyes. "Daisy. The man watches Married at First Sight with you and your fat dog—who, let's be honest, has his own set of issues—and he owns three types of oat milk because you once said you liked 'variety.' He's not going anywhere."

Daisy smiled.

Just then, the door clicked open.

Sam stepped inside, jacket slung over one shoulder, tie loosened, looking like the cover of GQ.

"Hey," she said, voice three octaves too high. "How was your first day? Normal? Uneventful? Full of… men?"

Sam paused in the doorway, brow raised. "Full of… men?"

"Just, you know, masculine energy," Daisy said quickly, waving her hand like she was brushing away the awkward. "Power ties. Spreadsheet banter. Football chat."

He stepped closer, eyeing her with amused suspicion. "Okay. I'd say it was about 70% small talk, 20% tech issues, and 10% someone showing me where the fancy coffee machine is."

"Oh good," she nodded, far too quickly. "Glad no one flirted with you by the Nespresso pods or anything. That would be wildly inappropriate."

Sam tilted his head. "Okay… what happened?"

"Nothing," Daisy said, far too loudly.

He dropped his bag. "Daisy."

Lance gave an awkward wave from the kitchen table. "Hi."

She folded her arms, then immediately unfolded them again. "Okay, fine. I may have called earlier and a woman answered—a beautiful, highly competent woman named Luisa, who probably moisturises daily and keeps her receipts."

Sam blinked. "You mean… my PA?"

"Oh, now she's yours," Daisy muttered, shaking her head.

He stepped closer, softening. "So you panicked and assumed I was secretly in love with her."

"Obviously," Daisy said, as if it were the most logical conclusion in the world. "I mean… she probably has SharePoint folders, Sam."

He gently cupped her face. "Dais. You are bloody ridiculous. And I adore you."

"No, you don't," she scoffed, trying not to smile.

"I do. Every weird, messy inch of you." He kissed her forehead. "You encouraged this, I assume?" He pointed at Lance, who was approaching the fridge to grab more wine.

"Absolutely," Lance smirked back.

"Luisa is twenty-four and terrifying. She asked if she could 'curate' my inbox and then told me my email signature was 'weak branding.' I was genuinely ashamed."

"Okay," Daisy said, following him to the sofa. "Sorry I freaked out."

"It's okay. I still love you." He kissed her again. "Even when you interrogate my PA over the phone."

"Ah," she said, looking at Lance and wincing. "You're not worried I'm… too chaotic?"

He laughed softly. "Daisy. You're chaotic in the best possible way. I'm obsessed with all of it."

Her eyes filled. "God, that's so hot."

They kissed. Lance groaned from the kitchen. "Ugh, at least let me pour more wine first."

Sam glanced over. "You've been here all day, haven't you?"

"Yeah. It's kind of my second home now. You should start charging me rent—or emotional damages."

Whilst Daisy's life was finally finding some sort of rhythm, Prim's was spiralling in the opposite direction. That weekend, after the dinner, she stormed through the front door like a woman possessed — if Hurricane Katrina wore designer heels and could fling a handbag with sniper-level precision. A scented candle went flying, the hallway mirror rattled, and a decorative bowl of pebbles met its untimely end.It was the kind of dramatic entrance that would suggest they'd just been ambushed by the FBI or sat through a four-hour dinner with Donald Trump.

But no.

Just a nice, quiet meal with Daisy and Sam. Family. Civilised conversation. A perfectly roasted chicken. So why the foul mood?

Grant had no idea.

Prim had no idea.

It was like the evening had irritated her on a molecular level. Like just sitting across from Daisy and Sam—happy, settled, smug—had made her skin itch.

Grant followed her into the kitchen cautiously, like she might suddenly combust.

"Prim?" he tried, tentatively.

She spun around, hands on hips, eyes wild. "Don't."

"I just—"

"Don't," she repeated, sharper now. "I cannot have a debrief. Not tonight."

Grant blinked. "Okay," he said, raising both palms. "No debrief. Just... maybe some basic clarity on why you're moving through the house like a wrecking ball?"

Prim exhaled, as if just being looked at was exhausting.

"I just don't get it, Prim. It's a football game. Why is this such a big deal?" Grant's voice was calm, confused more than anything, but with the slightest edge of frustration creeping in.

Prim was standing by the kitchen island, arms folded tightly across her chest like she was holding something in. "It's not about the bloody game, Grant. It's the timing. Two weeks after our wedding and instead of—I don't know—talking about our honeymoon or just being together, you're scheduling a lads' day with Sam to go eat overpriced hot dogs and yell at men in shoulder pads."

Grant frowned. "You said you didn't want a honeymoon straight away. You literally said, 'I'll combust if we don't have a buffer month.' Your words."

"Yes," she snapped, "because I thought we'd be adjusting, nesting, having breakfasts in bed and making joint decisions about tea towels. Not immediately separating like we're applying for time off from a job we don't like!"

"It's one afternoon, Prim. In London. And with Sam. You like Sam."

"I do like Sam. This isn't about Sam."

"Could've fooled me."

"It's about you not getting it. It's about how it feels."

Grant stared at her for a long beat, then leaned against the counter. "Okay. Then help me get it. Because right now it feels like I'm being punished for… having friends?"

Prim turned away, opening the dishwasher even though it was empty and spotless. "I just feel like everything's… happening all at once. And I can't catch my breath. And then you're adding more stuff, more plans, and I'm already drowning in wedding spreadsheets and colour-coded napkin options and whether or not Malcolm Donaldson will be offended by salmon."

Grant stepped forward. His tone softened. "Hey. Then say that. Say you're overwhelmed. But don't make me the bad guy for booking a few hours with my mate. I'm on your side, you know?"

"I know," she whispered, still staring into the dishwasher like it held life's answers.

"You sure? Because lately it feels like I'm on the outside looking in. Like you're… I don't know. Somewhere else."

She turned to face him, and for a second, her eyes flickered—like maybe she wanted to confess something, something she hadn't even told herself yet. But then her face shut down. The mask slipped back on. Shrug.

"It's just wedding stress. That's all."

Grant hesitated. "Okay," he said quietly. "If you say so."

Prim turned away again, but the air between them stayed heavy. The tension didn't lift. Her shoulders didn't relax. Her breath stayed shallow. And even though the room was silent, it felt like something important had been missed.

Or left unsaid.

Grant left and headed upstairs without a word, leaving Prim standing alone in the stagnant silence.

She blinked back a tear.

No. Absolutely not. She was not crying over this.

She rubbed at her face with the heel of her hand, furious at the sting in her eyes.

Come on, Prim. Get a grip. You have one week—one—until this wedding. You can get through it. You've survived worse than a moody fiancé and an empty dishwasher.

This is not something to cry about.

It's not. It's stupid. It's nothing.

She stood there a moment longer, surrounded by soft lighting and organised chaos—neatly stacked gift boxes, a wedding binder open on the table, the faint smell of vanilla and stress in the air.

But her chest still ached.

And the silence still felt heavier than it should.

Chapter 38:
Giant wedding cakes and ridiculous ice sculptures

And just like that, the morning of the wedding of the year arrived in a blur of hairspray, false lashes, and the soft clinking of champagne flutes. After a week of Sam leaving the company, spiralling into her insecurities, and generally feeling like a mess, Daisy was in desperate need of a win.

When the first glass of champagne was poured, she felt a tiny spark of relief—a brief moment of peace, like the universe was finally giving her a little something back after everything.

Champagne. It wasn't just a drink. It was her win.

In Prim's bridal suite—an enormous room that looked like Instagram had thrown up a fairy tale—final touches were underway. Plumping lip glosses were applied. Curls were fixed. And Lance, naturally, had somehow inserted himself into the girl gang for "emotional support" (and gossip, obviously).

"Honestly," he said, sipping pink champagne, "I admire you, Prim. You and Grant—perfect. Me? I could never do it. One man for the rest of my life? This gay can't be tamed."

The room exploded with laughter, except Prim, who blinked at Lance like he'd just said something in Latin.

Lance, oblivious, turned to Daisy. "Right, babes, I'm off. They're seating people and I need to pretend I'm helpful."

He gave Daisy a quick kiss on the cheek and disappeared in a swish of silk and sarcasm.

Prim stayed quiet. Too quiet.

Daisy clocked the change instantly. "Everyone out," she said, ushering bridesmaids toward the door like a bouncer at a club no one wants to leave.

When the room was empty, she turned back to her sister. "What's wrong? Prim—the day is finally here, you're getting married. This is your dream, remember?"

Prim's voice was small. "Is it though, Dais? What if I'm making a mistake?"

Daisy's heart stopped. "What? No. No, not at all. Is this about the other week? I thought we went through this. Things will work out, they always do. Come on, you love Grant. I've never seen two people more in love. He's amazing. And he's downstairs, waiting for you."

Prim sighed and then smiled. "You're right. For once."

Daisy laughed with relief.

"And you look absolutely beautiful. I think he might have a heart attack when he sees you."

"I hope not." Prim grinned.

"You good now?" Daisy checked.

"Yes. Go on. I need to make an entrance. You lot are the warm-up act."

"I love you."

"Love you too, Dais," Prim said softly. "Can you send up Dad? He's already late."

"Yep. See you down there."

She slipped out, leaving Prim staring at herself in the mirror.

Weaving through the corridor in search of her dad, Daisy finally spotted him. What she didn't expect to find was him—Malcolm Donaldson—chatting to Sam.

Huh.

Of all the things Daisy had imagined seeing today (including

Prim crying, Rachel's lashes stealing the spotlight, and Lance doing something ridiculous), this hadn't even made the list: Malcolm Donaldson and Sam Callaghan, deep in what appeared to be a semi-calm conversation.

Wait—was Sam laughing?

What is this? Malcolm Donaldson isn't funny.

"Hey," Daisy said, approaching cautiously.

"Wow, Daisy—you look beautiful," Sam said, his words catching just slightly.

"You look gorgeous, sweetheart," Malcolm added, leaning in to kiss her cheek.

"Thank you. But not as beautiful as the amazing bride upstairs who's currently waiting for you, Dad."

"Oh, yes—right. I'd better go. It was good talking to you, Samuel."

"Samuel?" Daisy repeated, smirking as Malcolm walked away. "Really?"

Sam rolled his eyes. "Don't start."

He grabbed her waist, pulled her in. "Give me a kiss, you."

Daisy giggled, melting a little.

"You look amazing," he murmured.

"Thanks. You do too. You like it?"

"I like it. I can't wait to get you out of it, but yeah, I like it."

They shared a few desperate kisses, like they'd been apart for months, not minutes.

"I've got to go round up the bridesmaids. It's time," Daisy said, flushed and breathless.

"I'll be over there," Sam pointed toward the drinks and fresh air. "Cooling off."

As she walked away, Sam watched her. And maybe it was the wedding, maybe it was the way she looked at him, but suddenly—briefly—he imagined their own.

Nope. Too soon. Definitely too soon.

Except what he didn't know was that Daisy had been imagining it too. Like all morning.

The guests were seated and patiently waiting for Prim's entrance. A soft piano cover of Perfect filled the air. Standard. The whole place looked like something straight out of a luxury bridal magazine: floral arches, fairy lights, a cake the size of Jupiter... wait, are those ice-sculpted pigeons?

It was all very Prim. A little too Prim for Daisy's taste, if she was honest, and there were far too many people. Daisy was sure that Prim didn't know half of them. But hey, it was Prim's day. If anyone was going to have a wedding that doubled as the Met Gala, it was her.

The bridesmaids gathered—a sea of sage green. Rachel looked like her usual supermodel self. Eloise, the only blonde, was flawless. Grant's cousin Candy looked wildly uncomfortable, likely because she wasn't in black for once. Lydia kept adjusting her dress every five seconds, whinging that "this thing just appeared overnight"—her pregnancy had suddenly popped, and the dress definitely hadn't been altered with bump-room in mind.

Daisy peeked through the curtain. Grant stood at the end of the aisle, fidgeting with his cufflinks. Poor thing looked like he might pass out. She felt for him.

Then the music changed.

The first soft notes of *At Last* floated through the air.

"Right. Ready, girls?" Daisy asked, counting heads. "Milly and Lydia, you're up first." She paused.

"Wait—where's Milly?" Daisy asked, glancing around with wide eyes.

Keep calm, Daisy.

"Erm, I don't know," Eloise answered, scanning the room, clearly panicked.

Daisy's stomach dropped. "I could have sworn she was literally just here…"

But even as she said it, something else hit her.

Her eyes flicked to the stairs.

Where was Prim?

"Actually…" she whispered. "Where's Prim?"

She turned, scanning the room—and just then, her dad appeared, descending the staircase. Alone.

Alone.

Daisy's chest tightened. Her dad was supposed to be escorting the bride. Not coming back without her.

"Dad, where is Prim?"

"Prim isn't up there?" Malcolm confirmed.

Realisation set in.

"What do you mean she isn't there?" Daisy shot back.

The music kept playing, soft and lovely and completely out of sync with the thunderclap of panic crashing through Daisy's chest.

Prim was missing.

And no one knew where she'd gone.

And her groom was waiting at the altar.

Daisy didn't wait. She kicked off her heels and bolted, down the corridor, past the confused wedding planner mouthing What's going on? and a cluster of distant relatives clutching Prosecco flutes like props in a play. The pianist was now on the third rendition of *At Last*.

"Prim?" she called, weaving through a maze of rose garlands and signs pointing to Love Is Sweet candy carts.

"Prim!"

No answer. No bride.

She tried the bridal suite first, heart hammering. Empty. Just a half-drunk glass of pink Prosecco, a lone earring, and the faint scent of Prim's perfume clinging to the air like a ghost.

Sam spotted Daisy running barefoot up the stairs and followed.

"Dais, what's going on? Why hasn't anyone come out yet?"

"It's Prim. She's gone."

"Shit." His face dropped, panic rising to match Daisy's. "What can I do?"

"Help me look."

Lance materialised, as if drama had whispered his name.

"What the hell is going on? Do we have a runaway bride?" he joked—until he saw their faces.

"Oh crap." His grin faded. "Should we tell Grant?"

"No, not yet," Daisy said, not willing to surrender to disaster just yet. "Don't worry—I'll find her."

She took command like a general in heels (or, currently, bare feet). "Sam, go find my dad and tell him not to panic. And tell that bloody pianist to play anything else. Lance, get the bridesmaids organised."

"What if they ask me what's going on?"

"Lie! Tell them Prim had... an issue. She'll be along shortly."

Bloody hell, Prim. Why do you hate me?

Daisy sprinted to the bathrooms and barged into the ladies'.

"Sorry!" she shouted at a startled Auntie Sandra adjusting her fascinator in the mirror. Crap, she really didn't have time for this, so she just shouted, "Bride emergency!" pushing past her.

One cubicle door was locked. Daisy knocked.

"Prim?"

Silence.

"Okay, if you're in there having a meltdown, I totally get it—but you have to come out! Grant looks like he's going to pass out, the music's already playing, and I—"

The door creaked open.

Not Prim. A child. Holding sweets from the candy cart. Looking entirely unfazed.

Daisy swore under her breath, spun around, and caught her dress on the sink.

Crap.

She yanked it free and bolted.

Frantic now. Her cardio was off the charts, and her step count was going to be elite.

Downstairs. Upstairs again. Garden path. Side entrance. Kitchen—because honestly, who knew where someone might go when they were maybe about to not get married?

"Has anyone seen the bride?" she gasped to a waiter carrying a tray of tiny Caprese skewers.

He blinked. "Um. No?"

Useless.

Daisy shoved open a set of French doors and skidded onto the back lawn. Her feet were killing her. Her lungs were threatening mutiny. And still—no Prim.

Panic tightened around her like a corset.

And then—

From behind a hedge at the far end of the garden—

A voice.

"I knew you'd bloody find me."

Daisy froze.

She stepped forward, heart thudding.

And there she was.

Prim. Sitting on the edge of a stone bench in her wedding dress, veil discarded, bouquet on the grass. Eyes red. Expression unreadable.

Daisy blinked. "Prim… what in the name of Jesus H. Christ are you doing?"

Prim looked up.

And whispered, "I don't know if I can do this."

Chapter 39:
Through rose-tinted glasses

Daisy stopped. Like she had an episode. Like her brain had short-circuited.

What does she mean she doesn't know if she can do this?

She was sure they'd already had this conversation. Sure, she'd literally just talked her down from the ledge, soothed the nerves, helped zip her into that ridiculously gorgeous, expensive lace dress. So why was Prim doing this again?

Stop being so selfish, Prim.

But then Daisy really looked at her—her sister's red, puffy face, the veil discarded like tissue paper, unpinned hair tumbling down her shoulders. The vacant expression.

Daisy's anger faded. Her heart cracked clean open.

Prim wasn't being a brat. She was broken. She was lost.

Suddenly, a flurry of movement behind the hedge—Milly resurfaced, scatterbrained and breathless, heels sinking into the lawn.

"I've managed to convince the driver to take us to St Pancras. Trains in a few hours—oh shit! Daisy, you found us!" She winced.

Daisy's temper reignited.

"Can someone please tell me what the bloody hell is going on?"

Prim stood, bracing herself. "I'm not getting married, Dais. I'm calling it off."

Daisy blinked. "Calling it off? It's happening, Prim. The guests are seated, Grant's at the altar, and At Last is on its third bloody rendition. Stop messing around."

Prim's voice shook. "I've made up my mind. I can't do this. I don't want to get married."

Daisy stared at her, the weight of it starting to sink in. "How can you do this—to Grant, to his family, to ours?"

Prim stepped forward and grabbed her hands. "You don't understand. For a while now, I've felt like I've been living someone else's life. Like I've been looking at myself through rose-tinted glasses—and I don't like what I see."

"But—" Daisy tried, desperate to hold on to some kind of logic.

"In a couple of days, I'll explain everything. You'll understand then. But right now, I have to go. And you need to tell Grant."

Panic surged through Daisy like a shot of espresso.

"No, Prim, don't do this. You can't do this to me. To everyone."

Prim gave her a sad smile. "I'm sorry. Okay. I really am, Dais. But I have to do this."

Then she was gone, slipping away with Milly through the back gate, leaving Daisy alone with nothing but the distant sound of love songs and the crushing weight of responsibility.

As Daisy trudged slowly back to the wedding—green feet, dress torn, dignity somewhere in a bush—she couldn't stop replaying the look on Prim's face. And for the first time ever, she didn't feel annoyance, or jealousy, or exasperation. She felt something new. She felt sad—for Prim.

She had her reasons, and Daisy had to support that, but why did she have to be the one to let Grant down? Everyone, actually. Prim denounced all responsibility and she had to be the one to face everyone.

This was really shitty of her.

Lance spotted Daisy walking across the lawn.

"No?" he asked.

"She's gone," Daisy choked out. Her throat tightened. Why the hell was she crying?

Lance swore under his breath and wrapped an arm around her, guiding her back toward the house.

Inside, she paused at the foot of the grand staircase, trying to steady her breathing.

Sam appeared beside her and pulled her into a hug. Lance mouthed "Prim's gone."

Daisy buried her face into Sam's shoulder. "I have to tell Grant," she whispered. "And I don't want to do it. Why would she leave me to do it?"

Sam squeezed her gently. "I know it's really shit, I know. But you can do this, Dais. He needs to know what's going on. Do you want me to come with you?"

"No, it's okay. Thank you. But I don't think he needs an audience while I stamp on his heart." She turned to Lance. "Can you go and ask him to meet me in the bridal suite?"

Lance nodded, already striding toward the altar—just a little too pleased to be part of the drama. Or maybe it was the rare satisfaction of having a clear role in the chaos. A job to do. A mission. A purpose. Like a very well-dressed wedding commando.

As Lance whispered to Grant, the poor bloke's face dropped like someone had yanked the rug—and possibly the entire floor—from under him. Confusion. Horror. Full emotional collapse, all in the space of a blink. He bolted toward the bridal suite, while guests turned in their seats, murmuring like extras in a particularly tense episode of Downton Abbey.

Lydia, Rachel, and Eloise tried to follow the commotion, but Sam stepped in smoothly, steering them toward the bar. "Just a quick toast while they sort out a little… hiccup," he said, all calm charm and subtle authority. And really, who were they to argue—especially when he looked that handsome.

Grant stormed into the suite.

"Prim? Where is she? What the fuck is going on?"

Daisy stepped in front of him. "Grant, sit down."

"What do you mean, Dais? What's happening? Where is Prim?"

"She's gone," Daisy said gently, guiding him to a chair. "I'm so, so sorry."

He stared at her. "This is a joke, right?"

"I wish it was. She's not coming down that aisle. Something about how her life doesn't feel like hers."

Grant's whole body sagged. He blinked fast, tears forming.

"She still loves you, Grant. But she's not marrying you today."

"Why?" he whispered, grabbing Daisy's hand like a lifeline. "How can she do this?"

"She didn't say much. Just that she'd explain soon. And not to contact her."

Desperately, Grant reached for his phone and dialled.

Across the room, Prim's phone buzzed on the dressing table.

Shit.

"Oh God, what do I do Dais?"

"For starters, don't go back out there. Stay here. I'll handle the crowd. Do you want someone with you?"

"Marcus," he said almost as if he didn't want to speak anymore and sat with his head in his hands.

Daisy opened the door to find Marcus already waiting—and Greg behind him.

"Greg, get whiskey."

He nodded and ran off as Marcus stepped inside with Grant, who was necking the half-full glass of pink Prosecco.

Daisy turned, mind racing.

Oh, Prim. I hope this was worth it.

Outside, Sam had managed to contain the chaos—barely. The bridesmaids were murmuring furiously.

"I can't believe it."

"Who just leaves?"

Sam pulled Daisy close. "How did it go?"

God, Daisy was so grateful for him right now, and she made a mental note that she would remind him of this and make it up to him later—if she manages to get through this ordeal with an inch of sanity left.

"Not great," she whispered. "He's gutted. So gutted. I've got to tell the registrar."

"I'll do it," Lydia said, stepping in. "You stay here."

"Thanks, Lyd."

Malcolm appeared; confusion etched across his face. "What's going on? What's happened to Prim?"

"You'll have to ask her. Though her phone's still upstairs," Daisy said, exhausted.

"She must've said something, petal."

Why was he being so kind? Didn't he get how furious she was?

"She said she didn't want to get married. That her life didn't feel like her own," Daisy muttered.

Malcolm and Sam exchanged a look, unsure how to respond.

Malcolm probably felt the weight of it, like it's his fault—like he should have been there more for Prim, and Daisy. Bit late now.

Lance arrived with Jessie and Nanna Jean, who were desperately demanding answers.

"Daisy, what's going on?" Jessie asked, fanning herself, eyes wide and glossy. "Is she having a meltdown over the flowers again or something worse?"

Nanna Jean looked sharper than ever. She narrowed her eyes. "Where's my granddaughter?"

Daisy swallowed, heart clanging. "Can we sit for a sec?"

They moved to a quiet alcove near the stairs. Jessie kept fussing with her hat, and Nanna Jean sat straight-backed, waiting.

"She's not coming back. She's gone."

Jessie blinked. "Gone where?"

"To the station, I think. She's not getting married, Mum. She… she left."

Jessie sat down slowly, like the air had gone out of her. "But… but everyone's here."

"I know," Daisy said softly. "I tried to stop her, I did, but she said she couldn't do it. Said she didn't feel like herself. Like she was living someone else's life."

"Oh, my girl," Nanna Jean said quietly, her voice like a crumpled tissue. "Why didn't she come to me?"

"Who knows how long she's been holding this in, Nan. We weren't to know."

Jessie's eyes flooded. "She could've said something, she could've—"

"She didn't want to hurt anyone," Daisy said. "But then she still did."

They sat in stunned silence for a moment, Jessie dabbing under her eyes, Nanna Jean stroking her handbag like it was a cat.

"Lydia's gone to let the registrar know," Daisy said, standing up reluctantly. "And someone needs to speak to the guests before they all start thinking the brides just lost an eyelash."

"I'll go help Lydia," Jessie said, steeling herself. "We need to handle this properly."

"I'll… I'll find Grant's mum," Nanna Jean said numbly. "She'll need someone."

Daisy gave them both a grateful look before they left.

Then—

Grant came bolting down the stairs like an award-winning greyhound.

"St Pancras," he shouted. "She's at the bloody station."

And just like that, he was gone—Marcus and Greg on his heels with jangling car keys.

Daisy sighed. Maybe she should have told him earlier. But he probably would've gone either way. Off on a romantic movie-style chase to win back the love of his life.

Except Daisy had seen Prim's face. She wasn't going to be won over that easily.

Meanwhile, inside the grand hall, the registrar had just cleared his throat and addressed the guests with forced calm.

"Ladies and gentlemen… unfortunately, there won't be a wedding today. The bride is…" he hesitated, as if grasping for a more palatable phrase "unavailable."

A ripple of confusion spread through the crowd like a dropped glass of Prosecco.

A beat later, Lance leaned and muttered under his breath, "The groom's now gone too."

The registrar gave an awkward cough and added, "And… yes, it appears the groom is now also absent."

Chaos.

Actual, full-scale chaos.

People gasped. Chairs scraped. A champagne flute smashed somewhere near the back.

"I can't believe this!" Grant's dad thundered, leaping to his feet as if someone had just insulted his golf handicap. "What the hell is going on?"

Grant's mum sat frozen in her seat, lips parted, mascara slightly smudged. "But everything's paid for," she murmured, shell-shocked. "The flowers. The catering. The band. The macarons."

The silence that followed was thick and uncomfortable—until Jessie, (so typically Jessie) raised her glass.

"Well… shall we party anyway?"

More silence. A whole room of people blinking in stunned disbelief.

Then Grant's dad huffed. "She's got a point. It's all bloody paid for. We won't get the money back."

"After that bombshell," Uncle Bryan added, loosening his tie, "we all need a drink. Maybe four."

A few murmurs of agreement. Someone near the back clapped. The band hesitated, looked at each other, then struck up an awkward jazzy number like they were on the Titanic.

Daisy stared around her, mouth slightly open.

They couldn't be serious.

But they bloody were.

There was no bride. No groom. And apparently, no plan B.

Just a bewildered registrar, a mountain of canapés, and two very expensive empty chairs.

And yet, slowly but surely, the room began to shift. Prosecco was poured. Shoes were kicked off. Someone shouted "Let's start with the speeches!" like it was a group holiday and not the remnants of a ruined wedding.

Daisy watched it all, half-horrified, half-impressed. Only her family could turn a runaway bride and a missing groom into a reason to crank up the DJ and pass around mini quiches.

Unbelievable.

She turned to Sam, who was already accepting glasses of Prosecco from the staff, handing one to her.

"Are we… actually going to a non-wedding wedding reception?"

He raised a brow and clinked his glass against hers. "Looks like it."

Daisy couldn't believe that they were all actually serious. It felt like a bad dream; she was waiting for someone to pinch her or jolt her awake.

But they bloody were. They were going to have the wedding party without a wedding.

Chapter 40:
Life is trying to tell you something

Prim arrived at the station with Milly. The train to Paris was leaving in an hour and forty-five minutes.

Milly joined her in a flurry of energy, waving something triumphantly in the air.

"I've got it! My brother just dropped it off. Phew, that was close."

Her passport, clutched like her life depended on it.

"You're so lucky you had yours with you, Prim, or we wouldn't be going anywhere. Why did you have it again?"

Prim laughed. But decided against actually answering the question.

Because the truth was… she'd been planning this. Not consciously, maybe. But the idea had been growing, whispering to her in the quiet moments. The passport was key. If she was going to escape her own wedding—run out on the love of her life—she wasn't going to stay in the bloody country. She was running from the music, not facing it.

So here she was, heading to Paris with Milly—her new best friend and probably the worst influence imaginable—in a £4,000 wedding dress.

"I've got my credit card too," Milly chirped. "We'll find a hotel, get you some clothes the second we arrive, babes."

"Thanks, Mills. I'll pay you back," Prim said, grateful and slightly stunned.

"No problem, babes." Milly winked. "Honestly, this is way more exciting than the wedding. No offence."

Prim smiled. But inside, something shifted. A twist of guilt. The devil on her shoulder. She kept telling herself: Life is trying to tell you something.

But then she reminded herself—of the thoughts she'd been having for days now. Weeks. Months, if she was being honest. A slow-burning itch under her skin. A whisper. A devil on her shoulder.

Life had been trying to tell her something: it's not time to settle down.

She hadn't lived enough. Not really.

If she had to pinpoint when it started, it might've been the day she let herself into Daisy's flat and accidentally walked in on her little sister and her absurdly fit boyfriend having sex on the sofa. Middle of the day. No blanket. No shame.

Prim had practically choked on her own gasp. Mortified.

But later—after the initial horror wore off—she'd felt something else, something inconvenient and sharp.

Jealousy.

Not of Sam—not like that. Though, yes, he was ridiculously hot (well done, Daisy), and she was genuinely happy her little sister had found someone who looked at her like that. But it wasn't about him.

It was about the spark. The spontaneity. The fun.

Daisy and this handsome ex-footballer, completely swept up in each other, unable to wait. It was sexy. Messy. Alive.

Prim couldn't remember the last time she'd felt that with Grant. Their sex life had become… scheduled. Predictable. Something slotted in between discussing paint samples and whether to upgrade the Dyson.

Grant got more animated about his golf swing than a Saturday morning shag.

And it wasn't really his fault. After eight years together, the fire had slowly fizzled out. They were… comfortable. Safe. Predictable.

Which, once upon a time, had sounded like everything she wanted.

But you weren't supposed to feel like this about the man you were about to marry… were you?

Maybe she should've said something. Maybe he would have understood. He always had, before. But she didn't. She kept it quiet, kept it tidy. And now?

Too late.

Because then life threw her a curveball.

She'd been headhunted—by Liliana bloody Lemoine, Director of Art Curation at the actual Louvre. At first, she thought it was a phishing scam. The Louvre? The Louvre?

She'd been at the Tate for nine years. She had a good thing going. She was stable. Respected. Settled.

But Paris…?

The Louvre…?

It was dreamy. Seductive. The kind of opportunity you fantasised about, but never actually got. The full Parisian fantasy.

At first, she brushed it off. She was about to be married, after all. To a man who adored her, who wanted to build a life with her. Who gave her monogrammed towels and spreadsheets about mortgages and asked if they should go for quartz or marble worktops.

It was everything she'd always thought she wanted.

But now it felt... beige.

She told herself she was just curious. One conversation. Just to see. But the conversation turned into another. Then an interview. And then a job offer. A real one. A handsome salary. A position as an actual Curator, not an assistant. Accommodation allowance.

Enter a new dream for Prim.

Not the Pinterest-perfect wedding. Not the forever home. Not the matching "his and hers" towels.

But this. A flat in the Marais. Croissants and fancy galas. Falling asleep to the hum of the Seine, not the sound of Grant snoring in his Arsenal pyjamas.

A romance of a different kind. One with herself.

She really liked the idea of this life.

She'd already typed the acceptance email. Hovered over send a dozen times. It was still in her drafts. Liliana had given her until the end of the month.

But deep down, she already knew.

She wanted to go.

She had to go.

She owed it to herself, right?

Maybe she should've told Grant. Maybe he'd have understood. He was good like that—steady, decent. He'd never held her back before. But she hadn't given him the chance.

And now?

Now she'd bolted.

Out of the wedding. Out of the life that was never really hers. Out of the mould she'd carefully pressed herself into for years.

Now, she just had to live with the consequences.

"Here's the train!" Milly squealed beside her.

Prim blinked; the spell broken.

"You ready, Julia Roberts?"

Prim stood and exhaled, lifting her wedding dress off the ground, bunching it in her hands.

"As ready as I'll ever be."

They boarded the Eurostar and collapsed into their business class seats—thank god for the extra legroom.

But she wasn't really ready, not even close.

Just as the train pulled out of the station, Grant came tearing down the platform, Greg hot on his heels.

He skidded to a stop, watching helplessly as the train disappeared into the tunnel.

"Shit."

He crouched, hands on his knees, like the air had been knocked out of him. Defeated. Gutted.

But not crying.

And not giving up.

He straightened, jaw clenched and marched to the ticket counter. He changed both his and Greg's tickets to the next train. Cost a small fortune.

Didn't care.

He was going to Paris.

And he was going to find her.

Chapter 41:
This wasn't how any of it was supposed to go

Back at Prim and Grant's non-wedding, Daisy and Sam stood holding each other as the band played on. Guests clinked glasses like nothing had happened—clinging to the free champagne, the canapé platters still doing the rounds like clockwork. Sequins shimmered, shoes were kicked off, someone's aunt was already barefoot and doing the Macarena like it was 2004.

The mood was surreal. Like everyone had silently agreed to pretend the wedding had happened—just to avoid the collective awkwardness of admitting it hadn't.

It felt like emotional theatre. A full-cast performance of Denial: The Musical.

It hadn't been a fun evening for Daisy. More like a rollercoaster—and not the good kind. The kind you find at one of those sketchy pop-up funfairs, rickety and clearly one screw away from disaster.

Why did she have to be the one tasked with all the horrible things? Telling people. Fielding questions. Lying through her teeth with a smile that barely stayed on her face.

"Prim's just taking a moment."

"There's been an emergency."

"Yes, the groom is still here."

All while glued to her phone, praying for a message from her runaway sister that never came.

She'd reassured Grant's mum, calmed the caterers, gently convinced Nanna Jean that no, it wasn't the end and they would work it out, so she could still eat her salmon.

Another lie. Because Daisy had no bloody idea what was going through Prim's head, and right now, she wanted to throttle her. More than when she made her do an impromptu speech at the engagement party.

And yet, despite the chaos—the confusion, the drama clinging to the air like the scent of peonies and Prosecco—here, in Sam's arms, Daisy felt… strangely happy.

Not ecstatic. Not euphoric.

But grounded.

Steady.

Like, in the middle of this bizarre hurricane, she'd found one small patch of solid ground.

Him.

"Come on. Let's dance." As the music shifted, Sam took her hand and led her to the dancefloor in a bid to calm Daisy's mind. They moved slowly, swaying in quiet rhythm.

She leaned her head against Sam's chest, her hands looped loosely behind his neck. The steady thud of his heartbeat anchored her. Strong, familiar, constant. A sound she hadn't realised she'd come to rely on.

"This is insane," she murmured, her voice muffled against the fabric of his shirt. "We're dancing at a wedding that didn't even happen."

Sam smiled, soft and knowing. "I know. So bloody weird. Definitely the strangest wedding I've ever been to."

He looked down at her, eyes warm. "You okay?"

"I think so," she said quietly. "I just... don't get it. How could she do this?"

"I don't think you have to get it, Dais. She had her reasons. She'll come back when she's ready."

"You really think so?"

"Of course." He brushed her hair gently from her face. "These aren't your pieces to pick up, remember."

There was no judgment in his expression—just calm understanding. Like he knew instinctively that this wasn't a moment to fix, but one to quietly hold.

Then a new song began to play—slow, familiar, unmistakably theirs.

Their song.

Daisy froze for half a second, then smiled as she recognised the melody. Sam's hands tightened slightly at her waist.

"This is our song, Dais," he whispered, pressing a kiss to the top of her head.

"Yeah." She nodded, eyes glassy. "You're right. I love it."

"And I love you," he said simply.

His voice was low, certain. No performance, no grand gesture. Just truth. He kissed her—gentle, sure—and then they melted into a slow, contented embrace.

Daisy's arms wrapped tighter around him. She closed her eyes, letting the moment hold her—until it crumbled, as if by magic, the second Marcus appeared.

"Daisy, there you are."

She tensed, still holding Sam's hand. "Marcus… did you find her?"

He shook his head, slightly out of breath. "No. We missed her. She's on a train to Paris."

Her stomach dropped. "And what about Grant?"

"He and Greg missed hers, but they got the next one. Don't worry, Dais—they'll find her. They'll bring her back." And with that, Marcus gave her a reassuring look before heading to the bar, like this was just another odd twist in an already surreal evening.

Daisy nodded slowly. "Thanks for telling me." she said, voice quieter now, her gaze lifting to Sam's. Her expression was solemn.

"Well… that's it then? I guess I should tell people."

"She'll be fine," Sam said gently. "There's nothing else you can do now. Grants on his way to her."

Daisy tried to breathe. Tried to let it go and stay in the moment with Sam. The music, the softness of his hands at her waist, the warmth of his chest beneath her cheek.

But she couldn't.

Because guilt trickled in, uninvited.

Her eyes drifted across the room. Grant's mum was trying to laugh with a friend. Lance was chatting up a waiter. Jessie danced with Malcolm—oh lord—and Lydia was giggling with Luca. It was strangely sweet, the way he was sticking by her, even though she was very publicly in a relationship with someone else. Mad to think they'd be parents soon.

Everyone was pretending. Keeping up appearances. But there was no bride. No groom. Just a swirl of sequins and confusion.

Daisy felt bad for letting herself feel happy right in the middle of it. Happy in his arms. This man, who kept showing up for her, again and again. Even as her sister's carefully curated day unravelled around them, Sam had drawn her into this cocoon of calm.

It felt like a stolen moment of joy.

But maybe that was okay.

Maybe it didn't mean she didn't care.

Maybe it just meant she'd found someone who made the chaos feel survivable.

She rested her chin on his shoulder, watching the dance floor. Some guests were still swaying to the music.

Her gaze landed on the head table—decorated to perfection, now awkwardly vacant, like a stage abandoned mid-scene.

Prim's mess. A big, bold, beautiful mess that had somehow turned into Daisy's quiet moment of clarity.

It was strange—surreal, even—how the roles had reversed. Eight months ago, Daisy had been the disaster. The one crying in supermarket aisles, piecing herself back together after sleepless nights and professional rejection. She was the one with the shattered heart, trudging through a job she hated and barely affording her rent.

Meanwhile, Prim floated effortlessly through her engagement, her life wrapped in ribbons and Pinterest boards. Perfect Prim. Together Prim. The sister everyone pointed to when they needed an example of how to get it right.

And now… this.

Daisy, dancing with the man who made her feel seen. Rooted. Whole.

And Prim? Gone. Vanished from her own wedding in a puff of cold feet and confusion, leaving behind a trail of raised eyebrows and uneaten cake.

It should have felt ironic. It should have felt smug.

But it didn't.

Because all Daisy could feel was love. For her sister, who would return when she was ready. And for herself, for surviving the wreckage of her own undoing and quietly rebuilding something new. Something stronger.

And maybe that was the biggest surprise of all. Somewhere between the late-night panics, the disasters, the heartbreaks, and the botched speeches, she'd stopped being the Daisy who always crumbled. She'd started becoming someone who could stand back up. And Sam—bloody Sam Callaghan—had been there, not to fix her, but to steady her. To remind her she already had it in her.

She looked up at Sam, her chest tightening with the kind of gratitude words could never quite hold.

Maybe the chaos never really went away. Maybe it just shifted. But somewhere along the way, Daisy had stopped trying to outrun it.

She tightened her hold on Sam just slightly.

No, this wasn't how the day was supposed to go. This wasn't how any of it was supposed to go.

But maybe, just maybe…

It was how something else could begin.

Acknowledgment

To my family and friends: thank you for surviving the emotional rollercoaster that was my writing this book. Your patience, encouragement, and perfectly timed deliveries of tea and snacks kept me going whenever my brain threatened to give up.

To my husband and children, you truly deserve medals. Thank you for pretending not to notice when dinner once again turned into take-away because "I'm nearly finished this chapter." Your support (and tolerance) made this whole journey possible.

And then there's Liv. Honestly, this book should probably have her name on the cover somewhere. Her brutal honesty, unwavering encouragement, and refusal to let me quit, even after I dramatically announced I was done at least seventeen times, kept this whole project alive. I couldn't have written it without her, and I certainly couldn't have survived writing it without her.

Huge thanks to Daisy, Lola, Adele, Mathew, Mark, Laurel, Gemma, and Amy for cheering me on, listening to my rants, and politely pretending to enjoy my chaotic voice notes. And to my book club — thank you for your enthusiasm, your feedback, and for not staging an intervention during my temporary obsession with plot holes.

To everyone in between who offered a push, a pep talk, or a caffeine boost: you're a part of the reason this book exists.

Thank you.

About the Author

Lori Laine is a British rom-com author who resides in the peaceful landscapes of Western Norway, where she creates stories brimming with heart, humour, and the delightful chaos of modern life. She's passionate about exploring love in all its messy, unexpected, and often humorous forms, writing about smart, ambitious heroines who navigate careers, friendships, and romance with wit and charm. Her stories are filled with swoon-worthy leading men, quirky side characters, and laugh-out-loud moments that embrace the unpredictability of life. Lori finds inspiration in everyday moments, the excitement of new beginnings, and the awkward, tender, and sometimes messy journey of discovering love and oneself. When she's not writing or balancing life with her family, she enjoys walking her dogs, reading, reluctantly hiking, and travelling across Europe with friends.

Published in Collaboration with Noble Legacy Publishing

<u>www.noblelegacypublishing.co.uk</u>